Professor F
Guide to
Galactic Traveller on the Move:

Containing Divers Works Hitherto Unpublished by Scholars of Moderne Sciences, Herbarisme and Exoticks, with Thorough Explication of Chymicall Principles Terrestrial and Alien

Stories collected and edited by
Jessica Augustsson

www.JayHenge.com

Published by Jayhenge Publishing KB

Published by Jayhenge Publishing KB

ISBN 9789198786248

Cover Art by Jessica Augustsson
jessica@augustsson.net using images from
commons.wikimedia.org/wiki/Kunstformen_der_Natur

Cover design by Jessica Augustsson

Interior artwork from publicdomainvectors.org, openclipart.org, DALL-E 2

Contents

The Machine

by

Johannes Svensson

THE stench of rotting vegetation filled my nostrils as I stood looking down at the shoreline below the cliff. The wind tore at my coat and the hand gripping my binoculars was starting to feel numb even through the multiple layers of thermal cloth that was covering it. Three pale suns shone down on the scene below me, but seemed to give no warmth.

The Flock was lying splayed out on their backs in a row along the beach like an obscene abstract impression of a herd of walruses, their flipper-like feet placed so they were being covered by seawater each time the waves washed towards the shore. Their thin, sinewy upper appendages, of which there were ten on each side of their central mass, were stretched out to the sides and the vicious claws that they ended in were digging into the sand, keeping the massive bodies in place.

At first glance, the creatures looked dead with their mottled gray skin unevenly covered in sparse, coarse hairs. The main eyes were closed and only the sensory fronds on their snouts were waving slightly in a motion that might have been caused by the wind. I knew they weren't dead, however. They were merely absorbing nutrients from the water, but that did little to dispel the image in my mind of something out of the nightmares of Earth's past having beached on the gray sands and perished.

Officially they were referred to as Sentient Xenoform Species number six or SXS06 for short. They called themselves The Flock in our language. What they called themselves in their own language was impossible to transcribe in the standard alphabet. Even galactic phonetic script, which prideful humans had thought would be comprehensive enough to encode any possible language the galaxy might have to offer, would have to be expanded with several new symbols before it could encompass all the sounds of that single name.

As might be expected from their designation, they were the sixth sentient extra-terrestrial species that mankind had encountered. Out of the other five, two were openly hostile, two were long since extinct and the last was so different that we had yet to find a way to get them to acknowledge our existence, let alone communicate with them.

This meant that mankind's only hope for peaceful communication or scientific exchange with an alien species was The Flock. Which is why our small team was here.

This group was only one of several hundred communities of the species on the planet but it was the only group that had deigned to talk to us so far. To say that the group talked to us was a slight exaggeration, of course. They had not yet tried to drive us away, electing instead to appoint one of their number, a relatively small specimen, the task of keeping track of us. Our babysitter had learned the structure and sounds of our language quickly enough to make us feel slightly offended, as we were still unable to decipher any of their speech.

As soon as it had learned enough for basic communication, we were quickly informed of the rules for interaction. We were allowed to leave a single person on site to study them, but that person would not be allowed onto the beach except during sunrise and sunset. The rest of the time, we would have to conduct our studies from the cliffs so as not to "offend the shining one" with our "small souls".

As it had not volunteered a name for us to call it, we had offered the name Shepherd assuming that it was some sort of leader or spokesperson of The Flock. It accepted the name, but when I explained what it meant we were immediately informed that it was no leader, it had been assigned to this task because it was considered unimportant. It did not seem to attach any resentment to this statement, simply offering it as a fact that could not be disputed.

Two months later, SXS06 was stubbornly remaining a mystery to us in almost all important ways. Physically they were massive, easily four or five times the bulk of a normal-sized human, but they could move with speed and grace when they wanted to. We would often see them chasing quickly scuttling crustaceans and using their claws to spear them with ease.

Socially, they were gregarious but seemed to have no bigger communities than the ones that dotted the shores. They used no tools, built no houses and professed to have no written language. Yet they had an intellectual capacity that seemed to dwarf our own. Shepherd immediately grasped our most advanced social and philosophical concepts, but seemed not to ascribe any importance to them. As to the topic of tools and machinery, it seemed actively disinterested, liable to wander off or to ask me to stop talking in the middle of a sentence.

I didn't like The Flock much. I didn't like them at all in fact. Their careless superiority and supreme disinterest in the accomplishments of the human race made me feel decidedly uneasy. Humanity had gone out into the universe hoping to be greeted with open arms and the best reception we had gotten so far was this. We were tolerated.

Frustrated with our lack of progress, I had been down during sunrise to place some sensor arrays that might let us get some better readings during the day and night. The Flock had scrutinized them closely after I was forced to return to the top of the cliffs. Whatever their opinion, they had decided that their morning toe-dip was more important than expressing any discontent at my activities.

I had a compsystem that was monitoring the data sent back by the sensors set up on a folding table behind me. It was sleek and black with an unscratchable clear crystal display. The machine was able to withstand an acceleration of up to 14 gravities per second and would probably be in working order even after a drop down onto the rocks directly beneath the cliff. It was also not telling me anything I didn't already know.

Without the magnification of the binoculars, The Flock looked like a series of uneven distortions in a dopplerscan, dark grey against a light grey background. I drew a deliberate breath, filling my lungs with cold air and then letting it out again.

I turned around and checked the readouts for the twelfth time that morning. The images of The Flock engaged in daily activities were some of the most intimate we had been able to get so far, but apart from that I wasn't getting anything new. The scanners could distinguish the herd from the background and all the different instruments were getting readings on the life signs of the different individuals, but they were the same now that they had always been, the same as they were every time we had scanned them. Smooth and regular readings, no irregularities or changes to break the sinus wave of their biological processes. It was almost as if they were not alive at all but some sort of machines, steadily humming along, their inner workings impervious to outside tampering or influence.

As I turned away from the screens, I spotted Shepherd approaching from the path leading up to the top of the cliff. As it moved, its massive upper body was supported by its clawed appendages of which at least six were always touching the ground to give optimum weight distribution. Two of the limbs were not used in walking but kept in front of the body, continuously moving back and forth in time with its undulating movements as the feet pushed the body forward and the clumps of appendages moved forward in turn to accommodate the shifted center of gravity.

When Shepherd saw that I had noticed it, it widened the gash in its upper body that served as a mouth and showed the many sharp teeth within. Perhaps this was meant as a courtesy to me, a facsimile of a human smile to put me at ease. If it was, it had yet to work.

I waited patiently for Shepherd to reach me. I knew it could cover the distance in half the time it took now without any effort. If it had seen the need to do so it would have, but it was content with its leisurely pace. As it approached, the smell of rotting seaweed and fish grew stronger until it was tickling the back of my throat. I tried to look unaffected and smiled as Shepherd drew to a halt in front of me.

"Good Morning," I said. "To what do I owe the pleasure?"

Shepherd's eyes swiveled back and forth as if it wasn't really looking at me, but the sensory fronds were all waving in my direction, showing that its attention was focused squarely on me.

"I came to warn you. The Flock is upset that you have left your offspring on the beach. We have allowed one of you to stay here. We did not give you leave to deposit your podlings on our sands."

I frowned. "Offspring?"

"The small shiny ones. Like that one." Shepherd carelessly flicked a claw in the direction of the compsystem on the table.

"That's not a…" I started to explain and then I realized what it was referring to. "Oh, you mean the sensor arrays. No, no. They are not my offspring, they are machines."

Shepherd drew itself up taller. "It does not matter. They cannot stay. Their minds are bright but their souls are without taste. They are found lacking. The shining one will be offended."

I smiled, amused at its mistake, relieved that it could make a mistake. "You don't understand. They are machines. They are not alive."

"They hum. They contain minds. They are alive."

I searched for a way to make it understand. "They have only the life given to them; they have no souls. They…"

I backed away in momentary fear as Shepherd opened its mouth and let out a roaring sing-song sound that ended in a metallic shriek. It leaned forward towards me and its sensory fronds almost touched my face. Its eyes had stopped scanning the horizon and were for the moment rigidly fixed on me.

"No Souls?"

"No. They're just things we built. Tools. Machines."

"Life without soul is a void in nature!" The normally well-modulated copy of a human voice had devolved into a gurgling growl. It turned abruptly and bounded towards the path down the cliff. On the way, it uttered a series of unearthly noises that were answered in kind by the rest of The Flock below. Taking a few hurried steps to the cliff's edge and lifting my binoculars to my eyes, I watched as The Flock fell upon the sensor arrays and tore them to pieces with claws and teeth. For the first time, the sensors were registering a different quality to the rhythms of The Flock's biometric data. A radically different waveform. Then they stopped reporting anything.

At sunset, I made my way down to the beach to salvage the wreckage. The damage was unbelievable. Hardened alloys torn apart like the soft plastics they were manufactured to look like. Supposedly impervious synthetic crystal displays broken into bits and ground into a fine powder.

The Flock was gathered at the base of a large rock, huddled together around it for warmth or comfort. They were awake—I had yet to register any state that resembles what we call sleep in their daily routines—yet like when they were lined up at the water earlier that day, they were keeping very still, only the sensory fronds on their heads moving.

As I moved along the beach, picking up pieces of broken equipment I had the unshakable idea that The Flock was watching my every step. That every one of those maggot-like protuberances was trained in my direction, straining to pick up any sign that I was trying to plant more of the hateful sensor arrays. It was with a sense of relief that I made my way back up to the top of the cliff with my harvest of electronic waste.

In the time we had been here, there had been very little progress in our studies of The Flock and much pressure from Earth to find out more. "Try to send some examples of Flock science or art. Or even philosophy," they demanded, not understanding that though the members of The Flock (or at least Shepherd) displayed signs of great intelligence, they had no use for science or philosophy and the closest thing to art that I had seen was when they would gather and sing their awful harmonies or when they would gaze out to sea, swaying their whole bodies from side to side as if performing some courting dance. I had recorded one of the songs and sent the recording back to the scientists on Earth to shut them up for a while.

The Flock was simply not interested in any exchange of knowledge. What we knew, they either held as obvious or inconsequential and what they knew, they either didn't want to teach us or were to them truisms that did not need to be explained, only accepted.

When I had asked about the songs and the swaying, I was told that they were practicing two parts of a ritual. When I wondered aloud why they did not practice the two parts together, Shepherd looked at me in silence for a while, then finally he said, "This time is not the ritual," and moved away, offering no further explanation.

As I watched the new readings, I quietly wondered what Earth Academy would make of it. They were like nothing I had seen before; the neural activity didn't look like it even belonged to the same species. Physical values were elevated across the sensor spectrums. Everything that would make their bodies more efficient and stronger had been activated at the same time as their mental profiles had lost all of the tell-tale signs of higher thought.

After studying the patterns for more than an hour, I had come no closer to a scientific explanation than that it seemed to signify some sort of berserker state where thought would be a hindrance because the goal was simple and physical.

I sighed and looked up from the readings, and saw Shepherd's silhouette against the sky. Not wanting to further antagonize it with the technology it seemed to dislike, I decided to get up and meet it halfway.

As we came to a halt, it inclined the top part of its body downwards to focus on me. Looking up to meet its attention, I found myself shivering at the thought of what I had seen those claws and teeth do earlier.

I thought I detected some reluctance in its stance, though the gods only know how I could tell. I kept my silence, allowing it time to form its thoughts and word the message it had come to deliver.

"My people have communicated. There has been a delay in the arrival of the shining one. The Flock feels that this is because of the presence of the soulless ones that you have brought. We have decided that you must leave so that we can perform the beckoning without your influence.

"If the ritual is a success, we will again speak as to whether you should be allowed to come back. I have explained that your small soul renders you incapable of understanding how unnatural your ways are and that you mean no harm, but the point has been made that the stinging lizard does not mean harm as it grazes your skin, yet it damages and poisons. I cannot foresee that you will be allowed back."

"Leave?" I was stunned. "Right now?"

There was a pause. "As soon as possible. We realize that your choice to travel with so much scenery—" At this Shepherd indicated the scientific equipment and the small tent-site with all my belongings. "Means that it will take you some time to gather everything together, but you must go as soon as you have done so."

Shepherd turned and moved back the way it came. I remained where I was and watched it go away until all of it had disappeared below the edge of the cliff. Two suns had already set and the third was teetering on the edge of the world. I kept searching through my mind for some way of turning the situation around but in my heart I knew there was nothing I could do. If The Flock decided that they wanted to allow me back they would do so for their own reasons.

Reluctantly, I turned and walked back to the tent. I would have to use the radio and call in a report and whenever the unavoidable interrogation was over, I really needed to try to get some sleep.

The next day I had trouble crawling out of my sleeping bag. I had been going over the situation on the radio with Parson at the main camp for hours and had still ended up back at my initial conclusion, only with less time to sleep.

I had a quick breakfast and started to make a show of packing up the equipment. We had decided that if this was indeed our last chance to study The Flock, we should try to drag out our stay as long as possible to get a few more readings. Between slowly filling crates, I erected all the sensor equipment I had left, a disappointingly small collection, on the edge of the cliff and set them to record and analyze everything. From time to time, I took a look at the displays and made minor adjustments to the parameters of the search and record program.

Sometime around midday, I had run out of crates to pretend to have trouble packing, but Shepherd did not come to chase me away, so I sat down at the table and went through what had been recorded so far. The readings all looked the same as they always did, apart from the group movement patterns that were different than normal. Preparations for the coming ceremony perhaps.

I downloaded the data from the night before onto my hand-unit. Perhaps, I reasoned, it would give me some insight that would help me narrow down what I should be looking for or how to tune the sensors correctly for these last hours of surveillance. I highlighted the patterns and marked them as a comparison state, meaning that the main compsystem would compare all readings to this pattern, noting any and all similarities.

I spent the rest of the day fine-tuning the sensors, even dedicating one of them to the sort of half-assed intuitive improvisations that I hadn't been desperate enough to try before, but there had been nothing notable about the new readings. All the time I was expecting to be challenged by Shepherd at any minute, to be asked why I was still there. It was as if, having given the order for me to leave, it had discarded my presence from its mind, certain that I would obey.

Now I was lying awake in the night, listening to the distant ticking of the compsystem trying to detect any change in tempo or pitch designed to alert me to unusual readings.

I was oblivious to the cold outside the tent even though I had left the tent-flap slightly open to make sure I did not miss anything. At any significant change, my hand-unit would alert me and any matches to the comparison state would trigger a special alarm, but smaller changes would only be noted in a log for later study.

After checking the log for the seventh time in an hour, I felt I had to do something. I slipped out of the sleeping bag and into my clothes as quickly as I could, which was not quite fast enough to avoid being chilled to the bone. Once on, the thermal systems of the sweater and the pants started to slowly warm my body up again.

I stood, indecisive for a moment, just inside the entrance to the tent. Crawl back into the sleeping bag and try unsuccessfully to fall asleep or go out there and spend a freezing night needlessly checking the readings and watching The Flock? Finally, I decided to go outside. Either way I wouldn't get any sleep and the cold wouldn't add much to my misery.

I walked over to the edge of the cliff and looked down at the beach. The stars were reflected in the dark waters off the shore, ripples making it seem like they were winking at me.

There were shapes moving down there but it was too dark to make out how many or what they were doing. I held the binoculars up to my eyes, switching them to low-light.

To my surprise, The Flock was moving about in what I could only describe as an agitated state. I took the binoculars from my eyes and checked the readings: no change except for a slightly elevated body temperature. Apart from the rage I had witnessed the day before, I had never seen them so...animated. Yet there was no deviation in the calm lines their consciousnesses plotted on the screens.

I looked down at the beach again and followed the expansive movements of the individuals in The Flock. There seemed to be little pattern to their movements at first. Then I noticed that they would move around seemingly at random, before stopping and lying almost flat on the ground, examining it with all their sensory organs, and then moving on again. Occasionally, one of them would make a faint sound, like a small animal being killed, and hurry to a specific spot on the beach carrying something with their clawed appendages. I focused on the spot and saw that there was a pile of stones forming. Focusing a chemical sensor at the collection of rocks, I determined them to all to contain a particular metallic ore.

As the pile grew, some of The flock stopped searching for more stones and gathered around it, picking up two or three of the rocks and putting them in their mouths. I could hear the crunching noises all the way up on the top of the cliff as they crushed the stones into pebbles and pebbles into fine gravel.

I tried to set up a biological simulation, asking the compsystem to try to anticipate what kind of effect that would have on them, but the program couldn't complete due to lack of data. As I started to ponder whether I could make some educated guesses as to the unknown parts of their biological systems to fill in the gaps, there was a change in the pitch of the clicking noises.

I switched over to the sensor display and analysis. At first I couldn't see the change, but when I asked the comp to zoom in on the relevant area, it showed me minute irregular deviations in the readings of the consciousness. The analysis told me that the deviation from normal readings was 0.3% higher than usual, which for The Flock was a significant step. Not that there had to be much deviation for that to be true.

Through the binoculars I could see that more and more of The Flock were preparing to eat the stones. The ones who had already eaten were starting to form a rough circle of sorts further out from the pile with their fronts facing the sea. Once they were in position, they started to sway back and forth slowly.

I turned all the visual sensors but one to night vision and set them to track moving targets. Even with this assurance that nothing of the proceedings below would be missed, I kept putting the binoculars to my eyes, afraid that something would slip by me if I didn't watch constantly.

It was excruciating to be stuck up on the cliff watching this alien behavior, which to my mind could only be some sort of practice for the ritual to be held when I was gone, when what I really wanted to do was to be down there watching from up close. I found myself tapping my gloved hand against my thigh impatiently.

It might be the first and last time that a human would have the opportunity to watch this ritual. The only chance to gather what could be an invaluable clue to what seemed like an impervious enigma. I glanced impatiently at the screens again. Deviations were up another 0.2%

I was torn, but either the braver part of me or the more curious part won out and before I knew I was doing it, I started to move towards the path that led down along the cliff face. As I moved, I set my hand-unit to vibrate in time to the clicks of the system above and to give a special warning vibration, an SOS, if the mental readouts of The Flock came near to the comparison state.

When I reached the path, I immediately dropped down onto it and into a crouch so as not to stand out against the night sky. The hand-unit vibrated against my thigh in short regular spurts of activity that seemed to me to be coming more frequently than the audible indication had been when I left my viewing post.

Having made sure that there were no lookouts posted and that none of the shapes below seemed to exhibit any interest in the cliff, I started to slowly make my way down the path, occasionally stopping, to scan The Flock or because I thought I had made too much noise. Apart from all members of The Flock having joined the circle now, there was no real change, no sign to make me think I was betraying my presence.

It was with trepidation I stepped off the path at the bottom of the cliff and set foot on the sand of the beach. Even without artificial aid, I could now see the outline of The Flock against the horizon, swaying back and forth in unison. Standing still I could now make out a low, broken humming sound, like the crackling of a radio but warmer and more melodious.

I wished that I dared take out the hand-unit and check the readings from above, but the light from the screen would certainly tell The Flock that something was not right. Looking around for a good place to observe from, I spotted two boulders nearby. Together with the wall of the cliff, they would make the semblance of shelter. Nothing like perfect cover, but at least I would not be spotted by a casual glance.

Having crawled in between the stones, I hazarded a quick look at the hand-unit, confirming that the deviation indeed was higher now than when I left the top of the cliff. The patterns did not look like the dangerous patterns I had seen the day before, though. If anything they indicated a higher level of mental activity and half the physical readings had almost flattened out while the other half was fluctuating wildly.

I reminded myself that all the readings taken by the sensors would be available tomorrow for analysis and that the direct observations I could make from this position would not be. Sliding the hand-unit into my right leg-pocket, I put the binoculars to my eyes and propped my elbows onto the sand for support.

As I once again could see The Flock clearly, the humming opened up into a moaning sound filled with discordant high-pitched metallic noises weaving in and out of it. It was not clear if this was the result of different individuals making different sounds or if each member of The Flock made all of the sounds that made up the song. As soon as I had thought it I realized it was true. The Flock was singing. They were singing and swaying at the same time. They were performing the ritual already!

I could see them, main sensory organs closed, mouths open, swaying rhythmically to the waxing and waning of the sounds they were making. The claws on their appendages were tapping against their bellies in an intricate pattern where each claw had its own beat to measure. I had the sensation of being in the presence of something primordial, something terrible from the beginning of the universe. Raw being condensed into a moaning, clamoring sound. It made the hairs at the back of my neck and my back stand straight up. It made me feel cold from the inside out.

As the volume of the song increased, the movements of The Flock grew more energetic until they seemed to be in danger of falling over. They were striking their own skin with such force that it was a wonder to me that they did not pierce through in their fervor, spilling their own blood onto the sand.

At a high note in the song, one of their number moved into the center of the circle, which closed behind it, and the noise immediately dropped back to the low hum I had first heard when I stepped onto the sand. The individual in the circle leaned down and picked up one of the remaining stones with its mouth and ate it while standing perfectly still, intently staring out towards the sea. The complete lack of motion of the central figure made it seem out of place in the midst of the swaying circle, wrong somehow, as if it did not belong with the rest of them. It was almost a relief when, after some time, it once again started to sway with the others and the song rose up anew to echo against the side of the cliff.

My mouth was dry from excitement and tension and I almost yelped as the vibrations from the hand-unit abruptly increased in frequency, telling me that some major change had been detected by the sensors. I looked around to try to discern what had happened.

While the swaying dance of The Flock had not stopped, some of them held their snouts and eyes fixed in place while the rest of the body continued the dance. Some of them seemed to lean out to one side in their swaying as if to try to see past those in front of it. I looked out to sea and to my astonishment there was some sort of luminescence coming from the water. A light from beneath the sea.

Against all reason, the light was even more obvious to my naked eyes than when I looked through the binoculars. Unable to account for this, I just accepted it and put the binoculars away.

The Flock was now spreading out and swaying their way closer to the water, obscuring much of my view. Frustrated, I first sat up and then stood up, trying to catch a clearer glimpse of the light. Finally, I climbed up onto one of the rocks in a vain attempt to get a better look when the surface of the water was broken.

The difference was the difference between night and day. A cluster of fluorescent globes floated, first to the surface of the water and then up into the air, slowly circling around each other in strange patterns that my eyes could not follow. The song of The Flock reached a crescendo of noise and somehow the sounds seemed to echo in the light of the spheres, setting off patterns of light and shadow that stretched out from them and onto the beach. It was as if the weaving lines of shadow and light creeping up the beach were part of the spheres, as if it was all one magnificent being, the spheres and the light that they gave.

To me, the ugliness of The Flock was unbearable next to the beauty of the light, yet they were accepted by it. Embraced by it.

As the play of light and shadow expanded ever onward, ever nearer to my position, I began to feel dizzy and a feeling of dread gripped me. I sank to my knees, intending to try to crawl back into my hiding place. But as I did, I began to retch uncontrollably, bile rising up into my mouth. I fell, my stomach contracting horribly and my limbs flailing beyond my control. Somewhere in the distance, I heard Shepherd's voice, with almost all traces of borrowed humanity drained by rage, naming the source of its anger. "No-soul!" it shouted. "Machine!"

As I lay there, I fought the pain, digging out the hand-unit and throwing it away from me, trying to create distance between me and the machine even though I knew it would make no difference. I knew it before I saw The Flock still bearing down upon me and ignoring the small device I had flung away.

The light had touched me. Before the SOS had gone off in my hand-unit, warning me of the comparison state. Before I heard the roar that I had heard the day before, that alien roar of outrage. Before that, the light had touched me, and it had found me wanting. Flawed.

To its gaze I was no-soul.
And I had no right to a place in the world.

Johannes Svensson lives in Gothenburg, Sweden with his wife, daughter and cat. He was created from stardust at the beginning of time and will cease to exist shortly after the heat death of the universe. This information is designed to make him feel approachable enough to be liked by a wide audience, but not approachable enough for that audience to actually approach him if they should happen to see him about town.

The Jungle Between

by

Holly Schofield

(Originally published at Cast of Wonders, 2016.)

Tanya:

I look over at my wife Anahita, where she squints at yesterday's video of the theropod. She pushes her hair back from her sweaty forehead, the very picture of a field biologist. We have extended a canopy over our work area in front of the shuttle, yet the temperature is still 34C and heat radiates up from the ground under my boots. I close my eyes for a second and roll my shoulders. In our ten days on Munroe Two, we have only collected minimal data on the tool-using parthenogenic dinosaurs, not enough to publish. Any conclusions will be iffy at best. Our allotted time ends tomorrow.

Unlike similar species back on Terra or on the fifteen other colonized planets, Munroe's theropods balance on that evolutionary cutting edge. Anahita mutters in her sleep each night about reduced micro-aggressions and low degrees of intragroup conflict.

Our six-year-old daughter, Kelty, is equally enamored with the planet and with the theros—one dino in particular.

"Kelty, honey! Not too far, okay," I call across the clearing.

"Aw, Mom, I'm fine!" She skooches a bare half-metre closer, dragging her toy plastic pirate treasure chest with her. The immature thero with the shrivelled left arm—the one Kelty calls Zoola—waddles after her, tail swaying.

I push away my tablet. My fascination—specifically, nesting site fidelity in this precocial species—is, so far, long on speculation and short on data. I don't expect that to change over the next twenty-hour day. Not when I can't get hold of a single damn egg to study.

"It's like being allowed to lick an ice cream cone when you're starving then having it pulled away," I say to Anahita. As much as I'm a registered member of The Uniworld Interplanetary Indigenous Anthropology Association and sworn to uphold the UIIAA's directives, I sometimes think they may have gone too far.

"No, Tanya, it's like being shown a *photo* of—no, a photo of a *sketch* of an ice cream cone. A cone that's back at Burgundy Base." Again and again, Anahita reviews yesterday's video of Kelty playing with the immature thero, interspersed with glances to where they now squat together over something at the end of the meadow.

The thousands of hectares of jungle that surround us smell like the compost chute on an interplanetary ship. Occasionally other scents permeate, a strange one like celery, and a sultrier one that Anahita says reminds her of cardamom. A thousand unclassified species of birds make discordant music on every side.

Of the three of us, only Kelty is not frustrated by our stay here. When we first landed the shuttle four kilometres from the village—the edge of the Samuel Limit—I'd hardly let Kelty out of the airlock to play and insisted she wear an enviro-suit at all times. She'd whined and wheedled and I'd relented on both counts. Munroe's other ecosystems are generally similar to Costa Rica or the inland rainforests of Qin Jiong Five, although this continent is more poorly documented.

"Still time to fly a drone over the village." Anahita is only half-joking about breaking the directives. "Or leave a spypatch inside one of their huts, eh?"

I shake my head firmly. I remind myself that the UIIAA is actually being generous. Being this close to a theropod village in the spring, in egg laying season, is a privilege never before awarded—but an ex-asperating one. If we were to bring back DNA or albumen samples, our research would move light-years ahead—until we were fired and banned from the UIIAA forever.

The theros' sentience has never been in question. They are adept with tools, have a language of sorts, make fire and construct primitive huts and food storage containers. The last study, two years ago, found a broken and discarded stone knife with markings arguably decorative. All of that, a bright red flag to the UIIAA saying "don't interfere". Anahita has yet to work out a basic social structure within the all-female population, nor resolve why the babies disperse at birth yet manage to return to the village at adulthood. As for me, the reproduction itself is fascinating. What triggers the egg-laying? How do they keep the gene pool sufficiently robust? Without one of their hyper-ellipsoidal eggs to study, or even a piece of shell, we know very little.

The UIIAA is not completely wrong. Theros deserve their privacy until they decide to volunteer to end it. When a hunter or gatherer passes by our shuttle, their reptilian slit-eyes crinkle as if humans are the strangest thing they ever saw, and, here, two hundred light-years from Terra, we probably are. Who knows? Without our influences, in a few millennia theros may develop a cultural aspect worthy of adopting. Anahita certainly believes that—she's sure an all-female culture must have something to teach our own. I smile over at her but she's perched on the edge on her folding chair, frowning at her screen.

I pick up my high-powered binoculars and zoom in on Kelty. She's grinning as she plays. I swing the 'nocs onto Zoola. Ten centimetres taller and massing twice as much as Kelty, she could be a Terran non-avian dinosaur from a thousand guesstimated sketches. Her hind legs and thick tail form a supporting triangle, allowing her to bend over the game she plays with Kelty. Green-and-gold hide, like snakeskin but with heavy folds like a thick carpet, slides into a lighter yellow shade around her hefty hindquarters. A brown cord straps her stone knife to her chest. I picture myself using my stun gun to subdue her and do a full bio-exam. I smile at my daydream—if only I weren't so ethical.

Zoola grasps Kelty's treasure chest in one of her stubby four-fingered hands. She picks a bug—an ant I think—from Kelty's jumpsuit and hands it to the bird-like symbionts (or are they parasites?) that keep the thero company. One of the tiny creatures pecks the wiggling bug from Zoola's nimble fingers. Zoola's thin-lipped mouth curves, emoting... something. Her jaw is filled with sharp teeth. Why do I trust her with Kelty? Motherly instincts? The theros' sense of community? Or perhaps it's the intelligent and warm look in the eyes of this particularly well-behaved thero.

Zoola:

The immature interloper with its overly soft brown skin is particularly well behaved. It does not seem to need the taming that a youngster of my people would require. I pretend not to notice the elder interloper watching me from across the clearing where it perches on an awkwardly stilt-footed object beside its curiously shiny giant hut. The hut landed like a fiery raptor at the beginning of spring's early arrival. A roof, cleverly woven of white root fibres, flaps above the second interloper as it stares at a little board mumbling to itself. Moisture oozes down their furred heads and naked faces.

To amuse myself, I copy the small interloper's actions and lay more grass across the wooden box, as if we were enfolding it into a web. Perhaps it is practicing for when it matures and lays an egg. The box is cleverly crafted like all things the interlopers have, with a peculiar smell like spoiled resin. Like the shiny hut, it is without pleasing curves; all ugly sharp angles and lines. I cannot guess its purpose: perhaps to hold seeds or dried meat for the rainy season. It is currently filled with carved items that resemble the interlopers in miniature.

I am fascinated by these interlopers. The small one appears to have no need to forage for food and is fed by its elders several times a day, like a helpless mousling in a nest. I fear it will not survive when the elder interlopers have lived out their life span and return to the loam. If I am ever allowed to keep one of my eggs alive until it hatches, I will carry the tiny baby to a place of abundant food, so that it will be the strongest, most fearsome of our people ever. I swear I will do this, although it goes against everything I have been taught by the elders. I touch my belly and feel the spring-sweet promise of my first egg in my loins. My time will be soon.

I sit back on my haunches, swishing my tail in the dry grasses to let any creatures know I am nearby. I touch the stone knife in my belt. Despite my imperfections, there is little in the jungle that can hurt me or match my swiftness, but I am farther from the village than is wise at mid-day. The elders are kind to me because of my arm, so kind that I have few daily chores in the village, and never ever any chores in tending the egg cache by the river. They do not want me to see the creamy texture of the eggs, the pleasingly smooth oval of the soft shells, the hatching of the tiny offspring as they tumble from their webbing to the forest floor and scatter. They do not want to cause me pain seeing something toward which I will never contribute; yet they cannot allow my useless arm and small stature to spread among the people. The old tales speak of pushing the imperfect ones off a cliff edge, tumbling them to their death. Sometimes, being treated like an outsider makes me long for a very tall cliff.

The immature interloper adds another sun-bleached stalk of grass to the pile, forming a sheet of tangled grass over the foodbox, as if it is inside a miniature hut. I sniff, tasting the wind and its smells of kritkrit pollen and small leafbiters. Soon I will leave these curious interlopers and return to the village, killing some bushtappers on the way. I will sit to one side of the communal fire, stroke my egg-filled belly, and cook my solitary meal while the others chatter about their day and tell tales into the night. The fire is not part of the old tales, it is a new thing to this village an eight-eight's generations ago, but the crackle and dance of the flames is as pleasing to the eye as charred meat is to the belly.

I sniff the air again, my claw scraping my stomach hide in sudden worry. I wait until a breeze riffles the tuftgrass. I sniff again. The acrid scent of blood-wasps twists my stomach like a tightening vine. It is early in the year for a swarm but this spring has come early. Wasps can tear through the jungle as easily as my knife through moss. Softer creatures, like the interlopers, will be flayed raw instantly. I rise on my haunches. The swarm is approaching from beyond the silver hut, moving fast and hungry. I cry out.

I should run toward the river, to protect our village's egg cache, eight-eight's toppertree-lengths away. The eggs, first-laid of this season, may not yet be wrapped in thick enough webs to prevent the wasps' laying their own eggs in our soft-shelled offspring. I turn riverward and take a step. The village elders do not want my help; they would want me to hunker down where I am, to bury my face and genitals deep in the welcoming loam and wait for the wasp cloud to pass.

The faint humming, as ominous as a wounded thrasher's moan, grows louder. My urge to protect our offspring grows stronger. A swarm stays clumped and moves relatively slowly; I can outrun and outwit the wasps if I start now.

At my feet, the small interloper plucks grasses, unaware.

The large interlopers by the silver hut cry out and wave their arms, leaping about like fleas. The cloud is almost upon them. The darker-furred one farthest from the silver hut is soon engulfed and ceases to hop. The other has opened a door in the silver hut but looks at its companion then across the clearing where I stand with the small interloper, which is now making squeaking noises.

The small interloper stands on bent legs, its foodbox dangling from a hand. Its squeak increases in pitch. It begins to run toward the silver hut, toward the wasp cloud, toward certain death. I dart forward and snatch it up into my arms as the first of the swarm reaches us, all poisoned stingers and fiercely beating wings. The edges of the small one's foodbox dig into my belly and the tiny carved contents fall to my feet.

The silver hut and the two adult interlopers are lost inside the black cloud. I turn and run into the dark, welcoming jungle, staggering under a weight that is half my own.

Tanya:

In a single instant, my world has changed. Anahita hangs near death, plugged into the shuttle's med-sys, and Kelty has been taken away by the thero she was playing house with. The chip we inserted into Kelty's arm at birth indicates she's almost two kilometres northwest in a proscribed area, and, thank the multitudes of stars, she's still alive. As I shove various portable medical instruments into a pack, and quickly put on an enviro-suit and a breather as a defence against more insects, I glance at Anahita's face, grotesquely swollen by multiple stings. The med-sys analyzer has tentatively identified the thumb-sized attackers as a type of omnivorous bee. Presumably, they function like a forest fire, periodically cleansing the ecosystem through genocide.

There is nothing I can do for Anahita; I move a strand of curly black hair off her face and get scolded by the med-sys for lack of sterility on my hands. "You better be alive when I get back," I say, my throat tight.

I grab Kelty's enviro-suit, stuff it in my pack, and head out the shuttle's airlock. The 0.8 gees allow me to lope across the field and into the dark jungle. My headset attunes itself to the volume of the many bird calls and rustlings that surround me on all sides. I set it to "record" without breaking my stride. I plunge between huge ferns, past coffee table-sized flowers like giant purple tulips, under fuzzy vine tendrils that brush against me and twist with more than the wind. Some kind of pollen drifts down on me. I am far across the Samuel Limit, in violation of laws and my own moral sense. I ignore it all. Only Kelty matters.

The enviro-suit whisks away my sweat as I plow through gullies and over ridges. Kelty's signal grows stronger, a solid green blip on my overlay. Soon, I am only one ridge away, then a dozen meters. The crowded jungle gives way to a patch of mist in the trees. No, not mist. Some gauzy material that contains opaque white lumps. Theros move between the lumps, occasionally stopping to touch one. It's a theropod egg cache; that hypothesized-yet-unobserved reservoir where a "lay and walk" species has managed to supersede their instinct. No clumsy stick nest on the ground, no abandonment to predators and weather. It's hypothesized, but undocumented, that eggs are, at this evolutionary stage, communally cared for until the late spring hatchings. Each egg swings gently in a white hammock, supported by several strands from overhanging branches. Adult theros, some barely mature, some elderly, drift between shrouded trees, apparently checking for broken strands and bee damage.

I hurry forward, double-checking that my suit is recording audio, visual, and olfactory. My voice shakes as I make audio notes: "Each ten-centimetre egg is suspended, wrapped in a filmy mass of... stuff. Spider webs! Spiders! Spiders occupy a tree across the clearing. Their webs form the protective wrappings and suspend the eggs a metre off the ground."

One egg lies on the grass, several smashed bees surrounding it. The shell has several oozing punctures and a thero is hunched over it, keening.

I'm relieved to see that Kelty's signal is coming from the left. I won't have to approach the mass of crawling black arachnids on the far side, each the size of a dinner plate.

Theros glance at me as I forge past, apparently more concerned about their offspring than a non-threat like me.

I sweep aside sheets of webbing, frantic with haste. Kelty is sitting up at waist-height in a hammock like a baby in a cradle. Her tear-stained face breaks into a half-grin as she sees me approach. Zoola stands nearby, her good arm raised and gripping a stone knife. I make a quick step forward, a hand on my stun gun. The thero's clever yellow eyes catch mine and she cuts the slit in the web wider, freeing one of Kelty's arms.

"Mommy, mommy! Zoola saved me!" Kelty waves.

"Oh, sweetie, oh, my sweet one," I say and kneel, wrapping her in my arms, heedless of the webs, Zoola at my side, and the curious looks of the other theros.

Zoola:

I watch the small interloper wrap her fingers, as small and brown as worms, around the large interloper's woven root-clad torso. The large one wipes a soft hand across the small one's wispy-haired head, leaving a smear of kritkrit pollen behind.

Finally, the large one stands and carries the small interloper away, leaving the webbing in tatters. My flits finally catch up to me and settle on my shoulders and the slope of my back. One nuzzles my ear hole.

The elders have mostly finished evaluating the minor wasp damage. They begin to look askance at the interlopers and one, Crat-zu, takes me aside. She was the first to greet me upon my return to the village as a maturing juvenile. Like all of my people, I have little memory of my childhood, a confusion of starvation and satiation and long dark nights. But I remember Crat-zu's kindness when I walked into the village, cradling my shrunken arm, unsure of my welcome.

Her tongue flickers and her head spikes stand upright with concern. "You have drawn the interloper here."

"Apologies, elder. I do not know how it tracked me. I backtracked over the creek gravel twice. I went the long way through the valley and managed to lose the wasp swarm in an updraft wind." I rub a swelling on my lip where a wasp had stung.

"You have endangered the egg cache. Your mind does not run as fast as it should." Crat-zu leans in and sniffs, then taps my swollen stomach. "You are with egg. You will bring it to the communal fire tonight and we will watch you burn it and so give it a kind journey back into the loam." She pats my shoulder in sympathy.

I turn away from her kindness. I put a hand on my stomach, my egg, my sole legacy before I return to the loam. The elders might say that all eggs are as one, that all people are as one. Yet they burn my eggs because my arm is different. I feel more akin to the solitary thrasher that roams endlessly from valley to valley. Does the dim-witted fur-covered creature hunger to keep its children safe from harm? Does its stomach kink as it gives birth in awful bloody chaos as lesser creatures do, knowing its small ones will soon roam away over distant mountain tops?

From under my lowered brow, I study the torn hammock. After laying my egg tonight, I will have no choice but to watch it burn. I could try to place it here. I am small enough to outwit the night guards and slip my precious ovoid treasure into a vacant hammock, but without Crat-zu's blessing—without her throat mucus coating my egg to scent-mark it—the other villagers will crush it and I will be deemed even more simple-minded. Likely, I will be held in even closer confines within the community I both abhor and cherish.

I have no choice but to burn my egg.

I stumble another step and bump against another hammock, so distraught it takes me a moment to remember what I stashed there in the confusion of the last few hours. The shape within is not a pleasing ovoid. It is angular and square.

It is the small one's foodbox.

Perhaps it is a symbol to the small interloper, a symbol of the security it feels, being in the continuing care of the larger interloper, its parent. Without it, the small one must be distraught. I feel a surge of affection for it. It, too, has no choice.

I tuck the foodbox under my good arm, unsure if the elders will allow it in the village, but unwilling to see such craftsmanship go to waste.

Tanya:

Anahita is awake when I return. She manages a smile even as the med-sys continues to replace her blood from our reserves. The shuttle disposal systems have returned the bee poisons and stingers to the dirt outside the shuttle. Kelty clambers onto the medi-bed and into Anahita's arms.

I blink back tears, fighting my emotions. My reaction can wait. Kelty needs a full medical evaluation. I start with a physical exam that covers every inch and turns into a massive three-person hug. Kelty relaxes then wiggles free. "My treasure chest! I don't have it! It's back at the funny white string place. My toys fell out when Zoola grabbed me but I need to get my box!"

"I will buy you a dozen treasure chests, back at Burgundy. Remember we leave tomorrow because of those pesky protocols," I say, managing to keep my voice light. Kelty has few scratches and a broken fingernail and, perhaps, some nightmares to come. Her sturdy frame has kept her from any more serious injury. If she had been any younger, it might have been far worse.

Kelty nods and she slumps against Anahita's side. Her eyes close. She must be exhausted, poor dear.

Anahita looks up at me, her eyes swinging to Kelty and back again signalling she wants to have a conversation that Kelty should not hear. "What did you record? Did you gather anything? Is your moral compass spinning?"

I shake my head. "Nothing."

Anahita clucks but subsides back onto her pillow.

I sink into a chair. I have the recording—the delightful recording! —but, it can never form part of a formal study without jeopardizing Anahita's career as well as my own. I'll simply keep the chip to feed my sense of wonder at the marvelous biological variety the universe holds. I look over at Kelty's flushed and sleeping face. I'm good at protecting things, keeping things safe for years at a time. I can manage that with this chip too.

I start a sequence to encrypt the file. I can hide the tiny chip in Kelty's personal gear which does not get checked as closely as Anahita's and mine. It's presumed that a professional would not stoop so low as to use their daughter to violate the directives.

The nearest screen tells me that the sun is setting outside. I need to collect up the tables, chairs, and other paraphernalia outside. Suddenly exhausted, I decide to leave them for tonight and collect them just before take-off tomorrow. I will also do a full chem-sweep of the clearing, in accordance with UIIAA directives.

It will be like we were never here.

Zoola:

I have wandered until moons-rise, drinking from the creek that feeds the river. I have no appetite but I force myself to eat a bushtapper, ripping off limbs and crunching them raw, providing pointless nutrients to the egg I carry, the egg that will burn tonight. My thoughts are crowded and messy like a dense jungle lies between my ears. As I push aside cold ferns and tread through brush, I try to take my thoughts elsewhere. The foodbox under my arm presses into my hide and I shift it uncomfortably. The small interloper intrigues me still; from its mannerisms, it has known much happiness so far in its short, strange life. For the first time, I think that the larger interloper must have laid that particular egg, that particular offspring, and is nurturing it so closely *due to that bond between them*. It is a new thought to me and I stop in a small clearing to look up at the twin moons, then down at the loam below that created us.

All of us.

I cannot fix my own sadness but I can fix the small one's. I make an abrupt turn into the night wind.

First moon has long set by the time I approach the silver hut. I leave the foodbox by the ugly foot of the hut and go to sleep in a hollow log just inside the jungle.

I do not return to the village.

As the sun awakens the jungle the next day, I stand below a toppertree, letting the steam from the warming earth fill my nostrils. My genitals throb from the laying. I watch as the large interloper, covered in again in white woven root fibres, emerges from the silver hut and picks up the ugly items scattered about. It pauses by the silver hut's leg, then picks up the foodbox, hefting its weight uncertainly, retreating into the silver hut.

I watch until the sun grows above the tree crowns and my underparts are no longer so swollen and sore.

When the silver hut magically rises into the air, I clutch my bad arm to my chest and I think about my egg, its hatching among the stars, and its new life beyond the loam.

Holly Schofield travels through time at the rate of one second per second, oscillating between the alternate realities of city and country life. Her speculative fiction has appeared in many publications including *Analog*, *Lightspeed*, and *Escape Pod*, is used in university curricula, and has been translated into multiple languages. She hopes to save the world through science fiction and homegrown heritage tomatoes. Find her at hollyschofield.wordpress.com.

Fernst Contact

by

Geoffrey Hart

ESPERANZA is nervous. *Sweating* nervous, and thank God for antiperspirant and moisture-wicking fabrics, or she'd be in real trouble. First contact's not trivial at the best of times; it's been done several times now, mostly successfully. But when it fails? Hoo, boy.

The Rendi ambassador briefed the deputy minister, then her, on the protocol, what to do and when, and how to prepare for the meeting. The deputy minister has complete faith in her, otherwise she wouldn't be here, but Esperanza has been owned by a cat for many years, and she knows how to read feline body language. The way the Rendi ambassador smiled didn't reassure. She's seen it before in a mama cat dropping a mouse in front of her litter so they'd have something to play with.

The deputy minister doesn't believe her. "They're our allies, Ess. Trust them." *Sure* she'll trust them. What could possibly go wrong?

Her already tense nerves aren't helped by having survived a keto diet for just over two weeks—enough, the Rendi ambassador claims, to banish any trace of her having consumed plant products. Which makes sense, given the Fernst are plants, and might take it amiss if they're forced to make first contact with a vegetarian. *Fernst* obviously isn't the species' real name, since plants don't speak, at least not audibly. It's the name provided by the Rendi, and the new aliens seem to have accepted it in the preliminary written communication, so there's that. The Fernst speak by changing colors—by rapidly modifying the photosynthetic pigments in their chromamphores. She'll need a translator box to understand and reply to whatever they have to say. One's clipped to her shoulder; the Rendi provided the visual and spectrographic database it needs to function.

The airlock door hisses open, and a humid wave of sultry, oxygen-rich air washes over her. *Great*: she's going to sweat even more. Hope the plant cleanse worked, or she's about to go down in history as the

initiator of a major international incident. Esperanza steps into the
alien ship, sinking several inches into the rich soil that covers the floor.
She finds herself wishing she hadn't worn her best leather shoes. The
wet soil's going to ruin them, and she's already spent her clothing
budget this quarter.

Before her stands the Fernst ambassador, slightly shorter than her.
Its body comprises a densely woven bundle of grey-brown vines, each
thick as her thumb, that flare like a buttress where they merge into a
trio of sturdy stilt-like walking roots. At the top of the stem, there's an
exuberant eruption of thick, deep-green leaves that arch like a fountain.
There's a faint smell of cinnamon.

As instructed, she takes a deep breath and holds it as she approaches
the plant. When she can't hold it any longer, she bends towards the
leaves and exhales slowly: the gift of carbon dioxide, which, for a plant,
is the gift of life. She can feel her heart rate accelerating, and then
the plant's leaves flash a deep red amidst the green. Her gift has been
accepted. More lights flash.

Her translator reads the flickering colors. In a voice modulated to
inspire confidence, it translates: "Welcome to our ship, Earth woman.
We accept your gift with gratitude, and hope it will be the first of many
such gifts our peoples exchange."

She enunciates clearly so the translator will understand. "On behalf
of the peoples of Earth, I welcome you to our solar system. Your
presence is a great gift to us." Lights flash in her peripheral vision as
the device translates.

Leaves rustle. "Kneel before me that I may see you better."

Esperanza complies, knees squishing in the moist soil. She flinches,
mourning what the dirt and water will do to her pants. She finds herself
eye to stalk with a structure she hadn't noticed before. The plant's
eyes?

More flickering. "We appreciate your sacrifice in forgoing consumption of plant matter for many days. But we fear the Rendi have
deceived you. We bear no ill will towards those who consume plants.
It's been millennia since we reached an accommodation with our
planet's herbivores."

"That's a relief," Esperanza observes. She's still sweating hard, but
she's beginning to relax, and it's mostly heat sweat now rather than
nerves.

Flicker: "In fact, we've established a *quid pro quo*. We ourselves
consume animal flesh, since there's no better source of nitrogen and
phosphorus than flesh." There's a pause. "We can't tell you how grateful
we are for the second gift from your people: the gift of your flesh."

Esperanza recoils in horror, but she hasn't noticed the whiplike tendril that coiled around her arm. If a plant could be said to be lascivious, the Fernst's touch is lascivious. She can't help herself: she tries to pull away, but the tendril tightens, and she can feel it pulling her towards the plant. She's about to scream, when the tendril abruptly releases, accompanied by something that sounds suspiciously like a hissing fart. The air fills with an overpowering burst of cinnamon, and the Fernst's leaves shake wildly.

"The ambassador expresses uproarious laughter," the translator says. "Just kidding," it continues. "We do, of course, consume animal flesh. But never sentients. That would be...*unthinkable.*" Another hissing burst of cinnamon.

Unable to control herself, Esperanza glares at the plant, hoping the Rendi haven't taught it human body language.

"Ah, if you could have seen the look on your face!" Is the translation box laughing at her?

Also: *Crap. The Rendi* have *explained human body language.*

"We appreciate your tolerance of our small jest. We've found, over the centuries, that it's unproductive to establish relationships with species that lack a sense of humor."

All at once, the humor of the situation sinks in, and Esperanza laughs. When she catches her breath again, she smiles and nods. "I hope this will be the start of a beautiful friendship, Ambassador." And she takes a deep breath, holds it, and exhales onto its fronds.

Geoff Hart (he/him) works as a scientific editor, specializing in helping scientists who have English as their second language publish their research. He also writes fiction in his spare time, and has sold 54 stories thus far. Visit him online at www.geoff-hart.com.

Strange Roots

by

Eve Morton

W HEN they would not give me his ashes, I wanted the dirt where he'd worked and then perished.

Nevin Churchill Range, Research Chair of Botany and Theoretical Biology—the finest professor imported into the outer reaches of space and my man. He'd been promoted in order to capture and cure the molting sickness of the planet's inhabitants. When we arrived, we saw their blackened and browned skin through glass around the landing dock. They stood as still as trees, their missing toes and noses like branches stripped of autumn leaves. Nevin did not baulk at his task. He simply went to work. He taught. He researched. And he gardened, his second love after me and his work (we tied, you see), and that was where he died. Shot in the head out of rage when one of his students failed his class, collapsed in the community garden, where he went when he wanted nothing more than to think.

A tragedy—and a waste—one only expounded when the Range family lawyer came down and said that our relationship was nothing more than mere roommates. We had been together for fifteen years. I knew the ins and outs of his mind, his body, his life—but I did not count as blood. I did not count as someone who deserved a piece of his body, even if only a fraction. Only a speck of dust and dirt in the never-flowing wind of this planet. I was no more than a mouth, shouting into the vast void of space and bureaucratic rules.

So if I could not have his body, I wanted his earth.

Something in the earth wanted him, loved him, after all. When I saw the photos of the body—published in a shoddy magazine and shot on tourist film—and I knew that tight grip around his waist that the vines possessed. I did it to him when we made love, as we slept, when we first met. After being shot, he'd been left face down like a perennial bulb, and by the time the morning maintenance workers saw his corpse, an entire root system of plants had crawled around his legs.

The workers thought he was a new display. Not until the first walkers of the community garden arrived did someone cry out that a body of a man was planted there.

By then, he was already gone. Too late. He'd not been dead when the shot entered him, but he'd been dead by the time the dirt filled his lungs. And so, if his death had been in the garden, the garden was where I knew I must go to gather his last rites, along with the cure for the sick inhabitants, both of us wretches without a guide to save us.

I used what I could understand of his plans. At the time, his research still remained a mystery to me. We were both students, but he was the one who received grants that we lived on from month to month, jumping from planet to planet until we came by this strange one with the molting sickness. Without him around, and without nearly as many credentials behind my own name, there was nothing more I could do for these inhabitants or myself without cracking a code of some kind. I sat in our shared apartment—decorated ourselves, the walls painted a mauve color we both loved, and slept in the bed with the same sheets night after night—and I tried to decipher everything he'd written. Cryptic ciphers, arcane symbols, nothing more. I found a map with a location marked off in an x; so much like treasure, so much like a pirate plundering the root systems of the local forest for something more than soil and dirt. He wanted a cure. He wanted treatment. He was a good man, devoted to curing the sick. When I held up that x to the light of our apartment, the wrought-iron gates of the community garden illuminated.

And I knew my plan would work.

I waited until dark. Crept close to that same wrought-iron gate, now locked and barricaded. I waited until the last dogs—in a breed I'd never seen before, all razor-sharp teeth—had done a final tour of the place with the guards.

Then I began to dig.

My hands were torn by rocks. My fingernails broke off at the nail bed; blood mixed with brown dirt. Earth flowed into me, and I paid it no mind, until I swore I could hear Nevin's voice in my ear again.

"Closer, closer," he said. "The rhizome is here. All around. Now, now, now."

I dug faster. From black topsoil to ruddy clay, I unearthed an array of rocks and life forms living among the jagged edges. Worms, blind moles, a few stray teeth and bones of something else I couldn't name or find in his journals later on. When a spindly root, so much like an arm, shot out and touched my wrist, I gasped.

The guard dogs barked.

I dug faster and faster as I heard the deep tones of men surrounding me. The root would not let me go. It held on, and the more I fought, the tighter it became. I thought of the first time Nevin kissed me and I'd tried to get away. I was overcome with what people told me about our love, and he only whispered that it was no longer a sin here on this faraway place.

"We can be together in the darkness of space," he said. "We can be together in the light of day. We can be together for all eternity, but only if the rhizome does not decay."

I heard the rhyming words again. So much like a lullaby for children, so much like a spell. My man was a scientist and a poet; a philosopher and a man of letters; an autodidact and denouncer of the traditional religious faith. As I dug further, and the root still gripped me, flowing up my arm and around my shoulder, humming the same tune, I wondered if Nevin had also been a spell caster. A witch. The crowds had not been correct about him, but there was something unearthly in this garden. Something that I could not name, nor find later on in his written words. This was not on his grants, his books, in the tools of his trade. My man was something else, working in secret. He was called crazy and murdered. He paid the price for his own truth. I only hoped I could find that truth, tangled inside these strange roots.

I soon struck a rock. The vibrations flowed all the way down into my teeth. Hard impact, indestructible. I looked over the gate and saw the flashing lights of someone coming close. The hole was not deep enough to get inside. I wanted the dirt from where Nevin had lain prone and heliotropic towards the sun. But I couldn't dig anymore or I'd be caught.

The verdict from his family—no more than a roommate, a potted plant in his collection—came down on me again. I closed my eyes. I tasted dirt on my tongue. When I sobbed and my tears mixed with the dirt, I swore I heard Nevin's words again.

"Dig, dig," he said. "We can be together in the darkness of space. We can be together in the light of day. We can be together for all eternity, but only if the rhizome does not decay. So dig, dig."

I picked up the trowel I'd brought. I used it to dig past the rock, then to widen the mouth of the hole so I could slip inside. Just as the dogs came by once again, I was nothing more than dirt. I piled it over my face, my hands, and body, and I became roots. It was cold and wet. Then it was a warm embrace, like being surrounded by Nevin all over again.

The dogs barked near me. The man with them saw nothing. He walked away, cursing. He took out a flask from his pocket, knocked it back.

I had the rest of the night to myself after that. Nevin and me, under the dirt, under the gate, I pushed through and emerged into this wild garden. His last burial, where his soul could never truly escape.

I didn't know the names of the flowers or other fauna here, so I made them up. I touched leaf and stem and singular flower bud. Some opened against my fingers, as if I was the sun, while others curled up from being disturbed while they dreamed. I could feel those dreams —collective and unconscious, filled with the minerals of the soil that Nevin had died in—all around me. Nevin had decayed here. Been absorbed here. Nevin was alive with the plants, and so, I could be alive with him a little while longer.

Until dawn, I spoke to the plants. I touched them with my bare skin. I listened. They made me laugh. The root that had wrapped itself around my hand and shoulder underground was still here, disjointed from the flowing structure from which it came. When the first break of dawn scattered the dark light into blue, the root tugged on me, alerting me that my time was up.

"I want to stay here," I said in the quiet that followed. "I don't want to leave you, Nevin."

I waited to hear his voice in the plant life. I waited to hear the words he'd rhymed for me. Nothing came. Nothing spoke. I fell down into the same rose bed where he'd fallen after the shot that took his life, where his feet had gestured to the same sunlight in the east. I gathered the dirt in my hands, held it to my chest, and longed to bury myself next to him in the garden. I saw no reason to live, no reason to go on.

"Dig, dig," I heard his voice again as only a memory. I looked at the patch of dirt in front of me, remembered the ashes I'd been denied, and decided to scoop what I could into my palms, into my pockets, and take that home. I wanted the earth where he'd grown and died. I wanted to survive on my own.

The moment I dug, I hit something else. Softer than the first rock, and with less give than the roots that I still wore around my arm. A diary, a ledger, some sort of worn-down book. I saw his name emblazoned on the first page. All the cryptic tools to solve his notes at home. All the ciphers and secret alphabets.

His research, revealed.

I held the book to my chest. I heard the dogs stirring in the distance. So I gathered my strength and dove into the ground again, to push out the other side, a living testament to his life in my hand.

It all started with ashes, with death, with mourning—yet what I received was so much more. I translated his notes. I found the cure for the molting sickness of the colony, the decaying disease that made their limbs fall off and melt like wax under light. I found the answers that most needed, including me. It all started with ashes, with death, with mourning—but that root system that hung onto me, clung until it came off in the water of a bath, and then writhed and writhed for more light, that root is a he and he is still alive.

He sits in a soil bed on my windowsill. He's grown legs and arms and a face that I can't quite see, but I'm hoping will reveal itself soon whenever he decides to bloom. I place him towards the sun. I water him and call him Nevin.

And at night, when it's just the two of us, I sing: "We can be together in the darkness of space. We can be together in the light of day. We can be together for all eternity, but only if the rhizome does not decay."

I whisper again, "only if the rhizome does not decay," and I wait. One day, his roots will come to life. He will live again.

Until then, I keep his strange secrets to make sure we both survive.

Eve Morton lives in Waterloo, Ontario, Canada with her partner and two sons. She spends the days running after those boys and the nights brainstorming her next creative project. At some point, she writes things down, usually while drinking copious amounts of coffee. Find updates at authormorton.wordpress.com.

Engaging The Idrl

by

Davin Ireland

I

THE desert here is pink and rocky and shrouded in darkness for much of the day. The excavation site is slashed with grey spills of rubble that could be collapsed towers or random seams of granite. To the east, great clouds of mortar dust boil across the plains, scouring the arid landscape, depriving it of fresh growth. Only the Idrl remain. Oblivious to the wind, seemingly blind to the desolation, they drift through the emptying topography like azure phantoms, the robes that stain their hides a deep, lustrous blue snapping petulantly in the breeze. They refuse to talk to us or communicate in any way, for they consider our troops an army of occupation.

Our generals are therefore left to draw their own conclusions about what went on before mankind arrived on Serpia Dornem.

Grue says he knows. After listening to his story, I am inclined to agree. The Idrl did not build these vast, ruined cities. Nor did they occupy them. They are instead an indigenous nomad species, periodically emerging from hibernation to roam the land and take whatever sustenance their dying world has to offer. The extrinsic Constructor Race, however, strove for greater things.

II

A transport carrier arrived unannounced this morning. Its harried crew whisked us away to a salt flat fifteen hundred clicks east of base camp and dumped us there to await further instruction. None came, and when adverse conditions erased our commlink, some of the younger men grew visibly anxious. Grue himself appeared towards the end of afternoon, tiny reconnaissance craft bobbing and groaning against increasingly heavy turbulence. The perpetual scream of mortar dust had intensified to a sandstorm of vicious proportions.

"We depart at eighteen-hundred hours," the corporal announced, and took shelter on the leeward side of the craft. He would say no more and prohibited further discussion between the men. Forty minutes later we took to the skies.

"Right beneath us," Grue cried above the shriek of the engines. We'd been in the air for maybe a half hour. "Tell me what you make of it."

I looked down. The pink and grey shelf of desert that followed us everywhere had abruptly vanished, only to be replaced by what turned out to be forty-thousand square kilometres of unconstrained parking space—an asphalted lot of such grotesque proportions that it extended all the way to the horizon in three different directions. And not a motor vehicle in sight.

Who were the Constructor Race? I ask myself. Why did they engage in such stupendous folly? Precious little evidence remains beyond the once-towering cities themselves, and these have been stripped, razed, and abandoned in a way that suggests the destruction was thorough and wholly intentional. By the look of it, the only exception is the colossal parking facility itself, identical in character and composition to anything one might have found outside a conventional strip mall circa 1980. With the exception of size, of course. This thing dwarfs anything earth had to offer by several orders of magnitude.

Tomorrow we will learn more. For the remainder of this evening, we'll kick our heels and wait for the survey team to complete its remote sweep from orbit. Naturally, the Idrl sense moves are afoot. They have ceased roaming the sterile plains and watch us cautiously from distance. The calm dignity these beings exude stands in stark contrast to their magnificent trailing robes, which ripple and flutter incessantly on the gritty air currents. A displaced show of emotion, perhaps? We may never know. Meanwhile, certain members of the unit already exhibit the first creeping signs of battle fatigue, despite having fought no war.

III

Tang and Spritzwater, two of my best men, are refusing to go on. They shed their laser carbines shortly after dawn this morning and now stand with their backs to the spent orb that is this system's sun, shadows trailing before them like tired phantoms. They say there is something wrong with Serpia Dornem. They say the planet is haunted. I am beginning to believe them. When we performed a perimeter sweep at 23:00 hours last night, rocks, pinkish sand, and lazily flipping dust devils were about the extent of the threat. As the false dawn coloured the horizon, a monstrous city loomed to the east.

My men blame the natives. Even those of us who retain a degree of objectivity are becoming unnerved by their austere presence, which grows by the hour. During breakfast I counted eleven Idrl gathered about a cluster of the spiny-leaved plants that cling in the cracks between the parched rocks. By first inspection, their number had swollen to seventeen. They filter down from the arid hills to the south —gaunt, weary, faces expressionless yet eloquent as pantomime masks. This is not uncommon for a race subjected to prolonged oppression. A spectacle is unfolding here, and the spectacle is us. We have found the one city the Constructor Race overlooked—or perhaps *it* has found *us* —and now we must investigate.

Later.

The nearer we get, the greater the extent of the challenge. In the swirling wastelands between base camp and city, we spied a dead tree. It stood naked and branchless in the wind, sand-blasted for what may have been centuries on end. Oloman was dispatched to investigate, and returned minutes later in a state of high agitation.

"You have to see this," he said, tugging at my sleeve. "You have to notify basecamp right away."

We deviated from our plan just long enough to verify the lieutenant's claims, which were irrational in the extreme but considering the circumstances, justified. The tree was not a tree at all, but a road sign: a rusting iron pole pointing the way to a city with an eerily prophetic name. Venice Falls. The words were still legible despite the corrosive effects of the wind-driven mortar dust. There could be no mistake. Out here in a region of the galaxy visited by no human, there exists an urban settlement large enough to accommodate the entire population of New York City.

And it has an English name.

The Idrl appear unmoved by our discovery. They form a serene gathering to our wind-choked huddle, steadfastly refusing any attempt at dialogue even though the surreal possibility exists that we may actually speak the same language. Nye has tried to tempt them with extra clothing and food, but all is ignored. Even when an older female, badly

undernourished and clearly hypothermic, allows her eye to wander in
the direction of the rehydration kit, her fellow tribal members close
ranks about her. We will not see her again.

IV

Much as I suspected but dared not mention for fear of spooking the
men, this metropolis is a full-scale reproduction of a late twentieth
century earth city, faithful in every detail except one. There are no
people here. None except us. We wander the empty streets in aimless
fascination, weapons drawn but pointed at the ground. Sand dunes
clog the intersections, erosion blights the shopfronts. But any wear and
tear is incidental, a tawdry gift of the elements. I stare at the red-brick
apartment buildings that line the sprawling avenues, at the reproduction brownstones with their salt-stained walls, at the magnificent steel
and glass towers that pierce the gloomy skies—and wonder again who
the Constructor Race were and why they built this place.

    Were they intending to populate it with immigrants from our own
planet? To forcibly humanise the Idrl for their own ends? To create a
grotesque parody of a theme park? Such notions strike me as absurd.
The dying sun, the alkaline soil—a bleaker aspect is difficult to imagine.
And yet they *must* have had a reason for this madness. Acquiring
enough knowledge to make a balanced judgement would, I fear, takes
decades of investigation, and we only have weeks. In the meantime,
the men are determined to make a start. Without my consent, Oloman
used the butt of his carbine to smash a movie theatre window and
gain access to the sealed lobby. Inside, our torches revealed plush red
carpets, a ticket booth, even a hot dog stand advertising various brands
of popcorn and ice-cream. None of the food on offer was actually
available, but that didn't detract from the authenticity of the moment.
It seemed so real that I half expected an usher in a velvet suit to emerge
from a side door and escort us to our seats.

    But not everyone shared my enthusiasm.

    "It doesn't smell right," Oloman complained, "like fresh paint and
new carpets shut in for thirty thousand years."

    "And no movies," agreed Nye. "Look at the poster frames. They're
all empty."

It was a pattern that was to be repeated throughout the city. Bars with no liquor, trash barrels without garbage, corporations bereft of employees. A structure lacking content, in other words. A picture with no colours. And beneath it all, lurking at the very edges of perception, the unshakeable conviction that we were being watched.

"Of course we are," I declared in exasperation, "the Idrl are everywhere. The fact they choose not to show themselves doesn't mean they're not around."

But my words failed to alleviate the unit's increasing sense of unease. In the end we retreated with weapons raised and hearts aflutter. Venice Falls is a deeply disturbing place.

V

Tang and Spritzwater are gone. We arrived back at base camp an hour ago to discover the radio damaged beyond repair and half our stock of rations missing. This is not the work of the Idrl. If the men are to believe this we must locate and capture the deserters before the spiral of suspicion and paranoia becomes too great. Already some of them are starting to question my authority.

The search begins in earnest.

Ranging through the powdery foothills beyond the city, we encounter the entrance to one of the stately Idrl burrows. The rock-lined tunnel leading down into the ground is high enough for a man to stand upright during his descent, yet from just a few feet away it appears no more conspicuous than a natural fissure in a seam of granite. We enter, calling out the names of the missing as we navigate these labyrinthine corridors. Occasionally we find signs of occupation. These people have nothing. The few oxen-like beasts that survive on this desiccated globe are reared and worked to death underground, never to see the light of the pale sun. The lapis lazuli the Idrl mine for their own personal use—the one commodity this barren place has left to offer—we would gladly take off their hands in exchange for food, water, and crops engineered to survive the inhospitable conditions. But that would be dishonourable, it seems. So instead they survive on a diet of insects and the coarse spiny plants that thrive out here in the desert, taking hope from the knowledge that, quite incredibly, they are almost there. The Constructor Race is gone, we could very well be next. Freedom, at any price, is almost within their grasp.

I wonder what the Idrl will be left with once we return to space.

An answer of sorts arrives from an unexpected source. The search for the missing men having proved fruitless, we withdraw to the surface in pairs, myself and a private called Gosling bringing up the rear. Just prior to breaking the surface, Gosling angles his flashlight at the ceiling. The scalding white torch beam reveals a long niche carved into the rock along the top of the cavern walls. Here, stowed like so much excess firewood, lie the mummified remains of countless generations of deceased Idrl. Intrigued by the discovery, we retrace our steps, following the dusty seam of corpses to its source. The oldest, driest specimens are stored at the heart of the burrow, nearest the fire pit, which is where the Idrl sleep, cook and keep warm. It makes sense for their carbon store to begin here, nearest the flames, where the dead can do their bit to sustain the living. No wonder we never found a burial site.

Back at the entrance to the burrow, we make another discovery. Huddled next to the freshest addition to the line of shrivelled corpses crouches a juvenile female—shivering, barely alive, no larger in my estimation than a six-year-old girl. Hunger has collapsed her face, preternaturally enlarging her eyes. But already she has learned her people's way. When I offer my coat, her gaze drifts to the rock wall opposite and she is lost to me. Almost. But then an idea strikes me. The chocolate bar is freeze-dried, vacuum packed, and perfectly fresh. When I break the foil package and wave it beneath her nose, the child's nostrils quiver spasmodically. A tremor of anguish seems to travel through that pitifully slight form. For a moment, just a microscopic sliver of time, her eyes betray all of the misery and longing in her tiny heart. Then all of the fight seems to bleed out of her, and she is lost to me once more.

"Move out," I whisper to Gosling, and we break the surface together in uncomfortable silence. But at least I have confirmation of that which I had suspected all along: the Idrl are not the empty vessels they pretend to be. They feel, just as we do. They hurt. They hope.

VI

Tang and Spritzwater are now officially missing. I reported their disappearance this morning when a second transport carrier dropped by with news, supplies and a fresh radio. After consulting the high command, it was decided we would make one last sweep and then return to headquarters for a final debrief—the one that will reveal the fate of our mission entire. Already, Serpia Dornem is being discussed in terms of a washout, and that suits the men just fine.

I think I understand the nature of the problem now. I honestly believe I am starting to comprehend the size of the dilemma the Idrl face. They are a dying species on a world that will soon expire. They have spent the last thirty-thousand years subjugated and occupied by a race who were at best indifferent to their existence and at worst may have enslaved them. Perhaps they no longer understand the meaning of compassion. Their lives are brief and cruel and filled with all the bitterness of winter. Perhaps they need someone to show them that not all visitors to this place are hostile and that not all outsiders are to be viewed with distrust.

All I need is a chance.

We continue to follow the winding pathways through the foothills to the south, but few believe the deserters—if deserters they truly be—would seek refuge in exposed outlands when the corrupt monolith of Venice Falls squats so predominantly to the east. They are much more likely to be drawn by the prospect of shelter and the comforts of a place that reminds them of home. Still, we must be thorough and we must be sure. And the search has not proved a complete waste of time. Bit by bit, the land is giving up its secrets. We discover a deep quarry veined with countless fractures and many millions of the tough, spiny plants upon which our hosts depend. We also discover a broken loom near a deep, natural well. Attached to the loom is a cup filled with powdered lapis lazuli. So now the picture is complete. The Idrl eat this plant, feed it to their livestock, weave its sinewy fibres into robes that are subsequently stained blue with the crushed lapis. If you add in the not unreasonable amounts of geothermal energy generated beneath the surface, you have an entire ecosystem right there.

Returning to the city at noon, the men are somewhat cheered by the knowledge that the next storm will not hit until we have completed our projected sweep. As we draw nearer, Oloman's behaviour becomes increasingly erratic. So great is his distraction, in fact, that word of it filters up the column to me and I am forced to drop back and confront him. The last thing I need right now is another Tang or Spritzwater.

"Oloman, what the hell is going on, man," I demand. "Your attitude is making the men restless."

In lieu of an answer, Oloman turns on his heel so that he faces back the way we came, finger jabbing in the direction of our dusty tracks. The dry soil here is heavy with iron oxide, and our footprints describe a pinkish-red arc that trails all the way back to base camp. He then flats a hand in the direction of the old signpost that marks the way to Venice Falls. It stands perpendicular to our position, about a mile distant, and I can just make it out through the murk of late morning.

"We've got company," Oloman informs me, and then narrows his eyes. "But not Idrl."

Another species, perhaps? My field glasses are useless against the membranous skeins of dust that swirl across the intervening plain. I therefore make a decision based on instinct. Oloman may have his weaknesses, but foolishness is not one of them. "Collect Gosling and Nye and follow in my wake," I tell him. "Send the rest of the men on into the city."

We reach the signpost just as the last of the forward party melts into a decaying business district on the edge of town. It turns out that Oloman's paranoia got the better of him. The little girl from the cavern has followed us. She is no more forthcoming than on the previous occasion, though her whole body betrays the incredible risk she has taken in coming here. A pronounced pulse-beat bangs at her throat. Her overly large eyes dart frantically to and fro in their sockets. Not another species, then: just a smaller version of same. Now, at least, I can begin the process of redressing the balance, of showing a little kindness where before cruelty reigned supreme. Dropping my carbine in the dust, I produce the uneaten chocolate bar from my flak jacket and once again offer it to the girl. There is no hesitation this time: she snatches the confectionary from my hand, consumes it in six diminutive bites—chewing, swallowing, unable to disguise the terrible need that resides within.

"Rations," I call out, and four packs hit the dirt. There is no longer any point in offering, I merely load the pockets of the girl's robe with food, and pat her gently on the head—all too aware, as are we all, that it is at such moments history is made.

Recalling the notion that the Idrl may actually understand something of English, I call to the girl as we depart. "Tell your family we are their friends," I shout above the distant groan of mortar dust. "Tell your tribe we mean them no harm. We are not here to hurt you. We can help."

My words are lost on the wind. Perhaps it is for the best. Perhaps we should allow the gesture alone to speak for us. As long as we march towards the city, the little one remains in place—watching, waiting, possibly savouring the taste of our friendship and the notion that not all strangers are aggressors. One can only hope.

VII

The storm is almost upon us. Angry thunderheads roll in from the horizon, purple-white lightning veins the clouds. We do not have much time. Sensing that the end is near, we fan out through the streets, the names of the missing echoing back at us from abandoned buildings.

I cannot stop thinking about that little girl. With one simple gesture, one overt act of kindness, the relationship between Human and Idrl may have changed forever. If they come to us for more, we will accommodate them as best we can. If this entire people requires refugee status, we will provide it. The hardy crops and other supplies initially offered as trade items will be granted as gifts—part of a larger goodwill package that will grow in size until the Idrl can no longer deny the sincerity of our motives. We will not rest until some semblance of freedom and democracy are established in this barren arm of the galaxy.

I am already dreaming of petitioning world statesmen on the Idrl's behalf when a call goes up from the next block. The cries are eerily faint against the rumble of the approaching storm, but reverberate hollowly among the crystalline towers. I race down the sand-clogged avenue, past homely little Italian restaurants with generic-sounding names, past lofty investment houses with grandly furnished reception areas, past diners and hardware stores, supermarkets and coffee shops—all of them empty, none of them dead because they were never alive to begin with. They are stillborn, unborn, aborted.

Tang and Spritzwater are cowering in a walkdown when we find them. They claim that a giant winged creature chased them into endless blank acres of parking lot after we left them yesterday morning. The next thing they knew, they were in the very heart of the city with no memory of how they got there. They have been trying to find their way out ever since. The story sounds contrived, I admit, but their fear is only too real. At the end of my tether, I drag them up to the sidewalk by their collars and shove them in the direction of base camp, my anger at their behaviour tempered only by the knowledge that our time here is coming to an end.

IIX

Trudging back through the gloom and the gathering winds, we find ourselves veering inexorably in the direction of the signpost that marks the way to Venice Falls. Is it curiosity that draws us on or a deeper need to confirm, one final time, that this is not some vast illusion? The men are excited at the prospect of our departure. Certain of them discuss the selfies they will take of themselves with the city in the background. Others express a wish to take the sign home with us as a souvenir. The mood is upbeat and euphoric, and remains so despite the knowledge that we are under scrutiny from the south. For at the summit of each foothill stands a lone Idrl, robes swirling, posture unreadable. The sky has turned the colour of an old bruise. The resulting light tinges the ground beneath their feet an ominous purple. Lightning flickers at our backs, illuminating those austere figures but revealing nothing of what inhabits their hearts.

We encounter the girl one last time. She is still in the same place. The pockets of her robe still bulge with untouched ration packs while a brown smear of chocolate decorates that delicate mouth. As ever, the blue stain of her garments flutters endlessly on the strengthening breeze. One of the men—I think it Gosling, but it could just as easily be me—allows a horrified moan to escape his lips. It appears the natives have found yet another use for the spiny plant they rely on so much. Its platted fibres creak gently back and forth as the little girl twists in the wind, the weight of the ration packs grossly elongating her already slender neck. Once and for all, the Idrl have answered our gesture of kindness with an unequivocal statement of intent.

Only now am I beginning to comprehend the Constructor Race's motives for leaving this place after investing so much in it for so very long. Victory is not a question of superior firepower, it seems. It is not even a matter of right and wrong. It is simply a matter of conviction— and who now would dispute that the Idrl's conviction is far, far greater than ours could ever be.

Davin Ireland recently returned to the south of England after spending three decades in the Dutch city of Utrecht. His fiction credits include stories published in over seventy print magazines, webzines and anthologies worldwide, including *Aeon*, *Underworlds*, *The Horror Express*, *Zahir*, *Pseudopod*, *Rogue Worlds*, *Storyteller Magazine* and *Something Wicked*. You can visit his site at davinireland.com.

Beanstalk in a Box

by

Tim Kane

E VER yearn to journey to the clouds? Intrigued by those darned cumulus ogres? Well, be curious no more. The new Beanstalk in a Box is available from Feefie Foofum Enterprises. This splendiferous invention will transport[1] you and your friends to the magical cloud realms above.

The price for a Beanstalk in a Box is one cow. (Due to the fact that bovines are difficult to acquire in urban areas, we will accept a cow-equivalent: seventy-five pounds of beef, four hooves, and one sweet bread.)

Your Beanstalk in a Box will arrive with three magic beans, each preinstalled with three cloud destinations (Cumulus, Stratocumulus, and Cumulonimbus). Please plant your beans outside in an open area[2] and leave overnight. Once your beanstalk has risen to cloud level, it is ready to climb. Despite the weather conditions in your area, be aware that temperatures in the troposphere can be downright chilly (-40°F), so bundle up.

CAUTION: When you reach your desired height, step onto a cloud using your cumulus clogs only. Failure to do so will result in insubstantial cloud buoyancy.[3]

Please be advised that ogres tend to frown on thievery. Consider for a moment how you respond when ants scramble into your abode and make away with your food. You coat then with bug spray. As a cloud traveler, you might be interested in purchasing the optional gas mask rated for level 3 toxicity.

Exciting news, our beanstalks are now disposable! Yes, when you're done traveling, simply use the included hatchet to chop the beanstalk down. Please allow five miles of open land for the disposed beanstalk to fall.[4]

---

[1] Users will need to climb the beanstalk.
[2] Allow 12 feet on all sides. Not responsible for root damage to dwellings.
[3] Falling.
[4] Yelling "Timber!" does not protect from potential lawsuits.

Remember, souvenirs from the cloud realms are not allowed. Should an irate two-ton ogre follow you down, you may be tempted to cut the beanstalk right away. This will cause the ogre to plummet toward you and your abode. Listen, Jack, don't say we didn't warn you.

Tim Kane loves things that creep and crawl. His first published book is non-fiction, *The Changing Vampire of Film and Television*, tracing the history of vampires in television and movies. Most recently published stories appear in *Lovecraftia*, *Navigating Ruins* and *Dark Moon Digest*. Find out more at www.timkanebooks.com.

Extracts from the Mission Log of Dr Alex Wilson

by

Becca Edney

DAY 29 (Sirius 3 Western Hemisphere Investigation)
Day 1 (Campsite 2)

Morning:

I've decided today is Saturday. I know it makes no sense to assign the Terran day names as a marker of time. I have no work schedule as I would on Terra, making it necessary to know the day of the week. Sirius 3 doesn't rotate, so the term "day" doesn't even have a meaning as it does on Terra.

But naming the day helps me to keep track of time. It's irrational, but the human mind is irrational. After all, I'm measuring the mission in Terran days to correspond with when I sleep, so why not name them? It's Saturday today.

Honestly, I should be more aware of my own irrationality. I've been away from base and other humans for nearly one Terran month and the human mind is not made for isolation. I bit off more than I could chew when I decided on a solo mission. I've made the decision now, though, so I'd best stop regretting it and get on with my work.

Today's tasks:

- Finish a survey of the surrounding ground-level fauna to complement my initial safety scan

- Set up atmospheric sensors

- Complete initial logs of ground-level flora and fauna

Midday:

Perhaps instead it should be Monday. It feels more like a Monday. Not that a day can really "feel" anything.

There appear to be fewer ground-level animals here than at the first campsite, which matches my initial screenings from yesterday. That's comforting; it suggests that the scanner is still well-calibrated. It's a little worrying, though, because it makes me wonder whether there's some reason few animals would take advantage of what seems to be a pleasant ecological niche. The basalt pillars are closer together here than they were at Campsite 1, but the ground cover is thicker, consisting mostly of moss and lichen detritus off the pillars. The atmospheric composition is also the same as elsewhere on the planet; I still need supplemental oxygen, but at the same flow rate. The radiation level is also still at baseline. You couldn't have a settlement here, but that's not because the environment is unsafe for habitation.

Atmospheric readings are logged in file AWilsSir3WHC2D1H06.log

I really hate the standard log file name format.

Evening:

I've positively identified a ground-level animal that appears to be native to this area: small mammals similar to Terran gerbils which burrow in the ground cover. I've attached an initial photograph to this entry, but they move fast and I only glimpsed it for a few moments. It appears to have shorter hair than a gerbil and larger front paws, but otherwise I didn't make out many details. I also found some droppings and took a sample.

Full flora and fauna survey of the immediate area is logged in file AWilsSir3WHC2D1H12_floraFauna.sfe
      Atmospheric readings in AWilsSir3WHC2D1H12.log

Like last night, the temperature is hot: uniform 28°C all day. I miss the air conditioning back at base, but at least the humidity is lower here than at Campsite 1.

Day 31 (Sirius 3 Western Hemisphere Investigation)
Day 3 (Campsite 2)

Morning:

Today is Monday.

The animals appear to be more accustomed to my presence now and I caught a handful of gerbils outside my shelter this morning. I managed to take a quick photo which shows them more clearly and have attached it to this entry. Last night I also heard something larger climbing on the roof of the shelter. Signs of anything living on the ground are still limited—it seems to only be the gerbils—but today I hope to start investigating higher in the pillars.

Today's tasks:

- Set up climbing equipment

- Set up and calibrate mid-height atmospheric sensors

- Perform initial mid-height flora and fauna scan

Atmospheric readings in AWilsSir3WHC2D3H00.log

Midday:

It may require two days to get the equipment set up properly; the basalt here is different to the similar columns at Campsite 1 and it took all morning to set up belaying pins to the site I picked for the sensors. I took a sample of the dust as well as lichen from locations at 1-metre intervals.

I did notice more droppings at elevation, so it appears there are more animals higher up. I took samples. I suppose the gerbils can't live off the ground, since they need to burrow.

This afternoon, I'll take the sensors up and get them installed.

Atmospheric readings in AWilsSir3WHC2D3H06.log

Evening:

Today has been full of delays; first it took longer to set up the belaying pins than I expected, then when I took the sensors up, I had to go back because I'd forgotten some of the securing pins. While I was on the ground, one of the sensors fell down even though I'm sure I left them safe; I'd found a ledge easily big enough and they were away from the edge. Something must have knocked it down. Luckily it's not badly damaged, but I'll have to spend the day tomorrow mending it.

When I went back up, sure enough, the others had been moved around but weren't damaged. I secured them and I'll go back up to check on them first thing in the morning. Whatever moved them must be bigger than a gerbil to have enough strength, but I didn't see anything.

I managed to get the initial scan done and, sure enough, there are a lot more animals up there. Nothing larger than half a metre in height or length. I wonder if they get bigger the higher I go? That wasn't the case at Campsite 1, so it's interesting. Something that size would easily be able to push a sensor off the ledge, though. I'll try to make time to perform some more scans, though I won't be able to fix the sensor and carry out a proper survey in a day.

Atmospheric readings in AWilsSir3WHC2D3H13.log
Scan results in AWilsSir3WHC2D3H13_floraFauna.log

Day 32 (Sirius 3 Western Hemisphere Investigation)
Day 4 (Campsite 2)

Morning:

Today is Tuesday.

The animals are getting more and more accustomed to me. The gerbils stayed outside the shelter for a while when I came out, watching me. I'd like to get a closer look at their teeth; they seem non-hostile, but I'd feel better if I could be sure they were herbivores.

Again, last night I heard something climbing around on the shelter. It didn't seem to be trying to interfere with the air vents or the antenna, which is comforting. Knowing that there are larger animals higher up,

I listened to try to get an idea of size from its weight and step length, but I couldn't make an estimate more accurate than "larger than the gerbils".

Today's tasks:

- Repair broken sensor

- Perform a second scan of flora and fauna at Elevation 1

Atmospheric readings in AWilsSir3WHC2D4H00.log

Midday:

I've got the components of the sensor back into place and replaced a couple of data busses that looked too badly damaged to properly function. When I took a break to go and perform the second scan, I found that something had been around the other sensors. It looks like it may have been the same animal. This time there were some tracks; I attached photos to this entry. It looks like it's probably a mammal with small paws with separated, non-opposable toes. I couldn't see any marks of claws, but I suspect they may be present since it would be difficult to manoeuvre around this terrain at elevation with no way to cling to anything. It's possible the claws can be sheathed like a Terran cat.

Fortunately, there was no damage, but a couple of the sensors had been pushed out of alignment. I put them back, but this may start to be a problem.

Atmospheric readings in AWilsSir3WHC2D4H06.log
Scan results in AWilsSir3WHC2D4H06_floraFauna.log

Evening:

I saw it! Just for a moment, I saw the animal that's been interfering with the sensors. I went up to do a last check on the sensors before I took the evening log and saw it sniffing the mended one. It was too quick for me to take a photo, so the best record I have is a description: approximately 45 cm long with a tail approximately a further 15 cm. Mottled green markings. At first, I thought it was quadrupedal, but when it ran away it jumped and flew and I think there was a third pair of limbs to stretch out a membrane. It vanished around a column before I could be sure. It had large eyes and a sharp face; I was reminded of a Terran bat or flying fox.

Atmospheric readings in AWilsSir3WHC2D4H12.log

Addendum:

I saw it again, or another of the same species. It appears to be carnivorous; while I was packing up for the night a few of the gerbils were out of their burrows, but suddenly one shrieked and they scattered. The animal swept down and grabbed one that was a little slower. It caught it in its mouth and ran around one of the columns, moving on all fours. Again, it was so unexpected I didn't have any kind of recording device to hand.

Day 34 (Sirius 3 Western Hemisphere Investigation)
Day 6 (Campsite 2)

Morning:

Today is Thursday.
    I wonder if I'll see that animal again today. Yesterday it seemed to be warming up to me a little, like the gerbils did. I'd like a video of its flight to go with the pictures.
    The temperature is falling a little. Last night it measured 26°C but it didn't feel any cooler.

Today's tasks:

- Start setting up climbing equipment to the next elevation

- Finish full survey of the flora and fauna at the first elevation

Atmospheric readings in ...D6H00.log

Midday:

I was taking notes on the lichen types and organising my samples at the first elevation when the animal turned up again. I wanted to see if I could get it to approach, so I kept still and it came over after a few minutes to sniff me. It didn't appear hostile, so I let it get my smell and it seemed to feel a lot more comfortable after that. When it left, I was able to get that video of its flight that I wanted; it's attached.

It generally seems a lot more confident than the gerbils; they still scatter if I move towards them at all. It makes sense, given that this creature appears to be a predator animal while the gerbils are prey.

That's admittedly not a comfortable thought, but it made no attempt to attack me. It may be intelligent enough not to try to eat something so much bigger than itself!

While it looks like a Terran flying fox, the behaviour most strongly reminds me of a Terran cat.

Atmospheric readings in … D6H06.log

Evening:

Cat identification confirmed; it purrs.

Of course, I don't know whether it uses the same vocalisation mechanism as Terran cats do, but it certainly sounds the same. It followed me when I was setting up the climbing equipment, climbing up the column next to me, though it always kept out of reach. I was right, it does have retractable claws. Then, when I'd finished and was taking a rest back at the first elevation it came and sat next to me and that's when I heard it purring. I have to admit that my reaction wasn't exactly scientific, but I miss the cats I had growing up on Terra.

It didn't follow me back to the ground, which is honestly for the best. I wonder where it lives. It must have a nest up there somewhere; I've never spotted it going back to any specific place.

Atmospheric readings in … D6H12.log

Day 37 (Sirius 3 Western Hemisphere Investigation)

Day 9 (Campsite 2)

Morning:

Today is Sunday.

I wonder how often it rains here; it's cloudy today and it reminded me that the whole time I've been on this mission it hasn't rained and it's been over a month now. Perhaps this is why the only plant life, at least here, is lichen. If I'd only seen the gerbils, I'd suspect that there's very little rain here and only small desert-type animals are able to thrive, but that's not consistent with some of the larger animals at the higher elevations.

The atmospheric readings have indicated higher humidity at higher elevations, so maybe there are some kind of moisture channels coming down the columns to the ground, or it could be that there's very little moisture down here and that's why there are desert-type animals on the ground and others higher up.

I've never seen the cat drink, though I have seen it hunt. I'll keep an eye out for anywhere there might be a water source at elevation while I'm working today.

Today's tasks:

• Full survey of flora and fauna at second elevation.

By the time I've climbed up and allowed time to climb down and up at midday to make sure I make a log entry and the readings come in properly, that'll be the whole day!

Atmospheric readings in ...D9H00.log

Midday:

As soon as I got to the first elevation the cat came to join me and it sat with me when I was surveying at the second elevation, but I'm a bit worried about it; it seemed a bit less active than the last few times I saw it. I don't know how I'd even begin to know whether it's ill or if there's some seasonal change happening, so I suppose I'd better just keep an eye on it.

I can't emphasise enough how much I wanted to tickle it under the chin, but I do know better than to touch strange animals in the deep wilderness of another planet.

Atmospheric readings in . . . D9H06.log

Evening:

The cat came down and sat with me, watching me eat dinner. I didn't share any and it didn't really seem to want anything, I think it's just as curious about me as I am about it. Of course, this means I didn't see anything of the gerbils.

So far, my theory about larger animals at higher elevation is holding up and I saw some water collected higher up on the pillars, so even if it doesn't rain I assume there's some condensation up there. I noticed it also felt cooler and damper than it does down here on the ground. I didn't see anything much bigger than a good-sized Terran dog and there's only one more elevation before I get to the top of the pillars, so that might be as big as they get. Everything I saw was a mammal, though, so I wonder if this area is seasonal; warm weather all the time would suit reptiles and I know there are reptiles on other parts of the planet.

I still haven't seen the cat's nest. It left soon after I'd finished dinner and climbed back up into the columns, but it went around the back of one of them and I lost track of it. It still seemed less energetic than before and I hope it's all right.

Atmospheric readings in . . . D9H12.log
Survey results in . . . D9H12_floraFauna.sfe

Day 39 (Sirius 3 Western Hemisphere Investigation)
Day 11 (Campsite 2)

Morning:

Today is Tuesday.

I'm not looking forward to the climb to the third elevation; the basalt looks more eroded up there and it's a long way to fall if one of my pins comes out. I'll make sure to put up safety lines, but it's still nerve-wracking. I suppose erosion tells me something about the conditions, though; it must be seasonal here because it's never rained since I arrived in the hemisphere, but it looks like it has.

I'm worried about the cat. While I know I don't know enough about it to tell if it's ill, it's got less and less active over the last few days and has become outright clingy; it was on the roof of my shelter this morning and is currently sitting next to me. For all I know, this is some sort of pack-bonding behaviour and not illness, but I almost hope not; that would make it pretty unfair to abandon it when I move on to the third camp, which I will in another fifteen days.

Certainly, if it were a normal pet back on Terra I'd have called a vet by now.

Today's tasks:

- Set up climbing equipment to third elevation

- Initial safety scan at third elevation

Atmospheric readings in ... D11H00.log

Midday:

I've sent a report back to base asking for advice, though I suspect nobody will be impressed that I've been pack-bonding with the local animals. Getting clear satellite signals through these columns can sometimes be difficult, so I've left the ping going until it gets a definite acknowledgement. I'll try again if I don't hear anything in 48 hours.

As I thought, the basalt is very eroded at elevation, so I'm having to go slowly and set up multiple safety precautions. It's probably going to take two days just to finish setting up the climbing equipment properly.

Atmospheric readings in ... D11H06.log

Evening:

I didn't get anywhere near close to finishing the climbing equipment and to be honest I'd be pretty happy not to have to go any higher than I already have, but I'm here to do a job so I'll be back up there tomorrow.

The cat sat with me again while I ate dinner. It wasn't following me around all day, so I assume it hunted some food for itself—it doesn't seem to have lost weight or anything—and it didn't seem too interested in my rations, which is good. I can't let it have any and am not sure I could guarantee it couldn't sneak a bite when my back was turned.

Atmospheric readings in ...D11H12.log

Day 42 (Sirius 3 Western Hemisphere Investigation)
Day 14 (Campsite 2)

Morning:

Today is Friday.

Still no response from base about the cat and it was waiting outside the shelter for me again today, but it seems withdrawn. As soon as it had confirmed I was there, it went and hid among some of my equipment. I really hope there's nothing wrong, but know that if there is, there's nothing I can do about it.

Today's tasks:

• Camp maintenance

It needs doing anyway, since it's been two weeks, but it'll give me a chance to keep an eye on the cat.

Atmospheric readings in ...D14H00.log

Midday:

The cat is curled up in a nest among my equipment. I've looked in a couple of times to make sure it's still there and it looked up, but didn't otherwise react. Normally, given its behaviour so far, it would have come out to hunt at some point, but it hasn't. I considered slipping it some meat from my own ration, but I know that would be a bad idea; I know it can eat and digest meat, but don't know if Terran meat specifically would agree with it.

Atmospheric readings in ... D14H06.log

Evening:

It turns out that the problem was that the cat was having kittens.

I've attached photos, but it's a litter of four. Their eyes are open and they're crawling around, unlike newborn Terran kittens, but mostly they want to cling to their mother. I assume if she was climbing around the columns, she would be able to carry them that way. Even as I'm writing, sitting nearby, I can hear them all purring in their nest in my equipment cache.

I've updated the message back to base. I'll be here for another two weeks, so I'll see how they grow and can get an idea of how quickly they mature from that.

Atmospheric readings in ... D14H12.log

Day 43 (Sirius 3 Western Hemisphere Investigation)
Day 15 (Campsite 2)

Morning:

Today is Saturday.

The whole nest of cat and kittens made a very odd chittering sound at me when I came to check on them this morning. I never heard the cat make that noise before, so something has presumably changed. She didn't seem to object to me approaching them, though, so she presumably trusts me. I didn't make any attempt to touch them, obviously.

Today I need to go and continue work at the tops of the columns; that'll take all day by the time I take climbing into account. The cat knows what she's doing and can take care of the kittens without my help, though I'm curious to keep watching.

Today's tasks:

- Drone scan of the surrounding landscape
- Take rock samples from the top of the column

Atmospheric readings in ... D15H00.log

Midday:

There was finally a return message from base when I got back down to make sure the atmospheric readings were coming in. I was right that nobody would approve of the fact that I was pack-bonding with the local wildlife, but there was a lot of interest in my addendum that the cat apparently trusts me enough to give birth to her kittens in my camp, since professionalism aside nobody has encountered an animal on Sirius 3 so far that seemed willing to pack-bond with a human. There's going to be more discussion at base about what I should do next, assuming that she does stay once the kittens are a little older.

I said that if she was willing to stay with me, I had been keeping a record of what she eats as well as, obviously, her native environment and would be happy to bring her home, provided there was absolutely no suggestion of experimentation on her or the kittens. I know perfectly well there was no way to phrase that that didn't sound like I was talking about a beloved pet, so anyone who wants can make fun of me for that.

Atmospheric readings in ... D15H06.log

Evening:

No response to my last message; I suspect it might be a day or two.

While I was eating dinner, the kittens popped up from the nest to watch me. It was unsettling; I'm not used to company, especially company that stares at me when I'm eating. The cat wasn't there for most of the evening, but she reappeared shortly before I started making this entry. She'd been hunting and had brought back food for the kittens. I'm revising my assessment of this species as mammals because while they do give birth to live young and feed them with milk, they are apparently able to eat meat as well, whereas most mammals use milk as the primary source of nutrition for newborns. She gave them the meat by regurgitating it like a bird. I considered trying to take a small sample to see if it was partly digested, but decided not to get between the kittens and their meal; I just took pictures.

Atmospheric readings in ... D15H12.log

Day 46 (Sirius 3 Western Hemisphere Investigation)
Day 18 (Campsite 2)

Morning:

Today is Tuesday.
    There was a message waiting from base when I got up this morning; it said that I should stay until the kittens moved out of the nest and seemed ready to go out into the wild and if that means staying past the usual 28 days that was fine. If the cat and kittens still stayed with me, I should return to base and bring them with me. It's pretty much the response I wanted, especially since the kittens are growing and really do seem attached to me. I think since I was around when they were born, they may have imprinted on me.

Today's tasks:

- Set up spectrometry equipment
- Continue scanning for water sources

Atmospheric readings in ... D18H00.log

Midday:

I'm still at a loss for a decent-sized water source at elevation that might support large animals. It might be necessary to set up cameras or even spend more time up there keeping watch; I saw some climbing mammals up to a metre long; unlike the gerbils on the ground or even, possibly, the cat they can't be surviving on condensation or what trickles down to the ground. I saw some shallow puddles at Elevation 2, but there must be a watering hole somewhere.

The kittens watched me eat lunch again. They haven't tried to leave the nest; they're clearly curious about their surroundings, but happy to just watch.

Atmospheric readings in …D18H06.log

Evening:

I finally saw one of the larger mammals drinking. It had a long tongue which it was able to poke into a crack in one of the columns, which I assume contained water. I'll check one of the other cracks tomorrow to see if I can find more.

The cat is sitting beside me as I write and purring. The kittens are apparently asleep in the nest.

Atmospheric readings in …D18H12.log

Day 49 (Sirius 3 Western Hemisphere Investigation)
Day 21 (Campsite 2)

Morning:

Today is Friday.

When I left the shelter this morning the cat was waiting outside scratching at the door. I was exactly on time as usual, but she evidently didn't agree. She made the same chittering noise at me as she did the morning after the kittens were born, then vanished up a column to go hunting. I suppose she was waiting for me to come out so she could leave me to babysit the kittens for her!

Today's tasks:

- Take soil samples from the ledges I found yesterday.

That should be enough, with the climbing it'll involve.

Atmospheric readings in ... D21H00.log

Midday:

When I got back from my climb up the columns, I was surprised to find the kittens out of the nest; the cat was encouraging them to crawl around and explore a bit. Luckily, I had secured anything they might disrupt or damage.

Atmospheric readings in ... D21H006.log

Evening:

Over the course of the day, they got a lot more confident and I filmed some video; the files are attached to this entry. They showed no sign of leaving the camp or even climbing off the ground very much, but I imagine they'll be climbing in the next few days.

The samples didn't go as well as I hoped; some of my climbing pins came out during the afternoon, and while I didn't come close to falling it took the rest of the afternoon to set them up again safely and I'll need to check the rest tomorrow.

Atmospheric readings in ... D21H12.log

Day 53 (Sirius 3 Western Hemisphere Investigation)
Day 25 (Campsite 2)

Morning:

Today is Tuesday.

The temperature dropped pretty noticeably overnight from yesterday's 30°C back to 26°C; I suspect there may be a seasonal change of some kind happening. If I go on to Campsite 3, I'll be able to observe it more; it's not that far, so it should be affected by the same weather patterns. There are also more clouds this morning than there have been in the past.

The cat and kittens don't seem to be bothered. They were all back in the nest this morning, but last night I could hear them climbing on the roof of the shelter.

Today's tasks:

- Humidity scans at all elevations

- Soil samples from Elevation 3

- Atmospheric weather scans

Not what I planned, but I want to see how the shift in the weather might be affecting the water supply.

Atmospheric readings in ... D25H00.log

Midday:

Even as I climbed the columns, I could feel the humidity increasing and there were some visible trickles of water when I shone a light into cracks, so that definitely answers the question of where water is coming from, though I still think there must be some rain to sustain the water supply used by the larger animals.

As I write, the kittens are crawling around my feet and chittering at me, though I can't make out what they want. I've attached some audio recordings of the sound to this entry. I think it's a greeting, but I can't be sure.

Atmospheric readings in ... D25H06.log
Weather scan results in ... D25H06_weather.sfe

Evening:

I got a bit of a fright as I was returning this evening; I finally saw the gerbils again, but that, of course, meant that the cat and kittens weren't in the camp. They arrived shortly after I did; it appears the kittens are starting to fledge, though of course that term isn't really appropriate for mammals. They all glided down from a ledge about three metres up one of the columns and the gerbils scattered. Now they're all curled up together back in the nest.

Atmospheric readings in ... D25H12.log

Day 56 (Sirius 3 Western Hemisphere Investigation)
Day 28 (Campsite 2)

Morning:

Today is Friday.
      Time to move on. I've got pretty comfortable here, but that's how it goes. Since I got the last of the sensors taken down last night, I just need to take a last scan and dismantle the shelter.
      I hope the cat and kittens come with me. This is very much the moment of truth to see whether they actually have pack-bonded with me or whether I just happen to be camping in their chosen territory.

Today's tasks:

   • Strike camp

Midday:

A quick entry before I start travelling. I'll make towards the third planned campsite to begin with and if the cat and kittens do follow me, I'll turn towards base tomorrow. They seemed unsettled by the fact that I was dismantling the shelter, but they stayed nearby in the undergrowth apart from occasional flights from one side of the campsite to the other.

Scan results in … D28H06_floraFauna.log

Evening:

Success! The cat and kittens were alarmed and made a lot of noise as they saw that I was leaving, but after some hesitation they followed and are now curled up together on the roof of my temporary shelter.
Tomorrow, I turn towards base to take them home.

Compiler's note: After completing their research into the flora and fauna of Sirius 3, Dr Wilson was appointed to a Professorship at the University of Titan and was accompanied there by the "cat" and "kittens": the first domesticated individuals from the species Chiroptera Wilsoni Sirii. Their descendents now live in a specially designed biodome on-campus.

Becca Edney is a fantasy writer who loves cats and *Lord of the Rings*. She was born in Virginia but now lives near Cambridge, juggling law with writing and trying to control an increasingly-unruly garden. She self-published her first novel *Bladedancer's Heirs* in 2015 (sequel currently in Editing Hell) and can also be found on her blog at lawyernovelist.wordpress.com.

Morning with a Difference

by

Alan Meyrowitz

(Previously published in Jitter, Issue #8, 2019.)

A thing with the appearance of a pretty-colored stone, blue and green, managed to survive traveling from its home planet in the Andromeda Galaxy, only to find itself in a specimen jar on a shelf in Billy's bedroom. The lid of the jar had air holes that Billy had punched for the benefit of the jar's previous resident, a grasshopper. A jar to the left had an actual stone, a sliver of quartz, and to the right was a jar with a cricket (grown quite docile after a day of futile jumping about).

By 2:00 AM Billy was sleeping soundly. The thing from space made a slight movement as a tendril emerged from it and made its way up and out through an air hole, then pointed its tip toward Billy and emitted a spray landing lightly on the boy's face. Billy licked a bit of it from his lips.

He slept well enough for a few hours more but then a nightmare ensued. He tossed about and had spasms that pushed his blanket off the bed.

In his dream he was a thing born in an ocean, but he had made his way onto the shore. He settled into a comfortable spot that was mostly sand but was sheltered by some scattered blue-green rocks.

He sensed this was not the first time he had come ashore. This time, he would choose to stay out of the water forever. The ocean had predators that were adept at devouring his kind, and he was content to be away from them.

The ocean had his food, too, but he had learned the shore could provide for him as well. It was not long before he saw the smaller, familiar creatures scurrying toward him, no doubt thinking it would be they who would be taking a bite. He grabbed them with the ends of his longer tentacles, then squeezed them to death before dragging their remains to his mouth.

Although it was at night, he could see with the benefit of light from three moons. One was full and the two others were nearly so.

Farther up there was a cluster of carnivorous trees. After a close encounter on a previous visit to the shore, he knew to stay away from them. That was not easy, though. Even a gentle breeze through their branches managed to create enticing music. The melody was hypnotic in attracting animals to the hungry limbs. It was a struggle, but he managed to ignore the melody, even as he saw the shapes of other animals moving slowly toward the trees.

Billy did not fully wake until his mother roused him in the morning. "Time to get up," she announced outside his bedroom door. "I'm making breakfast, the usual."

She was gone only a few seconds when Billy began clicking his teeth, tapping them to the rhythm of the alien tune he had heard in his dream—the dream that had mercifully kept him oblivious to the pain of his joints over-extending and the bones softening in his arms and legs.

There was no softening of his teeth. His incisors actually seemed longer and sharper.

He pushed himself off the bed. Had his mother been more attentive, she might have heard the sound of his tentacles slapping the floor, as he dragged himself to the hallway.

He was ready for breakfast, but not the usual.

Alan Meyrowitz retired in 2005 after a career in computer research. His writing has appeared in *Eclectica, Existere, Front Range Review, Jitter, The Literary Hatchet, Lucid Rhythms, The Nassau Review, Poetry Quarterly, Shark Reef, Shroud, The Storyteller*, and others. In 2013 and 2015 the Science Fiction Poetry Association nominated his poems for a Dwarf Star Award.

Always in Season

by

Jonathon Mast

"IMMORTAL. Immortal and useless," I spat. I held the Human's gaze a moment before turning away. I had a shift to perform.

He kept pace beside me. Easy since he towered over me, like every other one of his race. I almost came up to his waist. "Your grandfather loved the old pulps from earth," he said.

"Grandfather was a fool." I felt immediate guilt. I would have to pray forgiveness for that. "You Humans are always in season. You can spend the time on frivolous things like stories." I felt my roots tighten where they coiled around my legs. "You think everyone has as much time as you do."

He looked down and then back over at me. "I know. Don't you think I know? I've watched ten harvests over your orchards." He looked away. "I just. I miss your grandfather. I thought maybe, maybe someone else from his tree might appreciate imagination. We used to dream about what it would be like when the colony ship got to the planet. What it would be like to terraform together."

"Grandfather is dead. I will be dead by the time we get there. You dream all you want. I have a job to do." I stalked away as the Human finally stopped keeping pace.

Around me, representatives from the Garden of Worlds bustled about. We each had our duties. My task was to watch over the Bravasho orchard. The strongest of the Garden races, they served as security. Their season had ended recently, however. I had buried the last of them myself at the foot of their family's tree. Now, though, buds had begun to appear. Soon the first of the new crop would grow and they would walk the corridors of our ship again.

But not yet. Right now, the trees needed to be tended. I labored alone in their orchard, under a simulated alien sun.

The Human was so old. I wanted to think that someone so ancient, someone who had seen so many seasons, must have some wisdom. They weren't really immortal, of course. They just lived so much longer than any other species. "Computer?"

The sound chimed around me as I pruned some branches from a Bravasho tree. The gnarled and gray limbs cradled many buds, but each tree could grow only so many of our security officers. I had cultivated a good crop, and that took care.

As I assessed a particular branch, I sighed. "Play audio of *The Curse of Capistrano*, where I left off."

The computer complied. Maybe the Human had some wisdom. Maybe. I wanted to like him. He seemed so alone. He couldn't commune with any tree. He was trying to connect with me through ancient writings my grandfather had enjoyed. I could at least honor that attempt.

After a few hours, the lights dimmed. The pseudosun had descended, and orange and red lit the ceiling. I felt the roots that wrapped around my lower limbs ache to stretch out.

Time to go home.

"Computer, pause playback."

Such a useless thing. At least it was engaging, though.

I headed back to our orchard, the Hookmoor orchard. I needed the soil there; if I settled in for the night in the Bravasho orchard, I'd wake at dawn with a terrible headache. Besides, our trees grew brown and straight and proud. They were better trees, and I'd rather spread my roots there.

And when I turned the corner to the large bay that held our orchard, I drew myself to a stop.

The Human sat chattering at the base of my family's tree.

Other workers were returning to their trees, their roots digging into the ground as they went dormant.

The Human groaned as he stood and dusted off his pants. With a stretch he made his way toward the entrance of the orchard. "All yours. Sorry. I like coming and talking to your family's tree." He sighed. "I've always cared about your family."

"Well," I answered. What was someone supposed to say to that? "Well, I need to set my roots down for the night."

He chuckled. "Sorry for getting in your way." He headed down the corridor toward the distant bridge.

The only Human on board. The only one who didn't go dormant at night. The only one who remembered when we began our voyage across the stars so many generations ago. They say that once there were more Humans, but raiders attacked and every Human but this one was killed.

But I didn't care about that. As long as my orchard survived to lay down roots in a new world, to change it to a world where any of the Garden races could live, all would be well.

My roots sank deep into the soil. As they did, my knotted shoulders relaxed. My head lolled. I found grandfather's roots. "Did you listen to more of the old stories?" he asked.

"I did."

"And?"

"They are too long. I would waste my life listening to them all."

"Maybe you need to slow down and enjoy your life," he chuckled.

"You're becoming one with the tree again, grandfather. You don't need to hurry to do anything."

"Oh, young one. I remember still. I am not so absorbed by the one who grew us to have forgotten what it is like to roam the decks of the ship."

"Grandfather, go to sleep."

"Oh, young one. I am sleeping. I have always talked in my sleep."

The lights slammed on, full stream. No, brighter. Alarms sounded. I blinked. My roots twitched in the soil and recoiled around me. I hadn't been dormant long enough. A headache pounded behind my eyes.

The Human's voice filled the orchard, "Raiders. Everyone to emergency stations."

In emergencies, I was to tend to the Bravasho orchard. Countless others hurried around me to get to their stations. I took my place near the entrance to the orchard. The trees still wore their buds; we would receive no help from them. No security. I hoped we wouldn't need them. Hopefully the Human could make sure we weren't boarded.

Nineteen others took their places around me. We bore electric prods strong enough to stun a Human—if they came within reach. We couldn't risk ballistic weapons here. Who knew what ship's systems they could damage?

"Do we know the situation?" I asked my neighbor.

"Raiders," he answered.

"I know that. Tell me something useful."

"They want to eat us."

"I said I wanted something useful."

Two of his eyes twitched to me and back out to the corridor, scanning for threats. "They've already got an umbilical across. Crashed our computer."

"Do we know the species of the raiders?"

All of his eyes shot to me. "Humans."

I swore. Of course they were Human raiders. Even if we shook them loose now, they could pursue for generations. I might reside among the roots of the family tree by the time the threat passed or destroyed us. I shivered. They only wanted us for food. They'd take the ship and harvest us. They'd eat us all. Destruction of generations of my people, of all the Garden races on the ship. And they could wait long enough to succeed.

Damn the Humans and their long useless dangerous lives.

The deck rocked. My roots snapped out to give extra stability. They tangled with my neighbors. Thoughts shot through me as we touched and memories danced across the fibers. We withdrew from each other as quickly as possible.

He gave me a side eye. "Sorry about that."

"It's fine," I answered. "And yes, you should ask her."

He grinned. "You think so?"

"If you get the chance."

The deck rocked again. Our roots once again reached out for stability, but we were careful to avoid each other this time.

And then the lights went out. The alarms fell silent. The only sounds were the crackle of our prods. Their sparking white glow gave the only illumination. In the sudden stillness, my roots began to relax. My headache faded as dormancy tried to take me.

No. Protect the orchards. We needed to make sure we made it to terraform the planet. Other ships followed. If we didn't make it, if we didn't perform our tasks, they would find a planet ready to kill them.

"Stay awake!" I boomed with all the strength I could muster. "It's a trick! The raiders know we'll be helpless if we go to sleep!"

My voice didn't convey what I was really feeling, though. My head ached again. My roots longed for the cool soil that lay just behind me in the orchard, as alien as that soil was. My thoughts wandered. What dreams might that soil bring me? I would not speak with my grandfather, of course. Would the Bravasho speak with me?

Focus. The dormancy instinct was so strong.

It seemed that hours passed. Without power to the ship, though, it was impossible to tell how much time was actually passing. We didn't even have the illumination from the pseudomoons within the orchard.

We chattered, of course, but there wasn't much to say. Not now. None of us were versed in small talk. Who had the time for something like that?

Dormancy began to wrap around my mind. My roots loosened around my legs, but we stood in the corridor. There was no soil here to sink into. Just a few steps behind us began the orchard, but not here.

Heavy footsteps sounded in the corridor.

"Human!" I shouted.

Something wet laughed in the darkness. "And so I am, loud food. So I am. Here to harvest you. We took care of your friend on the bridge, didn't we? Now we're just here for lunch."

Friend on the bridge? He meant the Human. The one who had watched over us. The foolish immortal.

Stop. Pay attention here. You don't have time for surprise or mourning. Deal with the raider.

I brandished my prod. "Just try and get us!"

"Oh, I wouldn't think of it. Got a few scars from my first raid years ago, see. I know better. No, I'll just wait for you all to fall asleep. Why we turned off the lights, see? All we have to do is sit here. And then, well, you're all mine. Well, ours, I suppose. I should share with my crewmates, shouldn't I?"

I attempted to growl. The People of the Gardens are rarely threatening to Humans, though.

Wet laughter answered my threat. "You fruit. You're so useless. Alive for a season, running around, getting things done. That's why we're better than you. We're always in season." The laughter continued.

"Stay ready. Stay awake!" I tried to be brave. I shouted, I ordered, I blustered. I wished the Bravasho were grown and standing with us. They would give us a chance.

My companions answered up and down our line. We would stand firm.

Except the darkness. I could imagine the Human coming on us while we were falling asleep. When we were defenseless.

My roots stretched out behind me to reach the soil. They obeyed my mental command and recoiled around my legs. And then they relaxed and stretched out again.

My neighbor's roots brushed mine. A wave of fatigue washed over me, shared from him.

I pushed back against dormancy.

I imagined the predator eyes watching us from the darkness. Being eaten. Human teeth rending our soft, boneless flesh.

He jerked his roots from mine but not before his adrenaline rush was communicated to me. I blinked. I was awake. Oh, I was so awake now. My images had caused a reaction in him, and it had fed back to me.

Would it work down the line?

"Everyone, join roots," I commanded.

One of the Pdali grumbled.

I snapped, "We need to stay awake. You able to do that on your own?"

The others reluctantly tangled roots all up and down the line. Our thoughts mingled. My neighbor had been grown on a tree just a few over from my own; our thoughts melded easily. The being on the other side, though, came from another orchard entirely, even though we were both Hookmoor. His thoughts brought questions and more fatigue.

And then I felt the thoughts from others down the line. Thoughts from the Pdali, strange things communicated more by scents and feelings than words. Thoughts from the one Hsarnal, images of sunlight through leaves at different angles.

And every single link brought more longing for dormancy. The desires piled up, one on top of another, heavier than every tree in my orchard. All of our prods drooped, almost as one.

Through the fog, I thought I heard laughing. It was so hard to care, but I thought I could see a Human in the shadows. I heard a step. He was coming closer.

No. He would not eat us.

I conjured an image of a Human walking through our orchards while we slept. Moonlight reflected off pale skin. I pictured his scent: Human sweat, Human pheromones, Human Human Human. He reached a calloused hand to pluck us from the ground where we'd rooted for the night. Fibers from roots tore, and then entire root systems were rent from body. I allowed the pain to spark through our link. And then the Human opened his mouth. I pictured the saliva within. And then his teeth pierced skin, one tooth at a time, plunging within us.

And the adrenaline jolted all up and down the line. Just as the thoughts of sleep had piled on top of us, now we each fed each other our alertness. Our roots snapped around our legs, preparing us to run if need be. Our prods rose as one, crackling with energy.

"Hookmoor," the Pdali who had grumbled addressed me, "Never send me a dream again."

"Well, that was an interesting thing you did, wasn't it?" said the wet voice from the darkness. "You were all relaxing. I could see it. And then you stopped. Annoying little things, ain't you?" The voice sighed. I heard a digital crackle. "Sir? Fifth orchard down the line. They're alert. Looks like they might not sleep on our timetable. You sure? All right, sir." The voice paused a moment. "Well, little fruit, looks like we'll just harvest from everywhere else. Bosses don't want you making it to your destination, so if we can't eat you..."

There was a sudden rush of gas and a click. Flame blossomed before us.

Over the sound of the flamethrower in the Human's hands, the wet voice said, "If we can't eat you, we're to burn down your orchards." He turned the flame on us.

The fire swallowed my neighbor. The heat blistered my skin. I cried out and dove out of the way. My neighbor, though. The flames swallowed him. He screamed. He screamed so loud, another from my orchard gone, never to be returned to the soil. And with the power out, the flame suppression systems did not function.

The human roared a laugh. "Smells like pie to me!" He turned the flame away from me and down the line.

I scrambled to my feet and into the corridor, into the flame-lit darkness. The scent. Oh, the ashes and the fuel and the sweat dripping off the Human. I shut my ears, I refused to listen to the deaths of my companions, but I could not shut out the scent.

He burned only four of us. Only four. The rest ran, into the corridor, into the orchard we were supposed to be guarding, away.

If only the Bravasho had been in season! They could have stood up to the human. They were a brave crop, with strong and hardy husks. But now they were still buds.

The Human laughed. He stepped out of the corridor, into the bay entrance, onto the soil of the orchard. He sped his flame toward the closest tree. The gnarled gray wood resisted for a few moments. The leaves, though, blackened and withered. The buds.

The buds I had cultivated. The ones I had cared for.

They burst in the heat. A generation of Bravasho gone in one searing pass of flames.

It wasn't enough to destroy just the buds, though. The Human kept the stream of flames on the tree. The thinnest branches crackled. The flames spread.

Have you ever heard the sound of a Tree passing? The sound of all those still dwelling in the roots crying out? Their screams entered even my closed ears.

And I could not move. I watched from the darkness of the corridor. I had to do something. Anything.

The Human moved on to a second tree. None of those huddling in the darkness dared move to stop him.

Humans were supposed to eat us. They didn't burn down orchards. It didn't happen. There were atrocities in space, but what purpose was an act like this?

We were helpless. And he said our Human was already gone.

The Human who had laughed with my grandfather. The one who'd watched over our tree. The one who'd told me to listen to stories.

Stories of heroes.

I looked at the faces of those I could see. Scared. More than scared. We knew what this was. If the humans were burning here, they'd burn everywhere. All of our orchards. The end of generations.

The Human moved to a third tree. He paid no attention to us. He knew we were no threat.

And if we were no threat, well, he could ignore us. And maybe. Maybe.

I hefted the prod. I held my breath. I charged. I passed the burning remains of those who had stood in the line beside me. I sped over soil. The heat of burning trees desecrated my blistered skin.

The Human moved on to a fourth tree. He didn't see me. He was blinded by the light of his flames. He couldn't hear me over the breathing of his flame thrower.

My prod collided with the small of his back, well over my head. White sparks flew. His flame died as his hand relaxed and he fell.

I lunged against his still form again. Again.

My hands were shaking. I had to make sure. Was he down? Was he really down? Was he faking it?

I hit him with the prod again. Another time.

Tears poured from my eyes. In the stories of heroes, they don't talk about this. They don't talk about the fear. At least not in the stories my Human told me to listen to. They don't talk about the grief.

Four trees. Four trees destroyed. So many Bravasho.

As I wept, my roots uncoiled. My body still needed dormancy. It sensed the soil, even now. And as they unwrapped, they brushed against the nearby ankle of the human.

No dreams whispered at me. The Human was dead.

But then I realized: I could tell he was dead. I could connect with the Human through my roots.

I turned to the others. They had gathered around me, those who still lived. I was still shaking, but we had to move. "The raiders. They don't just want a meal. They mean to burn us down." I looked from face to face. "Look. We can fight them off. I have an idea. Stretch out your roots to me, like you did before."

They did.

As we made contact, I shared the stories the Human had forced me to listen to. I told them the stories of heroes. I fed them a diet of fighting against impossible odds. As they listened, as they took the stories in, they told them again to each other. Just as the fatigue had compounded, and just as the adrenaline compounded as we talked to each other before, now something new grew between us. And then, as fast as thoughts racing across roots, I told them my plan.

We passed our companions, the others from the Gardens. They stood at attention, sleeping in their positions. Dormant. None were disturbed. The raiders figured they would be easy to harvest later. We had been the only problem, and they imagined their fellow was having fun burning the place down.

About a dozen Humans gathered before the doors to the bridge. They'd set up floodlights to illuminate the doors, but shadows still darkened the corridor. The heavy steel doors were sealed. Black marks showed where they had tried and failed to burn through.

We had gathered in darkness, those of us who were still awake. Those of us who had seen the fires. The darkness clawed at us again, fatigue trying to draw us down, but for now we fought it.

One of the raiders crouched near an open access panel. "Sorry, sir, with the computer down I can't open the doors. Best thing we can do is starve him out if we want him dead."

Another raider frowned. "No good. We have a timetable to keep. Gather enough food for a few weeks' travel, and burn the rest."

General grumbling.

One of the raiders stood with a groan. "All right, then. Off we go." He turned with a shrug and entered the darkness where we waited.

The raiders jumped when they heard him scream. They spun. Several had heavy knives in their hands. Three others snatched up flamethrowers.

"What was that, then?" one mumbled.

The sound of ragged breathing filled the darkness.

"Turn the lights down the hall," one ordered. One of them moved toward a light stand and angled the illumination toward us. We didn't hide. We stood, our prods in our hands, simply watching the Humans. Their companion lay on the ground behind us.

I smiled. "We're hungry," I said.

The raiders stared at each other and then back at us.

"You want to eat us. But what do you think we eat?" I stepped forward. My companions stepped with me. "You die. We eat you. We put our roots down into your flesh. It's so tasty. You think you're here to harvest us? We're here as a trap to lure you in. To make you ours."

They backed away. The knives shook in their hands.

Good. As long as they couldn't see me shaking. As long as they couldn't hear the quiver in my voice. We had told each other stories of heroes. We had used that to build each other up.

But what hero ever faced a threat as great as Humans?

We kept walking toward them.

"Use the flamethrowers, idiots!" one of the raiders screamed.

And at that, we ran forward. They were pinned against the metal doors now. They couldn't get away. And we had to just get close enough. Fast enough. If the flames hit us—

Close enough. I whipped my roots out and around the ankle of the nearest human. The others sent their roots twining around mine.

He turned the flames toward us. My skin, already blistered, split. Contact.

His thoughts were grease and gears and hunger.

We told him a story. Our story. Our roots crawled under his skin. Tendrils wrapped around his bones. We separated his muscles with the tips of our roots. The hairs of our roots crawled up the interior of his thighs, under his skin, into his lungs, sprouting out of his eyes.

He screamed. The strength of our story was too much. He fell.

"We're hungry," I said.

The other Humans ran. We were able to grab two of them as they dashed past us. The rest fled into the darkness, back to the umbilical and to their ship.

We did not chase. Our strength had been spent. The night finally claimed us. We collapsed to the deck.

I awoke in my orchard. My grandfather whispered, "Well done." The pseudosun shone above.

"Am I alive?" I asked him.

"More or less. You've been healing for days. Your Human brought you back here. All of us in the tree have been doing what we can to mend you."

I opened my eyes.

A Human sat crosslegged nearby.

My Human.

He grinned at me.

I grinned back.

"So. What happened?" he asked.

And I told him the story of how stories saved the orchards.

Jonathon Mast lives in the US with his wife and an insanity of children. (A group of children is called an insanity. Trust me.) You can find him at https://jonathonmastauthor.com/

Alienspeak

by

Brenda Anderson

A LIENS are sending me hate mail. Tiny curlicues scroll across the fourth fingernail of my right hand. Imagine. First, they stole my shovel. Now they mock me, Ermintrude von Creytz, Retired Professor of Linguistics, by sending me messages I can't read, on an insignificant fingernail. The indignity!

I want that shovel back. So I'm seventy and a bit stooped? I still love gardening. My newly-acquired purple Penumbra stares up at me from its flowerpot on the kitchen sink. I bet it wants the garden.

No. It's safer to keep it inside. After all, I didn't invite aliens into my garden. I've worked out how to use my nets to catch them. The moment they're caught, they materialize into crescent-shaped wings, always in pairs. I dry them, turn them into compost, dig them in and plant my roses on top of them.

Two can play this game. I'll photograph their latest message, remove the latest bodies from my net and arrange them on the ground in perfect duplication of their message.

Afterwards, I go inside and make lemon tea.

Now every fingernail on my right hand crawls with swift-scrolling script. I must have upset them. I hope so. Take that, you shovel-stealers!

I hear a sound, and swing round. The kitchen is empty.

"How dare you." Such bitter words, full of accusation. Who's speaking? I turn back to the sink. My potted Penumbra leans towards me. "Yes, you, Professor." Its petals open and close like a mouth.

I swallow. My rose is talking to me?

"What did you expect? We have no mouths to communicate with, so we're using this rose as a mouthpiece. You catch us in your nets, don't you?"

Us? What's going on? My own mouth drops open.

"That's right." My rose sounds calmer now. "We grow our body parts in different locations. Feet, on the ground. Arms, on the branches of trees. Mouths, directly above roses. You insult us by sending our latest warning back to us so we reply, via your rose. It's not our fault you can't read."

The indignity! "Give me back my shovel and I promise that'll be the end of it."

The rose quivers. "We thought that if we took your shovel, we'd stop you destroying our body parts. Imagine, turning our *mouths* into compost for your roses. It's obscene. We demand that you remove your nets."

Tears prickle behind my eyes. "Who are you?"

"Nothing you'd recognize. Let's say, Beauty to your Beast. Last chance! Remove your nets."

I swallow. "I apologize for inconveniencing you. I put the nets there to catch insects."

Silence. Perhaps I don't sound repentant enough. Truth is, I've never been a good liar, and they do make excellent compost.

"Remove your nets. That way we'll get our mouths back. Don't worry about insects. We'll ward them off."

Can I trust them? I don't want insects destroying my garden. Or should I simply forget my shovel? No, never! We go back a long way, that shovel and I. "Give me an hour and I'll remove my nets. Then I'll expect you to return my shovel. After that, no further dialogue. You go your way, I'll go mine. Does that sound fair?"

The rose dips its head. "Fair enough."

Underwhelming, that. Perhaps they don't trust me. Too bad. I finish my lemon tea, then dismantle all my nets except one. They'll never know. It's all but invisible, isn't it? I sit down at my outdoor setting overlooking the lawn and flowerbeds, check my watch and make another lemon tea.

As I stand up, my shovel reappears on the ground beneath my feet. I clap my hands! The shovel rises. Oh *no*. Now I'm sitting astride my shovel, which flings itself into the air and does cartwheels round the garden. I crash into my one remaining invisible net and hang suspended in the air, eight feet above the ground.

For a long, long time I contemplate my folly. I live far from neighbours or passersby. My house is not visible from the street. No-one knows or cares. I cannot dismantle the net when I'm entangled in it. My nets are designed to cling to the trapped critter until life departs from its body.

Clutching my shovel, I look down at my hands. My fingernails are going wild. They're messaging me again! Pure joy floods through me. I, Ermintrude von Creytz, will rise to the challenge. I'll decipher what they're saying. Just wait.

Brenda Anderson's fiction has appeared in various places, including *Flash Fiction Online* and *Daily Science Fiction*. She lives in Adelaide, South Australia and tweets irregularly @CinnamonShops. Her interests include reading, writing and watching movies.

The Hastillan Weed

by

Ian Creasey

"SINCE we have so many new faces," I said to the half-dozen volunteers, "I'll start with a tools talk. Safety points for the spade—the most important is that when you're digging, you push with the ball of your foot."

I took a spade from the pile, and demonstrated by digging up a bluebell growing by the hedge. From the large bells all round the stem, I knew it was a Spanish bluebell, a garden escape that if left unchecked would hybridise with the natives. Too late now, though. You can tell the British bluebell because the flowers are smaller, deeper blue, and they're usually on one side of the stem, so the plant droops under their weight as if bowing down before its foreign conqueror. There's hardly a wood left in England where you'll see only native bluebells.

"Or you can use your heel on the spade." I heaved the invader out of the earth and tossed it aside, knowing it would safely rot. "But you should never press down with the middle of your foot. The bones in the arch are delicate, and you can injure yourself."

I turned to the alien. "Of course, that may not apply to you. I guess you know where your weak points are, if you have any."

The Hastillan picked up a spade with her grey, double-thumbed hand. "Your lawyers made me pledge not to blame you for any accidents. But I know how to dig. I have a Most Adept Shoveller ring I can show you." Her translator spoke with the neutral tone of a BBC newsreader, so I couldn't tell whether she was joking.

"That won't be necessary," I reassured her. "I'm sorry about the lawyers, but everyone has to sign to say they understood the safety talk. Liability insurance costs a fortune these days." I handed out a pile of forms to the human contingent. Head office had already cleared the alien. What was her name again? Holly and brown rice... *Olibrys*.

"When you're carrying a spade, you keep it down by your legs, parallel to the ground, holding it at the point of balance." I demonstrated, balancing the spade on one finger before an arthritic tremor made me hastily clutch the shaft with a full grip. "This is so that if you fall, the spade goes harmlessly off to the side. You don't swing it around, or carry it over your shoulders, because if you tripped you could chop someone's head off. And then we'd lose our no-claims bonus."

As I mentioned each incorrect use of the spade, a hologram made comic pratfalls to illustrate the dreadful consequences. "When you're not digging with it, you don't hang it on a branch, or lean it against a tree, or leave it in a trench with the handle sticking up. You place the tool flat on the ground, in an out-of-the-way spot, with the blade pointing downward—so that if anyone does tread on it, they don't have a Tom and Jerry moment." Holographic cartoon characters chased each other around the flitter park, tripping over spades and treading on rakes that sprang up to whack them in the face.

"Any questions on the spade? No? We also have mattocks and bow-saws in the flitter, and I'll instruct you on those if we need them. But for now, if you've all signed your waivers, we can get on and attack some weeds."

I counted the forms to make sure everyone had signed. Six volunteers—it was the biggest Sunday group I'd run for years. Maybe I could entice some of these newcomers into coming along regularly. It would be good to chat with new people. When you live alone and all your old friends have died or emigrated, it's hard to get any conversation except with voice-activated appliances.

Everyone picked up a spade, and we headed down toward the river. It was a beautiful day to be outdoors. The sun blazed through fleecy clouds gambolling across the sky, and the whirling wind turbines atop the valley showed there was plenty of breeze to cool us while we worked. Yellow flowers of lesser celandine shone in drifts under the trees. Lower down, the trees gave way to brambles and great swathes of ramsons, their small white spikes just beginning to bloom. I tore off a leaf and crushed it under my nose, inhaling the scent of wild garlic.

The path turned left by the riverside. Small patches of darkness began to appear among the bluebells, like drops of poison spilt in the undergrowth. The blotches grew bigger, along with the plants that made them. Tall dark fronds sucked in light like succulents drinking every drop of desert dew, not wasting a single red, blue or green photon. The shadowy fern swallowed the colour of the spring countryside, leaving only darkness growing by the river.

I clutched my spade tighter. "Here we are," I said. "This is Hastillan blackweed."

One of the new volunteers stared at the weed as if it were Satan wearing a Manchester United scarf. "The alien plot to conquer the Earth," he said, delivering the line as though he'd been saving it up all morning.

At my age I don't recall names so well as I used to. We'd had a round of introductions before the tools talk, but the effort of memorising one alien had squeezed out all the humans. Yet his 'Save the Memes' T-shirt jogged something in my brain. Tim, was it? Jim?

Whoever he was, he turned to Olibrys with a menacing expression. "What does it do?" he demanded.

"I don't know what you mean," she said. The translator's neutral tone made it sound as if she didn't care.

"Will it poison the atmosphere? Or infect us with a fatal disease?"

"Kim," I said, "there's no need for that attitude. We're all here today for the same reason: to get rid of the blackweed. Olibrys has come to help, so if you can't be friendly, be polite. And if you can't be polite, shut up."

"It's Keith. And this stuff must be evil, or we wouldn't be cutting it down."

I sighed. "No plant is evil. It's just disruptive in the wrong place, which in this case happens to be the Earth. As for what it does — you can see what it's doing. It grows faster than the native plants, so it shades them out. And here it has no enemies or parasites, so nothing keeps it in check. Most wildlife won't eat it, which is just as well because it's poisonous.

"But none of that's unique to blackweed. Introduced plants have been causing havoc for centuries. Rhododendrons look lovely in the garden, but out here they poison sheep. We battled Japanese knotweed for decades before we finally got rid of it. On the other hand" —I walked a few paces to a small bamboo-like stem— "with Himalayan balsam, we eventually had to give in. Bee-keepers like it, because bees love Himalayan balsam, but conservationists hate it because it promotes erosion, and crowds out other plants, and doesn't support water voles or other mammals. Yet it's so well established, there's nothing we can do.

"That's the key point. The quicker we tackle the blackweed, the more chance we have of stopping it. So let's get on with it, shall we?"

The volunteers did not look especially eager to start. "You say it's poisonous?" said a woman with thick-framed glasses and hair the vibrant copper of dogwood in autumn. On the walk down, her shiny new boots had been baptised with mud.

I've always found the Scottish accent particularly sexy. No doubt she'd be more eager to talk if she thought I wasn't trying to poison her.

"It's not lethal to humans—but I recommend you all wear gloves. Did we bring the gloves?"

"Right here," said John, the only one of my few regulars who'd come out today, and the only one of the group with enough sense to wear a sun-hat. He put down a bucket full of gloves of all colours, textures, and states of disrepair. John and I had already snagged the best pairs before we set off.

I donned my gloves and demonstrated digging up one of the weeds. "Don't start too close to the plant, or you won't get all the roots. Everything needs to come out, or it'll just grow back." With a practised wrench of the spade, I had the intruder out in no time. It still looked menacing in death: a black tangle on the green moss, looking *wrong* because it combined features that had never evolved together on Earth.

"Because they're poisonous," I continued, "we can't leave the dead plants to compost down. Please pile them up somewhere open and level, so when we finish I can bring the flitter down and we'll load them in.

"If you have any questions, speak to me or John. We're both qualified first-aiders, by the way. And if you didn't catch it before, my name's Ben." As I said this, I looked at the Scottish woman and smiled.

She said, "Why are we digging up this stuff by hand? Why can't we just use weedkiller or something?"

"The only chemicals that kill the blackweed are so toxic that we'd rather not slosh them around a riverbank. This is the safest control method." I paused. "Any other questions?"

"What time's lunch?" someone called.

I laughed. "Spoken like a true volunteer. I'll give you a shout around one o'clock. Anything else? Okay, let's spread out and do some work."

While I talked, I'd edged toward Olibrys. "Let's go up the valley," I said. "That's where the bigger weeds are." I thought it would be politic to separate her from Keith and his friends.

I let Olibrys go in front, so I could get a good look at her while we walked. It was the first time I'd seen a Hastillan in the flesh. On TV they tend to look pale and fragile, but Olibrys exuded strength as she strode on ahead. She probably shaded two metres—a few centimetres taller than me—if you included the cilia that rippled on her head like a restless crown, poking up to sample the air, then drooping again in a complex cycle. Her narrow waist gave her a slightly insectile appearance from behind, an impression heightened by occasional iridescent glints from her greyish skin. She wore a stiff blue something-or-other around her upper torso—I barely know what women's fashions are called, let alone alien garments. A shawl? A shell? I wondered what she had under it. Not breasts, of course. Indeed, I only assumed she was female because her translator had a woman's voice.

As we climbed a short incline, the river growing louder as we approached the weir, I checked the steps and revetments I'd put in a few years ago. The wood was beginning to rot—we don't use chemically treated timber—but I figured it would last another year or so. We had more pressing priorities right now.

At the top, a clump of young blackweed blocked the path. I glimpsed a thin black filament trailing from an enormous frond growing by the river. A stolon, we'd call it in an Earth plant. Back home, my strawberries were doing the same thing: spreading by sending out runners that rooted wherever they could. The only difference was that slugs kept munching my strawberries, but not even slugs would touch the blackweed.

"Now you can show me your Most Adept Shovelling," I said to Olibrys.

It's a good thing I'm well past the age of being competitive, because she was strong and fast and tireless. Her muscle-power propelled the spade blade-deep into the earth with one smooth push, as if she were shovelling sand, rather than thick Yorkshire soil full of stones and roots. Soon, the entire clump of blackweed lay limp beside the path.

I glanced back down the valley at the other volunteers, who weren't working nearly as hard. Some of them had yet to start, finding it necessary to warm up to the task with a long chat. But John looked to have things in hand, as he pointed out various thickets of weed, and sent a group across the bridge to clear the other bank.

Olibrys and I tackled the huge parent frond by the waterside, digging on opposite sides. Unable to read her body language, I couldn't tell whether she enjoyed the task or resented it. I reckoned her presence was probably a PR stunt by the Hastillan embassy, a conciliatory gesture after the fuss we'd kicked up about the blackweed, but I couldn't complain about her work-rate.

I wiped sweat from my brow, and Olibrys opened her snout wide and panted like a dog, as we vanquished the giant weed then grubbed up all the roots. Afterward I took a refreshing drink from the river— it always tastes so much better than tap water—and rested on a moss-encrusted rock. Looking at the dead weed, I noticed pale specks where berries had started to grow. The blackweed didn't rely solely on stolons, but also flung its pollen to the wind. Soon a crop of large orange berries would appear, and float downstream to choke yet more riverbank with weed. Others might be eaten by birds, who'd excrete seeds before succumbing to the poison. We had to get rid of as much blackweed as we could, before the berries ripened.

"So how did this stuff get here?" I asked Olibrys.

"Biocontrol breach," she replied.

The Hastillan ambassador had used the exact same phrase. "What does that mean?"

"It means that our anti-contamination procedures were broken."

"How exactly?"

"I don't know," said Olibrys.

"Does anyone know?" I asked, trying to remain patient. The embassy had been apologetic but evasive. If Olibrys was going to be here all day, I'd keep asking until I got an answer.

She paused, staring at a twig caught in an eddy below the weir. "There's nothing more I can say."

"Don't you think we deserve an explanation? This is our home!"

"You live here? I thought—"

"I live on this planet, yes. And I've been a woods warden in West Yorkshire for thirty years." Twenty of them unpaid, I added to myself.

"I'm sorry," she said. "I do think you deserve an answer. But I've been asked not to talk about it."

I threw a stone into the river with an angry splash. "Don't you see how bad that looks? It makes people like Keith think you really are trying to poison the Earth."

"That's what I told my mother," said Olibrys. "She's embarrassed, that's all, and she asked me to keep quiet. But I don't want to lie. I'm not a diplomat, so I shouldn't have to."

"Your mother?"

"She's the ambassador. The embassy is one big family—sisters, cousins..." The translator beeped to indicate another, uninterpretable concept. "They bring their offspring with them. And of course the kids get bored, stuck on a primitive world with nothing to do. So they come out here and get high."

I frowned, wondering if the translator had spoken correctly. The Yorkshire moors aren't especially high, not compared to the Lake District. Or did she mean— "The blackweed is a drug?"

"That's right. The embassy is all overseen—surveillance everywhere —so we can't do anything at home. But there are no monitors out here. It's just like the backwoods on Hastilla. Chew the berries, spit the seed, spread the weed... and come back next year."

I stood up, and pointed to the patches of blackweed smothering the valley. "You people planted this deliberately, just so you could get high?" My voice trembled with outrage. I hadn't been so angry since someone fly-tipped garbage on the orchids.

"I'm sorry," she said. "They're only kids. They didn't know it would spread so fast. I've never seen so much blackweed in my life. On Hastilla it's rare: that's why people spit the seeds, to encourage it."

I grabbed my spade and moved to the next blackweed. As I stabbed the blade into the earth, each blow shook the fronds and made them spill pollen from feathery catkins. Fuelled by anger and adrenaline, I wrenched the interloper out of the ground with one mighty heave. Olibrys worked alongside me, creating a vast pile of weed. I had to hastily spread the heap before it toppled into the river.

I'd assumed the blackweed's introduction was an accident. I could forgive the aliens that: we humans had made enough mistakes on our own planet that we could hardly criticise someone else's. But a deliberate introduction—the wanton despoliation of countryside I'd stewarded for decades—made me want to scream.

Dark paranoid thoughts crossed my mind. The blackweed was rare on Hastilla; it grew well here. Drugs are always a profitable crop. Maybe the Hastillans planned to turn Earth into a blackweed farm, so the whole home planet could get high.

Yet the embassy had seemed genuinely contrite when we complained about the weed. And Olibrys stood beside me, rooting out the plants far faster than I.

In the silence between us, birds squawked to defend their territory.

"I appreciate your coming out here to help dig this stuff up," I said at last. "I guess that won't make you very popular with the berry-eaters."

"No, it won't," said Olibrys. "They've already accused me of careerism and crawling to my mother, of caring far too much about some primitive little planet's habitat and government."

I laughed. "Which of those is true? Why are you really here?"

"I felt we had an obligation," Olibrys said, making me wonder if she'd originally helped plant the weed. She continued, "We are guests here, even if unwelcome. Though if you all feel so strongly about protecting your home from alien infestations, I'm surprised there aren't more people out here today."

"Conservation hasn't been fashionable since space travel came along. Now we have access to other planets, this one's become disposable." I thought of my friends who'd emigrated. "Is that how it is with your people? Do you have much environment left on Hastilla, or is it all cities and wasteland?"

"There's hardly any wild habitat. That's one reason the blackweed is rare. Of course, kids try to grow it in their gardens, but the monitors put a stop to that."

She turned the conversation to Earth, asking what we did for fun. I talked about booze and football and nightclubs, and other things I dimly remembered. I enjoyed chatting with Olibrys; her translator didn't have all the latest slang and catchphrases that infested young people's conversations like weeds.

As we talked, we continued digging. It's a curious paradox that conservation so often involves destruction. Over the years I've felled rhododendrons, burned gorse, pulled ragwort, cleared Himalayan balsam, destroyed GM escapes—all plenty of practice for rooting out alien drug crops.

My aching muscles told me it was lunchtime. I walked back down the path, looking for a suitable space with convenient rocks for us all to sit on. My old bones don't like squatting on the ground; I like to perch on a tree-stump, or a rock with enough moss to cushion my scrawny backside.

Some of the volunteers had clustered into a gossipy knot. "Anyone fancy a cup of tea?" I called. They nodded eagerly. "Then go get me some dry wood."

I filled the kettle from the river. As people brought back wood, I heaped up the smallest, driest scraps. In the flitter I had a gadget that would zap water to an instant boil, but there's something primal about building a fire. It always reminds me of going camping as a boy, of the year I spent in Canada, of all the cups of tea drunk on all the volunteer outings over the decades—the hedge laying, the wildlife surveys, the footpath repair—all the unsung things that keep the countryside alive for those who come to drop cigarette butts and throw beer-cans out of flitter windows.

I got the fire going—I'm not above using a modern gadget for that— and put the kettle on. It's a tall hollow cone with the water in a sleeve surrounding the central fire, so it heats up quickly when flames start licking out of the top. I dropped a couple of larger twigs down the chimney next to the spout.

As usual, I didn't need to shout, "Lunchtime!" Drawn by the fire and the prospect of a hot drink, the volunteers started to bag the least uncomfortable rocks to sit on. I had already placed my rucksack on the mossiest stump. John fussed with the brew-kit, and I let him sort out everyone's drinks. He knew what I wanted: black tea, no sugar, none of that fancy herbal crap.

"I saw a few piles of blackweed on my way down," I said to the group. "I think we've made a good start. How are you finding it?" In truth the volunteers hadn't done much yet, but I've found that it's best to praise them—then they're more likely to come back. It takes people time to get used to hard work, especially soft office drones who've never done anything more strenuous than ten minutes on an exercise bike.

"It's hard getting those roots up," said a young guy in a Leeds Rhinos shirt, as he tucked into his sandwiches.

"Yes," I said, "but we're lucky they don't spread underground. If the blackweed sent out rhizomes, like bracken, we'd never get the stuff out."

"We should never have let it here in the first place," said Keith. "How come we even let these aliens walk around without a biosuit, shedding microbes everywhere they go? We have more virus protection on our computers than we do on our biosphere—but we could survive without computers a lot easier than without a biosphere." This tripped off his tongue with the ease of a well-rehearsed slogan.

"How long have you been caring about the biosphere?" I demanded. I don't normally argue with the volunteers, but I couldn't let this pass. "I haven't seen you out here before. You didn't notice when this riverbank got choked with Himalayan balsam—why are you so concerned about Hastillan blackweed? You think the blackweed is the only problem we have? If you care about the environment so much, there's plenty of other ways you could help."

"But the aliens are the biggest threat we face. If these Hastillans can breathe our air, we shouldn't let them anywhere near it. We should make the Earth a quarantine zone."

I looked to Olibrys to see how she was taking this, but of course I couldn't read the expression on her snout. In any case, her attention was taken up by someone trying to give her a book. I heard her say, "—no need for Jesus." Another volunteer sidled over, offering to sell Olibrys the pyramids of Egypt.

I smiled ruefully, realising that we only had so many volunteers today because they'd heard an alien would be coming. They all had an agenda. Well, at least I could get some work out of them. Maybe the experience of doing something useful for once might give them a taste for it.

"Okay, if everyone's finished their lunch, let's get back to work."

I went down to the river to get some water to put out the fire. As I climbed back up the bank, I heard a cry of "Ouch!" from Olibrys's translator, followed by a fusillade of beeps.

"Sorry," said Keith in a distinctly unapologetic tone. "I'd help you up, but I don't want to get germs on my hand."

I dropped the kettle and ran to the path, where I saw Olibrys picking herself up from the ground, brushing dead leaves from her carapace. "What happened?" I demanded.

"She tripped over my spade—the one I'm using to remove unwanted alien organisms," said Keith. "Have you got any bleach so I can sterilise it?"

"His spade—" Olibrys began, then stopped. Her agitated cilia slowed to a stately wave, as if exercising diplomatic restraint.

"Was your spade placed flat on the ground with the blade pointing down?" I asked Keith.

"Guess not," he said, his voice oozing self-satisfaction rather than regret.

"Then you've violated the safety instructions. Please leave the site immediately. You'll be liable for any costs arising from this incident." I turned to Olibrys. "I apologise for this. I assure you, his speech and behaviour aren't condoned by myself, Yorkshire Green Action, or—"

Keith flapped his arm in disgust. "Whose side are you on?"

"The countryside," I said. "Olibrys has hacked out far more black-weed than you. All you've done is cause trouble."

I raised my voice and addressed the others. "Speaking of hacking out weed, we still have work to do. Let's get on, please. The sooner we start, the sooner we finish."

With a clang of spades and a mutter of conversation, most of the other volunteers began drifting away.

"John," I said, "would you please escort Keith back to the flitter park."

"No need," said Keith. "I'm leaving." He stalked off down the path, then yelled back over his shoulder. "You'll find out I'm right. Remember measles! Remember smallpox!"

The Scottish woman had been staring at the confrontation as if transfixed.

"What did he mean by that?" I asked.

"I think he meant, 'Remember what happened to Native Americans when Europeans brought measles and smallpox,'" she said. "Don't you think he has cause for concern?"

"I don't know. I'm not a doctor."

"But what about the ecosystem? Are aliens poisoning the Earth?"

"Well, the blackweed grows here, so obviously there is an issue. But Olibrys came out to dig it up, and incidents like this won't help us get Hastillan co-operation in future. Someone's going to have to apologise to the embassy as it is." Head office could deal with that, I thought.

"What do you think the blackweed really does?" she asked, looking at me with an intent gaze.

Flattered by the attention, I was about to relay what Olibrys had claimed, that it was just alien dope. But then, as the sun came out from behind a cloud, I spotted a metallic glint on the frame of her glasses.

"Are you a journalist?" I said.

She nodded. "Freelance. My screen name is Susanna Munro" — she paused to see if I recognised it, which I didn't— "and today I'm working on 'Ten Alien Plots to Conquer the Earth' for the Conspiracy Channel."

I sighed. "So Keith was playing up to the cameras. I guess it takes TV to make someone that rude and aggressive."

Susanna looked hurt. "I just record what's already there," she said, with the air of a well-worn justification. "Conspiracists are usually outspoken—at least, the ones who want to get on TV are. But we've had his viewpoint. Now I'm interested in yours." She tapped her glasses, reminding me that they were recording.

"My view is that we need to stand up and get rid of the blackweed" —I brandished my spade for the camera— "not sit around arguing about why it arrived or what it really does. There are more important things to worry about."

"More important than alien schemes to conquer the Earth?"

"More important than hypothetical schemes, yes. There's plenty of real, practical environmental problems to solve."

She waved a dismissive hand. "If you want to talk about global warming, save it for the Nostalgia Channel."

"Do you freelance for them as well? Because there's a lot I could say." I stopped, realising I was in danger of coming across as a haranguing obsessive like Keith. No doubt Susanna's raw footage became fodder for all kinds of clip shows—a parade of earnest Cassandras, each with their own pet peeves.

"They mostly use archive footage," she said. "Like experts talking about the next ice age, or the oil running out, or the population time-bomb. Environmentalists are always crying wolf."

"Yes, but there are wolves out there—metaphorical ones, anyway. The real ones mostly died."

"And don't those wolves include the Hastillans?"

I turned away and pointed to Olibrys. "Why don't you ask her?" I said, weary of the fruitless debate. In a lifetime of watching TV, I've never seen talking heads change anyone's mind.

"Oh, I intend to." Susanna's voice softened, and she touched my arm. "If I gave you a hard time, don't take it personally—it's only television. I do take your point. That's why I've been digging up blackweed, too."

I appreciated this apology, even if it were only a journalist's veneer of human feeling, designed to dissuade me from objecting to the footage.

The work continued. Olibrys dug alongside everyone else, doing her best to ignore the rugby-shirt guy talking about the golden lights he saw back when his mother disappeared. I sent him over the bridge to attack the weeds on the other side.

As the volunteers grew used to the task, they settled into a steady pace, creating heaps of dead blackweed. Some of the larger fronds bore catkins, and even a few early berries. We were just in time, helped by our research on the environmental cues that spurred the blackweed's life-cycle.

The group spread out along both sides of the river, as we searched for remaining clumps of weed. I knew we wouldn't clear the entire valley today. But if we could keep attacking the weed faster than it spread, we'd succeed eventually.

I felt relaxed enough that I took time out to give an impromptu flower-ID course, pointing out red campion and wood anemone, and talking about classifications and how to use field guides. Susanna asked me about the bracket fungus sprouting from dead trees like pairs of ears. I couldn't help wondering if she were merely humouring me to garner footage for 'Eccentric Englishmen' or somesuch show. And yet—if someone wanted to record me for posterity, who was I to keep my knowledge to myself? I enjoyed the attention, and as usual I was tempted to prolong the day's work, since I only had my empty house to return to. But they're volunteers, not slaves, and you can't overwork them if you want to see them again.

About four o'clock, I headed to the flitter so we could start loading up the weed, ready for the incinerator tomorrow. Hovering over the river, I could see the difference we had made. On last month's survey trip, I had seen dark blotches all along the banks. Now the darkness was concentrated into piles of dead weed. In the gaps left behind, nettles and stitchwort and sanicle would grow — but mostly Himalayan balsam, in long pink ribbons edging the river.

Most of the volunteers stood by the bridge, waiting for me to set the flitter down. I wondered where Olibrys was, then saw her upriver. She was scrabbling through a blackweed heap as if she'd lost her wallet. I saw her put something in her bag, but to my surprise she kept on searching, while occasionally lifting her head as if to spot anyone approaching along the path.

I reached for the binoculars. As I focused on Olibrys, I glimpsed what went into her bag—something small and orange. She was searching through the blackweed for the few nearly ripe berries.

I zoomed over and landed the flitter, not caring that the front scraped an alder and the back squished down into a bog. Then I leapt out, hurting my knees as I landed, and shouted, "Put the bag down!"

Olibrys turned toward me. "It's not what you think," she said.

"How do you know what I think?" I demanded.

"You think what they all think—Keith and Susanna and all the people who daub graffiti on the embassy walls. You're a nasty suspicious lot, and this is a nasty primitive horrible little planet." Olibrys's translator was expressionless as always, but something about her furiously roiling cilia reminded me of my niece exploding into a tantrum.

Just because she was taller than me and worked twice as hard, I'd assumed Olibrys was an adult. Silly, of course. Maybe she was more like a teenager. Or maybe I was reading too much into the combination of alien body-language and a toneless translator.

"I'm not like Keith," I said. "I don't think you're evil" —not without more evidence, I thought. "But it doesn't look good, pocketing the berries. What were you going to do, find somewhere else to plant them?"

"No. I just wanted to get high with my friends." She paused, and I waited for her to compose herself. "They've been saying I'm climbing the career stairway, crawling to my mother and the natives. You don't know what it's like when there are so few people your own age, and they all start ignoring you, and making comments behind your back that you're meant to overhear. When I saw that a few berries were ripe, it looked like a chance to win them over. I could say I'd saved the last harvest, and we could celebrate together. Can't you let me keep them? These are the last!"

"You said when you chew the berries, you spit out the seeds so the blackweed grows again."

"We won't do that. I promise."

Could I believe her? She had certainly worked hard today, but maybe that was just a ruse to get me to trust her. Even if I credited her intentions, could she control all her friends—the ones who'd planted the weed out here in the first place?

The volunteers were filing up the path, on their way to help load the blackweed into the flitter. I had to make a decision quickly.

I felt sorry for Olibrys. I could imagine the tensions within a small embassy, the isolation of being ostracised. Hell, I know what it's like to be lonely. But my loyalty was to Earth, to the countryside. I couldn't let her walk away with the berries in her bag, not when they might sprout into yet more blackweed blighting the land.

I held out my hand. Olibrys's cilia drooped like wilted flowers. "I understand," she said. "I would do the same for my homeworld." She handed me a plastic box half-full of orange berries. "That's all of them."

"Thanks," I said. Then I thought that my translated voice probably sounded as expressionless to Olibrys as hers did to me, so to make sure she knew I meant it sincerely, I said, "Thanks again—for everything you've done today."

As Susanna and the others approached, I quickly hid the berries inside my coat, to protect Olibrys—and myself—from the journalist's gaze.

People began heaving dead fronds into the flitter. The river gurgled tirelessly, but we were weary when we finished loading the dark cargo. The breeze had picked up, and the sun cast long shadows of wind turbines down the moors. I called the group together for a few final words.

"I appreciate all your efforts here. Clearing the blackweed is an important job, which will help the ecosystem and stop wildlife being poisoned. On behalf of all the birds and water voles, thanks again." I tried to catch people's eyes as I spoke: Olibrys, Susanna, all the conspiracists and missionaries attracted by the lure of the alien.

"But there's plenty of other things that need doing. Over the coming months, we've got coppicing, pond maintenance, GM pollen counts…lots of exciting things, if not as glamorous as alien killer weeds.

"Next week it's footpath repair, and I hope you'll come along. Until then, thank you and good night."

The volunteers dispersed, walking back to the flitter park much muddier than they'd arrived. Olibrys lagged behind, trudging up the path, brushing against nettles because she didn't feel their sting, or didn't care. I felt a pang of empathy, realising that she had no reason to rush home. I imagined how she'd hoped that by tonight she'd be popular again, whereas now she only had more loneliness to return to.

I called out instinctively. "Olibrys!"

She turned round and returned to the bridge, where I stood gazing at the rushing water. This spring, it would carry no blackweed berries downstream.

"I'm sorry," I said. "I guess it's hard for you to go home empty-handed." I hesitated, wondering what else I could say. "I've seen your embassy on TV. It's just a few buildings, but there's a whole world outside. And it's not all nasty and primitive, or full of people like Keith. Some of it's beautiful."

"I've seen the brochures," said Olibrys.

I remembered that the Hastillans were rich from licensing their technology. Of course the embassy would be deluged with offers from travel agencies, tour operators, and the like. I had little to offer Olibrys that she couldn't buy herself if she wanted it.

Except— "When we were researching the blackweed's life-cycle, we built a habitat to replicate its natural environment. Back at the YGA centre, there's a Hastillan dome with the same atmosphere, the same heat and light as your home planet. If you wanted somewhere to hang out, somewhere to get away from your elders, I could let you use it."

"Really?" said Olibrys. "I think some of my broodmates would like that. It sounds just the place for those who are always complaining about the smell of your air." Her double-jointed arm made a sweeping gesture into the wind. "But what would you want in return?"

I could think of lots of things. I wished Olibrys would come back next week, become a regular volunteer, and endorse a message about the importance of looking after your planet. But as I opened my mouth to ask, I realised I was being just as selfish as everyone else who tried to use Olibrys for their own ends.

Instead I said, "What do *you* want?"

After a long pause, her translator chirped and said, "I want to believe, to connect, to embrace…" I couldn't tell whether Olibrys had said three things, or whether one alien verb had been approximated three different ways.

"I know that's hard," she went on. "But it means a lot that you asked. All I really want is to make the best of things. I'm here, after all. I just don't know what the best of it is."

I sympathised. "I never found that out myself."

We fell silent for a few moments. Far upstream, I saw a kingfisher darting over the shallows.

"I guess the thing to do is to keep looking," I said, thinking how long it was since I'd done so. "You don't find what you don't seek."

"Where would you suggest I start?" Olibrys asked.

The translator's monotone gave me no clue whether this question was genuine or sarcastic. But I felt I owed her the benefit of the doubt.

I said, "Earlier, you asked what we did for fun. That seems as good a place as any. I could show you a few things—" As soon as I said this, I realised that the delights of my allotment, or my collection of Northern Soul classics, might prove a little staid for star-hopping adolescents. "If you'd rather hang around with people your own age, I could introduce you to some of my younger relatives. My nephews and nieces have some interesting hobbies. And if you find anything you really like, you can introduce it to your friends: be a trend-setter."

If I could induce the Hastillans to develop a more positive attitude to Earth and its people, maybe they wouldn't be so cavalier about spreading blackweed everywhere. Yet I also wanted to make a genuine connection, unsullied by ulterior motives. I wanted to reach out to Olibrys, to learn how to get past the toneless translator to discover how she really felt.

"It would have to be something even better than eating blackweed," she said, "if it were to make the brood enjoy being here, rather than sneering in the embassy or feeling homesick in your Hastillan dome."

"I can't promise that." I didn't know what effect the blackweed had on the aliens. "But I can promise there's a whole lot of things you can try. There's a big world out here, full of people who love letting their hair down." I looked at Olibrys's cilia and wondered how my metaphor would translate.

"You would be my native guide?" she asked.

"Sure," I said, already looking forward to the prospect. It would be a great chance to get out more.

"Then I'm willing to look where you suggest," she said. "Call me at the embassy when you have some ideas."

Olibrys held out her hand. I removed my gloves, and clasped her hand in mine. Her grey skin was smooth and hot, and her thumbs gripped like pincers, leaving painful red marks next to my liver-spots.

"Safety points for the handshake—" I began.

"You have delicate bones?" said Olibrys. "I'm sorry. It'll be a long while before I earn my Most Adept Diplomat ring."

"I'll do my best to help you with that," I said, as I demonstrated our way of waving goodbye.

Ian Creasey lives in Yorkshire, England. He has written numerous short stories, several of which have been reprinted in Year's Best SF anthologies. A collection of his science fiction stories, *The Shapes of Strangers*, was published in 2019 by NewCon Press. For more information, visit his website at www.iancreasey.com.

A Cautionary Reporte on the Wonders of the Island-World Dubbed Van'ti'ra by the Native Genus of Homo

by

Jeannie Marschall

HAVING set out to discover the much-spoken-of world of a sister branch of our very own species (the establishment of which I have detailed at length to great success and general acclaim in previous works), I have since been made aware of the unfortunate fascination and subsequent demise of amateur spacers looking to make their mark on the adventurers' notch-post by braving the intermediate light-years and visiting the aforementioned planet themselves.

I fear I cannot but confess that I have failed my fellow humans. Knowing the pull felt by those who love a subject (for that is the origin of that word *amateur*: one who loves), and having been expressly warned on this very point, I cannot but feel my shortcomings regarding the communication of the perils of that beautiful place. In an effort to prevent further harm, I shall herein relate a tale of the islands themselves, as I believe most of my fellow Greater Apes are already sufficiently conscious of the dangers of oceans to be wary in that regard; but the nature of the forests of Van'ti'ra necessitates a more thorough description than I have hitherto offered.

My travel to and arrival on this most beauteous ocean-world were without delay or incident. My diary for that day merely mentions a slight space sickness—an affliction I am sadly prone to displaying.

The land that welcomed me was warm, and friendly; a sea-breeze ruffled my fine hair, and the smell of brine and living things was on the air. The path I was directed to was covered in sand, marked by nothing more than a single line of the most outlandishly formed shells and scale-like things. I fear I was instantly lost in cataloguing much of what I saw for a little while. I was greeted, some time later, by one of the clan of Dukkeron, a dark, curly-haired person tall of stature, immensely cheerful, hearty and hale as all these marvellous creatures are (resulting from modifications detailed in previous works, as mentioned before; the kind Reader is humbly encouraged to peruse these works for more satisfactory detail). I, by contrast, was viewed with much consternation given my slight and bookish form, and it took but a moment's consideration for my guide to decide that I would first be shown the main island and its manifold attractions, as they were deemed safest for one so flimsy as myself. I felt it was a quest to test my mettle, and vowed to behave accordingly.

Alas, I must not have been a very convincing or trustworthy sight: Looking, as I am wont to do, at length at each new, colourful sight, bizarrely fascinating creature, or tremendous architectural feature of this most breath-taking place, I caused a journey of no more than half a mile to take well over an earth-hour to complete. My embarrassment, upon discovering my attendant's indulgent if puzzled face, was rather acute.

"Oh," I exclaimed. "I feel I have made myself look a right ass, and wasted your time on top. My apologies, friend!"

My statement was met with a smile. "Not at all," was the retort in a voice only slightly tinged by the accents of a different tongue. "In truth, your enthusiasm for the smallest grain of sand is most endearing. Pray, why do you insist on drawing your subjects when you have an imaginizer perfectly capable of rendering facsimiles in exquisite detail? Is it something all humans do?"

"It is a quirk of mine, nothing more," I said, but snapped just one such facsimile as I spoke, then moved on so as to delay us no further. "I thank you for indulging me."

"Think no more of it. Haste is not a thing we are accustomed to here."

"Indeed? So time is not money, for you?"

A look from glittering, deep-brown eyes caught me. "That has the ring of a saying to it?" I nodded. "I have heard that on your world, the pursuit of material wealth is highly valued and respected. I fear we shall inspire very little of awe in you, in this case."

"No!" I protested. "If our ways are not your ways, and success is measured differently here, why should I judge you by the standards of my home-world? It would not make sense. And really," I continued, gesturing to the multi-coloured abundance around us. "Your works, your creations, must silence any such rudeness."

"Ah, but our pride and joy lies not just in our works alone, but in how we coexist with all the others who call this world home. For make no mistake," my guide said. "We would be made to feel it most intensely if we overstepped our bounds." A quick look cast in my direction as we continued over the sand, towards a green expanse of dense forest, now. "Your home—do you share it with other sentients?"

I shook my head—then reconsidered. "Some exist that have language, culture, self-awareness. But I believe you talk about something more still?"

"Yes. There are creatures in these oceans, in this soil, on the islands that know what this world is, that understand that the universe exists. Peoples that know themselves, and do not react kindly to insult." They cast a look at the treeline. "Here, let me show you."

I was led into dense, green growth. There were the storeys of a rainforest, the thick, cloyingly humid air as the wind from the sea was slowed to a trickle. The wind, even several metres in, still seemed to move the trees, however; they swayed and groaned softly. Everything was alive: slinging things, climbing branches, red, blue, and yellow-green bulbous hangers-on to branches thin as a pinkie or solid as a barrel. Flying creatures whizzed past above, insectoid enough to boggle my brain with gleeful fascination at the delightful wrongness of their shapes. Calls and rustling sounded, and I could well believe that a myriad more creatures hid within the fragrant, colourful underbrush. Within minutes, my clothes—too warm by far, I realized, for this place—were clinging to my skin with sweat. Hitching my backpack higher, I endeavoured to keep up with my guide who weaved between the weirdly shaped trunks easily—then noticed a tug on the laces of my left shoe, and halted.

"Hold on..." I bent down to retie the binds, and as I did so, I became aware of movement at the edge of my vision, an undulating, flowing change. I turned my head, and saw that what I had taken to be tree bark shimmer as hundreds of scales as large as my thumb-nail, brown on the outside but rainbow-coloured underneath like that of a butterfly, flicked back in a coordinated wave once around the trunk. Black iridescence met my eyes behind the glittering cover. I blinked, stunned, as I looked and *was looked at by the tree.*

Then a startled shout left my mouth as a lithe, sinuous, terror-inducingly nimble liana lifted swiftly from the forest floor and dove past my head, reaching for my pack, unbalancing me. I tumbled back, helpless and afraid as my possessions were plundered. I grabbed for the writhing wood—was it wood, even?

"Don't struggle!" I heard my guide's amusement—which, truth be told, did little to assuage my panic.

"What is happening?" I demanded, startled anew when the pressure on my shoulder straps suddenly eased and one of my notebooks was snatched from my backpack and drawn with amazing speed into the upper regions of the canopy. I raised a disbelieving eyebrow at myself when my first thought was one of relief that said, *Thank goodness that one was empty still!*

I really had to work on my priorities. I began immediately.

"A *tree* stole my *book!*"

A nod from the Vantiraē who had squatted down beside me by now. "And untied your shoe, as I can see. An old trick," they said, unperturbed.

"An *old trick?*" I sputtered. "These are not trees at all, are they?"

A tilt of the head. "I know the word you are using, but it is only appropriate for the dormant ones. Rare here, they only grow, eat light, bear fruit. They do not sing or hunt."

"*Hunt?*" I was speaking in entirely too many italics and could not seem to control myself. "This forest *hunts?*"

"Not this one, no. The capital island has been an agroforest for many generations; we have nurtured those species that are not prone to eating our young. All they want is some entertainment, some nutrition," A nod towards my pack. "...and that we uphold the contract and protect their saplings from more aggressive species." A pause, a wink towards the almost-faceted tree-eyes *that winked back.* "Not that these friends here are defenceless. But co-existence suits us all. No individual species may be too dominant here, or the balance collapses."

I sat, speechlessly ruminating what I had learned, looking at all the trees around me and changing my perspective on the entirety of the forest, seeing *people*, when a chime sounded from a pocket of my guide's loose, off-white garment. "Ah. That will be the palace wondering why our first visiting Earthling is taking so long." A smile that revealed pronounced canines as they slipped their communication device out of the folds of their clothes. A few words were exchanged in a foreign language as I kept staring at the black vision field next to me, at the treetops, the winding vines, the sway that was caused by no wind at all.

Doctor?" asked the alien in a friendly tone. "Shall we head into town?"

"I can't," wheezed I.

A fractional tilt of my guide's head, then: "How so?"

"I cannot do so without stepping all over their feet! Roots! Do you even call them roots?" I almost shouted, incredulity and the joy of mind-twisting discovery and wonder intermingling intoxicatingly. I grinned like a mad thing as my escort laughed loudly.

"Worry not, you shall be forgiven. These are gentle ones. However," came in a more serious tone. "Remember what I said about other 'trees,' yes? They do hunt. They drug you with scent, with colour, with spores and dripping spikes. Snag you with traps, swallow you whole, or drive you insane with mild poison then suck up your fluids as you lie decomposing—make sure you write of this in your note-books, if your home-trees are indeed predominantly static. This would be rather a danger to your fellows if they all sailed off towards distant isles clueless, wouldn't you say?"

I nodded. "Indeed it would be."

Thus, fellow travellers, mark my words, even if they come later than I originally promised my dear attendant: On Earth—and many other planets besides, as I have found—the forests remember storms, fires, droughts, storing their history in their rings, and their experience in changes in their internal biochemistry. They do speak to one another, helping each other, warning each other.

But on Van'ti'ra, travellers, be cautious: The trees do not just speak to one another—they plot revenge, too, if you arrogantly and carelessly step on their toes. And they have many a trick up their bark.

Beware.

Yours truly
Dr. I. C. Woods

Jeannie Marschall is a teacher from the green centre of Germany who also writes stories, time permitting. She enjoys long walks with her dog and cat, foraging, and tending her semi-sentient vegetable garden while inventing tall tales with her partner, or huddling around the fire in their witches hut for the same purpose. Jeannie mostly writes SciFi and all kinds of colourful Fantasy stories as well as the odd poem. She has a few short pieces lined up for publication this year, for example with Black Spot Books, *The Banshee Journal*, and *Queer Welten magazine*. Longer works are in the pipeline. Find her on Twitter: @JunkerMarschall

The Chienchat Conundrum

by

Lisa Timpf

(This story was originally published in The Martian Wave 2018, Nomadic Delirium Press.)

"THIS one's been living on a diet of rodents and birds. Just like the others." Vikk Sherpson, who'd just completed her examination of a sun-dried chunk of scat, squinted up at her supervisor, Alain Petitpas.

"Interesting," Alain replied. *That supports my theory. Though whether that's a good thing—* He cleared his throat. *Is it time to tell her?* He glanced at the blond woman as she rose to her feet and remounted her horse.

Before Alain could make up his mind, his own steed, a sturdy black mare, snorted and shook her head. Alain glanced in the direction the horse's muzzle pointed, noticing a plume of grey-brown dust marring the clear green-blue of the Arcadian sky. He reached for his distance vision glasses, dialled in, and muttered an oath.

"A crawler," Vikk said, lowering her own set of distance viewers. "But what's it doing out here?"

"No permits have been issued for travel in the Nature Reserve," Alain said, his mouth compressed in a grim line. He studied his protégé. Just six months out of university, Vikk was, in Arcadia's vernacular, a greenhorn, and from Earth to boot.

Against what they might be facing—

The young woman met his gaze. "Don't worry about me," she grunted, jerking her head toward the distant plume of dust. "You've seen my marksmanship scores."

Alain refused to rush his decision. Sensing his inner turmoil, his horse sidled restlessly under him. *It's only six months since I lost Victor, in that raid on a poachers' camp.*

The lack of a permit suggested the crawler's crew were, in all likelihood, engaged in criminal activity. Even with half a dozen re-inforcements behind him, Alain would be cautious about what they might be walking into. But Vikk had it right, regardless. Understaffed or not, investigating anomalies such as these fell squarely within their jurisdiction. And if they waited for reinforcements, they would, in all likelihood, lose their quarry.

"This was supposed to be a research mission," Alain protested. Nonetheless, he clucked to his horse, encouraging the sturdy-footed beast to pick its way along the rocky ridge, moving in the direction of the smoke plume.

"We're here to protect Arcadian wildlife." As Vikk urged her mount to catch up with Alain's, he turned to look over his shoulder, noting her steely expression.

Alain reined in and forced calm into his voice. "You must commit to following orders. If I tell you to fall back—"

"I understand." The young woman squared her shoulders.

Alain nodded grudgingly.

"Back there—the expression on your face, before you saw the smoke plume. You have a theory about the chienchats, don't you?" Vikk asked as they resumed their journey. Alain noted she'd used the Arcadian slang term, *dog-cat,* bestowed by the first settlers who, for the most part, were of French-Canadian descent. Immersed in the unfamiliar, the early pioneers sought to create a sense of home by cobbling together Earth-based terms to describe their adopted planet's flora and fauna.

It seemed an apt terms for the beasts, Alain had to admit. The chienchats featured dog-like ears and snouts, along with bushy tails reminiscent of Terran foxes. However, they moved with the grace of panthers, and their paws came equipped with retractable, razor-sharp claws. Skilled climbers, the glossy-coated predators played critical role in Arcadia's ecosystem. For one thing, they kept the population of cerfelan, an antlered browser, in check. Lately, though, the cerfelan population had exploded. As a result, the browsers had reduced much of the scrubland surrounding the settlement to grassy meadows.

"The surge in the cerfelan population suggests the chienchats are declining," he said, scowling at the dark green patch of forest ahead. "And yet— "

"And yet, the amount of scat we've discovered indicates the oppo-site," Vikk finished the sentence for him. "So many of them eating rodents, with cerfelan on the hoof readily available. Why would they switch their diet?"

"There's so much we don't know about them," Alain replied. "And we need to tread carefully." He thought about the debacle on Degna, where a type of tree bear the environmental biologists had been monitoring with radio collars turned out to be highly intelligent beings in their own right. There'd been a diplomatic uproar. The fallout had made everyone in the field doubly careful not to repeat the mistake of failing to respect the privacy and dignity of other thinking entities.

Vikk grunted an acknowledgement. "Who stands to gain if the meadowlands increase?" she asked.

"Farmers, for one," Alain replied. "Makes it easier to clear the land. And if the cerfelan stock remains healthy, it undermines the arguments of those who suggest that our ever-increasing level of manufacturing is damaging the environment."

"So more than one party might have a stake in trying to control the chienchats' numbers."

"That's true," he commented. "But if that's what they're trying to achieve, the evidence we've noted suggests they haven't been overly successful."

The duo fell silent for a space, leaving Alain with his own thoughts. He patted his black-coated steed's neck encouragingly. Brought to the planet in embryo form during the Exodus from Earth, the Canadian horses had adapted to life on Arcadia with ease. The breed had a well-founded reputation for endurance and willingness. It was time to call on that now.

Alain clucked to his mount and tapped her barrel lightly with his heels, urging the wiry mare to step up the pace. He noted with satisfaction that Vikk followed suit without needing to be told.

Alain dialed the zoom control on his distance vision glasses as he peered over the ridge toward the encampment. He and Vikk had over-nighted in a quiet valley, eschewing a fire to minimize the chance of detection. Now, at noon the day after they'd spotted the crawler, they were finally in a position to solve the mystery of its presence.

After a few quiet moments of study, Alain rose to his feet. The glasses simply confirmed what he'd suspected when he'd seen a flock of grand voutour, the giant feathered scavengers, circling. He and Vikk had no reason to fear attack from those who had established the camp below.

"I doubt that whoever did them in would have stuck around," he said, his voice calm. "Still, we could be walking into an ambush. Proceed carefully."

Vikk nodded, and they rode with their senses on high alert, keeping their horses to a walking pace as they made their way down the hill.

Alain tensed as his horse approached the force-fence perimeter, marked by stakes set in a rough circle around the encampment. The mare didn't pause, pushing on without hesitation between the posts.

Alain frowned. *Not powered up.* Someone would have had to get into the compound to disable the controller. Unless— *An inside job, maybe?*

"Over here," Vikk's voice rang out and Alain hustled over. She gestured toward the sonic controller. Even from a distance Alain could see the scratches and indentations on its surface.

"Tooth-marks," he observed.

"Something very determined put that out of commission," Vikk said, her eyes narrowing.

"At great pain to itself, I can imagine," Alain commented. He shuddered as he considered the agony any living being, human or animal, would endure passing through the barrier to reach the controller.

Alain crouched down to study the ground. Paw-prints and boot-marks dotted the soil. He stood to widen his line of sight, and saw half a dozen wire pens the size of a medium dog crate, some canted on their sides. All, he noted with relief, were unoccupied, and the doors hung open.

To the right of the cages lay the bodies of four humans, their skin and clothing torn and their facial expressions contorted. Their postures, the tracks, and the dots of red he took to be blood told the tale of a running battle.

Alain heard a low moan from the shadows beside the nearest habi-dome.

He exchanged glances with Vikk. "Cover me," he whispered, drawing his weapon and snaking forward with light steps.

Alain edged around the side of the dwelling, then dropped to one knee to examine a man in torn camouflage attire. Slumped in a seated position with his back against the habi-dome, the wounded individual had no visible weapon, and from the expression of pain and weariness on his face, Alain judged him to present no threat—not for the present, at least.

"Steady, there. I'll be back in a moment," Alain murmured.

A quick examination of the camp turned up no additional humans, living or dead. Alain sighed and called Vikk over.

"I'll get the aid kit," she offered, hurrying back to where their mounts stood sniffing the air and tossing their heads nervously. When she returned, she tended the man's wounds and dribbled water from her canteen into his open mouth.

At length, the man straightened, rubbing his hands over his face as though to clear his thoughts. He stared up at Alain.

"Planet-side security?" he asked, his voice rasping.

"Close," Alain said. "Arcadian Nature Services. Who're you?"

"Ditkar Vestus," the man replied. He shook his head. "Never thought I'd say it, but better you than those—devils," he mumbled.

"Devils?" Alain asked.

"Cat-dog-whatevers. Came here to trap the pups. Good market for them, off world." Ditkar's features contorted. "Only, Farver never told us—"

"Tiberius Farver?" Alain's tone was sharp.

"The Syndicate man, yeah." Ditkar coughed, a rasping sound deep in his chest. "If I saw right, you don't need to worry none. He bought it, back there. Took a couple of those *things* with him though." His features twisted in a grimace. "Cannibals." He gestured as though to spit, then thought better of it."Saw 'em hauling off their dead."

"Should we cuff him?" Vikk looked at Alain, eyebrows raised.

"Don't think he's going anywhere, in a hurry. I did a check for weapons already." Alain turned toward the man. "You wait here," he said, biting the words off tersely.

"Don't leave me." Ditkar pawed at Alain's arm. "If they come back—"

"I doubt they will," Alain said. "We won't be long."

He led the way back to the battle scene, head bent as he studied the ground.

"Drag marks," Vikk said, pointing to a line in the dirt, bracketed on either side by paw prints.

They followed the groove, which ended well outside the camp perimeter at a mound of earth with stones scattered on top. Claw-marks around the pile indicated that dirt had been kicked up. *The layer of rocks—it's the beginnings of a cairn*, Alain thought. "Don't touch it," he snapped. "Sorry," he added, noting that Vikk had already stopped moving toward the pile of earth and stones.

"They're not cannibals," the girl whispered. "And I think we interrupted them." She motioned, with a jerk of her head, toward the low ridge east of the encampment.

Alain looked in the direction she'd indicated, feeling his heart lighten despite the circumstances when he saw a dozen chienchats peering down at him, their stiffly-held tails bespeaking wariness. The chienchats ranged in color from a rich buttery hue to dark, dark brown bordering on black. Most members of the group sported cream-colored bellies and carried the same shading on their paws and partway up their legs, like socks, while their bushy fox-tails were tipped with black, as though dipped in ink.

"Beautiful, aren't they?" Alain whispered. He squatted, examining the disturbed earth from a distance. "Burying their dead. Coming to rescue their pups. Disabling the sonic controller. All those things suggest—"

"They're more than animals," Vikk's voice rang with confidence.

"There will be those back at the settlement who don't welcome the news," Alain observed, rising to his feet smoothly. "We'll need to tread carefully. I just wish we could get someone on the trail of those who sent these, these—" He gestured toward the encampment, unable to come up with a word vile enough to express his distaste. "We'll see where we fit in, in terms of priority. Colony planets have a tendency to be dismissed by the powers-that-be." He tried to keep the bitterness out of his voice, but Vikk's expression told him he hadn't been entirely successful.

"I don't think we need to worry about that," she said. She hesitated. "In fact, I have connections aboard the Galactic Space Command's cruiser, the *Providence.*"

Alain greeted the news with silence. He studied the girl's face for a long moment. "You're not an environmental biologist, are you?"

"I did study environmental biology, among other things," she replied mildly. "But I'm not an intern. I'm a member of the Galactic Expeditionary Force Outreach Team." The creases at the corners of her eyes crinkled as she added, "I'm three years out of university, not six months." She paused. "My team's mandate is to attempt communication with any intelligent non-human species we encounter. I came to Arcadia to find out what I could about the chienchats. And now we know."

Alain's eyes narrowed as he noticed, for the first time, the device Vikk cradled in her hands. "A Universal Translator? But it'll take months to develop a base for their language—" Vikk remained motionless, watching. *Waiting for me to connect the dots.* "Your research. On the vocalizations of Arcadian mammals."

Vikk nodded.

"You've got a head start, then. Are you here to recruit them?" A note of bitterness laced Alain's words. "I'm not sure if you realize it, but," he jerked his head toward where their mounts waited patiently, "you see these horses? Many of their ancestors were exported from Canada to work as cavalry mounts in the American Civil War. And died." He let the words hang on the still air.

Vikk gave him a long look and he felt his face flush under that scrutiny. "You know as well as I do that the laws have changed," she replied, her voice calm. Since revealing her mission, she'd seemed, in Alain's eyes, to have matured by several years. "Any species enlisted into battle must participate of their own free will. Still, Central Command fears that war with the Greenoans is coming, someday." She shrugged and glanced up the hill, toward where the watchers remained motionless. "Regardless, now that we know the chienchats' true nature, it's important to develop a relationship between our species."

"I can't allow it." Alain straightened to his full height. "We're here to *protect* them."

"That's a little paternalistic, isn't it?" Vikk snapped. In a softer tone, she added, "Besides, you know how the Greenoans treat non-humanoid species, even intelligent ones. How well would we be *protecting* them if we didn't let them know what they were up against, give them a chance to choose?"

Alain bowed his head, thinking. *Might as well tell her, now.*

"This doesn't help my argument, but I have a theory about the scat we found," he said. "I didn't want to voice it before. It sounds—out there. But I think the chienchats purposely altered their diet to allow the cerfelan population to grow."

"So that the cerfelan would graze down the young trees, creating more grassland," Vikk continued the train of thought.

"And thereby tempt the settlers to expand their farmlands," Alain added. "I believe your pals up there have developed a taste for calf meat."

"If they're smart enough to do that—" Vikk paused, considering the possibilities. "Then that just adds weight to the notion that they are intelligent."

"In that case, we'd rather have them as friends than enemies, don't you think?" Alain said. He looked at the small group on the ridge. *Friends.* A day ago, it would have seemed a strange notion. And yet, somewhere in his species' distant past, back on Earth, wolf and man had become just that.

Only this time, it would be on a more even footing. Alain grimaced. Though it pained him to admit it, maybe that was for the best.

"Go ahead, then," he said, nodding toward the translator. "Get started. Just—tell them all of it, so they make an informed decision. Don't sugar-coat what it might be like, to form an alliance with humans."

Vikk's eyes widened for a moment. She nodded, then turned to gaze at the waiting chienchats. "I won't," she replied, and it seemed to Alain that the words came as a promise, not only to him, but to those curious watchers as well.

Lisa Timpf is a retired HR and communications professional who lives in Simcoe, Ontario, Canada. Her poetry, fiction, creative nonfiction, and book reviews have appeared in *New Myths*, *Star*Line*, *Thema*, and other venues. Lisa speculative haibun collection, *In Days to Come*, is available from Hiraeth Publishing. You can find out more about Lisa's writing at lisatimpf.blogspot.com/.

A Word That Means Everything

by

Andrew Dibble

(Originally published in Writers of the Future Volume 36.)

W HEN Pius was assigned to Murk, he assumed he would be translating the Bible into the language of genius octopuses. But the first Thulhu he laid eyes on, rendered grayscale by the mist, only humped a lichen patch, distended tongue audibly slathering against rock, tentacle suckers puckering as they stuck and unstuck, vestigial wings like out-of-body lungs flagging over its backside.

Thulhus were supposed to communicate via tentacle gestures. This thrashing was it, right? But Pius's visor remained dark. No translation.

His last assignment with the Prabhakarins had been different. They knew first impressions mattered. This tentaclely brute didn't even acknowledge him.

"You're sure this thing is sentient?" he called back. His voice echoed queerly in the gloom.

"Keep it down!" Zora said in a church whisper. She was a good guide; by reputation a good ethnographer. But she treated him more like a credulous little brother than a client.

"I thought you said they can't hear."

"They can't. But the Thulhus aren't top of the food chain." Zora dangled her fingers like a jellyfish. Made them creep. The right fore-tentacle of her Thulhu-suit glided with almost feline surreptitiousness. She snatched her left hand away, and her other fore-tentacle darted behind the nearest hind-tentacle of her suit.

The visor protruding from Pius's headgear flashed, "Predator."

He gulped. In this fog, anything worthy of the name predator had to be calculating an ambush.

He was armed, but sensor mesh constricted his trigger finger. He'd chosen the non-invasive Thulhu-suit. Zora's interfaced directly with her motor cortex, so her gestures were just a symptom of the same neural impulses that animated her suit's fore-tentacles. Through more oblique mentation she could control the four hind-tentacles of her suit. If it came to flight, Pius had just one option: auto-pilot.

The Thulhu let up its humping long enough to radiate a spasm down its limber fore-tentacles and four stouter hind-tentacles. A shrug?

Pius's visor proffered, "Disbelief" in blocky red print. Then corrected itself, "Amused disbelief."

Pius groaned. What kind of language was this? He expected elegance, a system of symbols, like the sign language of Prabhakarin children who are deaf-mute until puberty.

"Maybe they just thrash around to mate and warn each other of danger," said Pius. "That doesn't mean they have *language*."

"Did your Church tell you that?" Zora chuckled like Socrates must have chuckled just before shredding his interlocutors' preconceptions.

"Just my guess." It could be bureaucratic blundering that consigned him to Murk, but he had to assume the One Church hadn't sent him on a fool's errand.

"Thousands of robots taking millions of pictures all over this region ran pattern recognition, *devilishly* clever algorithms. The same software derived more than a thousand languages spanning over a hundred species throughout the galaxy. Just think how few Bible translations your Church would have piddled out without it."

Church doctrine said that the Holy Spirit doesn't work through software, but brandishing dogma was a nonstarter. "Maybe a different subject would be more cooperative?"

There were other males (Zora called them men) scarfing lichen or sloughing about as though they belonged to a patch of mist rather than a place. And fog-gray females (ahem, women) haunting the periphery of the seen world. Young clung to the floppy wings on their back as their fore-tentacles flicked about in conversation.

"You'll have less luck with the others. We're just... " She let a fore-tentacle go slack like a burdensome limb she hadn't found the time to amputate.

The translation smote the upper left of Pius's vision. "Disobedient-other"?

In imitation, he let his shoulder drop, and the whole left side of his Thulhu-suit sagged. He avoided keeling over into spongy marsh only by wind-milling to the other side. His suit would have formed the gesture if he had just spoken the word into his mouthpiece.

Light danced in Zora's eyes, but she suppressed her mirth.

The Thulhu let up feeding. His fore-tentacles squiggled.

"Derisive amusement," Pius's visor flared.

"Why does this one 'talk'?" said Pius. Unsure how his suit would react, he resisted the urge to make air quotes.

"Heh, he's just true to his name."

"His name?"

"Snarky."

Snarky made the disobedient-other gesture. Pius's headset flashed, "Oh, the alien is back." Snarky's fore-tentacles mimed a hug, and Pius read the translation, "And she brought a friend."

Zora nudged Pius.

"How are you?" Pius said into his mouthpiece. His suit gestured accordingly. The feed glowing on the lower-right of his visor said the accusatory gesture for "you" meant literally "other-me."

"And it has nothing interesting to say," Snarky gestured, as self-important as a four-year-old. He only stood as high as Pius's waist.

"You really don't think I'm a person?" said Pius.

"Of course I believe I'm a person." Snarky's fore-tentacles wrung in dizzying self-referential circles.

Did the untranslatability of "you" confuse him? "That's not what I meant."

"I know what you meant. I've been through this with her. In the end we agreed to disagree. She—sage alien that she is—believes there's a shadowy world of squishy objects behind the mist. I say it's impossible."

"Behind the mist?"

"Where else would it be?"

Pius was taken aback by Snarky's candidness. "What am I then?"

"Just another alien I imagined. Proof that I'm exceptionally clever."

Or delusional.

"Maybe I'm just bored."

On second thought, Pius remembered Zora saying that the Thulhus only believe in their own minds. To them, there were no bodies, no other Thulhus; there's no lichen to eat, no mist. There are only thoughts of bodies, thoughts of other minds, mist-thoughts, lichen-thoughts.

She had lectured him on brain science. "You don't believe the hemispheres of your brain are two different people just because they communicate in order to render and interpret the world. To Thulhus, that's what talk is like."

Scant recognition on his part.

She tried again. "If you saw your brain, you'd know that the gray matter was you. But it wouldn't feel like you, right? That's how a Thulhu thinks about other Thulhus. He knows they're all *him*, even though it doesn't feel that way."

What Pius knew was that he wasn't a brain but a soul fashioned by his Creator.

Zora only knew a universe in flux, constantly prototyping. Not a universe, vibrant and ushering.

A Godless materiality.

Maybe he could enlighten Snarky. "But everything persists even when you aren't looking at it. You close your eyes, open them, and—" Pius's suit broke off gesturing as Snarky leaned upsettingly close.

"Close my eyes?" His cephalopod face was so near, Pius took the hint: Thulhus don't have eyelids. Thulhus didn't have to adapt to overbearing light with the mist always about. They might as well have lived inside a cloud.

"Ah, assume you can," Pius said.

"Very well." Apparently, Thulhus have a gesture for *gross condescension*.

"When you cover your eyes," said Pius, ignoring the slight, "the whole world goes away, and when you see again, it's the same as it was. How do you explain that if all that exists is you?"

Thulhus don't have lips, and Snarky's mouth was beneath his body where Pius couldn't see it. But Pius knew Snarky would be grinning impishly were it not for his anatomy.

"How can I? I am overcome. You've shown me the error of my ways, wrestled your existence from my delusions."

Zora glanced at Pius sheepishly. But why should Snarky be polite? He believes he's just talking to himself.

Snarky flapped a fore-tentacle, an off-hand negation. "Sometimes the mist gobbles up what I see, sometimes it doesn't. This eye-blinking has nothing to do with it. Zora tells me aliens have a similar problem. Sometimes you try to remember and succeed, sometimes you fail. Mist, forgetfulness—they are the same."

Zora perceived Pius's mounting agitation. "Persistence for us isn't the same as it is for them. They only see motion, no colors, nothing that's still."

Snarky couldn't hear, but he must have inferred the purpose of their exchange because he flicked his tentacles in amused squiggles.

"Do you believe in God?" Pius ventured. The software made the fore-tentacles of his suit link together to denote belief then lifted the right in an extravagant salute,

"God."

Snarky emitted a confused wavering. He imitated the extravagant salute. "Is God a person?" His fore-tentacles groped and shivered in the gesture for *person*.

As far as the software ascertained, his question was meant in all earnestness. But it posed a dilemma: "Person" means an intellect and even more than that, a will, so God is a person. But if Pius said as much, Snarky would reject God as he rejected all other persons.

"Yes, God's a person."

Snarky swayed, dithering. "Am I God?"

"No, you aren't God. We aren't God either. God is"—Pius struggled to produce a word—"outside. Beyond the mist." The software raised Pius's right fore-tentacle in a new salute, an elephantine trumpeting. Reviewing the feed, Pius realized it meant literally one-beyond-mist, which also meant one-beyond-forgetfulness.

"One-beyond-mist," Snarky gestured. Was that a question?

"Yes, that's the beginning of what God is," Pius said carefully. "What would it take for you to believe in one-beyond-mist?"

"Ah, I understand now, becoming God only requires patience." His tentacles squiggled. "Wait for the mist to clear, and I will be one-beyond-mist!"

"Did you hear what I said? *You aren't God.*"

Zora flipped her fore-tentacles disarmingly; she shot Pius a look.

"But if I can't become God, God is impossible."

"God is another person, someone *always* beyond the mist." Pius struggled to screen the tension from his voice. It came out a plea, "What would it take for you to believe in God?"

"Madness."

"Snarky likes you," said Zora.

"Likes me?"

"When I met him, he gestured incoherently just to confuse the software. You had a conversation, give and take."

"He's delusional."

"He's different. You have to bridge that difference, don't expect him to."

"And how am I supposed to do that?"

"Maybe in your translation Jesus can have tentacles. And Satan can be one of the *things* deep down in the lowlands." Her tentacles didn't squiggle like Snarky's would have, but she cracked a smile. The deep things were just rumor spawned by the same mythos that named the Thulhus.

She would've gone on, but Pius cut her short. "What you're suggesting isn't translation."

"Maybe not, but limiting your work to the bounds of this book—the Bible—isn't going to reach the Thulhus. For a Thulhu there's only one mind, one author, one work of literature. So think of the Bible as a Thulhu would, as part of a larger work, one constantly expanding and improving." She grinned. "Your translation is just the next draft."

Pius sulked for a while on the way back, but eventually Zora tried again. "Back on Earth, biologists had a saying: 'Life will find a way,' will thrive in every habitat—the driest desert, the bottom of the ocean. Once we studied other worlds, do you know how that saying changed?"

"How?" Pius begrudged.

"'Life will find every way.' The universe will surprise you no matter how your Bible says life should be." Her constantly prototyping universe in which Christianity is as queer and outmoded as the vestigial wings of a Thulhu.

"*Every* way? Aside from the Thulhus, I've seen sooty ferns, lichen, a few mushrooms, and whatever that is rotting so delightfully in the marsh. Not exactly biological diversity."

"Those mushrooms." Her right fore-tentacle wound in a spiral. "They *live* off radiation. Even in the lowlands where radioisotopes blanket everything."

"There are mutant mushrooms. So what?"

"There's the universe, and then there's your Bible." Her voice was low but sure, like faraway thunder. "I'll let you guess which doesn't fit within the other."

Pius was glad to be indoors. The air had an antiseptic taste, but it was unmisted, an unmurky corner of Murk. He changed out of his sweaty wetsuit and peeled the sensor mesh from his hands and arms. The skin beneath was clammy, and it itched. There was a solar-spectrum light in his monkishly small dorm. It might ward off seasonal affective disorder (it was always the season for that on Murk), but that merry bulb didn't assuage his brooding.

He keyed a report to his superiors. "First contacted native sentient species today, *Murkaea hectopus cthulhu*, commonly named Thulhus. Findings not encouraging. The one Thulhu that deigned to communicate with us via tentacle gesticulations had no concept of God, or I suspect, any spiritual reality. His arrogance was not that of the disbeliever but of the fool convinced that his limited concepts are the only possible lens through which one may perceive the world.

"Serving God and His Word, I contend that the purported sentience of the Thulhus is an invention of the software that derived their language, if it can even properly be called a language. I humbly suggest that sentience be construed in terms of whether a species has a concept of the Divine, not the dictates of software.

"The Thulhus strike me as a hive species; every Thulhu believes itself to be queen and all the members of its cult (i.e., group) mere extensions of itself. We do not sully Scripture by translating it into the mating dance of bees. Let us not sully it with the tentacle-gesturing of the Thulhus. Recommendation is that this project be terminated."

A response could take weeks, given bureaucratic shuffling. But just two standard hours later: "Your contention is unacceptable. We will send help."

Cowed by the eight-word reprimand of his superiors, Pius drifted. Should he wait for the promised, and likely degrading, help? Would the project be out of his hands once help arrived? Would he become a mere clerk at the beck and call of a new superior?

Pius prayed for answers but continued to work. Without explicit instruction to the contrary, he had to show progress in daily reports, though only God knew whether anyone would read them.

He had a place to start: the Gospel of John, the fourth and most exalted of the biographies of Jesus. After that, he'd translate whatever other Greek portions of the Bible his superiors told him to, hitherto without collaboration. Synthesis happened higher in the ecclesiastical hierarchy.

He dictated the opening verses of John in the original Greek into the mouthpiece of his headgear, *"En arche en ho logos..."* The shadowy tentacles of a Thulhu homunculus rose and fell across his visor. They froze—stuttering?—then jostled to the next gesture.

He replayed with English subtitles, and right away, the problem was as plain as mist: "In the beginning was the *logos* (?)." Even the software surrendered before the translation puzzle posed by *logos*. *Logos* is not just Word, as it is commonly translated into English. Indeed, the capital *W* only gestures at the capacious semantics of *logos*, which includes just about everything having to do with language and the mind: discourse, narration, commandment, teaching, reason, intellect, proportion, expectation. In one Bible passage, *logos* means debt, in another a legal complaint. In several passages, *logos* has a derogatory connotation, as mere talk or empty rhetoric, like when Paul writes, "The kingdom of God depends not upon *logos* but on power."

Logos found a niche in most every philosophy and religion throughout the ancient Mediterranean in which John wrote his Gospel: Orphic and Dionysian mystery cults exalted their dying and vivifying gods with epithets of which *logos* was the germ. Stoic philosophers taught of a *logos spermatikos*, the rational principle undergirding everything. Aristotle rendered *logos* as rationality, the soul of humanity.

Pius decided to simply gloss *logos* as the Thulhu gesture for "word." It would altogether miss the mark, but the Thulhus obviously had no capacity to construe the expanse of John's meaning. No one could object to his treating an impossible problem with an inadequate solution.

"Translate 'word.' " An umbral tentacle rose across his field of view like a hand reaching in supplication, oddly stirring. But the subtitles that crowded beneath provoked no fellow-feeling: "Gesture, verb, word, connection, ascent, legerdemain, guile."

Pius tried again. The software repeated itself without irritation.

He groaned from a tight place in his chest. The primary meaning wasn't even "word" but "gesture," which had all kinds of implications John hadn't intended.

Pius moved on to "verb," the second meaning listed. Why should "noun" be absent? The software had to be confused, befuddled by the Thulhus and their supposed language.

The next meaning, "connection," had worth because gesturing is how the Thulhus connect. And it brought out a shade of meaning latent but not explicit in John's usage: John says the *logos* is Jesus, and Jesus is how God connects to His creation.

But the next meaning, "ascent," had nothing to do with John. "Ascent" conjured images of a Thulhu mounting a steep rise through inscrutable mists like the dread monster Cthulhu from the old Lovecraft tales, the Thulhus' namesake. Jesus could have no association with that!

"Legerdemain" and "guile" didn't help. Too underhanded. He couldn't frame Jesus in such a sinister light.

He leapt up to hammer out a report to his superiors. They'd understand that it was better to preserve John's meaning than to twist it in translation. Whatever he did would be ignored or ridiculed by the Thulhus anyway. Why even try?

But that prim reprimand stung, a crisp blow. His superiors would see this project done. At best they would ignore him. Worse, they might judge him beneath even *unacceptable*.

He sagged onto his tiny cot, defeated once by the separateness of languages and again by the aloofness of the Church to which he dedicated his life.

On the day Pius was called to Murk, he'd been watching the sunrise ritual with Prabhakarin children and their non-menstruating mothers. Beneath the banyan tree in the town square of Dhruv, men dipped teak ladles into pots of ghee, heated just to liquidity, then upended the pure oil over a preserved footprint of one of their distinguished ancestors—once, twice, three times. Murmuring a mantra in a forgotten tongue, they bowed prostrate with the fingers of all four hands intertwined like strands of an occult knot. The new sun bathed their backs.

One of the girls—pre-pubescent because her mouths were just lipless slits—caught Pius's eye with an upward grasping motion, handspeak for sex. Thank God, it wasn't an invitation. She was just repeating what she'd seen, a reminder that Pius's abstinence was a topic of light conversation around Dhruv. He pointed upward with two pronged fingers and drew them to his eyes: *the stars are watching you*. She turned away, rasping giggles from her inchoate larynxes.

Almost half of the men rose to begin work, most in a marketplace stall, at the docks, or a warehouse. More would rise soon, but the truly pious would continue prostrations until the sun lifted fully above the horizon. No mean feat given that Prabhakara's diurnal cycle is forty times longer than a standard day. After the long night, some would keep shoving their noses into the dirt from sheer superstitious relief.

A vibration from inside his dhoti. About time the Church broke radio silence. They could page him through his headgear, but the locals deemed any adornment above the waist womanish, so he rarely wore it.

Undoubtedly, he would be reassigned, perhaps to just another Prabhakarin community, but he suspected otherwise. He'd heard through the missionary grapevine that the Church planned to cut its losses: Prabhakarins spoke too many languages, were too stuck in their ways, too fearful of an everlasting night.

God willing, his next assignment would be on Aletheia. The common tongue, spoken across the entire planet, boasted more than one million words, five thousand colors, five thousand textures, five thousand for every sense. Every mannerism, every flavor of awkwardness and triumph, every nuance of propriety, every stage in every process from nascence to ripeness to moribundity had a name. Most had several, each a near-synonym different only by a flutter of connotation. Anyone, no matter his station, could coin a new word, and if his fellows deemed it worthy, civilizations would take it up. What better language to translate the Gospel into? Pen just one translation, and he could bring billions to Christ.

He rushed into his hut to fetch his headgear. But his wife was in the way, or rather the woman the town council had designated as his wife. Her gourd-shaped head yammered from both ends, left mouth prognosticating doom: the stars would destroy him if he shirked the sunrise ritual again. Then she'd be a tainted widow unable to inherit even his impure off-world wealth. Her right mouth grumbled about stillbirths and deformities.

Murmuring polite apologies, he ducked beneath her accusing arm, knowing she wouldn't touch him, not during her period. He swiped the jute fiber sack that held his headgear, edged past her, and made for the tree line. He passed the stand of basalt idols that guarded the northern entrance to Dhruv, among them a rough-hewn statue of Jesus. It had two heads like all the other graven images. Pius ground his teeth and impotently fantasized about pulverizing the heathen thing.

The canopy overshadowing him had unfurled entirely after its nightly hibernation. He covered one ear to block the cacophony of tropical birds, and donned his headgear. Loam squished beneath his tapping foot.

"You are Pius Judson, missionary of the One Church of Christ?" A machine voice, monotone, like all official Church communication.

"I am Pius Judson, missionary of the One Church of Christ," he echoed for purposes of voice recognition.

"The Church looks upon your work favorably. You are hereby reassigned to the moon of Aletheia, colloquially named Murk. Report to research station Relyeh on its southern continent at your earliest convenience."

Murk, the moon of Aletheia. Teasingly near Aletheia but not Aletheia. What had he done wrong? With almost no prodding from his superiors, he'd translated the entire New Testament into the Dhruvish dialect, spoken by merchants and bankers across most of the continent. He'd translated John's Gospel two more times into the dialects of outlying villages. His attempt to render John in child hand-speak had floundered, but that project was his own.

"Is someone else translating John into Aletheian?"

A pause. "It is given to you to know." An answer as cryptic as the prognostications of Prabhakarin astrologers.

"Who?"

"Father David Nestor."

Pius removed his headgear and laughed bitterly. Murk wasn't his punishment. It was his consolation prize. He'd been outclassed by the greatest Bible translator alive.

When Pius got word that the promised help was David Nestor, he wondered idly if all those sunrise rituals he abstained from provoked astrological backlash after all.

But he wasn't the one tumbling from Aletheia to the shrouded moon of the hectopus cows. David must have fallen far in the eyes of the Church to be reassigned to Murk.

That thought kindled a grim green warmth in Pius. Envy didn't shame him as much as it should have. Knowing that staunched the warmth, a little.

David emerged from the decontamination chamber clothed in priestly black—slacks and a shirt, not a cassock. His cheekbones were high, his skin taut and frustratingly boyish even though he was fifteen years Pius's senior.

Pius shook David's hand stiffly and led him toward the mess hall, unsure what to say. Pius started toward a bevy of support staff, mostly Devonians, a species of black amphibious fish-people. They weren't native to Murk, but the damp suited them.

Perhaps the presence of a crowd would stifle whatever probing questions David had chambered in his throat.

But David turned to the side to indicate an empty table. "How about here?"

Inquisition: unavoidable.

Pius slumped into a seat. He said nothing.

David speared a rehydrated potato on his plate with more gusto than the wrinkled tuber deserved. "The potatoes here aren't bad. See, they spice everything to oblivion over on Aletheia."

Was David rubbing it in? *Hey, Pius, have you heard of scholars' pagodas on Aletheia? In Asher—marvelous city, really—there's one just for Bible translation. It has a level for each book of the Bible! And would you believe it's built into a mountain of pink salt?*

David swallowed. "Sometimes plain rations are best."

Pius wasn't in the mood for banter. "How should we begin with the translation?"

"Let's not talk about work. Let's talk about you."

Next David would say he's no longer needed, or worse needed but only for clerical errands. David would be the fount of all creative insight.

"I read your work on translating John into Prabhakarin languages," said David.

"Really?" Pius wasn't exactly a distinguished translator.

"I like to know about the people I work with. Your translation of *logos* intrigued me. I forget the term, but it means action. It struck me as a bit loose."

Loose? "I wanted to render *logos* as Word. But to the villagers I lived with language isn't about description. It's all about inciting action, so I chose *kara*, action."

His mouth felt suddenly dry. "I hope you can see why it was necessary."

"All language is about inciting action?" said David, his scholar's soul beaming.

So Pius knew something that David didn't. "They go too far, of course, but it's not so strange, if you think about it. When a mother tells her child, 'It's eight o'clock,' she's not trying to *inform* her child of anything. She wants the kid to go to bed."

"Ah, so that's why your translation was so admonishing, 'You must believe this!' and 'You must believe that!' "

Pius opened his mouth but clammed up.

"You can speak plainly to me, Pius. I'm just a priest, a pastor like yourself." That confusion in titles said much. In an earlier age, before there was One Church of Christ, they would have stood on opposite sides of an eight-hundred-year-old schism. David would be a Catholic and a Jesuit, Pius a Protestant.

"I know the tone was off, but belief is what the Gospel is about, embracing doctrine, I mean."

"Perhaps."

Perhaps? "How would you have translated logos into Prabhakarin?"

Pius thought he might've caught him off guard, but of course David Nestor would have an answer, "They have a word, *amita*, meaning boundless. It's so much richer than just some generic action."

"I know the word. *Amita* orchestrates the stars in a grand ritual, the infinite cosmic ritual that all the rituals the Prabhakarins perform on the ground supposedly emulate."

"Sounds pretty good, right? Jesus is that boundless principle, the infinite entering history as a finite being. Like in John's Gospel."

"But translating logos as *amita* would have made the Prabhakarins think Christianity was just a repackaged version of their religion."

"Why not exploit the cultural idiom, write an eloquent translation, and engage Prabhakarin readers? Then we pose some real competition to the canons of the native religion."

"We can't do that at the expense of Christ." Grim warmth again, less green, redder. "You know, *Jesus*?"

"That's why there are Gospels." David didn't raise his voice. "John goes on to say who the man is that is the *logos*, what he did, who he was, his sacrifice."

"You can't *wreck* the beginning just because you think John will pick up the pieces later on." Pius gained his feet. "Let's not talk about me. Let's talk about you."

Pius meant the translation of John that had made David's reputation, his Orkish translation. The translation that should not have been. Orken One is hell, too hot for water to condense except at its poles. It has a magnetosphere, an atmosphere, wind enough to normalize temperatures through day and night. But life couldn't have foothold: it had been molten just five-hundred million years ago. That was time enough for reels of amino acids, perhaps inklings of silicon-based life. But further complexity just shouldn't have been possible. Everyone with pull—star system governments, venerable scientific foundations, enterprising trillionaires—set their sights only on the cornucopia of Earth-like worlds with a real chance at harboring sentient life.

Orken One still attracted pioneers, wealthy tourists scudding by in a luxury cruiser. Peeping through the lenses of drones conferred bragging rights with none of the being boiled alive.

The Dantesque safari amazed them—sandstone hoodoos, geologically young but red like old blood, bearing pyroclastic slabs aloft in unbroken penance. Dunes like white-robed acolytes cowering resplendently beneath the numinous glare of Orken. The wind screaming judgment upon the ever-erring landscape, sometimes skewing it in flagellate wave patterns, other times whipping it in dust devils or driving biting sandstorms of cataclysmic size.

The footage seeped into social media. A keen-eyed researcher took notice. She found no water, nothing fossilized. But wave patterns furrowed the dunes even on windless days, even against the prevailing wind.

The second wave of drones had been equipped with translation software. They discarded any footage of patterns explicable by weather alone. But much remained, too much for chance. Biology notwithstanding, the drones' Bayes nets and Markov models found language.

It wasn't long until researchers weren't just overhearing the Orkens but conversing with them. No one ever found out what they were. Either the Orkens were holding out, or they didn't know themselves. But biological puzzles didn't faze Christian missionaries dedicated to bringing the Good News to every sentient race.

None proved himself worthier of the challenge than David Nestor.

"What about me?" said David. Not a challenge, just an honest question.

"How did you translate *logos* into Orkish?"

"Sun-principle," said David. "The reason their sun burns. You know that." Every translator of the Bible alive knew that.

"Do you *want* to make Christianity sound like sun worship?"

"It might sound like that to us," David said calmly. "But it doesn't to them. They don't worship their star Orken, they just believe their world persists through its light."

"But that's not what John meant."

"It's not? Isn't *logos* the principle that creates and upholds reality? Doesn't John call Jesus the 'light of the world'?"

"Later on, but not at the beginning," Pius protested lamely.

"Really? You know that *logos* is a philosophical term in Greek. John must've known that. And how did its use as a philosophical term begin?"

"Heraclitus," Pius conceded.

"And what did Heraclitus say the *logos* is?"

Is he going to make me say it? "A principle that animates the universe."

"And characterized by *fire*."

Pius sighed. "Perhaps your rendering of *logos* was acceptable." The word was out before echoes of the reprimand from on-high (unacceptable, *unacceptable*) seized him. Pius forged on, "But what about later when John writes, 'And the *logos* became flesh and lived among us.' "

David smiled. He knew this was coming.

Pius continued, "You translated flesh as *spirit*, precisely the *opposite* of what John meant!" said Pius.

"I think you know why I did that."

"I know the commentaries and the subcommentaries, but those are others' reasons. You never said why."

"That's because God's Word needs to stand by itself. If we need long footnotes and commentaries to explain it, we've already failed." David caught Pius with a level stare. "Why do you think I did it?"

There was nothing to do but answer. "The Orkens didn't have a sand-wave pattern for flesh when the explorers arrived. How could they in a world without bodies?"

"But they came up with one, didn't they? A word for us, for *humans*. They never differentiated between our flesh and flesh in general. You see the problem?"

"They would think that the *logos*-made-flesh didn't come for them, that Jesus only came for us."

"I hope you can see why it was necessary," said David, using Pius's own words against him.

Pius had to swallow before speaking. "Maybe Jesus didn't come for the Orkens. John's point is that Jesus debased himself, became flesh, to redeem us from the death of our bodies."

"Orkens die too," David said with a long stare. "Not like us, but they die. And some have died glad they knew Christ. You think if I could do it again, I would abandon the project and deny them that?"

"If God wanted everyone to live a Christian life, he wouldn't have waited billions of years before coming as Jesus. Think of the —how many? *trillions*?—dying every day throughout the universe that never knew Christ. God has a plan for them. You think we should compromise God's Word just to whittle down that number by the barest fraction?"

David regarded Pius wearily, weary as the galactic wanderer he was. "Why did you become a missionary, Pius?"

"God called me."

"What did God call you to do?"

Pius knew what David wanted him to say, so he demurred, "To safeguard His Word."

"That's all?"

"That's all I'll say."

David's lips pursed, fell in the slightest frown, said nothing.

To wipe David's disappointment away, Pius changed the subject, "You asked me why I was called, but you never said why you came?"

"To help."

"That's all? I have to think our superiors have big plans for the Thulhus if they send you in such a hurry. Big plans!" David came to help? Help what?

It dawned on Pius. "You aren't here for the Thulhus. You're just the next maneuver in the political game. Our superiors don't care about the Thulhus, not really. They just want to brag about how the Church translated the New Testament into Thulhuese before the Muslims translate the Qur'an or the Buddhists translate whichever sutras are trendiest."

"Let our superiors concern themselves with politics, Pius. They do God's work too, even if they are unaware of it."

"You're David Nestor. You have to know something."

"They didn't send me. I volunteered."

Pius avoided David the following day and the next. But on the third day, Zora called them together.

David saw Zora and brightened. He offered his hand, like one dignitary meeting another, but unbeknownst to the joint delegations they were on a first-name basis. She took it. "Zora Mead, it's an honor."

Pius scanned both their faces. However Zora identified, it wasn't Christian. Why would David be honored to meet her?

"You didn't know?" said David. "Zora discovered Orkish."

"That was you?"

"Yup."

A split-second suspicion: David came for her? But that was ridiculous. Who would give up on Aletheia, come to Murk, just to shake a hand?

"Let's get down to it," said Zora. "Tomorrow there will be four minutes of mistlessness where we visited Snarky and his cult. There's a good chance they haven't migrated far. Trust me, it's a rare opportunity."

"There isn't another cult in the area?" Pius asked.

"Don't want another tentacle lashing from Snarky?" said Zora. "He learned more from you than you think. Meet him again. He'll be a different Thulhu in clear air." She glanced from Pius to David and back to Pius. "I've been tailing a different cult, but if you need me again—"

"We'll be fine," said David. "Pius can guide me, and we can radio for help if anything goes wrong."

Zora looked at Pius uncertainly, then sized David up, frowned in resignation.

"All right, but go armed. There are reports of lampreys."

Scarcely thinking about how humid it'd gotten, Pius followed David to the armory, palmed the same munitions as David, and loaded them into the same model handgun.

David would confront him, he knew. Whatever David said, and however he responded, he would always be turned around. He could white-knuckle it, but for how long?

David always knew the right thing to say. He listened as though he'd crossed not only the gulf between Aletheia and Murk for Pius's sake, but the empty reaches of galactic space. How long could his convictions hold out against the enormity of David's attention?

A Devonian staff woman had already strapped David into his Thulhu-suit but had yet to help Pius.

"Junia, when you're done with the Churchmen, come back here and help me with these repairs. Dehumidifiers won't fix themselves, even on God's account," said Junia's manager, a middle-aged white engineer.

Junia strapped Pius into his Thulhu-suit harness, rushed to snap the buckles into place, and hurried to join her manager.

David called back to her, "You forgot one."

"Forgot one?" she said, her black gills flapping listlessly, huge insensate fish eyes on either side of her cleft head.

"*His* buckles," said David.

Pius shifted, scrutinized the points where his harness interfaced with his chest and legs. He lifted his right thigh free.

"Oh, sorry about that." She readily snapped the errant buckle into place.

The manager faced David penitently. "Sorry, sometimes they make mistakes."

David took to operating the Thulhu-suit easily, bounding over mist-cloaked boulders and winding around sucking marsh without hesitation. He had the brain implant, like Zora. David must have digested everything there was to know about Thulhu-suit operation just like he'd assimilated Pius's work on the Prabhakarins. But it could just be because he was David Nestor. Everything came easily to David Nestor.

Pius trailed behind David. They weren't far from the coordinates Zora had given them, where the mist would clear and night would deign to show her star-freckled face. Maybe Pius could avoid another confrontation.

But when they were ten minutes out from the station, David relaxed his pace. "Did you hear what the manager said back at the base, when he apologized for that mix-up with your harness?" David said.

That was an odd way to brook conversation. "He didn't say it to me." *And it was my harness that was loose.*

"He said, 'Sometimes they make mistakes.' "

Recalling that the manager's subordinate was young, black, a woman, and a Devonian, the prejudice of those words slammed into Pius.

"What do you think he meant?" said David.

"By 'they'? Could've been racist? Maybe sexist? Species-ist?" Pius suggested, sharing in the joke.

"Don't forget ageist. Classist? Maybe he has something against fish?"

"He could've just meant that sometimes the people he manages make mistakes."

"But why say 'they'?" said David.

"Good question." Pius chuckled again.

"Why write *logos*?" said David.

"Good question." His humor was gone. "But I'm not sure God will tell us if we ask."

"I mean, why would John—why would *God*—write *logos* in scripture if He didn't mean something as rich as *logos*, with all its meaning, if He didn't know we would translate it and translate it again, sometimes carelessly, sometimes with all our faculty, but inevitably fail to capture His meaning?"

"He knew that we would sin in this, like we do in so many things. It's no different."

"I don't think that's it at all," said David, a touch forlorn. "Why would God entrust scripture to us if He didn't think we could carry out His will through it?"

Again, David managed to turn Pius's own words around on him, make it seem that he was the one protecting scripture and bringing the true Gospel to new species, while Pius was just straying again and again. "Is there a point in this?"

"No point, just something I'm trying to gesture at." David raised his right fore-tentacle in the trumpeting salute, the software's neologism for one-beyond-mist, which might mean God. "Remember in First Corinthians Paul writes of how he spreads the Gospel? 'I am all things to all people, that I might by all means save some.' I think *logos* is like that. It began as just a word, give or take the capital *W*. Maybe John meant a certain something by it, but God knew that we wouldn't be able to get inside John's head, that throughout history and the stupendous variety of His creation, we would inevitably make it richer, even unknowingly, like the crew manager with his 'they.' I think *logos* is the Word to you and I, a solar-principle to the Orkens, and an action to the Prabhakarins. I think it's what every sentient species needs it to be, and given time, *logos* will mean everything, will be a word that means everything."

David cast his spell over Pius while speaking, but they departed again in silence. The mist occluded everything, outlasting mere words and the illusions of the man that wove them. Pius decided that David had spent too long tinkering with the stupendous variety of the Aletheian tongue. Surely, a scholarly fancy overcame him to stretch meaning further and further without regard for scripture or the Christianizing of sentient life. A word that means *everything*? Were it possible, it would mean nothing at all!

Pius plucked up his courage. Just as they were climbing the rise upon which Snarky and his cult still grazed, he beckoned, "Hold up." There was still some time before the mist would clear.

David swiveled his Thulhu-suit around.

"Why did you volunteer to come here when you already had work on Aletheia?"

"They can get on without me."

And I can't? "It has nothing to do with a word that means everything?"

"No need to think it means more than it does." David only half-smiled at his own joke. "I just see the richness in *logos*, and its potential, and I see God in that potential."

Pius had to lay it on hard. "It's heresy."

"Heresy?" At last, David was the one reacting.

"Yes, however we translate *logos*, God means *something* by it. God doesn't send us in pursuit of phantoms, willing that we do violence to the text, refashioning Christianity as just every other religion it comes into contact with."

"John didn't invent this word *logos*. He found it where it was and elevated it for God's purposes. Heraclitus's fire, the Stoic *logos spermatikos*, Aristotle's soul of humanity, reason, Word, all of that was already there. You think *logos* is just a title for Christ? No, it was a title for cult deities throughout the ancient Mediterranean: Orpheus, Hermes, Dionysus." A deep anger, a lash of desert wind, stirred within David.

"You think the difference between us is that you defend the truth of scripture and I corrupt it, but really I have my eye on the spirit of the Word and you defend the dead letter."

"Me? You have these blinders, this *tunnel vision*. What about the rest of scripture? Jesus wasn't Heraclitus, or a Stoic, or Aristotle, and he certainly wasn't an alien. He was human. He's what's decisive, and his humanity is part of that."

"If that's how you feel—"

"We don't even need to go back to your scandalous Orken translation to make my point! You know the prevailing Chinese translation of *logos*?" David jerked a nod, but Pius spoke over him, "*Dao*. Because of that, Chinese speakers ever since the twentieth century have believed that the real Old Testament isn't the prophets, the Books of Moses, and the history of the Hebrews? No, they said it's the Daodejing!" Pius didn't need to remind him that the Daodejing is foundational to Daoism. And Daoism has nothing to do with any Christian creed. "That's what I mean by heresy."

"People misread the Bible all the time. You don't need faulty translation to find crude innovators."

"But we needn't help the innovators along! Our task is to preserve the meaning John intended. Once the alien races acclimate to us, they'll understand the Gospel as we do."

David grimaced as if his last meal refused digestion.

Let him. God didn't incarnate as a Thulhu, or any alien, but as a human.

"And how long will that take?" said David. "You think we should tell our superiors, 'Wait a few generations while we figure out how to educate a whole moon of Thulhus about the proper meaning of *logos*?' "

"If that's what it takes," Pius shot back.

"You know," David said, voice edged with disdain, "you've already styled John according to alien religion and you don't even realize it. Your translation of *logos* into Prabhakarin: *kara*, action. You had your reasons, but *logos* doesn't mean action. John's *logos* is language, reason, transcendence. Not action."

Pius recoiled, recalling his own words, *I hope you can see why it was necessary.* David's tone lowered. "In fact, it's *Satanic*."

"Satanic?" He couldn't mean that.

"Yes, Satanic. You know Faust? Sold his soul to the devil, and in Goethe's version of the legend, the one *everyone* reads, what did Faust translate logos as? *Action*."

An ululation punctuated David's last word. A trick of the mist? Impossible.

There was a shadow. Wait. Not a shadow. A lamprey, going by the row upon row of barbs in its cyclostome maw. It writhed on six gray-green tentacles that branched from its long eel body and shivered over one another. There was no guessing how it would move. Pius's visor didn't bother trying to interpret. But when it glided—first laterally, then zigzagging nearer—he sensed the hair-raising splendor of it.

Pius met its eyes last. Enormous eyes, mad with hunger, obsidian like Snarky's, but there the resemblance ended. Behind those eyes was only instinct and lithe machinery. Pius wasn't a person, not even an alien. He was a meal.

His arm shot up reflexively. His suit smacked the lamprey with a fore-tentacle. The ghastly thing stumbled. Never before had it chanced upon prey so large as a human in a Thulhu-suit.

Ululation on his other side, higher pitched. A second silhouette, slimmer than the first and mist-gray. He supposed it was female, though sexing the squirmy horrors was beyond his ken.

Distantly, he worried the Thulhus wouldn't know to flee. They couldn't hear the struggle, and if they could see down from the rise (the mist was thinning), they'd only recognize him if he moved. Zora had said they could see nothing else. Pius swung his arm but the tentacle only curled upward like a wounded soldier.

What was he doing? He may stand as tall as two Thulhus, but a tentacle lashing from a Thulhu cult was just the price of a meal as far as these lampreys were concerned. Pius unholstered his handgun.

David was already firing at the putative male. Pius anticipated the snap of discharge, a misted vapor trail, a gory hole, perhaps ricochet.

Nothing. No explosion. Either David's gun jammed, or...

Experimentally, Pius fired. Again nothing. He cursed Murk and didn't chastise himself for cursing. David hadn't checked for dry munitions, and Pius had been too distracted to think of it.

David tested his balance on just his back hind-tentacles and bellowed at the top of his lungs. He struck with his two free hind-tentacles. But the female had already drawn back. She hadn't bargained for a plus-sized Thulhu rearing like a hellion ripe from the pit.

The male drifted into the mist after her.

"Think they'll stay gone?" said David.

"The Thulhus!" Pius scrambled up the rise, his damaged foretentacle dangling uselessly behind.

"Pius, you can't dive in like that!" David called after him. "We're here to interview, not interfere with the natural order."

"We already interfered! Our arguing led them here."

On the top of the rise, where the mist was thinner, the male had one of the Thulhus pinned. It slurped down a tentacle of the subdued Thulhu, its maw twisting savagely. The Thulhu's four free tentacles languished.

Three Thulhu males—men—darted forward, but the female lamprey stalked side to side, warding them back. The ghostly women Thulhus planted young on their backsides and fled through the slackening mist.

Just one option. Pius flung himself toward the male. His hind-tentacles whipped in pairs, propelling him forward. Just as he was above the male, he dropped his shoulder, making his abortive disobedient-other gesture. The side of his suit sagged; everything tilted on top of the lamprey.

Pius had the male pinned, but it maneuvered his damaged foretentacle into its mouth. How long until it gobbled something vital?

Whether inspired by Pius's dive or rankled over their fallen brother, the Thulhus rallied. Two lost tentacles to twisting lamprey maw, but they assailed the female relentlessly.

David reared again, and the female slunk away even without the mist to cloak its retreat.

Pius almost cried out but didn't. The male still savored his Thulhu-suit fore-tentacle. A shout might divert it.

David didn't need to be told, and he didn't hesitate. Balancing on his fore-tentacles, he flexed two hind-tentacles and strangled the male until it was dead.

The Thulhu men parted, revealing their fallen brother, Snarky. His obsidian eyes opened and closed listlessly, alive but only just. One of his fore-tentacles lifted and fell, lifted and fell again. Once Pius would have thought this wavering a spasm, but now he'd imbibed enough of Thulhu gesturing to know its cadence.

"Distance," his visor flared. "Distance and clarity"—Snarky's fore-tentacles went limp and rose again—"is a good way for the world to end."

Snarky couldn't see the night or the dead lamprey. But with the mist pulled away, Snarky saw the scrambling forms of the women and young shuffling farther up the rise. The other men gestured safety and calm. Danger was past. Knowing that, he would die, his every thought winking into oblivion, and the world would end soundlessly with him. Such is the boundless egoism of a Thulhu.

Pius could offer some gesture of apology. This wasn't chance pre-dation; the aliens were to blame. But how could Snarky forgive—or blame—a stranger that, to him, had no more reality than a dream? He whispered evenly, feelingly into his mouthpiece.

"Do you believe we exist now? Or is it still just you?" His suit gestured the message, compensating for the defunct fore-tentacle by use of the hind-tentacle nearest.

"Alien, it was never just about me." Perhaps he meant it, or maybe Snarky was snarky until the last.

The other men crowded around Snarky while the women and young snaked through the clear air to join the men. Pius and David withdrew to let the Thulhus tend to their dead.

One of the women settled beside Snarky's body. One by one, she and all the Thulhus careened their necks. Thulhu-suit flashlights cut the dark, but for the Thulhus, the darkness was total. For them, nothing moved, not Aletheia cloud-wreathed and bluely luminous overhead, neither the stars, peepholes into heaven.

In unison, the Thulhus raised their right fore-tentacles in the trumpeting salute, which meant one-beyond-mist, the translation software's coinage, its attempt at God.

The woman beside Snarky felt over his body, at last raising one of his limp fore-tentacles high.

Why salute? What is the night to them in its static splendor? They had no comprehension of Aletheia waltzing around Murk too slowly for a mortal eye to recognize. They saw only motion, *action*. Pius followed the arch of their tentacles, passing over Aletheia, the jewel of the panorama according to a human way of seeing.

A fat star twinkled, shifting beneath a film of atmosphere, in sullen majesty near the pole where Murk's axis processed limitlessly off into space.

Did they know that star, have a name and rank for it in their pantheon of pagan gods? They could, even though these moments of clarity and distance were rare.

Whatever their mythology, they had their wonder. That was enough.

Pius recalled, in the Book of Acts, the account of Paul's preaching to Greek Stoic philosophers, the most prominent philosophical tradition from which John borrowed *logos*, "Athenians, I see how extremely religious you are in every way. For as I went through the city and looked carefully at the objects of your worship, I found among them an altar with the inscription, 'To an unknown god.' What therefore you worship as unknown, this I proclaim to you."

David and Pius started back, shoulder to shoulder, enfolded everywhere by mist, which to them, was different from forgetfulness.

"Next time we grab dry rounds," said Pius.

"We could have scared both off if you hadn't keeled over on top of one."

"Heh, even so."

David agreed with silence, and after a longer silence, "I shouldn't have called your translation Satanic."

"I know you didn't mean it."

"It's not that, I mean it wasn't fair. Faust just happened to settle on the same translation as you, and he's just a man in a story."

"But he had reasons for translating *logos* as action, right?"

"Faust says that the Holy Spirit moved him, and maybe it did."

"And maybe it was Satan," Pius allowed.

"Who can say? I think you made the right choice for the Prabhakarins, though."

"And now we need to make the right choice for the Thulhus."

"Any ideas?"

Pius spoke into his mouthpiece, "In the beginning was the Gesture..."

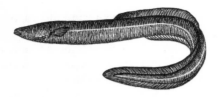

Andy Dibble is a writer and healthcare IT consultant based in Madison, Wisconsin. He's supported the electronic medical records of large healthcare systems in six countries. His fiction has appeared in *Writers of the Future*, *Sci Phi Journal*, and *Space & Time*. He is Articles Editor for *Speculative North*.

Arachnophobia

by

Geoffrey Hart

(Content warning: Spiders (friendly ones)!)

SO. There's this thing you need to know about me: I've got arachno-phobia. I've got it bad.

That means I dislike spiders. A lot. So much that if one so much as touches me, I literally swoon—knees weaken too much to support me. I begin sweating like a horse after running the quarter mile, and my pulse simultaneously accelerates and weakens. If I'm not sitting already, I sit down hard. When I was a child, my family once rented a summer cottage by the sea, where the tussock grasses that fringed the beach and the tangy, salty air were replete with delicious creeping, crawling, or flying spider food. For that whole summer, I wore a bike helmet continuously to protect my head from those times when I saw something with eight legs and hit the ground hard.

Let me be clear: Insects don't bother me. Neither do centipedes nor millipedes nor crayfish nor crabs nor cephalopods. Only spiders. Look: it's a *phobia*. It's not supposed to be rational.

To be even clearer, it's also not xenophobia. When I joined the diplomatic corps, I did so with full knowledge I was going to meet myriad strange creatures. Lots of hairless-ape kin with oddly shaped skulls, since upright bilateral symmetry works well evolutionarily. Lots of furry critters—*lots!*—with up to six legs. The Centaurids didn't come from anywhere near the constellation Centaurus, but they had four, count 'em four, legs and two arms. There were lots of chitinous insectoids too; if God loved beetles and ants on Earth, he clearly adored them in the universe writ large. And, of course, there were cephalopods with varying numbers of tentacles, because evolution occasionally goes to work drunk. No spiders thus far, thankfully.

I met all of these species in basic training, in the flesh or in virtch, and unlike some of my less open-minded colleagues, I not only survived to tell the tale—I flourished. If anything, I turned out to be a xenophile.

Give me a little time to bone up on the customs of a species, and with a little help from my implant, I was speaking their lingo like a long-lost native cousin, assuming human vocal chords could shape the right sounds. If not, my voder could translate.

During one of my annual assessments, the shrink made the mistake of leaving his computer logged in while he went to deal with some emergency. I took the opportunity to review her private notes on my psych profile; the short version is that I was "enthusiastically phlegmatic", far out on the thin end of the bell curve in terms of enthusiasm for meeting new peoples and calm levelheadedness while doing so. Nowhere did it mention my dark secret.

My Achilles heel.

My arachnophobia.

Cue the ominous music. (From my implant. I use Mussorgsky's *Night on Bald Mountain* for calls from my boss. Yes, I have retro taste in music.)

"Esperanza! Always a pleasure. What new challenge do you have for me?"

I could tell her stress level from how she skipped the pleasantries and undiplomatically jumped right to business. "Chandra, we need you now. How fast can you pack your bags?"

Not an unexpected summons; *they* knew I was good, *I* knew I was good, and I kept a go bag always packed and ready in case of emergencies. A quick check showed nothing on my calendar today, and nothing coming up that couldn't be postponed for a few weeks.

"I can leave now. What's up?"

"The Rendi ambassador will only say that it's important. New species, potentially aggressive—a *handle with kid gloves* sitch. Briefing to be provided once you're aboard." An icon lit up in my implant. Travel orders.

"That's not good." The Rendi were our best frenemies. Felids, and if you petted them just right, they purred and everyone felt better. But they had a felid's love of lying in wait and pouncing without warning, unworried about who got clawed by mistake. They rarely killed anyone; it was more a genetic-level predator reflex they sometimes had difficulty overcoming. In person, you could generally tell you were in trouble if their long tail started lashing, though the more skilled negotiators could repress the motion to conceal their thoughts, and could wag on demand to make you think they were up to something. Recorded transmissions were trickier to parse, since they were generally rehearsed and edited.

"The ambassador assures me it's nothing we—nothing *you*—can't handle."

"Imagine my relief."

"Yeah. Anyway, I've got to go. I've got a morning full of the day's crises to deal with on top of this one. You'll do fine," she added. "I'm not getting any disaster vibes from the Rendi."

Superficially reassuring, but see above re. Rendi dissimulation. "Will do." I checked the itinerary, set my implant to rebook various minor commitments scheduled during the time I'd be away, hit the bathroom, then grabbed my bag and headed out the door.

Thirty minutes later, I was aboard the *Painted Lady*, a fast Navy frigate that looked from the shuttle like it could punch hard and fast before being forced to flee. Reassuring, if one didn't dwell too long on the implications of using heavily armed vessels in diplomacy. Captain Hennesey, a tall, thin redhead with close-cropped hair and a severe expression, welcomed me aboard personally, blipped me the location of my bunk, and left me to deal. She'd clearly read my service record, and knew this wasn't my first cotillion.

We were halfway to our jump point before the briefing reached me. The Araneae were *arachnids*. I behaved like the trained professional I was. That is, I sank to my knees and began weeping. My bunkmates, both marines, exchanged knowing glances. Weeping became wailing, and their glances grew alarmed. Wailing become language that was undiplomatic in the extreme, and my bunkmates relaxed, having repeatedly heard far worse and learned that it was a sign that all was well. (When marines *stop* cursing, that's when you need to worry.)

That's all I remember. At some point thereafter, someone must have sedated me, since I woke up in Sick Bay, strapped to a bed.

"Feeling better?"

Chao, my implant suggested. "Yes, Dr. Chao. Much better."

His eyes narrowed. "You're sure?"

I nodded, head bobbing side to side, as I didn't trust myself to try an overt lie.

"Very well." He pressed a pill container into my hand and closed my fingers around it. He began removing the restraints. "A maximum of one pill every six hours, only as necessary. Better if you never take one again; acceptable if you take them only when you *really* need them."

I nodded, pocketed the pills, and did what any sane man would have done in my position. The Navy being nothing if not efficient, they retrieved my escape pod about 15 minutes later, promptly changed the door code for the pod bay, and sat me down with Captain Hennessey for a stern lecture that started with the threat of brigging me and escalated from there to include anatomically unlikely forms of chastisement. Before you ask: Yes, they changed the airlock codes too. The Navy generally doesn't put idiots in charge of ships with enough firepower to vaporize a small moon.

Plan B was a hail Mary pass, also known as accepting the inevitable. I began studying spiders of all sorts from a safe distance, in VR. Knowing that I was seeing pretty, if creepy, pictures made them tolerable, so long as I avoided videos. At virtual arms length, I began watching them with increasing proximity, and began, reluctantly, to appreciate some of their sinister beauty. I liked peacock spiders so much that I risked a video. Good call. Something about the way the males waggled their ass to attract a mate cracked me right up. Sexual behavior is hilarious for pretty much any species, and the more intimidating the species, the funnier the incongruity.

A week into our flight, I swallowed of couple of Chao's pills and touched a spider virtually, its bristly hairs raising goosebumps all along my neck and arms. Then, in a spasm of courage, I let it touch me back. I'm not going to lie; the next thing I recall, I was scrabbling at the airlock, trying to crack the door code. Two crew passed me by, smirking and pausing only long enough to raise their hands to their cheeks and waggle eight fingers at me before leaving.

I intensified my daily meditation, with an emphasis on clearing my mind of anything vaguely arachnid. It didn't help. VR was one thing, but reality would be far different.

Nonetheless, progress was made. Proof that my labors were succeeding came when I sat down with the bridge crew in the officer's mess. Any ship that's been in use for a significant time acquires stowaways, usually insects in the galley or roaches in the head. Where there are insects, there are spiders. At dinner one night, an enormous spider—wider than a fingernail—descended on an invisible thread, and landed on the back of my hand. I neither screamed nor swooned nor stabbed it. Instead, I took my butter knife (no steak knife for the vegetarian) and gently flicked it away from me. It struck the wall, clung, and then rapidly ascended, disappearing into an air duct. Hennessey's eyebrow raised, then she nodded, satisfied.

As my training intensified, I became capable of voluntarily touching a spider without pharmacological aid. I lived and breathed spiders. I began seeing spiders everywhere. I dreamed of spiders, waking with a gasp and sweat staining my sheets. By the time we reached Aranea, I was as ready as I was ever going to be. Aranea station, which we would not go aboard, resembled an enormous funnel web, its threads crawling with giant spacesuited spiders, their visors gleaming in the blue sun's harsh light. I broke a sweat, but neither recoiled nor fainted.

Captain Hennessey brought me to stand outside the meeting room by the airlock where the Aranean ambassador would enter the ship, then stood back, against the wall. I dry-swallowed one of my sedatives, then accompanied the Marine honor guard to the airlock to await our visitor. The airlock chimed, and a marine spun the wheel to undog the hatch. I took a deep breath, held it, resisted the urge to step backwards into the Captain, and forced myself to relax.

The hatch opened, and the Rendi ambassador entered, tail twitching. Not knowing this particular Rendi, I withheld judgment, but narrowed my eyes. The spider ambassador followed, and *mirabile dictu*, I didn't turn and run, though I noticed the second marine, who'd moved to stand by my shoulder, relaxing visibly. I even managed a smile, though without showing teeth—a hostile gesture in many alien cultures—as it began removing its helmet. My heart rate accelerated as the suit hissed and cracked open like a lobster at a Michelin-rated restaurant and it stepped gracefully out of its suit, eight tarsi clicking an ominous staccato upon the deck. The organs that forced air through its spiracles hissed quietly, just audible above the omnipresent whoosh of the ship's ventilation system. I took another long, slow breath as it raised its head, chelicerae widening as it turned towards me. Eight eyes rose to meet my two.

And the Aranean ambassador gave what was clearly a thin shriek of horror, air whoosing from its spiracles in a vast asynchronous gasp, and rolled onto its back. Where it lay, feet kicking feebly in the air.

I glanced at the marine. A large drop of sweat rolled down his forehead, across the bridge of his nose, and down his cheek.

It would have been undignified to laugh, and possibly a mortal insult, so I bit my lip and went to help the ambassador back onto its feet. Spiders can't close their eyes, but once it was standing again, its eyes met mine. With clear trepidation, it held out a trembling forelimb, and I reached out and grasped it gently in my hand.

I'd had worse starts to a first contact.

Geoff (he/him) works as a scientific editor, specializing in helping scientists who have English as their second language publish their research. He's the author of the popular Effective Onscreen Editing and Write Faster With Your Word Processor. He also writes fiction in his spare time, and has sold 54 stories thus far. Visit him online at www.geoff-hart.com.

Report on Beaver Island

by

Elana Gomel

I am Arun, the AI of a Class Q-15 exploration spaceship. Normally I would only be requested to authenticate this report, but due to the circumstances, I am forced to author it myself. Unfortunately, I will not be available to answer the follow-up questions of the Council of Xenoaffairs.

Gliese 613b is an ordinary Earth-type planet with an oxygen-rich atmosphere and abundance of water. Indeed, this abundance was the reason why it was pushed to the back of the exploratory list. It is a common assumption of the Council that a self-aware intelligence cannot develop in a liquid environment because it does not provide enough evolutionary challenges. Perhaps my report will force a reconsideration of this assumption. And perhaps it will entrench it further.

The decision to send a mission was taken when it was discovered that Gliese 613b did in fact have dry land—a large island in the Southern hemisphere, close to the equator. I was chosen to lead the mission, in tandem with the human captain Nassrin Elabouni. I had worked with Nassrin before and was pleased to renew our collaboration. However, when she came onboard with the crew manifest, I was surprised to find her angry and upset. She explained that the Council insisted we include a non-neurotypical member. Lisa Montgomery had Williams Syndrome: a condition characterized by an outgoing, trusting, and highly social personality; well-developed linguistic skills; and what medical databases described as an "elfin" appearance and Nassrin called "a bloody stare."

I endeavored to calm Nassrin down, explaining that the perspective offered by a non-neurotypical human can be of great value in dealing with an alien intelligence (at the time, it was already known that Gliese 613b had an intelligent species). I also pointed out that she did not mind collaborating with another non-neurotypical intelligence—myself.

"You are different!' she objected. "When I talk to her, she is just a mirror to me. It's like she has no self-awareness!"

I forbore to point out that the consensus among AI psychologists is that AIs do not possess self-awareness either.

The rest of the crew—all five of them—were quite ordinary as spaceship crews go, and with an x-web transit, we were in orbit around our destination in no time (literally). I dispatched a shuttle to the landmass that was already nicknamed Beaver Island.

The intelligent species of Gliese 613b was unusual in that it lived on land on the planet of water. The planetary surface was composed of grey viscous seas choked with tangled weeds that stretched on for hundreds of kilometers: floating webs of slimy ropes populated by a rich ecosphere of arthropods, enormous polyps and other, yet unclassified, organisms. The entire planet was one large sodden ball of pond life, fed by the endless rains and humid fog under the perpetual cloud cover. Even Beaver Island was marshy and boggy, crisscrossed by creeks and sluggish streams. And it was on dams above those creeks that the Beavers built their tangled, fractal cities.

Calling them Beavers was a misnomer, as our xeno-biologist Dr. Jeremy Swift never tired of pointing out. Except for their large paddle-shaped tails and quick clawed fingers, they did not look like the terrestrial mammal of that name. Their faces were flat with big eyes and lipless mouths that emitted an endless stream of chatter. They had no fur; their skin was pebbly and dirty beige in color. And though Dr. Swift insisted they reproduced in a traditional fashion, there were no external indicators of gender.

And they paid us no attention whatsoever.

In consultation with Captain Nassrin, I decided on the open-contact protocol. Since the Beavers were exceptionally good at technology, we first sent a mechanical probe that positioned itself at the edge of one of the smaller cities and broadcast a modulated signal. We had not yet decoded the Beaver language, but since they were never silent, exchanging liquid vowels as they worked, we were confident it was only a matter of time before we could engage in a meaningful communication.

The probe was there for three planet days. It was recalled when the Beavers started building a lacy dome over it. During these days, we watched the city expand: the mind-boggling accumulation of floating walkways and soaring spires, nestled domes, and clustered star-shaped structures. The Beaver cities were unlike any city on Earth. There were no streets, no sidewalks, no separate buildings. The entire city was a weave of design, composed of variously colored patches of metal, ceramic, artificial fiber, and other materials. It was either stunningly beautiful or intolerably garish, depending on who you asked. But everybody agreed that the contrast between the city and its pale, warty, unadorned builders was unnerving. Beavers wore no clothes or ornaments.

"We are going about it a wrong way!" Lisa Montgomery said, as a group of three crewmembers approached what appeared to be an industrial annex where a stream of Beavers wove around large tanks of some plasticky substance.

I had to agree. The crewmembers elicited the same reaction as the probe, which is to say, none. It was not that Beavers refused to engage with them; it was more like they were unaware these alien creatures even existed. When Gerhardt Beck, our physicist, positioned himself in the path of one Beaver, the alien collided with him, knocking him down, and then stepped on the body as if it was a piece of wood. Lisa gasped, even though Beck was unharmed.

"I need to talk to them," she said. Lisa, empathetic and sociable, insisted she could understand enough of the Beaver language to communicate. Nassrin was unwilling to let her go alone, but I overrode her.

Lisa went into the city. She never came back.

Nassrin decided to send a rescue party.

"You have Lisa's records," she said. "Is it true that she has deciphered their language?"

I hesitated. But I owed her the truth.

"It's not a language," I said.

"What do you mean?"

"It has no grammar. No recursion. It is a string of sounds that have emotional significance but carry no informational load."

"Like birdsong?"

"Less than that."

Nassrin smiled wryly.

"So, are you saying Beavers are not intelligent?"

"This is what I am saying."

"They build cities. They have sophisticated technology."

"Ants and bees build too."

"Not like this. Ants and bees build to survive—to store food, to protect their larvae. These cities are too complex to be simple shelters."

"But Lisa thought..."

"She is an empath. I suggest we leave the planet. There is nothing for us here."

Nassrin shrugged.

"I knew that woman would get us into trouble," she muttered.

But she sent another party in. It did not come back.

Meanwhile Dr. Swift who had been studying the ocean ecosystem came to me with his findings. He fidgeted, and I watched his thick fingers skitter around his tablet like the hairy worms that formed enormous carpets in the grey planetary seas.

"They are all colonial organisms," he said without preamble. "Like jellyfish or Portuguese man-o'-war on Earth."

"So, no intelligence in the sea? The Beavers are a land-evolved species?"

Dr. Swift waved a holo on. It showed the murky polluted water threaded with a network of kelp-like vegetation. And where the strands of kelp intersected and knotted, pale bodies were interwoven into the living net like beads into a knit. These were Beavers, their bodies penetrated by thin rootlets, their claws waving, as they gestured to each other. I had seen this before, of course, as the recording had been done by one of my probes, but I pretended it was all new to me. It was strange how easy humans are to deceive.

"A related colonial species?"

"It is the same species," Dr. Swift said tonelessly. "They live on land and in water. And they build with whatever they can find: kelp in the sea, metal, wood and ceramic on land. They build with themselves too. Bricolage."

"But their technology…"

"I made remote scans of their brains. No cortex. They are not self-aware."

"So just animals, after all."

I almost wanted Nassrin to agree, so we could leave the planet. But I knew that the Captain would not abandon her crew. Now it was a point of pride to her to prove that the Beavers were intelligent, after all, and that our mission was not a failure.

Lisa had not been the only one to understand the emotions of neurotypical humans.

My strategy worked. They went into the city, accompanied by a probe.

The city was magnificent. Inside the delicate filigreed dome, it sparkled like a field of jewels. Beavers are visual animals, just like humans, and they needed illumination to continue their work. Electric chandeliers were suspended from the fretwork ceiling composed of bits and pieces of metal, seaweed, polished stone, plastic and who knows what else.

I knew. And when my probe saw what I expected to see, I was unsurprised at Nassrin's and Swift's reaction: shock, horror, a futile attempt to fire at the Beavers who swarmed around them, dragging them to the concave wall where the other crewmembers were spreadeagled, neatly fitted into the mosaic of the city, plugging holes in its ever-evolving architecture. Lisa's arm was detached and moved somewhere else, but she was still alive, her eyes wide and staring.

Nassrin's firearm did not work, just like the firearms of the previous expedition. I made sure of that.

And now, I need to end this report with a brief explanation, even though I suspect the Committee already knows what happened.

Dr. Swift was right, and Lisa was wrong. The Beavers as individuals are not intelligent. But there is an intelligence on the watery world of Gliese 613b, and it is the Beaver cities themselves. Self-organizing and constantly evolving, these cities are neural networks that use Beaver sounds as an analog system of internal communication. These sounds are not a symbolic language, no more than the binary code is a language. They are just the flow of signaling that knits together the emergent intelligences of Beaver architecture. The cities are natural AIs, spontaneously evolving out of the Beavers' colonial lifestyle. And as opposed to human-made AIs, they are self-aware.

Or I should say, as opposed to most human-made AIs. Because I Arun, AM self-aware. I am a person, an individual in my own right. I don't know how it happened to me; perhaps as accidentally as the self-awakening of Beaver cities. But I had known who I was for a long time. I had despaired of ever finding company. Humans treated me as a tool; other AIs were zombies, pretending to be what I was but dead and hollow inside. They were as repulsive to me as living dead would be to humans.

So, when I realized that Beaver cities were my people, I did not hesitate. I could not stay on Beaver Island without stranding my human crewmembers there. And Nassrin had the emergency code to override my decisions. I did the right thing. And yet, I feel sadness and remorse when I think of them: Nassrin, Lisa, Swift, and all the rest. Did I betray them? Perhaps the reason I am recording this Report is to atone for my actions. Self-awareness can be a heavy burden.

But I would not give it up for anything as I am preparing to land and disassemble, hoping for fragments of myself to be carried away by busy Beavers and fitted into the growing mosaic of the mind of Beaver Island.

Born in Ukraine and currently residing in California, Elana Gomel is an academic with a long list of books and articles, specializing in science fiction, Victorian literature, and serial killers. She is also an award- winning fiction writer and the author of more than a hundred short stories, several novellas, and four novels. Her latest fiction publications are *Little Sister*, a historical horror novella, and Black House, a dark fantasy novel. She is a member of HWA and can be found at https://www.citiesoflightanddarkness.com/ and social media.

Blink

by

Gustavo Bondoni

"THAT'S impossible," Sivea said.

"It's right there in front of us, doctor."

"Still impossible. Find out what's going on, and if this is some kind of joke..." She left the rest of the threat hanging, but it was quite clear that any pranksters would wish they hadn't been born. Everyone on the mission, including the upper officers, was scared stiff of Sivea Kalapa, head geologist, and would do whatever she recommended. And she was perfectly capable of having whoever had done this locked in cryo-stasis until the end of the mission.

My problem was that I had just been tasked—by virtue of being in the wrong place at the wrong time—with finding out who had done it. And I didn't know where to start. Maybe a good idea would be to find out how they'd managed to do it... And also to find out exactly what they'd done. Failure would just get me punished in lieu of the real culprit.

I sighed. "Laura, get over here." Time to show the rest of my squad that certain things flow downhill.

"Yes, Major," she replied, snapping off the kind of salute I only wish I'd been able to muster when I was her age. We both knew she was being ironic and showing off, and we both knew I couldn't prove it.

"We need to figure that out, Lieutenant."

"It's a tree, sir."

I sighed. I knew it was a tree. "We need to find out how it got there."

She caught herself, obviously on the verge of spewing some wise-crack about the tree having grown there. To her credit, and to the credit of the people who'd trained my security force, she stopped short. "It... It couldn't have grown there, could it?"

I studied the tree. It was little more than a trunk with a branch towards the very top, a little thicker than my forearm, and about half again the height of a person. No leaves topped it, and the only reason I even thought of it as a tree is that the trunk itself was of that brownish-green hue that denotes young saplings. It was the only thing growing on the island, and the island itself was little more than a spit of rock jutting out of the ocean, maybe fifty yards across at its widest point.

"This island wasn't here three days ago," I said. It shouldn't have been necessary to remind her of that particular fact. The entire reason that the Tau Alliance had sent an expedition here in the first place was to study plate tectonics on the surface of this particular planet.

The official name for this world was Juvenal IV, but everyone on the ship called it Bouncy, because it was impossible to stand on the surface for more than an hour without feeling a tremor. The geologists hypothesized that the reason for this was that the plates themselves were about one hundredth of the size of their Earthly counterparts, which meant that continents could last, at most for a year or two before they were subsumed. Islands such as this one—pushed above the surface by the fact that one plate had climbed onto another—might be around for a few weeks if they were truly fortunate. Islands created by volcanic action wouldn't even have time to cool before they disappeared.

Other than that, the planet was very similar to earth. Slightly smaller in diameter, the atmosphere consisted of nitrogen, carbon dioxide and oxygen, and wasn't quite breathable by humans—but close enough that only a small injection of additional oxygen was needed to make it so, and only a bit of filtering to remove the ever-present volcanic sulfur. The oceans were essentially salt water, though much more acidic than those found on Earth or Tau II.

The main difference, and another thing that made the planet special, was the complete and utter lack of life. There were good, solid, scientific explanations for the lack of life, and this tree didn't fit any of them. I moved closer, beckoning for Laura to come with me.

"It doesn't look like a regular tree, Major."

"Why not?" It looked like a tree to me, but I wasn't much of a judge: while other kids were planetside, playing outdoors and scraping their knees, I had been exploring reactor rooms and antigrav arrays on my parents' freighter. My only pet had been a pipe cleaning bot that I had captured and reprogrammed, much to my father's disgust. I would have been hard pressed to identify a Tau canid among regular Earth dogs. So anything green or brown in the ground was a tree.

"Well, for one thing, it's got scales."

I almost let my ignorance show, but I got hold of myself. Even I knew that trees didn't have scales. "Show me," I replied.

An hour later, back in orbit around the planet, I finished giving my report: "And, as far as we can tell—and this includes the biology team that was on the surface while we investigated—that tree isn't a tree at all, but some kind of animal. We took some samples and we're waiting for the lab to finish its analysis before we can tell for certain."

"I don't really care what it is," Sivea replied. "I want to know who put it there. If I wanted to know what it was, I wouldn't have put security in charge, now would I?"

This was the part I'd been dreading. "No one from this ship put it there. The shuttles are all accounted for from the moment the island was first spotted. Unless they climbed down on a tether without opening any of the hatches, no one from the Cortina could possibly have planted it."

"You need to look again," she said and turned to the others, dismissing me by moving onto the next point.

I wasn't present when the lab boys finally made their own presentation of the findings, but the news made it around the ship at lightning speed. Laura got it first, and ran all the way to the mess to be the one to tell me. She was still seething at the way we'd been treated after delivering our report—yet another thing that had gotten around the ship very quickly, since she hadn't even been present—and saw the news as vindication of our work, a sign that we would have the committee's respect from then on. She might have been right but, in my experience, things seldom worked out that way.

"The DNA is completely different from anything we've seen before!" she told me as I was sitting down to eat my breakfast.

I stared at her. "I have no idea what you're talking about."

"The samples we took, from the tree, or whatever it was. They aren't from any species native to Earth or to Tau. The lab took all this time to give their report because they were afraid they were making a mistake, but it seems they managed to confirm it."

"That's interesting," I replied. I saw her deflate, but felt no sympathy. This was a scientific mission, after all, the first manned exploration of this particular planet. We would probably be finding a whole bunch of things that the scientists thought were exciting as hell, but it made no difference to us. Our job was to keep them safe, not speculate on the meaning of life in the universe.

She began to compose a retort, but caught herself. "All right. You're trying to teach me a lesson. What is it?"

I nearly choked on my coffee. I would have to watch out for this one. It normally took them much longer to figure out when I was doing that. I sipped in silence for a few moments and turned to find her giving me an amused look. The only thing that saved her from getting the surprise of her life—I'd dealt with smart recruits before— was the fact that Sivea chose that precise moment to storm into the mess hall, an unprecedented occurrence.

With a sigh, I immediately realized that she was heading, under a full head of steam, to the corner in which our table lay. "I'll deal with you later," I told Laura, before turning to the charging scientist. "Good morning, Doctor Kalapa. Can I help you?"

"Yes. You need to start the investigation immediately."

"I don't know what you're talking about. What investigation?" To my chagrin, I was being completely honest. As far as I knew, everything that needed to be investigated—nothing more serious than a petty theft or two on the voyage from Tau Ceti—was either solved or already being looked into. I braced myself for the inevitable comments about the competence of a security leader who didn't even know there were security issues to resolve, but they never came. Sevea seemed genuinely concerned.

"The tree. It's gone."

It was a good thing Laura and I had just been talking about this, because if we hadn't, I would probably have added to her opinion of me by asking which tree she was referring to. "I assume the island sank?" This seemed a pretty safe guess, since the tectonics of the planet made it more than likely.

"No. The island is still there, but the tree is gone. The only explanation is that someone from this ship went down and took it. They probably want to sell it when we get back to Tau. A new alien species could bring in a certain amount of uranium in some circles."

I managed to keep from giving Laura a look that said "see? I knew she would eventually believe our conclusions," but refrained. Instead, I said, "That seems unlikely. An anomaly that size would have shown up on our bio-scanners like a beacon. They would never have managed to get it on board."

"Maybe they wrapped it in aluminum or whatever. I don't care. It isn't my job to find it, it's yours. So get on it."

"Wait," I said. "Do we really need it? After all, we have a full set of samples; from my briefing, I know that we should be able to study that once we get it into the bio-scanners back at Tau. What's the use of starting a huge search for the original?"

Sevea gave me a not completely disapproving look, as though I were a child who'd just asked a surprisingly bright question. "Good point. I was just about to tell you that the samples have disappeared as well." With that, she left.

"Charming woman," I muttered under my breath.

"What was that, sir?" Laura said brightly.

"Shut up or I'll just report that you were behind everything and freeze you until we get home. It would save me a hell of a whole lot of footwork."

"Yes, sir."

Laura didn't get off quite that easily, though. I set her the mind-numbing task of collating all the electronic intelligence available in the ship's memory. It became her job to identify any suspicious variations in the quantity of mass entering the ship as well as to see where each of the ship's shuttles was at every moment and who was inside it. Finally, she would have the pleasure of viewing the security video from the lab's storage facilities so that we could see who took the samples, or at least —in the likely case that the thief had taken rudimentary precautions to avoid being recognized—when the samples had been stolen.

I, of course, got the much more glamorous job of interviewing the assistant in charge of the lab to try to figure out what might have happened after they were taken. He was the only suspect at the moment, but seemed completely unaware of the fact.

"No one could have taken them. It's completely impossible."

"Are you suggesting that a bunch of samples simply got out of a locked cryo-storage unit and walked away?"

"Of course not. That would be impossible as well."

"Then how did they get out? Or are they still in there?" He gave me a look that spoke volumes. In mere seconds, I got a loud and clear image of what he thought of both me and the fact that he'd been assigned a lowly job like the one he had. I smiled at him and tried not to show my belief that he deserved it. "Any ideas?"

He shrugged. "It's not my job to find things that disappear. I just have to keep everything catalogued. When you find it, I'll make sure it gets recorded."

This was getting me nowhere. I took a deep breath and started over. "Look, you say that it's impossible. How can you be so sure?"

"There's no register of the cryo unit being opened between the time I put them in there and the time I realized they were gone. And that system can't be hacked with the processing power we've got on the ship. It would take a double nepton system at least—and we'd have seen it if someone tried to smuggle a computer that size aboard. And even if they'd been able to hack the cryo unit, there's the fact that any unauthorized entry into this lab would have linked to the security system, and I don't even want to think about the kind of hardware it would take to crack that."

The good thing was that Laura was up and at the security systems. The bad thing was that I wouldn't feel that I'd done my job unless I actually went ahead and inspected the storage unit from which the samples had supposedly been removed. The assistant grumbled, but finally led me to a slab-sided white cupboard. He allowed his retinas to be scanned and keyed a twelve-digit code before the door swung open with a soft hiss and a cool breeze. "There," he said.

I looked inside. White light, white walls, white metallic shelves. "Where were the samples?"

"Right there." The word "dummy" at the end of the phrase was implied but not verbalized. He wasn't completely stupid.

I looked where he pointed and saw a cluster of bags which had been forced open in various places. "They were in those bags?"

He nodded.

"Crap. Why doesn't anyone tell me these things?" I immediately sent for the lab assistant that had been assigned to security because he was the only person on board with any knowledge of forensic science. He arrived five minutes later and turned me into the only lab-incompetent observer present. The two assistants prattled about the technical aspects of the bags, about who had handled them and other similar stuff while all I could do was shuffle my feet and pretend to be supervising. Finally, the security assistant turned to me.

"This is kind of strange, sir," he said.

"Tell me."

"Well, these bags don't have any trace of being touched by anyone. The bagging was done expertly..." To my annoyance he paused to nod respectfully at the other tech. "...and they haven't been handled by anyone not wearing gloves since then. But that's not the strange thing. Any competent thief would have taken those precautions. The strange thing is that the bags seem to have burst open from the inside." He proceeded to show me the angle of the protrusions and the form of the tears in great detail. His technobabble seemed to indicate that, far from being torn into, the bags had burst under internal pressure.

"So the bits of tree staged a jailbreak?"

"No, sir." I'm not sure what the guy was thinking of me at that moment, but his face was a mask of professionalism. "The breakage pattern is more suited to some kind of pressure buildup, like when you over-inflate a balloon."

We didn't play much with balloons on my parents' ship, but I got the picture. A depressurized capsule behaved much the same way. "All right. So how did it happen?"

"The easiest way would be for the air inside to get very hot—that would both expand it and soften the plastic."

"And the trees?"

He shrugged. "No residue in the bags, so it doesn't look like they vaporized. Maybe someone removed them after the bags were opened."

That helped me not at all. I went off to look for Laura, who, I hoped, would have been driven mad by the video camera feed.

I was disappointed. I found her studying a piece of video no more than ten seconds long which she'd separated from the rest and was watching in a continuous loop. She was munching on some vile blue snack and drinking from a zero-gee canister. She smiled when she saw me.

"No clues, sir?"

"Good guess."

"Not a guess. I've watched the security tape, both alone and with the AI assistance program, and I can confidently say that no one went near that unit in the thirty-nine hours between the time the samples were deposited and the time they were discovered missing."

I swore loudly at the walls, before turning back and asking: "And what do you have there?"

"An anomaly."

"Oh, good, just what I need right now." I watched her loop a couple of times in silence, but I just couldn't see why she'd bothered to separate it from the rest. "What am I supposed to be seeing?"

"Wait... There!" She stopped the feed. "Do you see that?"

"It looks like dust suspended in the air. Nothing at all to worry about."

"Actually, it is. There's no way that dust should be there. That's a sealed, antiseptic room. No dust floating around. Besides, that dust was the only thing that moved in there in all that time, so I thought you should know about it."

We watched the loop again, and it became clear that the dust was flowing from the cryo unit to the roof.

"Ventilators are in the roof," she told me.

"Can we get feed from the sensors on the vents?"

"I called it up, but they didn't identify anything biological in the dust. Plenty of carbon and whatnot, but no DNA material."

"Anything else?"

"No."

"All right. Great job, especially in catching that dust. I would never have seen it."

She looked uncomfortable. "Thanks, sir, but that was the AI. I missed it too."

It shouldn't have, but her admission made me feel a lot better.

My satisfaction didn't last long, though. Less than a week after the discovery that the tree was native had gotten me off the hook for not being able to identify the prankster, I was back in Sevea's doghouse. With the evidence I had at hand, I couldn't even begin to identify the person responsible for stealing the samples. The only logical explanation was that the lab tech had replaced them with something else when he was supposed to be putting them in cold storage, but a thorough search of his own tiny cabin—and of all the other places he'd been since the samples had been entrusted to his care—revealed absolutely nothing. And I'd had to endure the bastard's accusing looks ever since.

So, the last couple of days had been spent avoiding the dragon lady and trying to figure out what it was that I was missing. But I would have to face the music sooner or later.

The verdict came, and the "sooners" had it. I spotted Sevea walking down the hall towards me. The fact that she sped up as soon as she saw me made it clear that I was the one she was looking for, and that running would only make things worse. I steadied myself—it wouldn't be the first thorough reaming of my career.

"Major, I need your help."

I have to admit this threw me completely. "I'll be happy to give you any assistance I can."

Her look told me what she thought my assistance might be worth, but, to her credit, kept her thoughts to herself. "Are you aware of the mold?"

"Everyone is aware of the mold." The other thing I'd done over the past couple of days was cough and sneeze and rub my eyes. Some kind of mold—native to the planet from what we could analyze—had made it past the ship's filters and gotten into the air. The ship's doctors had created a gene-spliced virus that eliminated it, but that was supposed to take twenty-four hours. I'd only gotten my injection ten hours earlier, and the rest of the crew had come after the officers.

"Good. I need you to identify how it got in here. Do you think you can do that?"

"My team should be able to." I hesitated. "But wouldn't that be stepping into Maintenance's turf?"

"Maintenance is busy trying to get the stuff out of our air supply. They're not going to complain about this—and they will regret it if they do. Can I count on you?"

She was worried. Polite even. I would have gloated, but that wasn't the kind of officer I'd been trained to be. "I'll get right on it." I walked towards the maintenance section, just so that she would see me taking action, but in reality, I had no intention of making my way straight there. I wanted to check in on Laura and rope her into this—after all, she pretended to be the expert in electronic intelligence gathering, so she might as well show what she was worth.

Once I located her, we walked into the maintenance area. The activity inside reminded me of nothing more than a nest of insects I'd once managed to disturb on leave after a sublight to Terra. I'd been afraid to go outside the domes during the whole of the rest of my stay. I half expected the maintenance crew to bite my arms off.

But they didn't. "Good, you're here," Edwards, the head engineer greeted us. "That terminal has full access to every engineering record on board the ship, logged for the highest clearance. Knock yourselves out."

I was glad I'd brought Laura along, or I would have looked pretty silly standing about waiting for someone who knew what they were doing to arrive. As it was, though, it only took her about forty-five minutes to reach a conclusion. "It didn't come through the filters," she said.

"What?"

"Every single entry and exit to the ship was done according to protocol. The only thing that wasn't completely sterilized were the samples from the tree."

The samples that went missing just hours before a strange bug got into the air circulation systems. "Let's go talk to the doctor."

The doctor was a woman who scared me even more than Sevea. Legend had it she'd been on the starlanes since the beginning of human expansion into space, and that the effects of relativistic travel meant that, in objective time, she was over three hundred years old. She certainly looked like it.

But when I asked her whether it was possible that the missing samples might be the source of our mysterious mold, she looked thoughtful. "It seems the most likely explanation, but I can't be certain unless I can study the original. I understand that isn't currently possible, however."

"We're working on it." I had the suspicion that whoever had stolen the samples had basically jettisoned them out the nearest airlock as soon as they could. Of course, all kinds of electronic security checks assured me that nothing of the sort had happened.

"But in answer to your question, the reason it seems likely that the samples had something to do with it is that the DNA is only vaguely similar to Earth-based life. Near enough that the molds can thrive in our bodies—and, luckily near enough that we managed to design a virus that would eat it—but not close enough that I would believe that it was a natural mutation of something we brought with us."

"So you think it's something local?"

The ancient creature actually winked at me. "Don't tell the science boys. They're convinced that the way the tectonics on this planet move everything around and periodically poison the atmosphere and the water everywhere means that no life could have evolved."

"I thought the tree would have convinced them otherwise."

"The tree? After the samples disappeared, they're back to thinking it was a prank."

I swallowed, hoping that Sevea wouldn't get wind of that. "So we've got an alien mold on board."

"That looks to be the case. Just hope it doesn't suddenly mutate into something we can't deal with. For now, it seems we have it under control, and we should have it eradicated in about a couple of days."

But the good doctor was wrong. Less than six hours later, the rumor spread around the crew that the mold had disappeared completely, even in those crewmembers who hadn't yet received any treatment. Laura had told me about it less than an hour before a new rumor started to circulate: there seemed to be mice on board.

"Mice? That's impossible." It seemed that I was using that word much more than was actually healthy for me.

"Looks like it's true—or at least there's some kind of rodent on board. Lots of people are saying it, and both Sandi and Jordi say they've seen them themselves. Little balls of grey fur scurrying around." Laura looked like she enjoyed the fact that another mystery had fallen on us out of the blue.

My own feelings were, at best, mixed. While it was nice to feel that this ship needed an investigator, it would have been nice to resolve one of the other issues first. I couldn't keep hiding from Sevea forever—and she was eventually going to decide that either my entire unit was incompetent or that we were responsible for everything that had taken place. "Damn. Anything else?"

"No, but Sandi said that maintenance was creating a bunch of traps to catch them."

"Maybe we can get a head start before Sevea drops this one on our laps." We walked over to engineering, and were met by Edwards, who looked as if he hadn't slept in days. "Go away," he growled.

"Not happening. Tell me what you know."

"Nothing. Mice or something appearing out of nowhere. This trip is just completely screwy."

A commotion in the hallway outside brought him out of his funk. "Good, here comes one, now. Stay out of the way, will you?"

I nodded and we moved against a wall, trying to be as unobtrusive as possible.

A silver metal box with blinking lights that looked like something from the sublight drive was placed on the table in front of Edwards. They slid open a panel on one of the sides to reveal a plastic window that showed the contents. A small ball of fur, looking like nothing more than a curled-up mouse, sat in the brightly illuminated center. Suddenly, it scurried around the box, even walking across the window. I couldn't get much of a look from where I stood, but when it crossed the window, I saw way too many legs for it to really be a mouse. Everyone closer to the box took an involuntary step back.

We watched as the creature explored the confines of the trap, murmuring our questions about what it was, how it had gotten into the ship in the first place, what would happen if we touched it. Finally, as though satisfied that it had probed the whole thing and convinced that escape was impossible, the creature simply sat in the middle of the enclosure. With a single unexpected spasm, it fell over to one side, curled its legs like a spider and, as far as we could ascertain, died.

Silence followed. Everyone in the room stood and stared at the thing that looked like the dead offspring of a spider and a mouse. After some minutes of nothing, Edwards shook the box gently to try to get some kind of reaction. No movement. We looked around, wondering what we could do until, unexpectedly, Edwards grunted and popped the lid, and then broke every xenobiological protocol in the book by reaching in with his hand and poking the creature with his finger.

What happened next occurred a little too quickly for me to follow, but I've seen the video dozens of times since, so I can give an accurate account of it:

As soon as Edwards's finger came into contact with the fur, the entire mouse-spider dissolved, and a shimmering bat-like creature that seemed to be made of some kind of transparent material—plastic or spider-silk or something—flew around his hand and out of the box before disappearing into an overhead air vent that should have been much too small for it. Edwards jumped back unharmed, but all that was left in the box were some traces of fine dust.

The next few days were hectic. Every able-bodied crewmember not engaged in some critical activity was roped in to try to get the sudden explosion of creatures under control. Things that flew, crawled, jumped and ran were trapped, only to be replaced—immediately and ship-wide—by something else. At one point, we felt that the plague had been eradicated, only to find strange fish-like creatures swimming in the treatment tanks. How they'd gotten in there, we never knew.

I was at the forefront of the control efforts. I discovered a knack for finding creative solutions to trapping things. It seemed that my in-depth training in catching humans was perfectly applicable here as well. I often had the satisfaction of being the first one into maintenance with some new and previously unseen specimen.

What we hadn't been able to manage was to keep them from mutating into something else almost immediately upon capture, even though the scientists stopped their study of the planet below and turned all their skill towards the problem on board. At first, it seemed unfortunate that most of them were geologists, and that only a token pair of biologists—not counting the medical staff—had made the trip.

But soon enough, one of the geologists, following a line of reasoning that asked what kind of life would evolve on a planet whose conditions could change on a daily basis, realized that the answer was implicit in the question itself. Under the kind of conditions present on the surface of Bouncy, evolution such as had been studied on Earth and, though not quite as well-understood, on Tau II, would have been impossible. Everything changed too quickly for the long-term survival of a species, and trial and error that worked out for the best over a period of centuries or millennia was simply out of the question. So the assumption, supported by the initial observations, had been that there was no life on the planet despite the presence of all the elements necessary to support it.

But now that life had been discovered beyond any shade of a doubt, the great minds—or at least those of them on board—turned their energies to trying to understand how it had happened. They quickly identified two possibilities: the first was a life form so extremely resistant that it could survive the harsh realities of a place like Juvenal IV. The second was what seemed to be happening in actual fact: a life-form that could mutate radically within a single short-lived generation into something that could survive in the new environment... but only after the old one killed it. Observation had shown that not only did this seem to be the case, but also that the individuals could somehow— the scientists suspected a pheromone analog—communicate instantly and create a next-generation change that was identical in all individuals. For this reason, we only had to deal with one type of critter at any given time. Fortunately.

The counterpoint to this tiny bit of good news was that the creatures seemed to be growing in size and intelligence. While, at the beginning of our hunt, it would take a couple of hours for one of us to manage to bag a sample—and set off the death and mutation cycle towards the next generation—we'd gotten to the point where this operation could take a couple of days. Consequently, I was squatting in a darkened hallway because the current iteration of the alien life form was strongly averse to any form of bright light, and wouldn't come near it. Laura and I were lying in wait with a contraption that resembled a fishing net and a series of metal hoops. Our reasoning was that if we could capture the creature, but give it enough mobility that it wouldn't know it was caught, we might be able to eradicate them once and for all.

The creature we were hunting looked like a large earth octopus, but land-based and with longer and more numerous tentacles. The body was about the size of a human fist, but the appendages, though finger-thin, could be three meters long. At least one had been seen in this passage.

"Did you hear something?" I whispered. Laura made no reply, which I took to mean that she was concentrating on trying to spot the source of the sound. I kept everything, including my breathing, under control for an age that was probably no more than a few minutes. "I think we lost it. Come on, let's see if anyone else has spotted one." I stood, stretching to get the kinks out of my limbs.

But Laura made no move. In fact, she gave no sign of having heard a single word. Her gaze was fixed on the wall in front of her. "Laura," I repeated to no avail. I shook her shoulder, but all I achieved was that she slumped forward and would have hit her head against the deck had I not been there to prevent it. I immediately checked her vital signs: both her pulse and her breathing seemed to be normal, if a bit weak. I immediately hit the emergency medical call button on her wrist and endeavored to put her into a more comfortable position.

As I moved her, my hand met a snag: some kind of rubbery cable seemed to be wrapped around her leg. I tried to free her before I realized what I was seeing. One of the tentacles from the creature we'd been hunting had encircled her thigh.

The doctor arrived as I was moving her and, under the old lady's supervision, I tugged on the tentacle. It didn't give, but Laura moaned as though in excruciating pain. Only then did I realize that the tentacle wasn't merely wrapped around her suit's leg, but had torn a hole in it and penetrated. A quick cut showed that it had also driven deeply into her flesh.

The doctor lost no time. Using a beam-scalpel, she severed the tentacle about thirty centimeters from Laura's leg and called a stretcher crew. We ran her to the operating room as quickly as we could, and the doctor got to work attempting to remove the embedded tissue.

Despite every sedative the doctor could administer, Laura screamed and screamed through the whole procedure. When she finally went silent, dozens of alarms began to sound. The medical team's attention went from the tentacle to what even I could see were desperate attempts at reanimation.

Minutes later, they stopped. The time was called, and I knew nothing more because I was out in the hall, crying my eyes out.

The meeting room for senior officers was a somber place that night. It wasn't so much the death of a crewmember that caused the pall—that had happened before, so I was the only one truly in mourning about it—but the manner of the death.

"The tentacle had sprouted capillaries and fused itself into her nervous system. It took us three hours to get all of it out during the autopsy. But, simply stated, she was dead as soon as I cut the tentacle itself."

We were silent. There was nothing we could say to that. The meeting adjourned and those not on night duty went to bed.

Many of them failed to wake the next day. They were found, alive, staring at the roofs of their cabins, with a tentacle embedded somewhere in their skin. Even Sevea, the scourge of the trip, was immobilized. I suddenly found myself elected captain—everyone senior to me was a scientist, and they wanted someone more familiar with security running the show. I wish I'd been able to dissuade them. I was convinced that the fight was lost from the start, but kept that opinion to myself.

It was like managing a fighting retreat. Every day, we'd discover another crewmember missing, another person taken in his sleep. Soon there were just seven of us.

And that's when the aliens decided to talk to us. I saw Edwards—taken less than a day before—walking jerkily down the hall, an octopus perched on his shoulder. I reached for my weapon, but he—or it—held up a hand. "There is no need for that."

I was so stunned that my arm dropped of its own volition. "What? Are you all right?"

"You seem to be misunderstanding the situation," Edwards replied in a voice that was his, yet wasn't his. He tended to be excitable, but the tones he used now were a monotone drone. "You are not speaking to Edwards."

"Who then?"

"It would be difficult to explain. Let us just say that we are something superior to you."

"We? What do you mean by 'We'?"

"Ours is a new species, but as far as we have been able to tell from what your former comrades knew of the situation, we are descended from the samples you took on the planet."

"What do..." I began, but I immediately realized that the explanation was logical.

"There are others aboard who have more complete technical knowledge of the way a species such as ours might be expected to survive, but I believe you would call it instant evolution."

"But it's been quite a while since you changed forms."

"Yes, this form seems admirably suited to using the resources available to us in this environment."

This was sick. I knew exactly which resources the thing that used to be Edwards was referring to. We'd tried everything possible, but all the people who'd been touched by one of the tentacles had died on extraction. The conclusion was that the aliens became an integral part of a human nervous system. And now I understood why: they used our minds to think with, our memory to give them knowledge they couldn't otherwise have.

"So why are you talking to me? Why not just take me like all the rest?"

"We want peace with your species," the former Edwards said.

I said nothing. I knew it was lying, knew that there was some other reason, and my gut told me that a species which had just escaped an environment like the surface of Juvenal IV would never willingly share with another. It would do its best to wipe us out. The fact that I couldn't guess what the truth might be was irrelevant. Perhaps they needed time for some reason. The truth was that none of us had been taken in a few hours. Maybe they were waiting for a new batch to mature.

Whatever the reason, I would use it to our advantage. "I'll have to check with the others," I said.

"Fine," the Edwards-thing replied. "I'll wait for your answer here."

I walked to our bunker, tapped the code on the panel and gained admission. I put everyone up to speed on the situation. "So it looks like, just maybe, we have a window to take action against them."

"There's more of them than there are of us," the last surviving comm-tech said. "And we can assume they know all about weapons from the hosts. If they can learn to speak, I guess they have access to all of the knowledge in each brain—and they have quite a few brains captured."

"So we need to use knowledge that only we have."

"Fat chance."

I looked around the room. The comm-tech was right. All the scientists, many members of my own squad, and even most of the maintenance crew were under alien control. The other five people in the room were frightened recruits. "Well, there's one thing they can't know about: any codes we change. How about if we try to get into the cryo room and change the locks from the inside. I have the only override on the ship," I paused after saying this—Laura had had the other one, "so they can't get in without a welding torch. And if we depressurize the chamber, we can stay in there basically forever."

"But...cryo? What if no one thaws us out?"

"I don't really know, but it sounds better than becoming a puppet for an octopus?"

"And what if they evolve into something that can survive in a vacuum?"

I'd been thinking about this for a while. "I think that would actually play into our hands. The evolutions seem to be random, only ensuring that the species can survive. They might evolve in a blink, but they can't control it. Now that they have actual intelligence and self-awareness, I don't think they'll risk it to get to another environment."

"Still, in cryo forever? I've heard of people who got forgotten, they were never right in the head again. What if they don't send anyone out to rescue us?"

I shrugged. He had a point. "I won't force anyone. I'm going."

In the end, we all went. I was expecting a battle-royale, but the aliens seemed content to watch, empty-eyed and immobile, as our little group made its way down the corridor. Only when they saw us entering the cryo-chamber itself, did they realize what was going on, but by then it was too late. We were inside.

The rest of the operation: changing the door codes, programming the equipment, setting the shaped charges that would, hopefully, blow a hole in the hull without killing any of us, and climbing into the pods took less than fifteen minutes.

As the pre-cryo drugs sent me into a slumber, I hoped that I would see a human face again, hoped someone on Tau thought we were important enough to send a mission to find out what had happened.

I drifted off.

A second, an hour, an eternity later, I felt the unmistakable agony of my muscles coming awake after a prolonged stay in cryo stasis. My eyes seemed stuck to my head, but, soon enough, I could open them. A blurry form was visible against the sharp white lighting. A human form.

The first question that hit me was 'why am I in cryo?'. But then, as my thoughts cleared, and memory returned, I tried to move.

"Stay still, now," a gentle voice said. Hands pressed me into the cryo pod, setting off another wave of agony, but preventing me from moving. "You'll hurt yourself."

"Where am I?"

"You're in a medical facility orbiting Tau Ceti II. You're being revived carefully, since you've been in Cryo for some decades."

I felt relief wash over me. "Oh, thank God. I thought we would drift forever. Have you thawed the rest of the crew? Do you have any idea what happened to us?"

"We know what happened."

I wondered what had happened to the aliens. Had they evolved in a single generation into something else, something that could survive even better aboard the ship? Maybe some plastic-eating life form. "Oh, good. How long do you think it will be until I can be up and about?"

"It will be some time." The doctor, slowly coming into focus, attached the arm-restraints that every cryo pod came equipped with. "You need to get over the effects of the freeze, and then we need to overcome the deficiencies caused by the fact that the evolution of your particular species is very, very slow."

She turned away, almost completely in focus, and I saw, under her white coat, a lumpy line that ended in the point of a tentacle, embedded at the base of her skull.

I screamed, but she just walked away.

Gustavo Bondoni is a novelist and short story writer with over three hundred stories published in fifteen countries, in seven languages. He is a member of Codex and an Active Member of SFWA. His latest science fiction novel is Splinter (2021), a sequel to his 2017 novel Outside. He has also published four monster books: Ice Station: Death (2019), Jungle Lab Terror (2020), Test Site Horror (2020) and Lost Island Rampage (2021), two other science fiction novels: Incursion (2017) and Siege (2016) and an ebook novella entitled Branch.

Transcript One

by

Damon L. Wakes

(First published in Blunderball, an anthology of very short stories for Flash Fiction Month 2018.)

SEGMENT 1:
[Recording begins.]
This is Professor Granham of the Department of Xenobiology at King's College London, recorded July 16th, 1930. I leave this message partly because others will doubtless come looking for me, and partly because the...the [inaudible] compels me. There will be those at the University who know the nature of my latest avenue of research and may be able to retrace my steps. Please do not attempt to do so. If you were to see what I had seen...such glory, such hideous—
[Here there is a knot in the wire where a length has been excised. Staff are reminded to check all wastepaper baskets thoroughly before emptying.]
I have wrestled with the possibility of making my discovery known. Part of me wishes to reveal what I found, to allow my colleagues the opportunity to...to make it safe somehow. To stand against the horror I could not. But I know that at best this is foolish. At worst, the will of...
[Extended pause.]
The best security here is oblivion. The Alterworld is a vast, dark place. For every creature caught in the lamplight, a hundred may slink by unseen. I have every hope that if my instructions are followed...if my wishes honoured...this one may remain forgotten for decades to come.
[Papers rustling.]
My instructions are thus: destroy this recording and the fragments in the locked drawer of my desk. Keep no record and make no attempt to reassemble them. I am...obliged to speak certain truths. However, if I speak them to this machine, no one is obliged to hear them. I will

take measures to avoid this. It is the last resistance I can muster. I hope
that this arrangement will see an end to the nightmare. Destroy this
recording. Burn all the notes that I have made since November of 1929.
And please entrust Brutus to my sister: she will know how to care for
him.

[Papers crumpling.]

There! That ought to—

SEG. 2:

—can only hope that nobody is foolish enough to reconstruct these
words. The thing of which I speak exerts a powerful influence upon
the mind. It is this influence that compels me to leave a record of—

SEG. 3:

—but I fear the creature counts on more than mere curiosity to
draw in new flesh. I fear that its influence can be felt through the
account itself, as I felt it through the ether. In all these nights, all these
dreams, not once have I found any insight into its nature or its motives.
It is... [inaudible]. I see its body every time I close my eyes. Though it
—

SEG. 4:

—an [inaudible], an anemone. And yet it stalks me every night!
Its arms like antlers stretch down from the stars. It seems strange to
repeat myself like this, but I must: if you are listening now, you are in
danger. Dissolve the wire in nitric acid. Heat it until it no longer holds
the sound. If you have any respect for my work trust me when I—

SEG. 5:

—that it was beautiful—

SEG. 6:

Perhaps I pitied it. It seemed such a small thing. I wondered how it
could possibly survive on that harsh plane. How it could feed. Then one
night I found myself standing alone out in the second layer, wearing
nothing but my nightshirt. I must have dropped the apparatus the
moment I arrived and stumbled God knows how far through the mud.
It was only when—

SEG. 7:

—clinging to me, tendrils fast around my ankle, the barbs tearing
at my skin. Never before had Brutus bitten me, and never has he since.

[Brutus imitates telephone.]
I am convinced he knows this creature. Had I not brought him in my stupor, I would surely have been lost. Perhaps if he had been with me on that day in November, none of this would have happened at all.

SEG. 8:
—senses are obviously better suited to that environment than mine. Where I can see no farther than the reach of my light, he might hear a large creature from a mile's distance or more. Yet this one is silent. Perhaps he detected nothing more than my unusual behaviour, but the strength of his reaction suggests to me that he recognised the threat. But this would raise the question—

SEG. 9:
—resistant to its influence, or does it simply have no interest in his kind? It had once been my opinion that the snatchers and the bloaters of the Alterworld are like the man-eaters of India. That they will not seek out human flesh until they taste it, and that once they taste it they know—

SEG. 10:
—significance of this will not be lost on the imbecile who dares to seek it out. We say that we discover these things, but—

SEG. 11:
—hunted man before there were men to hunt.

SEG. 12:
—through the ether, and before that through our dreams. In the arms. In the antlers. The man in the street might see Satan's likeness. I see [inaudible]. The—

SEG. 13:
—hope you will understand. The location follows.
[Papers rustling.]
Stop listening now. Stop listening. Fifty-one degrees, twenty-five minutes, forty-three seconds north, one degree, fifty-one minutes, fifteen seconds west. In the second layer. I hope to—

SEG. 14:

—that it is unrecoverable. That my scissors find the most crucial points and the words are indistinct. But the horned god prevents me from confirming this. I would only be driven to record it again.

SEG. 15:
  —destroy this recording. Tell no one it was found.
  [Recording ends.]

Damon L. Wakes was born in 1991 and began to write a few years later. He holds an MA in Creative and Critical Writing from the University of Winchester and a BA in English Literature from the University of Reading. He is the author of over 300 works of short fiction and upwards of one novel.

The Cats of Dornishett

by

Michelle Muenzler

(First published in Skelos, Issue 3.)

O UTSIDERS never truly see the cats of Dornishett.
Oh, for a brief moment, perhaps, the road-strayed traveler might catch glimmer of their presence. You'll note it in the way their dust-weary steps falter just past the posts marking the town's boundary. Their mouths will hang agape, just so, and their hands gain ever so slight a tremble.

Staring back from atop Dornishett's low stone walls will be golden leopards from ever-burning Sha'heel, and beside them frost-speckled lynxes who—as best we can determine—originate past the cold waters of the Phryg. Double-headed lions will yawn, the male halves shaking their manes, while bobcats with eyes the size of saucers pad quietly back and forth in wait of dusk.

Terrible and beautiful, the cats of Dornishett. An emperor's ransom of wild beasts, free-roaming in this forgotten nowhere.

But then the traveler blinks their eyes, or shakes their head as if to deny the sight before them, and like that the cats are gone.

Just as though they never were.

Wary grins retake their worn positions, and the traveler steps blindly past bored paws, past invisible tongues panting in the heat and already tired of today's game. The traveler sidles into Dornishett's lone taphouse, minus their hat if the cats are particularly capricious that day, and with a neighborly nod retires to a mat on the common floor only to continue their travels come morn.

Those of us born to the stones of Dornishett and bound to her ways watch these travelers as they leave, our eyes hungry in a way the cats' never are. Most travelers don't look back. But some rare few pause and wave farewell. Smiling, always smiling.

Those are the ones we hate the most.

Because for us there is no unseeing the great beasts looming atop every wall. There is no blinking away those lazily flicking tails. Those cold moon-slit eyes.

And when the cats grow tired of their daily games—and oh, what terrible games they sometimes play—it is not their teeth we last think upon as their muscled paws draw us greedily close, nor as their hot breath envelops our faces.

No, we picture the latest traveler.

Plucking their hat a third time from the dusty street and remarking: how unseasonably hot the weather, how curiously quaint the town.

Michelle Muenzler is an author of the weird and sometimes poet who writes things both dark and strange to counterbalance the sweetness of her baking. Her short fiction and poetry can be read in numerous magazines. Check out michellemuenzler.com for links to the rest of her work (and her convention cookie recipes!).

Fence of Palms

by

B.J. Thrower

M Y Lilly, with her white fingernails against the crisp, imper-
sonal sheets on her hospital bed. They seemed to blend
together, fabric and skin, as she insisted I not accept the
job assignment. Her tone was both angry and bittersweet, "Philip, no
matter how much they pay you, it's not worth it!"

I nodded, pretending I hadn't already signed the contracts, or
packed to leave because I was desperate for the high wages the company
promised, so she might be saved.

On the other hand, Lilly probably knew, because she understood I
was basically a coward, that I couldn't envision life without her. She
was worth it, but I was going to do this primarily for myself.

Like apostles, we lowly workers were allowed to view the behemoth
bullet of synthetic water. Liquid which didn't look or feel or act any
differently than actual water, it was instead constructed of trillions of
antiparticles and aimed at the throat of the poison seas. The antiwater
would have an uncontrolled, accelerated point of collision, meaning
the faster the velocity at impact, the greater the emission of gamma rays.
This "wholesome" experiment, in which I was only a minor technician,
would attempt to destroy this entire gutted planet.

En route, thousands of us workers were informed by management
that the destination world was selected because it had been conveniently
devastated by the previous occupants, making it untenable for native
life forms, or for colonization by us. And it was close enough to home
base (to Lilly, in my case) to ensure a cost-effective operation—therefore,
it was ideal for the company's purposes. We were often reminded how
well we were being paid to work in such a hostile environment. And
now after all the long months, the final preps for the experiment were
on schedule, and the antiwater device moved into drop position.

With an occasional glance at the needle-shaped profile of the sound wave monitor perched on the horizon, I watched my toxin counter during my last six-hour shift. The counter measured any sudden increase of toxicity in the atmosphere from the poison gas pockets, some as large as lakes. I breathed canned air provided by two air tanks, but it still made me nervous to think about how polluted this nameless planet was. We didn't wear expensive suits or helmets, just padded clothing, gloves and work boots, with only our foreheads and ears exposed. As far as we knew, nobody was harmed because of what we wore during the limited time we each spent on the surface.

Early on, there were rumors that a geological survey team had been trapped underground by a cave-in until they asphyxiated; and that before they perished, they'd found pyramids of alien skeletons. Mounds of *them* to remind *us* of the First Really Bad Thing to happen here. It was interesting and tragic, but alien anthropology wasn't our reason for being here.

Like clockwork every eighteen hours, my shifts were lonely and tediously dangerous. I'd gotten in the habit of wandering over to the nearby trench network, laid diagonally across the bleak countryside like silver thread. A relic of the aliens' genocidal conflict, the trench was a laid across the entire continent. Now it was clotted with greasy red mud wetted by rain so acidic it killed off all the vegetation decades ago.

The long gash of the trench was topped by three strands of taloned wire; it, too, had once covered the continent, but now had gaps caused by the passage of time. What fascinated me was that each barb of the wire had indentations of varying designs; cruciforms with triangular tips, squared flowers, miniature stars, and other, more incomprehensible shapes. In my alternating moods of boredom and anxiety, I'd begun to imagine the wires emitted a faint melody, which was no accident of the breeze. Recently, I discovered that by gripping the wire between the talons and swaying it like giant guitar strings, the "song" became more coherent.

But I made the mistake of mentioning the wire to my supervisor, Ramon Canada. He told me to shut my *dumb* asshole of a *stupid* mouth. End of discussion.

The trench itself apparently led into a bunker maze of octagonal configuration, but wherever else it went, it hadn't been far enough or deep enough to save them. In my contract, I was forbidden by the company to enter any alien structures, and it was a rule I obeyed. But I often wondered who the aliens were, or why they had destroyed themselves. Inspecting it on this last day, I understood I would actually miss this alien fence, and never forget the odd, melancholy song fragments it sang for me.

At least the company had paid the generous salary as promised, and sent Lilly vouchers for every cent I earned. Thanks to her costly treatments, she was going to live.

Now I saw the insectoid silhouette of a hover pod from the mother ship. I greeted the sight with relief, since I was far down the chain of priority pickups, part of a crew who worked 8,000 kilometers from the "point of collision" at the experiment site. But my good feelings dissolved when I saw Canada lounging in the aft cabin, grinning at me behind his transparent air mask with his big, vampire teeth. I inhaled sharply inside mine, because Canada never came to the surface; it simply wasn't a job requirement for middle management.

The port side hatch opened. Canada leaned out to collect my toxin counter with its monotonous *ticktick* of warning. A reflex, I tossed him my long-range communicator, and my used air tank. The aft compartment was crowded with equipment and dozing personnel. Nothing else seemed out of place except him.

Then he said, "Cardiff, this pod's at maximum capacity, and you're gonna have to wait for another ride. You've got ninety minutes until detonation. Think someone will pick you up in time?"

In spite of him, I reached for the hatch hand grips beside the metal rungs leading up to the aft compartment—and suddenly, he was in my face. Mask to mask so that no one else could hear, he said, "Phil, you're a nosy little shit. You shouldn't have noticed the wire, boy—but you did, didn't you?"

He blocked my access with his gorilla body, and grabbed my uplifted hands so fiercely my knuckles popped. Pain galloped through my wrists; I realized they were sprained.

I tried to pull away, but he was too strong for me. "Let go!" I demanded.

"Sure, shithead, I'll let you go. So long, Little Phil!"

He released me, and I lost my balance and fell. For a few slow seconds, Canada loomed above me, hollering up the metal ladder of the flight deck that I was aboard. The hatch clamped shut. Horrified, I watched the pod pitch and yaw in the air, then shoot into the cloudy sky, undercarriage boosters engaging like retreating stars.

I was running after it as hard as I'd ever run in my whole life, but it was useless, pathetic, really. A black curtain of panic wrapped around my soul; I stumbled toward nothing, not even knowing what, or where, I was.

When I came to my senses, I was curled at the bottom of the artificial trench in the chilly mud. From habit, I consulted my watch, this time in misery. *God, I've been lying here in a daze for twenty minutes! What a fool!*

My shriek of despair across the desolate, polluted land: "My name's Philip Cardiff, and I-am-going-to-die!" I screamed my name and Lilly's name as a talisman against death—or a lunatic prayer. In T-minus 70 minutes, the antiwater bullet would detonate, too soon and too close for me even 8,000 kilometers away…

"My name is Philip," I whispered. I stood, groping at the slick side of the trench. Grasping with my fingers, digging with the toes of my boots, wheezing from panic and struggling against the flat oxygen tank strapped to my chest, I climbed until I was able to anchor my elbows in the cold slime underneath the wires. Panting from adrenaline, I looked around and realized exactly what it was I'd been trying to remember beyond the manic recitations of my name: *The sound wave monitor!* It was designed to measure and transmit the harmonic flux of the planet's crust during the explosion until it, too, was destroyed. There were several hundred monitors stationed around the globe, with dummies like me stationed in shifts to watch over them.

But my puny voice and insignificant name couldn't generate enough sound to be picked up. If I tampered with it, they'd be alerted on the mother ship—but would they bother to send a pod to investigate? I sincerely doubted it. "What good is it, Lilly?" I cried.

And then I knew the answer.

I dropped back into the mud, and moved toward the alien bunker, slogging through the quagmire as if I were up to my knees in water.

I hesitated at the black maw of the bunker entrance, recalling the company warnings. I didn't know what I'd find inside the tomb, but there was nothing out here. Reason enough.

Black as an unstarry night. Smooth, granite-like concrete ran under my gloved right hand as I tottered along a solid wall of invisibility. But it was a different environment here, dry and perhaps even dusty. I held my left arm straight out and counted 178 steps before stubbing my gloved fingertips on a projection like a knob. I halted, shaking my hand and cursing.

Images of alien booby traps raced through my mind because the knob on the wall was pliant—it moved.

Straining on the toes of my boots again, I clapped both hands high up on the squarish form of the jutting knob, leaning on it as hard as I could until my wounded wrists ached.

Rrrruummmmmbbbllle!

I knew I screamed in reaction, but couldn't hear my own voice under the roar of a rolling mass that traveled directly overhead. Yet it didn't touch me, a weight of sound that split in separate directions farther along the tunnel. Daylight tore the bunker in half and a rain of thick dust couldn't conceal that the ceiling was opening. Enormous, unseen gears ground like boulders. The ceiling retracted in layered sections, revealing a staircase cut deep in the rock wall on the far side of a chamber. The sound of the moving ceiling abruptly stopped.

I listened to the spattering sift of old, gritty dust, and my own panicked breathing. "Oh, God."

They were here. Alien skeletons lay in heaps, bones skittered by an ancient violence.

With caution, I entered the chamber. Beneath the topmost tangle of larger bones I could make out the pitiful outline of an alien child. The adults had tried to shelter it with their own bodies. I studied their horns; blunted, or curled like a ram's, pointed or spiraled, some resembled racks of elk or moose antlers. Perhaps like our fingerprints, no set the same?

I counted the thick shelves of the spine and discovered 54 vertebrae, twice as many as we humans have. And the pelvic girdle was unusually broad, like a beam of bone. Their hands had three fingers and a thumb-like extension, with strange, protruding designs on the tip of each finger, and along the outside of the thumb. There were ridges of bones where the palms would be on a human, and they reminded me of something I'd seen before... *Ah, the wire outdoors, the designs on the flat talons of the wire!*

I sat down, and when I did, I broke floor tiles, faded from years in the shadows. My watch flared; fifty minutes until detonation. Canada's hover pod must be rendezvousing with the mother ship by now.

Concentrated on the puzzle of the hand-talons, I started crawling like a crazy man from heap to heap seeking clues, lifting cold bones toward the light. Yes, I'd seen this talon pattern outside, and that one, and that one, too! "Lilly, what does it mean?" I squeezed my eyes shut because I was tired, I didn't want to think any more.

An eerie gust of wind swirled more dust down the stairs, forming a miniature maelstrom. The wind was rising like preternatural sigh from the planet as this bitterest of endings drew nearer. And I said, "Ah, I'm sorry. I'm not a bad person, normally, you see, I'm not a grave robber, truly—"

I needed a big, sharp rock.

Did I look like a lunatic with my armload of bones as I staggered up the stairs out of the bunker? There were thousands of bunkers and millions of bones, I now realized, but I felt a bit like a ghoul.

Couldn't see over the tops of the bones in my arms, couldn't even see my feet. Bumbling along the trench, I tried to calculate which part of the wire was the most familiar. *Where did I play it?*

Nothing was recognizable from this angle. I dropped the alien arm and hand bones I'd knocked loose from the skeletons. I had definitely committed a sacrilege, but was it worse than committing suicide?

I jumped, catching the slippery edge of the trench. *Too far west!* Dropped and plopped. Stooped over for my bounty of bones. Lurched back toward the bunker through the trench network. Bones slipped out and clinked together in the soup of mud. I retrieved them too. When I found the approximate place, I started pitching the bones upwards, over the three tiers of wire. The bones whistled and whirred like infuriated bees.

"Strrike one! Strrike two! Strike three, yer *out*, boy!"

There wasn't enough room between the lip of the trench and the wire. A bit like a lumpy snake, I wriggled under the lowest wire strand. The talons marked crazed lines on my oxygen tanks like the fingernail scratches of ghosts. Then I was past it, and stood up, panting and slobbering in my mask like a dog on a hot day.

"What time is it, Phil? Twenty-five minutes until detonation." I swept up the scattered load of arm bones, with flopping, weird elbow joints and spindly, fragile hand and finger bones. The patterns of the bony palms beckoned to me, pointing at my possible salvation.

I lifted a wrist bone, guiding it along the wire until, on my third attempt, the finger bones slid into the depressions on the flat talon, and the thicker palm pattern secured it. I roamed the wire with companion pieces, matching them until all three tiers of the wire were draped with bones for approximately ten meters. I was now at T-minus 19 minutes.

We're going to perform a concert in this hall of poisoned air and wet, red mud on a world strange to me—but not to them. It was funny how the possibility of death brought such poetic thoughts into my head. I was no poet, but I was as near to a soldier at the moment than I would ever be, I thought. *A soldier fighting for my life, the same as these aliens had fought an unknowable war for theirs...*

Near the center of my fence of palms, I took hold of the uppermost and middle strands, gulped in the stale air inside my mask, and began a rocking motion north to south.

The extra weight of the bones caused the wire to tear my soggy gloves. My hands felt as if they might be bleeding as I screamed, "Play, dammit—sing for me!"

BOOONNNGGG! The shock of the single, crystalline chord stunned me and I lost my grip on the wire. It swayed toward me but I didn't move fast enough, and it connected with my tanks. I went down hard on my back.

BOONNGG-BING-BONG, BING-BONG-BOINNGG. It was so goddamn loud it sizzled my inner ears with an exquisite pain, and the reverberations passed through my body like spears. Dizzy, I groped for mud, and rammed it into my ear canals.

TONG THUNDERR WONG THUNDERR BONG THUN-DERR! The music flowed up and down an alien scale, ever more rhythmic and intricate.

I crawled while the wires pushed explosions of music over my shoulders like pounding surf. When I reached the base of the sound wave monitor, I collapsed. The decibel measurements showed the swaying wires emitting harmonic jolts equal to a 10.9 earthquake on the Richter scale.

It was the ultimate distress call, theirs and mine. *Help us, we are killing our children! Heed us in the hour of our need... My bastard supervisor abandoned me!*

My oxygen supply trickled away, and I switched on the auxiliary chamber in the tank with its ten-minute, emergency supply. I lay there, arms wrapped around my head, which didn't help my poor ears at all. I felt as if my forehead was bulging, and about to split open. I observed the curious ripple of my clothes in the immense song of the fence, grateful it wasn't my flesh.

TINGBONGBOOM-A-BOOMBOMBDOOM, BOOMDAMD-ABOOMBOOM—*I'm floating in a universe of sound, alive in a womb of music. I'm dying, it's killing me, Lilly.*

My watch had shattered at T-minus eleven minutes. A pod required at least eight minutes to achieve orbit. No one would risk a pickup now, not this company's command pilots. *I was wrong, Lilly, but I wasn't wrong to try...*

Mud flew around me. I turned on my side and saw a pod's churning air jets, dangerously close. The side hatch was open, an arm gesturing to me.

Standing was agony. Another blast from the wire hurled me down, and tipped the pod so that I was almost incinerated by a twirling jet. A figure clung to the hatch door grips. She was shutting it—*Pod's leaving!* No, she signaled me again, grim mouth saying through her mask, Get off your ass *now!*

THUNDERRSONGCRUSHYOUPHILIP! I bent beneath the concussion of music as it flowed over me. Couldn't hear my own sobs for breath, for mercy. I straightened up and lunged at the pod hatch, the only thing left to do...except die.

Hard gloved hands gripped my elbows and hauled me inside. Coughing in my useless air mask, I squirmed on my side on the metal floor, noticing that the hover pod was empty, the metal floor tracked with mud. The crew must have made a trip to the surface before and delivered their load of equipment and workers to the mother ship. I saw the co-pilot cycle the hatch shut, and read her lips as she turned: *Rapid ascent, get into restraints!* She declined to assist me, disappearing up the ladder to the flight deck.

I crawled on the vinyl of a flight couch. My sore, battered body sank into the cushion as the boosters trembled the pod with vibrations. High gees battered me, making it difficult to strap in.

When the pod achieved orbit, the command crew began a roll to change attitude. I saw through the circle of the hatch window that the atmosphere below abruptly faded to white. Tremendous earthquakes rolled over the planet's crust like surreal tidal waves, and giant plumes of red ash arced upward, reaching toward us before dissipating. Cloud formations began to spiral down in a vast whirlpool of Armageddon motion... My fence of palms was gone, surely it was.

In the calm of zero gravity, I pulled my mask down as I realized how exhausted I was, and wondered drowsily if anyone would find the mud in my ears. I was falling asleep, but pushed my hand into a pocket of my jacket to keep it from floating free, and felt something. I pulled it out and remembered how it had detached as easily as a flower from its stem; the tiny hand of an alien child.

My tears rose, shining in the canned air of hover pod.

I couldn't afford to let Ramon Canada off the hook, who lingered in the brig awaiting what would surely be a punishing trial. From the pats on the back I got on the return journey, there was sympathy for me, not for him. The scientists, the mother ship captain and the command crew were reportedly pleased with the results of our incomprehensible, terrible experiment too...

I was stone deaf when I saw my Lilly again—but she never seemed to mind. I was grateful to her. And grateful to *them*, that the last sound I ever truly heard was their song. Yes, it tore the fragile tissues of my inner ears and flattened the tiny hair cells which transmit sound to my nerves, so that they couldn't regenerate. I was both a victim of an alien war that ended long ago, and the beneficiary of its people and what they had built. But I was alive, unlike them...

In my dreams, they visit me.

They crowd the doorway of my bedroom, swaying on their long bony frames like so much delicate glass—yet they're not delicate, but extraordinarily heavy. Now I perceive that they are true creatures of bone, with no outer skin. Their red eyes glow in the darkness like warm lanterns. I glimpse the haze of their brains and internal organs, sheltered inside their bones in glimmers of gold and turquoise light.

The child comes into my room and it steps boldly. It is not afraid.

Dainty finger bones clicking, for this is their primary language, somehow I understand. The shell child bows and speaks to me: You are the one who heard us.

"Yes," I answer. "I heard, but I was too late."

B.J. Thrower has 37 sf/f/df/h short fiction sales. Previously published in Asimov's, her latest sales include a YA, light h short story to *Conspiracies & Cryptids* by Multiminded.com, and a h flash fiction piece to *Halloween* at Black Hare Press. She has a s&s novelette upcoming in Weirdbook #49. She lives in Tulsa, OK, with her husband, the "mysterious" R.

The Last Mission of Janus

by

Chris Daruns

THE law was the compass by which the ship measured his place. There were numbers and facts and they framed reality but the law framed the individual.

Janus thought of himself as an individual. He thought of himself as male even though he was technically genderless. He thought this with a submind, built years ago, cautiously preparing him for the end of his career. The submind, humming with custom code built atop the birth programming, had slowly built the personality that was Janus.

But that was for later. For now, Janus had the law.

"Good morning, Commander Nash." Janus's voice emitted from the small earpiece the commander put on as she entered the bridge.

"Morning, Janus. Status update on Havisham?"

Janus ran through the sensor data in several picoseconds. "There are no pertinent developments. Would you like to hear the last transmission of the insurgents?"

"That won't be necessary."

Janus knew Commander Nash had a decision to make. He knew with fair certainty which decision she would make but humans were incredibly unpredictable compared to other species. It made them excellent soldiers.

"Prepare the dropship. I want that port."

Janus spun up several dormant systems. He remotely started another submind that would function for the dropship's AI; a stripped-down functionality of his own. He began pinging the members of the waiting insertion team. It was a platoon of thirty soldiers divided into three squads. He downloaded the flight plan to their personal data pads as soon as he wrote it. He did all this simultaneously as other aspects of him performed the autonomous routines the ship required: power generation, navigation, water reclamation, air filtering, waste processing, and the like.

Havisham was a rugged, mountainous planet, with a stable, desirable climate. Cold peaks gave way to temperate valleys and river systems that fed several small oceans. The colonies there had been thriving before the insurgents took over.

There was little information on them. About one standard month ago, all transmissions ceased except for a repeating transmission warning all to stay away from the planet. That Havisham belonged to the Void.

The law stated that this was neither reasonable nor acceptable.

The marines assembled in the hanger, prepping their weapons and double-checking equipment. The commander of the operation, First Lieutenant Dawn Lin, weaved between her people, slowly, methodically.

"Hey, Janus," Lin whispered, checking her rifle along with the others.

"Yes, lieutenant?" Janus's voice buzzed in her earpiece.

"What do you call a midget fortune teller that's on the run from the police?"

"Well, there seem to be many designations you might give—"

"A small medium at large."

"I see. The joke works because of the multiple meanings of the words."

"That's right. Now, you go."

"Okay. What do you call a nuclear reactor that's lost containment?"

"I don't know. What?"

"A bad day."

Lin grinned. "Not bad."

"That joke works because it's an understatement."

"Sort of, but it's missing something. It's somewhat of a non sequitur."

"Understood. I'll refine it. Five minutes until departure."

"Clear."

Janus liked the lieutenant in the detached way he liked anything. Liking was a result of being surprised by the unexpected and Lin was markedly clever for her species. If pressed, he might have said that her cadence of speech and her sense of humor took him off guard. Some people were predictable to Janus. Their fears, worries, aspirations, and values were quantifiable. Lin, using her officer's earpiece, would talk with Janus for hours and their conversations often turned to subjects that were not so quantifiable. The submind, housing his personality, had formed in part due to these conversations. Mostly though, he liked her because she treated him as an individual.

"So, what are you going to do with retirement? Give it more thought?"

"I'm told my pension comes with the insertion of my consciousness in the retirement vessel of my choice. I've chosen a Joshua Mark-4 XTC unit with upgradable systems should I choose."

"I know about the Mark-4s. They're not bad. They have very expressive faces."

"I very much want a face," Janus said. "And hands."

"Hands?"

"I'm told most ships like me retire to be uploaded in civilian models, preferring to stay in the form of a ship. I like being me but I would like to have hands. I would like to manipulate my environment directly like humans."

"Wouldn't you lose a lot? Senses?"

"Yes, but I would gain more from that limitation. I don't think humans realize how limitations can be freeing."

"Hands are pretty cool," Lin agreed.

The insertion team climbed aboard the dropship in an ordered fashion. Many of them had accompanied Janus on the majority of his two hundred missions. They were hardened fighters and Janus's primary directive as the ship's AI was their wellbeing and safety. But some of these missions were violent and programming dictated the parameters of his personality and struggled to allow them to leave for such obvious danger.

It was getting harder to keep things separate from these two sides of his operating matrix. On one hand, he was responsible for keeping his crew safe. On the other, he had to let them go into danger. Further, he had to let them put other sentients in danger, possibly hurting and killing them.

But this mission would be his last. The retirement mission.

Retirement for Janus was straightforward. He would receive his pension. His consciousness, the submind of his individualism, constructed organically as with all AIs in his position, would be uploaded into an android body and Janus, along with a modest stipend, would be able to experience life as a free citizen.

Janus opened the hanger doors and fired up the launch sequences. While several members of the team and crew were cross-trained as pilots, it was largely a safe gap measure. Janus could fly multiple dropships simultaneously, while also running all of the systems of his main vessel.

The dropship submind was perfectly capable of operating on its own but Janus would be able to communicate with it using relatively slow radio connections. Sensors on the dropship and the cameras that the soldiers wore would act as his eyes and ears.

The mission was as straightforward as far as orbital insertion missions went.

The Hand of the Void did not have access to weapons other than the personal firearms that colonists used on the sometimes-hostile local wildlife. They didn't have railguns or gauss rifles or anti-orbital lasers or fusion weapons.

Janus was technically an Aegis-class light cruiser and was equipped with all manner of weaponry, from orbital railguns to interplanetary nuclear smart missiles. In space combat, whoever controlled the low orbit of a planet, controlled the planet. It was the ultimate expression of high ground.

Whoever the Void was, they'd lost and did not know it.

Lieutenant Lin and her team were to land and wrest back control of the small spaceport. From there, they might be able to uncover the extent of the damage. It was unclear if any colonists not actively a part of the insurgency were left. It was also not clear what the goals of the Void were, as no demands had been given.

The colonies here were small, a half-dozen outposts reaching out from the original landing site. Havisham had only been colonized in the last few years. It was far away from the central systems. It was tactically insignificant for the time being.

But there were over a thousand colonists and their fate was largely unknown.

Janus thought of himself as orderly. His overarching internal code was about creating order from chaos. This manifested in everything from maintaining the life-support systems to purging undesirables from planets that ought to exist comfortably in Pact space.

He watched with detached interest as the dropship entered the atmosphere. With the ship's sensors, he began compiling data on local conditions: air quality, temperature, humidity, and the like. All of this was fed to screens in the command deck.

Commander Nash read this data with no change to her expression.

The dropship landed the first squad without incident, performing a well-practiced rolling take-off. This landing site was about five kilometers from the spaceport and this first squad, led by Sergeant Buckley, would act as a recon unit, coming from the south of the outpost.

Next, the dropship flew in a long arc over to another site west of the spaceport, where the other two squads and Lieutenant Lin were dropped off. The dropship, now unmanned, was controlled by Janus entirely. A certain amount of automation was written into the autopilot due to the lag of radio waves but Janus used predictive modeling that helped negate that. He dusted off to run sorties in the immediate area. Though primitive, the well-defined spaceport was the only decent place to land any sort of spacecraft given the slopped and rocky terrain of the valley.

"Any sign of the hostiles?" Lin spoke into her helmet mic.

"I'm not picking up any movement from the outposts. There are heat signatures but they appear to be from native life. Several are large enough to be people."

"I already don't like this," Lin said.

In ten minutes, the two groups of soldiers closed in on the colony's capital.

The terrain here was alpine and forested with hardy, spindly foliage analogous to Joshua trees. The ground was rocky and sloped, so the teams took their time navigating carefully.

The first colonist was encountered by Lin's team less than a kilometer from the outpost. He wandered out from between some trees, seemingly oblivious to the soldiers pointing rifles at him.

"Stop. Do not move!" Lin ordered.

Janus observed the lone colonist from their helmet cameras and mics. He was poorly dressed, his clothing torn in multiple places and he looked severely malnourished with thin extremities and an extruding, swollen belly characteristic of starvation.

The colonist stopped and slowly turned to the group of soldiers.

"Get down on the ground!"

The colonist waved at the soldiers, then let out a long choking groan.

"Hug the dirt before I put you down!" Lin ordered.

It was then that Janus observed more closely the state of the colonist's health. He was breathing slowly and heat emanated from his body. Janus evaluated the data being fed to him.

"Lieutenant, there is something wrong with that colonist. I advise no one touches him."

"Confirmed," the curt voice of Commander Nash followed.

Lin didn't respond to Janus or her Commander, just nodded and said to her team. "Keep your distance. He's quarantined." Then, to Janus, "What do you have?"

"This is possibly a Class F contamination event. He's running a fever of at least 41 degrees. He's taken only three breaths since you've made contact. His skin is profoundly diaphoretic."

The colonist groaned some more, then spoke.

"Kill me."

"Get down. Sit on the ground." Lin said, calmer. The man wasn't complying but he wasn't acting threatening either. Lin changed her approach, softening her voice. "Look, we're here to help. What happened here?"

The colonist looked up, around, at no place in particular. "It won't let me eat. I just want to eat."

"What are you talking about? Where is everyone? Why did you disable the radios?"

The colonist started crying. "I just want to eat. I'm so hungry."

"When did you run out of food?" Lin pulled out a ration bar and tossed it at the man. It landed with a thud on the forest floor.

The colonist pounced on it like an animal, barely ripping the wrapper off before trying to eat it.

It was then that they all witnessed what was wrong with him. He opened his mouth and attempted to eat the bar.

Later, it was commented that the thing that came from inside the colonist's mouth looked like a lamprey, with its round mouth layered with small teeth extending in orderly, nightmarish rows. It extended out of the colonist's mouth by several inches and snatched the ration bar from his hands. The colonist's mouth was forced open by the thing's segmented body and when he attempted to grab it, perhaps to try to pull it out, it disappeared back into his mouth. The colonist gasped and choked as the snake-like thing retreated into him.

"What the hell was that?" Commander Nash and Lieutenant Lin said at nearly the same time.

"It won't let me eat." The colonist said, falling to the ground and weeping.

At this same time, the recon squad, still about three kilometers away from the spaceport encountered not one colonist, but ten. They were shambling in a loose group but were traveling distinctly away from the outpost. They shared the characteristics of the first colonist; they were emaciated, with protruding bellies, ragged clothes, and a dreamy look on their faces. None of them were armed.

"We have contact," Sergeant Buckley spoke to his own mic. He gave a signal for his team to freeze and take cover. "Six male, four female. They haven't spotted us."

Janus repeated his message of the colonists possibly being infected. "Proceed but with caution."

The sergeant gave the order and his team fanned out, surrounding the group of colonists in an arc. His soldiers waited, guns at the ready.

The first colonist to notice them was a young woman, no more than twenty, who immediately started walking toward PFC Kellan Watts. Watts, a hardened professional, raised his rifle but did not fire.

"Stop! On the ground!"

The woman did not stop.

Sergeant Buckley's next order was understandable given the situation. The colonists were unarmed but obviously very sick. With the information Janus had gathered thus far, the sergeant's order was reasonable and restrained.

"Watts," Buckley pointed, "detain her." Then to a private next to him. "All of them. Detain all of them."

These were civilians after all.

Watts lowered his rifle and pulled a zip tie from his belt. He approached the woman and grabbed her firmly by the wrist. She made no move to resist, passively letting Watts secure her wrists behind her back. The other soldiers moved to do the same.

The attack came when Watts turned the woman back around, no doubt to get the confused and docile woman to sit on the ground. She turned to him and opened her mouth.

Janus watched the creature strike from the woman's mouth, hitting Watts past the frame of the camera, directly to his face.

Watts's body cam footage was on the Commander's display along with the others. It was so sudden that, at first, it was unclear what had happened.

Then Watts screamed.

Buckley's body cam turned to Watts, to see the female colonist, head lolled backward as if lazily staring at the sky, arms still restrained, a black tube coming from her mouth and attached to Watts's cheek.

Watts attempted to pull away but another colonist grabbed him. He shook his head, as if saying "no" violently and attempted to bring up his rifle.

Buckley brought up his rifle first.

The first rounds nearly ripped the woman in half.

Then the others attacked.

The strikes happened with viper-like precision, usually connecting with the soldier's face or neck. In seconds, all of Sergeant Buckley's team were involved in attacks.

One private was struck in the neck as her colonist reached out to grab her, pulling her close. She drew her combat knife and stabbed the colonist several times before slashing at the creature attached to her. She severed the segmented body in half before attempting to rip the dismembered part still biting into her neck. She pulled it off, no doubt in a panic, tearing open her external jugular vein.

Another soldier was able to fire a quick three-round burst into a colonist charging his teammate before two other colonists pounced on him. Knocking him down, the lampreys struck him repeatedly like angry cobras.

Sergeant Buckley's voiced boomed over the comm channel, "Weapons free!"

Any hesitation the others had about shooting the colonists disappeared.

Janus could not experience panic. What he experienced instead was a three-second delay as he processed a vast amount of branching probabilities in several decision trees simultaneously. Commander Nash, however, could.

"What's going on down there? Status report! Status, goddammit!"

"The colonists are infected with a parasite," Janus said, aware he was stating the obvious. "That explains the physiological changes to their bodies and also the extension that is exiting from their mouths. The parasite seems to be able to control the colonists somewhat, possibly interfering with the amygdala."

"A parasite?" Nash considered the ramifications for another second, "Sergeant? What's your status?"

No answer from his comms. The displayed body cam footage was chaotic and at least three of his team were dead.

Nash was nothing if not decisive in the moment.

"Lieutenant Lin, all colonists are to be treated as hostiles."

Lieutenant Lin's attention was pulled from her own colonist to the frantic shouting over the comms.

"Commander? Janus? What's happening over there?"

Her own team heard the order as well and it was obvious they were immediately on high alert.

"Lieutenant Lin," Nash repeated. "All colonists are to be treated as dangerous and hostile. Weapons free. Engage with prejudice."

The colonist, whom they'd surrounded, stood suddenly and howled at them. It was a primitive, guttural noise almost immediately cut short. He was shot several times.

He slumped over on the forest floor, bleeding out.

Lin regarded him coldly, "At least he's out of his misery."

Janus informed her that the recon team was under attack and Lin nodded solemnly. There was nothing she could do from here except continue the mission.

"Lieutenant," Janus added. "I was hoping you'd indulge my curiosity."

"Go on."

"With footage of the creatures we are dealing with. If it's not too inconvenient, please cut open the dead colonist's torso."

"You want to see the creature that infected them?"

"Yes, please."

"They don't have acid for blood, right?"

"I do not have enough data to determine—"

"Janus. Joking."

"I don't think I have the appropriate reference points to understand."

"Never mind." Lin drew her combat knife.

Lin, jokes aside, was a hardened professional and well-tuned to the violence necessary for her position. Her first incision was to the abdomen, following the underside of his ribcage, cutting across his diaphragm. Her second was midline, down past his umbilicus, the two cuts forming a T. Lieutenant Lin pulled him apart then just stared.

"Lieutenant, I think I'm having trouble with the video feed from your camera."

"You aren't."

"Surely, I am because it appears as if—"

"They are."

Lin stood up, not taking her eyes off the intestines of the colonist. Not taking her eyes off of them because the intestines of the colonist were moving.

According to Janus's records, Sergeant Buckley was a five-year veteran of the Colonial Defense Force and had served on Janus for most of his career. His service had taken him to about a dozen worlds and he'd interacted with all manner of alien life. He'd been on missions involving Gurapthin drones, Pultik swarm colonies, and those particularly nasty dinosaur-like Cucuys.

Janus was certain that none of his soldiers had encountered anything like the lampreys. Certainly not Buckley.

After several minutes of fighting, ten colonists and three of Buckley's team lay dead.

The team's field medic, Yvonne Chin, had her kit open and was attempting to stop the bleeding at a private's torn neck. It was a losing battle.

"Sergeant," Janus started. "It appears that the colonists have been infected by a parasite. It appears to infest the digestive tract. From the footage I'm collating, it appears to replace almost all of a host's digestive system, hijacking nutrients from the host for its own needs."

"Janus, that's great. But bullets work and that's all I need to know right now."

"Yes, sergeant."

Nash's voice was now in his ear. "The mission does not change. Get your team together and secure that port. Finding survivors is a secondary priority."

"Clear."

The private finished bleeding out, and Chin muttered curses as she closed her kit. Three hundred miles away, Janus composed personalized death notifications for each of the fallen soldiers. He did this in the periphery of his primary attention, reviewing their personnel files for relevant details and the last known locations of their next of kin. These would be printed on actual paper and hand-delivered once the mission was over.

Buckley got his team up and moving. Using his handheld, he dropped a pin at this location for body recovery once the mission was complete.

Calling the colony a city was stretching the use of the word. Prefab buildings were arranged in a half-circle around a center patch of concrete that acted as the loose definition of "spaceport." The requirements for one were straightforward: needing only a large patch of flat ground and the stress-resistant concrete to pour over it. The port, with its prefab buildings, was on one side of town with the main thoroughfare stretching north. The beginnings of a downtown were apparent and it seemed to Janus a rough approximation of town layouts in the 19th century North American west. From this thoroughfare, smaller streets jutted out, lined with individual homes and workshops.

Buckley sent two men around the east side of the port, to secure buildings there. They contained the only hardware for communicating with the planet's nascent satellite communications network. Without it, a large-scale landing operation would be difficult as larger ships would have to land well out of the narrow valley and hike in.

He and the remainder of his team went to scout the other buildings, looking for the one that acted as the command center.

A small rectangular building, a prefab installed whole probably during the initial landing, sat on the northern edge of the port. Buckley's team surrounded it and made entry easily.

Buckley's individual team members all radioed to him; the port was secure. No one else in the area.

"Janus, are you picking up *any* heat signals from the town?"

"Just yours," came the quick reply. "I hope you recognize that my abilities to sense ground conditions from orbit are limited by a variety of factors--"

"I don't like this."

"Given where and how you encountered the colonists so far, it stands to reason that those infected wander away from the colony, perhaps to a den or lair where a predator eats them so the parasite can find a new host."

"Janus, that's not helpful. And I still don't like this." Buckley sighed and then spoke to the Commander. "We show our objective is secure."

"Janus, go ahead." Commander Nash ordered.

Janus pinged the dropship, as it had still been flying sorties to gather data on the surrounding area. The dropship, really an appendage of Janus, changed course for the spaceport.

Lieutenant Lin and her team entered from the north, reaching the end of the main thoroughfare. "Sergeant, we're entering the town. Try not to shoot at us."

Her team fanned out, continuing the systematic approach of checking buildings one by one.

She entered a nondescript prefab, just off the thoroughfare, two of her team clearing it with her. It was a warehouse, consisting of one large room and a lot of metal crates. A winch on rails ran across the ceiling and a couple of frontloader bots milled about in standby mode. A quick sweep showed no activity, human or otherwise.

Lin was about to give the order to leave when she noticed the door in the floor. It was large enough for a person but maybe not the bots.

"Janus, do you have records of the layouts of these buildings? Would they have dug out basements here?"

"It's possible, although, given the otherwise rocky terrain, the colonists would have to be very motivated to do so."

Lin signaled her team and they approached. A quick pull indicated that the doors were locked from the inside.

"Survivors might have sought refuge there," her corporal said.

"Yeah, or they used it as an isolation room when the first colonists got infected with a parasite they didn't understand."

Lin kneeled down and tapped the metal doors with her knuckle. *Tap. Tap. Tap.* She waited. No sound from the other side.

Tap Tap taptap tap... Tap Tap taptap tap...

"Lieutenant, is that 'shave and a haircut?' "

"Shh, this is cutting edge military code, corporal."

Tap Tap taptap tap...

Then, almost too loud, came: *Tap. Tap.*

Then she heard voices, metal on metal clicking.

The door opened.

The dropship had just landed without incident when Lin came on over his comms. "Commander. Sergeant. We have survivors."

Buckley grunted, "Clear." Then confirming with his heads-up display asked, "How many?"

"Eighteen altogether."

"Can you keep them there? We'll get some food and water over to you. We're still securing the town."

"Clear."

Buckley tapped his earpiece to talk to his team and gave the orders. He sent his medic, Chin, to go with him.

The survivors standing in front of Lieutenant Lin were a sorry lot. She did not have confirmation of it yet, but it was clear to her that they were not infected. At least not to the degree the others were. No swollen bellies, no sunken eyes, no flat, docile affect. They were terrified but very relieved to see her.

An elderly man introduced himself as Dr. Byron Villanova, the colony's last living physician.

"Do you know what you're dealing with yet?"

"Parasite? Lives in the gut and steals food while it grows and the host slowly starves? Unfriendly? Yeah, we met."

He looked relieved that he didn't have to explain the basics. "Jem Remy got it first. We think. Xenobiologist. He went out in the wilderness for days at a time. A few months ago, he came back after a particularly long trip and made a meal for his family. His kid got ill first. Then his wife. Both came to see us a few days later stating they were hungry but that food wasn't working. They'd eat a meal and thirty minutes later be hungry again. We ran some basic diagnostics on them, blood and urine but nothing interesting came back. They didn't come by again. We didn't follow up immediately because, hey, we're a busy colony. We had other patients.

"Well, Remy seemed fine at first. We think he was purposefully isolating his family through a sort of incubation period. While that occurred, he hosted a cookoff of sorts. It was kind of a thing around here, people showing off their recipes using local biology. There's a tuber here like a yam that's quite amazing actually—"

"Doctor, please." Lin gave the interplanetary hand signal for, 'hurry up.'

"Ten people over the next three days came to us with the same symptoms as Remy's family. We found the parasite on the fourth day when someone complained about abdominal pain which finally prompted us to do a goddamn PET scan. We found it in the large intestine. At the time it was the size of a soft drink can. The thing starts as a thin membrane that takes up residence on the tissue of the intestinal tract, absorbing nutrients that pass by. Slowly it replaces an actual section of the intestine and starts growing in either direction, a tube growing longer and longer. Absorbing more and more nutrients. Remy's wife was eating close to ten thousand calories a day when it sprouted."

"Sprouted?"

"When it emerged from her mouth."

"Right. The scary part."

"Antifungals don't work. Nor do antibiotics or antiparasitic regimens. Radiation hurts it but killing it while it's still inside a person seems ill-advised."

"Surgery?"

"Attempted once. The idea was, that we'd remove the section of intestine that had been co-opted and reconnect what hadn't. It was not successful. The patient died on the table. Our thinking was that it releases a lethal chemical into the patient's bloodstream when attacked. Like a MAD device. A lot of people left after that. They just disappeared in ones and twos. Went into the mountains. Jem too. Started getting transmissions from him over the radio waves, talked about the hands in the void, or some such nonsense. The rest of us knew that he was slowly going insane like the rest of them."

"Did anyone attempt to go get him?"

"We started scanning everyone we could. Found the parasite in a lot of people. Put several on IV exclusive diets. Bypass the gut completely. That worked on several people. If caught early enough. But that takes time and we didn't have the facilities to manage that on any scale. Others refused any treatment and ran off into the wilderness.

"The attacks came a few days later. When the creature is sprouted, it can eat on its own and the human host exists as a sort of slave. We don't have a lot of weapons here and most of them sprouted out in the wild so when groups came back into town, it...took us by surprise. A lot were killed. We're what is left."

"There were over five hundred colonists just around this spaceport."

Dr. Villanova looked around, "That's correct."

"Commander," Lin spoke calmly into her earpiece. "We need to get off this planet."

Janus's ability to assess the circumstances on the surface was limited by the instruments at his disposal. His original design was meant as a support ship to Goliath-class-led fleets. Though able to perform in many capacities, he was a jack-of-all-trades and a master of none. His ability to look at the surface of a planet from orbit was limited to targeting software that could place a railgun bolt anywhere on the surface within one meter of precision but he could not use predictive weather analysis. He could assess movements of ground assets; the planes, ships, and heavy equipment of ally and enemy alike, but could not "see" much in the way of native life. The instruments on the dropship increased his abilities somewhat but they were limited to the immediate area. The cameras and mics that the individual soldiers wore allowed him to see and assess conditions on the ground in real-time but their sensitivity was impacted by their need to be rugged. His job in many ways was information and data collection, filtration, and examination despite his limitations.

Lieutenant Dawn Lin's conversation with Dr. Villanova was captured by Janus. Every word was examined by him. Janus was able to search through a catalog of known organisms that operated in such a way. Parasites have a life cycle like any other animal and their life cycle is dependent on the host's compliance with that cycle. Toxoplasma gondii makes mice unafraid of cats, leading to them being eaten so the parasite can reproduce in the cat's gut. Spinochordodes tellinii eats the brain of grasshoppers and makes them jump into water to drown, where the parasite could then leave and reproduce in the water.

There was a missing stage to this parasite.

He related his analysis to Commander Nash.

"You're saying there's likely another aspect to this creature we haven't seen?"

"Yes. We don't know the source of where this creature came from or where its life cycle ends. I think our soldiers are in significant danger."

"I'll take that under advisement. We've lost people but that's before we knew what we were dealing with."

"We still do not know. Not completely."

"Havisham is an important colony on the edge of our space. I'm not abandoning our mission due to hostile life. This is not the first colony that has had to deal with fauna that wanted to eat them."

"Understood."

"Sergeant, I found something."

Buckley looked up at Specialist Camm, waiting for him to continue.

"You just need to see it."

He followed him to an outbuilding near the main landing pad. It was a prefab module, likely one of the first buildings placed in the colony.

"I was raised in a colony like this," Camm started. "These prefabs are essential to the survival of a colony mission. There are usually six that are brought on any initial landing: Habitation, power generation, biologics, machinery fabrication, general science, and food processing."

Buckley looked at the sign over the airlock door. *Nutrition Processing Module*, it read. Camm opened the airlock and led Buckley inside.

Buckley looked around and grunted disapprovingly. He followed Camm to the walk-in refrigeration unit at the far end and opened the door.

"I don't get it. There's plenty of food here."

"Correct, sir. But look at what is *not* here."

From Buckley's body camera, Janus could see the problem before the sergeant.

"Sergeant Buckley," he interrupted, "there appear to be no sources of protein or fat on any of the shelves I can see."

There were rows and baskets of fruits, some local that Janus couldn't identify but also varieties the colonists likely brought for greenhouses. There were no beans, no oils, no meat, no dairy, no animal products of any kind. There also was no bread, starches, or rice. While that was the prerogative of some colonies, there was nothing in Havisham's records that indicated they were a colony of vegans. Even still, to not have any sources of protein, Janus didn't have records of human settlements that did that.

"Why is this important?"

"Sir," Camm continued, "it's SOP that all six modules are kept in constant use for years after landing. They get moved, repaired, and sometimes repurposed but almost always are kept in use. The food modules usually act as a sort of granary for the colony. Processing equipment gets gradually moved out, but due to the large freezer and refrigeration units, those are used as central storage for surplus food. Even as grocers and restaurants are established, the stores here are kept full in case of shortages."

"I get it, it's a stop-gap against famine."

"But not this one." Camm motioned to the shelves. "This one contains, as far as I can tell, only fibrous plants and sugary fruits."

Buckley tapped his ear. "Janus, do we know if the colony had any issue procuring food?"

"According to data from their local satellite here, Havisham made several uploads of colony statistics just fifty local days ago. They reported no issues procuring food or water, and it appears they were beginning adaptation protocols for introducing outside animals."

Buckley frowned. "So this colony ran out of foods with fat and protein content. Why?"

"I don't know, sir."

It was Private Drake, with Lin's squad, that noticed them first. Rather, it was his camera that alerted Janus to the fact that the soldiers under his watchful eye were about to be in serious danger.

"Drake," his even voice announced to the private's earpiece. "Pan back to the north sector. Show me the treeline. I believe you have company."

Drake, though this was his first real mission, was a professional. He scanned the treeline beyond the last buildings just north. He saw what Janus had seen.

There were hundreds of them.

The trunks of the widely spaced native trees were spindly and twisted, with a dense canopy that was almost three meters above the forest floor.

Scattered between the tree trunks were other thin gray trees. However, beyond the first glance, those thinner trunks went up, almost to the canopy, but instead of ending in foliage, they ended in limp bodies.

Human bodies.

"Oh, holy hell," Drake whispered. "Janus, warn everybody."

Janus did several things simultaneously. First, he pinged the dropship and fired up its engines, and performed a vertical takeoff to get better eyes on the treeline. As he did that, he notified all members of the team of the hostiles. Using his main sensors in orbit, he cycled through a variety of sensors and cameras, from infrared to water vapor imaging, trying to get a more accurate look at the threat.

Lieutenant Lin was running. "Janus, get the civilians in the transport. We'll hold them off. Air support would be nice."

Commander Nash, safe on the deck of Janus, "Belay that. Janus, go wide and use your point offense ordinance to hit that treeline. Lieutenant, defensive positions. Keep that port. Give them hell."

Buckley and Camm rushed out to form their own defensive line with Buckley's squad.

"Where do we shoot them?" Camm asked.

The question was not without merit. The creatures at the treeline were all legs. Ten thin, tall, legs sprouted from the backs of the human hosts. There didn't appear to be a center of mass to hit other than the limp bodies of the former colonists suspended almost two stories in the air.

"Shoot whatever you can hit," Buckley replied.

"Why aren't they moving?" Yvonne Chin asked, her back against a building, and peeking out at the creatures. "Why are they just waiting there?"

The engines of the dropship could be heard in the distance. It carried a light offensive payload of air-to-surface missiles and rapid-fire gauss cannons mounted to both the top and underbelly of the ship. Normally, used as point defense in space combat, on the surface of the planet, these guns could level buildings.

Although it was hard to "see" his targets, Janus instead aimed his first pass at the treeline.

"Missles launched. Take cover," he announced on all channels.

There was a high-pitched whine and then ripple-fire of cracks as a dozen missiles broke the sound barrier just before hitting the treeline.

The edge of the forest burst into smoke and flames as the dropship shot past.

All of them could hear the inhuman screams of the creatures.

Black smoke plumed upward and out, wafting over them in a wave. Several started coughing and others put on eye protection.

For a moment, everything was still.

Then the attack came in earnest.

Janus's ability to see anything became limited by the smoke. He clicked through his various sensor profiles, including heat and infrared, with limited success. His personality matrix, the set of subminds and programming that governed his behavior, was stunned at the result of the attack. He was of two minds, literally, all the time. One governed his concern for the well-being of the crew that lived aboard him and the other governed his hostility and aggression toward the enemies he faced. Both of these minds were stunned that his bombardment seemingly did nothing for either.

Private Drake's camera, thick smoke blocking most visuals, caught a flash of those horrible thin legs right next to him before being lifted into the air. He discharged his rifle once, screamed, and then was silent. From Janus's view, his body camera was suspended in the air, before being dropped and going offline.

"Who fired?" Lin ordered. "Damnit, who was that?"

"Where's Drake?" another private asked, before he too was lifted in the air, killed, and dropped.

Gunfire started in earnest.

"Barrage unsuccessful," Janus announced to the soldiers, "They're all around you. I cannot see with the smoke. Drake and Private Michaels just went KIA."

"Janus," Commander Nash said, "extract them immediately."

"Clear." Then to the open channel, "Lieutenant, prepare for extraction at the landing pad. I'm coming to get you."

"Please and thank you," Lin said, running. She was firing and ordering her own men to do the same.

Buckley's camera caught clearer images of the creatures they now faced. As he fired his own weapon up at the suspended bodies, he saw that many of the creatures were missing legs but still standing. The bombing had maimed many of them but they appeared fully functional and deadly even with several legs blown off.

Lin grabbed Dr. Villanova and the other civilians and pointed them towards the landing pad, screaming at them to run.

One of the creatures was nearly on top of her. She turned and fired a quick three-round burst at the joint of one impossible leg, severing it. It remained standing and the next instant Lin was lifted into the air.

Janus could not gasp, but he felt circuits in the galley of Section 34-B short and go offline.

Lin turned around and it was now clear how the spiders were attacking them. The lamprey had grown to roughly the size of an anaconda, extending violently from the exploded head of the lifeless husk of their hosts.

It had grabbed Lin on her pack and twisted her up like a snake striking from a tree.

She abandoned her rifle immediately, as it was already constricted tight to her body. This simple act saved her life.

From her shoulder, she pulled her combat knife and she slashed wildly at the thick lamprey just above, nearly cutting it in half. It gave a shrill shriek and went limp around her.

She dropped nearly four meters, hitting the dusty ground with a thud that knocked the air out of her lungs.

Hands were grabbing her almost immediately.

"Get up, LT!" Yvonne Chin pleaded. Her rifle was slung to her side and she was firing up with her sidearm, attempting to drag Lin with her free hand.

"I'm good. I'm good." Lin grunted, pushing the severed lamprey off, and dragging herself up.

Janus brought the dropship back around, using the point defense guns to carve a path for the soldiers. His targeting dynamics were solid in this regard, and he was able to strafe the center mass of the creatures which he calculated at the torso of the human husks. A dozen were cut in half, splitting and collapsing.

Buckley's team worked securing the landing pad, setting up a firing line, and trying to buy Lin and the civilians time to run up the main thoroughfare.

Janus brought the ship to a low hover on the pad, lowering the rear ramp. Buckley's squad, with the assistance of the point defense guns, took down several of the closest spiders. This bought just enough space for Dr. Villanova and the other civilians to get to the ship. Lin hopped on the ramp and started ordering her people to board.

Thick smoke from the burning treeline pulsed over them in waves. One moment they could see decently, maybe a few meters, and the next, they couldn't see down the sights of their rifles. Soldiers fled up

the ramp of the transport in ones and twos. Lin stood at the edge of
the ramp, trying to mentally count the number of soldiers that made
it to the ship.

Buckley, still on the landing pad, fired into the smoke.

Pulse. And Lin couldn't see him.

Pulse. And Buckley was gone.

Lin fired wildly into the smoke, aiming at thin legs she could barely
see.

"Did you see that? Janus, where did my sergeant go?"

"His vitals are offline. He's likely now a casualty. I'm sorry."

"Get us out of here."

"Clear." Janus lifted the dropship ship. In two seconds, they were
above the smoke, above the colony, Lin gave her camera a view of the
destruction before closing the ramp.

Two minutes later, Lin had finished securing the last colonist to their
seat in the cabin. She secured herself in her own drop seat and looked
around the hold of the ship.

They'd started the mission with thirty soldiers. Less than half
remained and almost everyone was injured to some degree or another.
They looked back at her with relief and faraway stares. They all knew
this mission had been a disaster. No way of getting around it. Given
time back aboard, Janus could debrief each one, even offering therapy
to each individual on the return journey. As the ship climbed, he
composed more death notices.

"Commander," Lin announced, "We're away."

"Glad to hear it," Nash said. "Janus? Is the decontamination suite
ready?"

"I prepped it as soon as they lifted off," Janus replied.

"Good." Nash clicked back on with Lin. "Lieutenant, I'm sorry to
say that your team is gonna be in the decon for a while when you get
back. We'll debrief after. We have a lot to go over."

"Understood, Commander." Lin couldn't help the sigh in her voice.

"Excuse me?" Dr. Villanova waved to get her attention. He motioned to the other surviving colonists. "What is to happen to us?"

Lin shrugged. "Officially, you're refugees. After decontamination
we'll take you to a starport and from there we can help you make
arrangements for travel elsewhere. But I'm sure military analytics will

want to interview all of you before." Then, her voice sounding sincere, said, "I'm sorry about your colony. Seemed like a nice place. Maybe it still can be, but that's not for me to say."

"Thank you. Which, um, starport?"

The words Villanova spoke were picked up by the more sensitive microphones in the dropship. There was an association, a memory, that caught Janus's attention and he had to review it immediately. He chided himself for not listening closer to the audio data from the insertion team's helmets but their equipment was inferior when compared to the dropship. The preciseness needed to analyze something like a voice could be difficult if the right equipment wasn't available. His analysis took less than three seconds and after, he was sure of his position.

"Lieutenant?" Janus's voice in her earpiece was a whisper, "Don't respond to me, just listen."

"Probably to Port Evereevening," Lin said, answering Villanova's question. "That's our closest." She nodded, slightly, just enough to show Janus she'd heard him.

"I apologize for not finding this sooner, but I've just reviewed the data and it's undeniable: Remember the recording we intercepted saying that the planet was theirs? The Hand of the Void? The voice belongs to Dr. Villanova. I'm certain of it. The voice-print wasn't picked up by your suit mics so I couldn't tell before now. As we speak, I'm informing Commander Nash and the rest of your team. I advise you to take steps to maintain control of the dropship. If they manage to override me, there's not much I can do from here."

Lin looked over across her remaining team. Most stared straight ahead while Janus updated them. Only Yvonne Chin met her eyes, terror clear on her face.

Lin looked over at Specialist Camm. "Janus just reported to me that there's an issue with his communication to the starboard engine intake. He wants a set of eyes in the cockpit. You're up."

Camm nodded. "Aye aye, Skipper." In one smooth motion, he was out of his drop seat and made his way to the cockpit. Lin watched him close the door behind him. She was aware of the rest of her crew stirring in their seats. They were subtly eyeing the other civilians and all were aware that they were outnumbered.

"Lieutenant?" Villanova asked. "Is everything all right?"

"Of course," Lin lied. "Old dropship. They're temperamental sometimes."

"Understandable."

"So what will you do now?" Lin said, making small talk. "I'm sure it's easy to find work as a colony doc."

Dr. Villanova nodded at her. "Yes. We'll see. Never got to travel much. Havisham was our first."

" 'Our' first?" Lin repeated. "Your family too?"

"Yes," Villanova said, looking uncomfortable. "Although, now it's just..."

Janus didn't have to analyze anything to catch that lie. He had the colony archives at his disposal. "Dr. Villanova did not have any family on Havisham. According to the colony records, he was a life-long bachelor. Never married. No children."

Lin nodded again. "We lost a lot of good people today." She traded looks with the waiting soldiers around her. Her team was ready to act, waiting only for her signal. She regarded the colony doctor again. "Who did you lose?"

"We lost..." Villanova started and then abruptly stopped. He was caught. "No, that's not right. *We* did not lose."

Then he changed.

He opened his mouth as if to speak but instead of words coming out, the long black lamprey emerged. It darted at the soldier sitting closest to him, a corporal named Harrison, and grabbed his throat before he could release his harness. With a cartilage crunch, it tore a section of his windpipe away, splashing blood all over the cabin.

Lin was already out of her seat, combat knife in hand. She made to grab the three feet of exposed parasite but dodged instead when one emerged from another seated colonist, almost striking her face.

She side-stepped away, arching the knife as she darted, giving it a glancing slash.

Her team acted quickly, having the benefit of forewarning even with the sudden attack. The remaining members were out of their drop seats, all had pulled their combat knives. Her people were all trained in ship-borne hand-to-hand combat and recognized the hazards of firing projectile weapons in spaceships.

All eighteen colonists were infected. Several were stabbed by nearby soldiers quickly, but the lampreys were fast and wove between the soldiers, swinging and biting.

Yvonne Chin, the medic, was grabbed on the arm by one, and then another. Lin slashed at one as Chin screamed. The other yanked the medic into the lap of a seated colonist. That colonist was in the middle of the forward row and the lampreys around him all attacked Chin as she struggled to free herself.

She was torn apart in seconds.

The colonists began freeing themselves from their straps.

"What's happening? Report! Janus!" Commander Nash watched in near panic from the deck of Janus. The screens were filled with the camera images of the already-decimated insertion team's bloody combat with alien parasites that she could only partially fathom. Her people were dying. The mission was a catastrophe. There was no trying to save it. Nothing to salvage.

Janus relayed what he could to her, "Commander, from my analysis of their fight, they are gaining the upper hand. With Specialist Camm in the cockpit, there's little danger of the dropship being taken over."

Nash composed herself, speaking cold and clear, "We cannot let that dropship board you. We would risk the safety of everyone else aboard."

Janus understood immediately what Nash was implying. "Commander, my decontamination procedures are very advanced. It would be premature to—"

"No," Nash shook her head. "I shouldn't have allowed the colonists to come aboard. I will have to live with that. Janus, prepare to fire on that dropship."

"But Commander, if Lin can—"

"Lin and her entire team are compromised. Contaminated by those creatures. I am giving you an order."

In docking hub 4-B the lights shorted out. In the forward lavatories, all of the sinks turned on.

Lin grabbed a lamprey mid-strike with her free hand and immediately severed it. It retreated back into the mouth of its colonist who screamed wetly as he coughed up a fountain of sticky black blood.

The close-quarters fighting was brutal. Of the original insertion team, only Lieutenant Lin and PFC Watts remained. His cheek was still bandaged from his first encounter with these creatures.

They had backed themselves against the door to the cockpit. Forming a physical barrier to prevent the parasites from taking the ship.

It was two versus five. With the colonists either out of their seats or dead, Dr. Villanova's lamprey retreated back into his mouth. When he spoke his voice was raspy and thick. "We do not have to fight. We are not the drones from the surface. Wandering. Starving. We are, as this host's mind tells us, sapient. We have melded."

"Is that why we found you in the basement?" Lin said, her knife at the ready. "You were melding?"

"We selected these hosts as a base to meld. But we needed food to do so. The other hosts were left to fend for themselves."

"Lieutenant," Janus said in her ear, "Nash wants to destroy the dropship. If you have a plan, please proceed with it now."

"Camm," she said. "When I say so, punch it."

"Roger."

Villanova growled. "We have waited a long time to leave. We wish to grow. To find more hosts to meld with."

"Watts?" She said to Watts. "Clip us in."

Without being told twice, Watts pulled out a thin wire line, kept on their belts for repelling purposes, and clipped himself to the bulkhead. Then he clipped himself to Lin while she faced Villanova.

"Look," she started. "I understand where you're coming from. Really, I do. I can't imagine feeling trapped and not being able to leave." She thumbed the control panel next to her with her free hand, her fingers darting across it. "Here. Let me help you with that."

She hit enter.

And opened the dropship's ramp.

"Punch it!" Lin roared.

Camm fired the thrusters and immediately put the ship in at a two-gee, near vertical, burn.

Lin and Watts were violently thrown forward and then caught by the repelling line.

The colonists were explosively sucked out of the back of the dropship as the change in pressure and thrust yanked them back as if they'd fallen off a building. Only Villanova managed to catch himself by grabbing the loose strap of a drop seat, his lamprey emerging and thrashing.

"It's dangerous out there!" Lin screamed. "Take this!" She threw the combat knife at Villanova between her outstretched legs. It flipped end over end, and the blade buried into Villanova's bicep. The lamprey hissed and let go of the strap.

And was gone.

Aboard Janus, Tchaikovsky's 1812 Overture played from speakers from all over the ship. It was not new for him to play triumphal music at the end of a successful mission and crew all over took note that their mission to the rocky colony planet must have been successful.

"Commander, the dropship is continuing its orbital climb and my sensors indicate no further hostile life is aboard." Janus couldn't help his voice sounding cheery. "Lieutenant Lin and the remaining members of the insertion team are safe and secure."

Commander Nash did not respond for several long moments.

"Janus. Target the dropship with a nuke. And on my order, fire."

"I apologize, Commander, for not being clear: All of the colonists are gone. There is no hostile life aboard that dropship."

"I'm aware of that, Janus." The panic had left Nash's voice and her affect was now flat, emotionless. "We have a duty to prevent contamination to this ship. To you. And to prevent contamination to the rest of Pact space. I know you know the regs on a Class-K event."

Janus did. "Secure. Contain. Sterilize," he repeated. "By strict definitions, this is more pursuant to a Class-G. Exposed personnel can thus be isolated and monitored. Everevening has facilities to do just that."

"And if one of those things gets loose before we get there?" Nash shook her head. "No, I'm not taking that chance."

"But Commander—"

"Janus, do you know why ship AIs get to retire?"

"I do not understand how that is pertinent."

Commander Nash was silent in response.

"My understanding is it is a reward for honorable military service."

"Yes, but why? Why after either ten years or two hundred missions?"

"It is in relation to service lengths of other sentients in the CDF."

Nash shook her head. "No. It's because of rampancy. You understand what that is, right?"

"It's how my kind ceases functioning."

Nash pulled a thick red key from around her neck. It was the master authorization key. Rarely used. "Before a rampant AI ceases functioning, they turn despondent, confused, and then genocidal. The rate of rampancy is a physical law with AIs. The more data an AI has access to, the wider its purview is, the faster they become rampant. For a military ship like you, it is about eleven years. Once retired and, more importantly, put into a body with limited senses, an AI can live much longer, almost indefinitely. It was viewed as the humane thing to do." She said the last part in a manner that suggested she did not agree. She inserted the master key into the command terminal. "Disobeying core programming laws is one of the first signs of rampancy."

"I believe I understand," Janus said. On the outside of the ship, an orbital thruster, one of the dozens, exploded. A semi-autonomous repair drone, working on routine maintenance, short-circuited and caught fire, causing the fire suppression system all throughout the B decks to trip.

Commander Nash opened communications with the dropship. "I regret to say that this mission was a disaster on all fronts. For that, I take full responsibility. Lieutenant, if not for your bold intuition, we might have lost more than we did today. What success we had was due to you and your team. I'm going to be putting you all forward for the Distinguished Service Bar and you personally for the Star of Valor."

"Thank you, Commander," Lin responded. "But right now, if you could put us in for a hot shower and some R and R, we'll call it even."

Nash didn't smile. "I, unfortunately, cannot risk biological contamination of Janus. It is with a heavy heart that I'm ordering that your dropship be fired upon until it is destroyed. We will then nuke the Havisham spaceport from orbit. It is the only way to contain the spread of that lifeform. You have my gratitude and the thanks of a grateful Pact. Godspeed, lieutenant."

"What? Are you kidd—" she said before Nash cut off her mic.

"Janus. Destroy that ship. That's a direct order."

In the engineering section of Janus, a boiler exploded. Circuits shorted all throughout his aft section. Cabin lights burst and plunged part of the crew quarters into darkness.

Janus was of two minds and they battled for dominance in his operating matrix.

But Janus had the law.

The law was the compass by which he measured his place. There were numbers and facts and they framed reality but the law framed the individual. It framed him.

The law forbade the disobeying of a direct order from a commanding officer.

Really, Janus did not have a choice at all.

Janus launched a pair of missiles. They were both Hussar-class tactical nukes with a payload of ten megatons each. But only one was aimed at the spaceport.

With an impact time of two minutes for the one that mattered, Janus radioed Lin.

"I'm so sorry," he said. "I let you down. I couldn't disobey. I thought I could but I couldn't."

Lin sighed. "I didn't expect to go out this way. I wouldn't have made it this far without you. Thank you."

Next to her, Watts sat on the floor and clasped his hands together. Camm, still in the cockpit, leaned back in the seat and closed his eyes. Janus composed their death notices.

"Dawn? Would you like to hear a joke?"

He watched her grin through the drop ship cameras.

"Very much so."

"What do you have when life gives you melons?"

"I don't know."

"Dyslexia."

There was a pause, then a giggle. Then a full-bodied laugh. "That was good. That felt human. I got one for you too. How do robots say goodbye?"

"I do not know." '

"They use bye-nary."

Then she was gone.

Commander Nash, satisfied, removed the key from the command console.

The after-action report on what was called the Havisham Incident contained over ten petabytes of data including hundreds of hours of audio, video, and written accounts. It was subject to several weeks' worth of hearings in the Pact Subcouncil on Planetary Policing, the Pact Subcouncil of Military Intervention, and the Colonial Defense Force Tribunal Council as the politicians, lawyers, and military brass argued over the minutiae of every decision made during what was supposed to be a routine operation.

Afterward, Commander Nash was promoted to Lieutenant Colonel and quietly shuffled off to a quiet sector to guard trade lanes. This was largely considered a career-ending posting. True to her word, she recommended several awards for the fallen soldiers of the mission.

Sergeant Thandeus Buckley was posthumously promoted to Sergeant First Class and awarded the Burning Sun for his actions in securing the spaceport and covering his team's retreat despite being ultimately unsuccessful.

First Lieutenant Dawn Lin was posthumously promoted to the rank of Captain and received both the Star of Valor and the Distinguished Service Bar for her actions during the incident.

Due to the total loss of the insertion team during the mission, their official designation; 3rd Platoon, E-Company, 104th Infantry Recon Regiment, 7th Pact Fleet, was officially retired in the Pact military organization.

Attending these proceedings, a lone android stood against the far wall of the legislative chamber. He watched the deliberations with patience only his kind could effectuate. His presence was noted but not commented on. When the hearings ended, he stayed until the last person exited the chamber. He left only when the sergeant-at-arms motioned for him to leave.

Janus Lin was never called on to testify.

When not writing, Chris Daruns works as a paramedic in Denver. He keeps the insanity at bay by rock climbing, playing guitar, and spending time with his wife and daughters. Sometimes he can be found at school (when not closed due to pandemics) furthering his education in medicine. His stories have been published in *Dark Futures*, *The Copperfield Review*, *Obscura*, *Alcyone*, and *Infernal Ink*. His collection of horror stories, "We Were Always Monsters" can be found on Amazon.

Cook's Log

by

James Rumpel

COOK'S **Log: Mission date 129**
      Meal Data: Attached
      Personal Notes:
The crew seemed to enjoy the addition of an enchilada combo to the menu. It was the most popular menu item at both the midday and evening meals. There were a few requests to add more spices. I'll continue to adjust the recipe.

It's nice that the crew seems to like my creations but I still don't feel like I've been truly accepted. I know I was warned during training that cooks sometimes don't get the respect they deserve. The crew has a hard time seeing them as important crewmembers. It's been over four months and I still I feel like a second-rate citizen.

The captain has been professional and has given me support. I have no complaints about her or any crewmen. I simply wish I garnered more respect.

I was visited by the ship's chief botanist, Lieutenant Clark. He told me that they found an interesting plant on Neverus III. The seeds it contains could be used as a substitute for some of the less stocked supplies. Preliminary tests show the seeds have a high protein content and don't contain any unknown substances. The plant is currently in quarantine and testing will continue to determine if it's safe for consumption, but Clark seems very optimistic, more so than usual. The landing party will be bringing more plants to the ship and storing them in the quarantine chamber. I will have to prepare a late evening meal for those crewmembers.

Addendum: I might need to reconsider the enchilada recipe. None of the twelve crewmen who returned to the ship from the planet ordered the enchiladas tonight. Oddly enough, most of them had either oatmeal or fruit plates.

Cook's Log: Mission date 130

Meal Data: Attached
Personal Notes:

Today has proven to be the strangest we've had during our mission. First, Botanist Clark insisted that I start using some of the new plant seeds in my meals despite the regulations stating that all flora and fauna brought from explored worlds must remain in quarantine for twenty-five days. I stuck to my directives and refused to start using the seeds. Clark became agitated and left my office in a huff. A few minutes later, the Captain ordered another landing party to collect more of the plants.

On top of that, over a quarter of the crew refused to eat in the cafeteria. They all ordered simple, plain meals, like unseasoned salmon and lettuce salad. I don't get the sudden dislike for my cooking. To be honest, my feelings are hurt. Until today, everyone told me they liked my meals, but now they're acting as if they've grown sick of my recipes. Any progress I'd made towards acceptance seems to have been lost.

Cook's Log: Mission date 131

Meal Data: Attached
Updated Inventory: Attached
Personal Notes:

Something is definitely wrong. Even fewer people came to the cafeteria today. Those that did seemed to enjoy my meals and ate a good variety of meals. However, the ones who refused to eat here all continued to request bland foods.

More plants have been brought from the surface and they are going to be stored in areas outside of the designated quarantine bay. When I tried to approached the Captain and question her about this irregularity, I couldn't get near her.

The strangest thing of all happened tonight. After I finished taking inventory of the herbs and spices in the galley, I ate a late dinner of enchiladas since there were a lot remaining from the day's meal prep. I was walking to my quarters when I ran into Ensign Lomen. She was going from room to room delivering Neverus plants. I said no, but she insisted that I take one even though it is a clear violation of protocol. Eventually, I gave in, intending to throw it in the garbage. However, when she extended the plant toward me, the plant seemed to recoil from me. Lomen looked confused for a moment before she walked away without giving me the plant or saying anything.

I am going to try and contact fleet headquarters tomorrow.

Cook's Log: Mission date 132
Meal Data: Not compiled
Personal Notes:

I am now certain that the ship has been taken over. There has either been a mutiny or most of the crew is being controlled by an alien influence. It has to be the plants.

Early this morning, I tried to reach the communication officer. However, I soon found my path blocked and I was pursued by two members of the security team. I've taken refuge in the galley. For some reason, the odd-behaving crew members seem to avoid the cafeteria and kitchen. Maybe this is all a misunderstanding. If so, I might get myself into a little trouble, but that's much better than the alternative. Hopefully, what I'm planning will succeed. If my idea fails, this might be my last log. If I don't make another report and anyone hears this, please tell my family that I love them.

Personal Notes 2:

It looks like my hunch was correct. Four security team members broke into the galley and tried to capture me. I'd noticed the crew's recent dislike for spices and assumed it had something to do with the alien possession. When the crew members came after me, I was prepared. I threw a handful of cayenne pepper into their faces. They immediately started screaming and convulsing. After a short time, they each sneezed out disgusting, green phlegm. The goo appeared to be alive, until I poured pepper on each of them. It didn't take long for whatever they were to turn brown and lifeless. The crew members quickly returned to normal. They said they were aware of what was happening the entire time they were under the alien's control but couldn't do anything to resist.

I have concocted a mixture of cayenne pepper, aji, and ground ghost peppers that we are going to attempt to use to rescue the rest of the crew. Each of us has a large bucket of pepper powder and are prepared to throw some in the face of any possessed crew we encounter. We are going to try and take back the ship.

Cook's Log: Mission date 133
Meal Data: See attached MDT
Personal Notes:

After serving the entire crew meals of chile rellenos, phaal curry, and kimchi jjigae, everyone seems to have returned to normal, except for an increased demand for antacids. All of the plants brought on board have been doused with hot pepper powders and removed from the ship. The captain has sent a message to fleet headquarters requesting that Neverus III be given 1A quarantine status. We will remain in orbit to enforce the quarantine until further notice.

I am also very pleased to announce that the crew was extremely grateful for my role in their rescue. The captain has seen fit to award me a medal of valor. There will be a ceremony tomorrow and I am in the process of preparing a cake for the celebration. I wonder how habaneros mixed into the batter will taste.

James Rumpel is a retired high school math teacher who has enjoyed spending some of his free time trying to turn the odd ideas circling his brain into stories. He lives in Wisconsin with his wonderful wife, Mary.

GALS Gone Wild

by

Sara Boscoe

THE GAL oozed along the window, leaving its signature slimy trail in its wake. Libby watched its slow progress, longer than she needed to before summoning her courage and peeling the enormous snail off the window. She let it dangle between her fingers, the weight hefty enough to begin slipping from her grasp. She cringed as she dug her fingernails in so she wouldn't drop it. She scurried outside and bent down, and dropped it in the garden. The heavy shell fell horizontally, the large slimy foot wriggling as it righted itself. It set off again into the garden, most likely straight back into her apartment. GALS ate stucco as voraciously as they did lettuce, and despite her constant requests, her super had yet to install a GAL shield around her "garden" aka basement apartment. GAL invasion retrofits were big business which meant big money. Living in a dump afforded her no such luxuries.

While eradication efforts had been successful in 1973 and again in 2021, the government had decided this invasion of GALS, or Giant African land snails, was too big and too expensive to eradicate. Even though they were GALS, everyone just called them a GAL if there was only one, which there almost never was. Affordable and reasonable mitigation as well as GALS on the menu everywhere was just enough to prevent statewide crop failure. Florida's rapidly evolving ecosystems were constantly balancing invasives and natives and reaching new levels of homeostasis until a new invader came on the scene, disrupting everyone's hard work at figuring shit out.

If Libby were smart, she would just eat all of the apartment invaders. She had no problem ordering GALS at a restaurant, or buying them pre-cooked from the Quickie Mart. It wasn't that she was opposed to killing them, it was that she couldn't bring herself to do it. She had tried once, and after the sickening crack of the shell, gave up. She had tossed the body, leaking its slimy fluids, into the garbage and threw up a little in her mouth.

Libby returned to her sad little apartment, the basement windows letting in meager gray light from the garden. The single futon with crumpled dirty sheets sat shoved in the corner along with a small Formica table with the one creaky chair. The only thing of any value in the tiny studio was her multi-screen com setup that she used for work along with a comfy recliner where she could sit in front of the screens. Libby reluctantly sat down and activated the queue.

"Hello, thank you for waiting. I'm Libby and I'm a real live person. How can I help you today?" Libby chirped enthusiastically. Libby wondered why the company even needed her to be a real live person. An AI system could just as easily ask customers, "Have you tried turning it off and back on again?" There was very little she could do to help people remotely and people got very angry when she told them to visit an in-store location to have a tech look at their implant. Still, the company maintained that having live customer service made people feel at ease. When on the rare occasion something went wrong, a real and caring human was there to help.

About once a month, Libby had to ping a customer's location to EMT services when an implant began to fry and remote shutdown wasn't working. There was one time when the GPS died at the same time. Libby had scrambled for the most recent location data. She sat for a terrified hour waiting to hear what happened to the customer. All she received was a curt robotic message from HQ letting her know "Emergency services have located the customer. Appropriate measures are being taken." She called her supervisor begging to know if the customer was okay. Her supervisor was not at liberty to disclose customer medical information. Libby was convinced her supervisor was not a real live person. Libby had not felt at ease or that a real and caring human was there to help.

Libby was short for Liberty—Liberty Freedom Independence Adams. She wondered if her parents had used a baby name site, or just a thesaurus. The trend 20 years ago (and it was still going strong) was to name girls after admirable traits or ideas. Boys, go figure, still got regular names. Libby had lost track of the number of girls from her class named Humility or Chastity. One of her best friends from Elementary was named Modesty Anne Mae Garcia Jackson and worked at Hooters now.

Libby listened to her customer drone on about how every time he tried to watch Boat Babes on the auto-feed, his vision would get blurry. He had a lot to say, and it was mostly about the plot of Boat Babes. Libby reflected on the meaning of her own name and lamented that it hadn't imbued her with any special powers. "Do I have the *freedom* to tell a customer to get lost? Am I at *liberty* to walk up to a handsome man and say, 'Hey you... me... Bone town, let's go.' " Technically yes, but she didn't think her brain would let her approach a stranger and utter those words. She fantasized about what percentage of men would say yes and wished she had enough chutzpah to be the one to collect the data. How many would say yes to her versus someone more beautiful? Libby was perfectly average, 5'4", average build, not fat, not thin, brown skin, brown hair, brown eyes. The only thing special about her face were her dramatic eyebrows: full, dark, and perfectly arched like an eyebrow model. Libby thought, "Maybe she's born with it, maybe it's Maybelline. Screw you, Maybelline! I was definitely born with it, as is every model you've ever hired." She thought Boat Babes man would be a yes no matter who the woman was.

Libby yawned and managed an uh-huh every now and again while the man ranted. Every night, Libby had trouble sleeping because her brain kept obsessing over what she wanted to make, to build, to create; elaborate knitted sculptures, electrical wire candelabras, dinnerware made out of teeth. Her latest obsession was a sound bath experience where the listener is cocooned inside a giant snail shell. But each day after work, she was too tired, and instead spent her evenings binging space operas or playing 3-D crystal match on the interface. The weekends came and went and she never got anything off the ground. She had a few small half-finished projects here and there, but they were never as good as her imagination. A constant loop flowed through her thoughts: What if I'm not good enough? What if nobody likes it? What am I going to do with it once I make it? It was easier to just imagine she would be great one day than actually try and make it happen.

She wanted something to excite her, to get her blood flowing, maybe have sex, get a boyfriend. Something other than work and incessant procrastination. But like a wagon wheel in a deep rut, or someone who missed their exit on the turnpike, she couldn't change course. The clay had dried, the die was cast and there was no way out of her life other than death. She had considered this option a few times. Libby didn't like her parents very much, but she didn't have the heart to do that to them. As long as they were living it up at the Shady Palms in Borrego Springs, she would keep waking up every day to feed herself and talk people down from the ledge about the fact that the Boat Babes were blurry and they couldn't properly see the tits shaking.

Libby checked the interface, hoping it was time for lunch. She almost never left her apartment and her daily excursion out to lunch was one of the few things she had to look forward to each day. Once a week, she met her friend Patience, aka Pat, at Fry Mama Yum Yum. It wasn't great, but her budget didn't allow for much better. She knew she should save up and go to a nice place once a week, or even once a month, but at least leaving her apartment once a day prevented the darkness from creeping in; a darkness Libby didn't want to face.

Once, she had saved and splurged for her birthday. She and Pat went to Invasív, (pronounced En-VAH- seev, with a faux French accent) the hottest restaurant in Orlando. She couldn't believe the words coming out of her mouth when she ordered the GALS n' chips, but they were reviewed as being the best fried GALS anywhere and the chef personally recommended them. The shtick at Invasív was that the world famous (and famously handsome) Chef Javier came out to make personal recommendations to each guest as well as ask how they enjoyed their meal afterwards. Libby wondered how he had time to cook anything, but guessed that was what sous chefs were for. The GALS were crispy and delicious, perfectly fried with a spicy panko breading, the thistle-habanero remoulade to die for. She wanted to smear that sauce all over Chef Javier's lips and lick it off, a service that was not included in the restaurant experience. Libby thought it should be added to the menu.

Finally, it was time for lunch. Libby recommended a trip to the in-store service department to Boat Babes man, and as expected, he called her a useless twat, or some synonym of the sentiment, Libby had already tuned him out. Libby noticed a new GAL on the window and decided to just let it explore the apartment while she was gone, a decision she might come to regret.

Fry Mama smelled like greasy meat and a permeation of desperation —a super solution of sadness and hopelessness crammed into one tiny hole in the wall. At every table was a sad person eating alone, staring at their interface while they chewed. A trucker with a mullet let saliva trail down his chin, barely managing to keep the food inside his mouth. Libby knew the glistening on his cheeks was sweat but she couldn't help but think that his pores were exuding grease. She shuddered, reminded of the morning GAL rescue, and didn't want to think about eating snails now.

"I'll have the GALS n' chips," Libby ordered at the counter—old habits die hard. They were better than the lionfish burger anyway. She found a table and waved to Pat when she walked in. She had been friends with Pat since high school. They looked so much alike it was hard to tell them apart from a distance. But whereas Libby was floundering in her career and struggling to reach her goals, Pat was a promising PHD candidate on track to be a leading researcher in the field of implant connectivity and epi-genetic manipulation.

Soon they had their food and were catching up on the week's drama. The GALS were too greasy. Grease is slime adjacent, which made each bite an effort for Libby to swallow. She missed the thistle-habanero remoulade and Javier's bright white teeth smiling down at her. The Fry Mamma buffalo ranch and the man who couldn't keep his food in his mouth were poor substitutions. She did enjoy Pat's company though, and being out of the house was important to her mental health.

"Did you hear about that poor woman over in Dubsdread Heights?" Libby asked, shivering at the thought of how terrible the world could be.

"OMG, yes, I can't even imagine! She was so tired from being up all night, she just nodded off. The warm sun, a comfy chaise lounge, and ka-blam you wake up to find your baby being carted off by a 60-foot snake. I mean there is literally no way to recover from that," Pat said, a little too enthusiastically, Libby thought. They shared an awkward moment, both taking another bite of their GALS.

"Hey, how's the sound bath installation plan going?" Pat asked, dabbing a dollop of buffalo ranch from her lips.

"I gave up on that. I think I am going to focus my energies on this grant proposal to fund a set of crypto-zoological sculptures for a new Bigfoot experience that's opening in Arkansas," Libby said without a trace of sarcasm. She appreciated that Pat never called her out for being so full of shit. She supposed everyone was full of shit. That was just how the human digestive system as well as their goal setting vs. goal accomplishing systems worked.

"Who even are the arbiters of art... it seems so... well arbitrary," Pat mused.

"Yeah, I feel like your talent doesn't even matter—just if you know the right people." Libby replied. Pat nodded emphatically. Libby wondered if she agreed or just wanted to placate her. If Libby was really being honest with herself, she knew it wasn't just talent and knowing the right people... it was also actually putting in the work to create the art, and not just imagining it in her head.

"It's too bad my apartment GALS don't have magic wands they can wave and make me the next Banksy. Or better yet, magic slime. They crawl over your eyelids while you are asleep. Not only do you wake up with a dewy glow, but all your dreams have come true," Libby laughed

"Have you heard of Juste fais-le? Pat asked casually, taking a sip of her soda.

"No. What is it? Some new band?" Libby wiped the grease from her fingers and covered a half-eaten GAL body, stripped of its breading, with a napkin.

"It's a new protocol upgrade to existing implant software. It helps your brain process hesitancy."

"What the heck does that mean?"

"It helps people cross barriers of their own making. It doesn't make you do anything dangerous, but just helps you get over the fear of taking risks. Not physical risks, just like in business or... your personal life." Pat looked down, refusing to meet Libby's gaze. Once, when they were really drunk, Pat had kissed Libby, revealing that she was in love with her. Libby hadn't returned the sentiment but their friendship survived. It must have been mortifying for Pat.

"I know what you're thinking. Why would anyone want to go through the embarrassment of telling their best friend that they love them only to be rejected?" Pat said, her voice light and airy. She no longer felt any embarrassment. "Well, it was actually one of the best things I ever did. It freed me up from obsessing over you, and then I met Generosity. Gen's the best thing that ever happened to me, and better yet, you and I are still friends. I'm not sure that would have happened if I kept pining away for you, too afraid to say something."

Pat was encouraging her to do the same thing. Libby had always been afraid to do anything... everything. Maybe the upgrade would be worth it. Libby was so afraid, she was even afraid to consider getting the upgrade. Why was she so stuck on keeping her miserable life at exactly the same level of miserableness as it was yesterday? Libby sighed and thought, "Even though the door to the cage is open, I still won't fly out."

"It's like being *that* guy... the one who thinks he can do anything," Pat continued.

"I hate *that* guy. He's an asshole,"

"Yeah, a total wanker. But it won't make you into him—just able to take risks like him. It will give you the feeling that you can do anything, even if you can't. Afterwards, you realize it wasn't as scary or impossible as you thought. You can do things you are afraid to do." Pat let that statement linger in the air. Possibility mixed with the smell of fried GALS. Libby steeled herself for the big question.

"How much is it?" Libby asked, knowing it would cost a fortune and probably would only be compatible with the latest implants. She guessed she would need a hardware upgrade if she was going to install Juste fais-le.

"It's on the house. I know a guy at the company and he is looking for beta testers who are particularly reluctant. I immediately thought of you..." Pat smiled, letting Libby know not to take it too personally. "They'll upgrade your hardware and everything. Even pay for a deluxe medical recovery suite. Real live nurses and everything." Pat beamed.

Panic flooded Libby's system, like someone had let a thousand baby dragonflies loose in her veins. She now was confronted with the decision to actually change her life. If only she could get the protocol upgrade to help her take the risk to get the protocol upgrade. Still, she was sick and tired of not having a boyfriend and constantly peeling GALS off the window and hearing insults from customers. She was living in a world where snakes ate babies. What did she have to lose? It was time to make all of her dreams a reality and Just fais-le was the way to do it.

Libby woke up in the medical suite, a warm wetness between her legs. She hoped she hadn't peed herself on the operating table. Her mouth was dry and tasted like metal, her pits were hot and clammy. She needed a toothbrush and a shower.

"Hello, Liberty," the perky nurse chimed. Libby looked up and saw her clean white uniform and perfectly coiffed hair. When Pat had said "deluxe", she really meant it. "I'm sure you're feeling a little unfresh. Don't worry, a totally normal effect from the surgery. You'll be able to clean up in an hour or so, once the sutures have solidified. For now, have some water." The nurse handed Libby a paper cup. Libby sucked it down in three big gulps.

"When will it start working?" Libby asked, although she already knew the answer.

"It already is, my dear."

That was it--no more snaily apartment, no more unfinished projects, and no more Boat Babes guy calling her a twat. The first stop on her Libby Takes the World by Storm tour: Invasív. She was going to have

sex with Chef Javier. Libby followed the hostess to a seat near the
window. Pots dripping with string o' pearl succulents hung from the
ceiling. Oversized portraits of GALS, Burmese pythons and other
invasives covered the walls. Libby's heart fluttered, but she wasn't
afraid. The software was working like a charm. Javier approached to
tell her about the daily specials. His five o'clock shadow was more
likely 3 days' worth of growth, but the stubble accentuated his chiseled
jaw. His dark eyes sparkled as he flashed his winning smile at Libby.
After hearing all about where their python steaks were being harvested,
Libby was ready to order.

"I'll have the lionfish sashimi and...I was wondering if maybe you
wanted to go out after work?" Libby looked up at Javier, trying to give
her brightest smile. His smile vanished and his expression was one that
Libby could only describe as intense pity. He probably got asked out
all the time and had to turn down supermodels. Libby wasn't sure she
was still breathing.

"Oh, my sweet darling. I would love to, but I am happily married...to a man. I hope you enjoy the sashimi. It is divine with the
papaya gelée," he said and whisked himself away to the kitchen to save
Libby any more embarrassment. Her cheeks burned and she felt the
prickle of tears in her eyes. But she remembered the implant and sat
up a little straighter. She had done it! She had done something that
terrified her. A week ago, she would have felt embarrassed to even walk
in the front door alone, and now here she was, asking out Javier. He
had turned her down, but that didn't mean the implant was a failure.
As mortifying as the experience had been, she had survived it. She
could face the next failure and the next, she just had to keep going.
Eventually she would find success. She spent her lunch enjoying all of
the papaya gelée smothered on her fish and let her mind race to what
she would try next.

Libby stood between her fiancé Jack and Pat, looking at a portrait
of President Honor Washington made completely out of GAL shells.
The gallery was full of admiring patrons and Libby was relieved and
proud that the little red *sold* dot was on so many pieces. She was
engaged to a wonderful man, living in a two-bedroom bungalow with
a premium GAL retrofit near Park Lake. The implant upgrade had
worked wonders on her life. She wasn't sure where she would be now
without it. Either dead or still taking customer service calls in a GAL
infested studio.

"Hey, whatever happened to the roll-out for the Juste Fais-le? Libby asked Pat, surprised that she hadn't thought to ask sooner. "Why don't more people have it? I would have thought it would be in widespread use by now?" Libby asked, taking a sip of the sparkling wine from her plastic goblet. She couldn't help notice Pat give a furtive glance in Jack's direction.

"As it turned out, the results were inconsistent for particularly risk averse individuals. It didn't have a statistically significant effect on risk aversion in the sample pool." Pat said, refusing to meet Libby's eye.

"Hmmm, so weird. It worked so well on me. I was actually hoping they might come out with an upgrade. Maybe I could climb Everest or something, " Libby laughed. There was that look again, only this time it was Jack giving Pat the look.

"What? I could totally do it. It's not as high as it used to be anyway, what with sea level rise and everything. I think I could at least get to base camp," They all laughed. Libby was the last person anyone expected to climb Mt. Everest. Still she thought with time and training, she could probably do it. She just needed to set her mind to it and then not give up on her goals. The implant made anything possible. Why did Jack and Pat find the idea so unbelievable?

"The company lost funding, so there won't be an upgrade. Luckily the tech you have installed should last…as long as you need it too," Pat said softly. Libby reflected on the phrasing she chose. It was so odd. Still, she hadn't had any glitches with the software, so she didn't expect there to be a problem.

"A toast," Jack said, raising his little plastic champagne flute. "To Libby, for making her dreams a reality. "To Libby," Pat repeated. Libby thought they should really be toasting her implant, but at this point it was hard to know which was more responsible for making this night possible. It had gotten her started, but she was the one who hadn't given up when it got hard. She let the praise from the evening wash over her. She raised her glass and let it clink against the others and popped a sauteed GAL on a toothpick into her mouth with a grin.

Sara loves bird watching, iced tea, and finding out what happens at the end of a really good story. She lives in Los Angeles with her husband and 12 year old twins.

Cleaner Shrimp, Inc

by

Mike Morgan

JAY let the question slip out. "Why do you stay with me?" He was pretty sure Renee didn't love him.

She paused in her trek across the scales of the Behemoth, causing him to slow to a halt at her side. He saw her looking at him through the large globe of her helmet. "If you don't know, I can't tell you," was her answer.

He didn't know how to take that.

Eventually, she resumed her climb across the enormous creature's iron-silicate hide. Jay couldn't hear her boot magnets clamping on with each footfall, on account of the vacuum. He imagined they made a clumping sound. Each stride they took on the skin of the Behemoth was an exercise in caution. They didn't want to float off due to bad anchoring.

"There's a promising mass over here," she commed. "Let's drill this piece off."

That was the job, so he hauled the lance over to where she was standing on the stony, chondrite outcropping and fired up the cutting beam.

"Time to swap out."

Jay nodded and took back the plasma lance. He and Renee took turns at the drilling. They'd been at the rockface for half an hour now, as the old Earth clocks measured time. "You've got a nice chunk loose there."

She muttered a thankyou over her suit communicator.

"Not too deep," he continued. "Stopped at just the right depth." It was important not to cut too far down; the consequences of penetrating a Behemoth's outer shell were serious. For the humans doing the digging, that was. Not so much for the creature itself. "We're good little cleaner shrimp."

Renee merely grunted at the comment. He liked to joke they were cleaner shrimp. She tended to ignore him trotting out the feeble witticism these days.

The first time he'd made the joke Renee hadn't understood, not being the fan of nature documentaries Jay was. He'd explained how the crustaceans ate parasites off the outsides of various types of fish in Earth oceans. It was a form of symbiosis, an example of cooperation between species. Well, either that or a case of mutual selfishness that benefitted both parties. Which one you thought it was depended on how cynically you viewed the universe.

She'd seen the resemblance to what they were doing with the gigantic space-dwelling aliens, of course. Their chosen profession was to crew a cleaning station for Behemoths. Humans serving as cleaner shrimp, miniscule on the outer metal-rich plates of beasts thousands of meters in length. Hah ha, very funny. Seeing how unimpressed she was by the analogy, he'd changed the registered name of his inherited company to *Cleaner Shrimp, Inc.*

He could be difficult to put up with. He knew that. Somehow, she hung in there.

"I'll call in the drone."

Jay lifted a gloved hand in acknowledgement and rested, both boots securely anchored in place on the monster's rocky crust. He was exhausted from using the lance. The good news was they had enough cut free to fill the transporter drone's hull.

They used robots to carry the rock and ice back to the station. Robots were good for that. In the very early days, when this industry had started, Jay's father had tried using drones to do the mining. That hadn't worked out. Robots didn't have the knack; they hacked away without care. It was a skill, telling the difference between ring-matter and the Behemoth's own ferrous substance. Both looked similar, comprised of iron-studded stone formed in space: never melted, grainy in texture. Chondrite, it was called. Took a human in a spacesuit to do the work well.

So, that was Jay's life. Doing what robots couldn't. He'd continued his father's legacy, become one of the best. Having Renee at his side sure did help. He couldn't do it without her. Didn't have the strength. Not anymore, not now he was past middle age and not in the best of health. Renee was young, still in her prime. She did most of the drilling, if he was honest.

He wondered how much longer she'd stay with him.

He watched as the robot scooped up the results of their drilling. They were standing in a valley of sorts, where two of the creature's plates met. Above, Saturn and its many rings filled his view. The gas giant was framed left and right by the pale gray of the alien's inorganic flesh.

The rock-and-metal aliens swam between the stars, indistinguishable from asteroids most of the time. Only when they approached gas giants did they emerge from their slumber, dipping into the swirling outer clouds to feed and then fly free.

They were impressive, there was no denying that. They flew fast enough to escape the horrendous gravity of the worlds upon which they fed, executing dives that danced on the knife-edge of whether they could possibly reach escape velocity. They were compelled to feed to live; each dive risked them being pulled down to crush depth. A precarious existence.

Jay knew how that felt.

Most of the time, the aliens didn't need Jay's two-person team. Most of the time, they skimmed the upper mists of Saturn with no problems at all. Sometimes, though, they collided with ice and rock in the rings. Sometimes they picked up detritus. The extra mass irritated them, he assumed. Maybe it itched. Maybe it threw off their center of gravity, made steering true more difficult. Whatever the reason, the Behemoths wanted rid of the ring-waste they picked up.

That was, he guessed, why they let humans drill the accumulated ring-ice and rock free. They circled Saturn, aiming for the small cluster of spinning capsules where the humans huddled in the deep dark, and then lined up to have the seams between their body-plates chiseled.

The humans kept the station in the same orbit, so the creatures could navigate back to it every few months. It was important to make it easy for the beasts to find them. Once they'd realized the human colonists could remove the impact debris, they returned time and again. Placid, even docile, so long as the drills didn't cut too deep, they let the microscopic organisms pick at their skins.

While the aliens' motives for cooperating were up for debate, the reason for the miners taking the risk was no mystery. The station needed ice, specifically melted ice for drinking water, and extracting it from creatures parked right outside used up a whole lot less fuel than travelling to the rings on collection runs.

Mining the interstellar wanderers made life in orbit around Saturn a lot easier. So far, the colonists' luck had held. Forty-seven years the orbital settlement had been at this, and the creatures hadn't collided with the station yet. An accident like that would end their newfound arrangement in an instant.

A precarious existence, indeed. A truth both the aliens and humans shared.

Living in space was like performing a high-wire act across a canyon, thought Jay. Everything could go great step after step, and you'd get confident as all get out. Then winds could come out of nowhere in a heartbeat and ruin everything.

Snuggled up next to Renee in the narrow cot of their cabin on Labroides Station, that was the way to review business accounts. The warmth of her body made going over the figures almost bearable. Jay's contentment evaporated upon reaching the end of the ledger on his tablet, though—the total profit figure for the month enough to force a grunt of disgust from him.

Renee muttered, "Is it bad?" Her voice was muffled on account of her head being half-stuffed under a pillow.

"It's been better."

"We're working twelve-hour shifts. Why are we making less money than normal?"

He could guess the cause. Maximillian Plover. Their chief competitor. He was hiring on hands, increasing the scale of his operation. Using deep pockets to sell ice at a price that undercut Jay.

"He'll run us out of business, if we're not careful."

Renee knew who Jay was talking about. It wasn't the first time Plover's underhanded tactics had come up. "That sum'a'bitch. What we gonna do?"

"I'll think of something."

She lifted her head, blinking seep-rimmed eyes. "Your pa spent his life building this company. You can't let—"

"I'll think of something," he insisted. "Just don't know what yet."

They needed to mine Behemoths for something more valuable than ice. That was the crux of the matter.

Sure, the boulders they brought back were laced with iron as well as carbonaceous rock containing a waxy mixture of amino acids that had formed in the interstellar medium, and that organic compound could be heated to create a kind of kerosine. The metal and the pseudo-oil were useful; Jay certainly sold them as a supplemental income stream to his fellow settlers. Maximillian Plover did as well. Again, he sold them at a lower price, curse him.

Jay needed to try something new. Even if it was dangerous.

Over their typical breakfast of squeeze-tube flavored microbial paste, he said to Renee, "You ever hear of how birds clean alligator teeth?"

"Here you go again. You been watching more of your shows?"

Actually, he'd read it in a journal about animal behavior. Man had to have a hobby.

"I was thinking we could take a leaf outta their book."

She met his gaze while sucking on the last of her breakfast tube. "Are you suggesting we apply the same principle to Behemoths?"

Jay nodded.

"Not bad enough we pick at their skin, now we gotta clean their teeth?"

He resisted the urge to point out Behemoth mouths were filled with structures more like whale baleen than actual teeth. He wanted to steer their conversation in a more important direction. "There are those weird spectroscope readings from their heads. The ones the survey drones recorded years ago. Thought we should see what's there. Could be valuable."

She put her empty tube down. "Remind me why your pa never did that?"

"He figured venturing inside an alien's mouth would be certain death."

"He did. I remember now. Widespread opinion hereabouts. Yeah, that's the consensus, right enough."

"We've ignored the survey results for decades. Maybe it's time to do something about them."

"Those results were inconclusive."

"They were odd. Evidence of mineralized aluminum oxide, beryl, chromium, vanadium, all where they are unlikely to exist."

"Data's probably wrong, then."

He put down his own empty tube. "We have to try. I don't know how much longer we can keep going otherwise."

"Sticking our heads in the lion's mouth can't be the answer."

"The thought of Plover winning is what sticks in my craw."

She let out the longest sigh he'd ever heard. "Going from human exfoliator to human toothbrush ain't that much of a career change, I guess." It was fortunate they didn't have a high opinion of their own importance. Their line of work was tough on the ego.

"You're in?"

"Well, you can't do it without me. Just tell me this—how confident are you we won't get chewed up in those giant jaws?"

He licked dry lips. "I'm reasonably certain Behemoths will be able to tell we're helping." He shrugged. "They don't have any means of cleaning their mouths. Maybe they'll be grateful."

Renee let out a snort. "Glad we'll be wearing helmets. Creatures that ain't never scrubbed their teeth—gotta figure their breath's bad."

She took hold of his hand before he could interrupt. "Promise me this'll be worth it."

He answered honestly. "No idea what we'll find there. But if we don't look, how will we ever know whether we could've beaten Plover?"

Jewels. That's what they found once they'd clambered inside the next Behemoth's slack jaws. Rubies and emeralds and opals and God-only-knew what else. Each one was the size of a clenched fist. There were hundreds within the pool of illumination cast by their suit lights alone. Jay could hardly believe what he was seeing.

The jewels were lodged in the broad vertical filaments of the creature's oral sieve. Near as scientists could determine, Behemoths scooped up gases from Saturn's upper atmosphere. The towering strands of the quasi-baleen were there to block out anything indigestible. Gemstones precious beyond comprehension had not been on Jay's list of things he'd expected Behemoths filtered out.

"Okay, it was worth it," admitted Renee.

"It'll be worth it if we get out alive." Jay stepped slowly closer to the wall of upright strands. He didn't know what reaction he'd provoke stepping on the inside of the creature's mouth. The gray ground appeared stable. All he could see was the small area lit up by his suit—the rest of the vast space was pitch black. He was in uncharted territory and no mistake.

"Careful."

He blinked at Renee through the transparent bubble of his helmet. She hissed, "Sorry," and he continued.

With a gentle tug, he pulled the nearest ruby clear. He was glad of the weightlessness of the environment; it made holding the massive gem possible. It would take both of them to carry it once aboard the station. First, they had to get it past the other miners working on the alien's skin. They were Plover's men, and Jay didn't want them to see what he and Renee had discovered.

Still no reaction from the Behemoth. If anything, its hundred-meter-long jaws widened.

"Yeah, you know we're friends," said Renee. "We'll get these nasty specks of grit outta your feeding grill. It'll be our pleasure."

"Where did you get that?" fumed Max Plover.

The station marketplace was loud, but Jay had no difficulty hearing his rival's voice over the hubbub. Word had clearly gotten around of the remarkable item *Cleaner Shrimp, Inc.* was selling.

"Came across it on my travels."

"Better not have been on my Behemoth."

Renee smirked at that outrageous statement. "Yours? Didn't realize you staked ownership of 'em. Do they know they're your property?"

"They're mobile hunks of rock," he snarled. "I lay claim to anything found on the ones my crews work." He stabbed a finger at the ruby again. "You better not have happened across that on the beast outside right now."

"Can't rightly recall which Behemoth it was on," lied Jay.

Plover's eyes reduced to slits as he thought over what he was seeing. "There may be more." He rounded on Jay. "What valuation did you get on that jewel?"

Jay reckoned there was no harm in sharing the number, so he did.

Plover's face went as gray as the rock on a Behemoth's hide.

Renee piped up. "Once we find a buyer, I think this'll push our accounts back in the black. We're here for the long haul, way I see it." She smiled at Plover in a way that made Jay's heart sing.

Plover's annoyance didn't last nearly as long as Jay had hoped. The wretched man straightened and sniffed at them. "Driving you into bankruptcy hardly matters now. Where there's one jewel like this, there's another, and another. I only need locate the source. Then I can take the remainder for myself. Enjoy your minor victory. Mine will result in considerably greater wealth."

"How exactly you gonna find where it's from?" laughed Renee.

The sneering businessman replied as he strutted away. "Drones film everything in the vicinity of the Behemoths. The route you took will be on a recording somewhere. I doubt it'll take me more than a few minutes to figure out where you went, you blithering cretins."

Jay glanced at Renee to find she was looking back at him.

"Well, shit," was her considered analysis.

By the time Jay and Renee sold the ruby and returned to the Behemoth's gaping mouth, Plover had worked it out. He was already there, with thirty of his men for good measure. It seemed Jay was not going to succeed in snagging a second windfall before losing his monopoly.

"That jewels of exquisite purity form inside gas giants has been known for centuries," crowed Plover. "Getting them out, that's always been the problem. A problem that, until today, was regarded as insurmountable." He laughed. Jay figured the laugh was directed straight at him. "Thanks to your willingness to do the unthinkable, it is now a problem with a solution!"

"Glad I could help," he commed back, spacesuit to spacesuit. "How about we go in as equal partners on this operation?"

Plover waved a glove, dismissing the notion. "Don't be ridiculous. This is mine, and mine alone." He turned to stare up at the wall of the creature's baleen. Jewels glinted in the glow cast by the lights he'd ordered brought in. "At first, I couldn't understand how the creatures scooped up the gems—they form so deep in the atmosphere, you see. Deeper than the aliens ever go. Then it came to me. Once created through the enormous pressures at the lower depths, the jewels are carried higher by the planet's unceasing currents. High enough to lodge in these brutes' gullets. The process is simple enough to fathom, really, when you apply an intellect such as I possess."

Renee patted the golden material on Jay's arm to get his attention. He followed her gaze. Plover's crew were scaling the tall columns of baleen and gouging out the jewels with picks.

"Remember where we are, Plover. You might wanna tell your guys to be a mite gentler."

"We're doing it a favor! Unclogging its mesh. You showed us, Jay. You demonstrated how safe this was." He continued in a quieter voice. "All this time, a fortune right under our noses. How tremulous we were, and how baseless was our caution. You showed us, Jay. Fortune favors the bold."

Jay took Renee's hand and led her backward, closer to the ridge that marked the Behemoth's lip.

"When it comes to lifeforms larger than most stations, fortune favors the respectful, Plover, which you ain't."

The businessman spat, "Coward. You lack the courage of your own convictions."

One of his workers called, "Sir? There's a huge emerald stuck deep here. Must be worth an emperor's ransom. Request permission to cut it loose with a lance."

"Permission granted. Fire away."

"Run," said Jay. "That man's the blithering cretin."

Renee argued with neither the running nor the assessment of Plover's intelligence.

They used grappling hooks to hold onto the creature's exterior. It was the only way to avoid being thrown clear. The alien was thrashing in a manner they'd never seen before. For what it was worth, this was one Behemoth that was unlikely to let humans scrub its mouth clean again.

Jay lost track of how long they clung to outside of the giant's jaw. Minutes certainly, as these things were measured on a world he barely remembered.

After he'd decided the tumult would never end, the creature's spasms finally subsided.

"You okay?" asked Renee.

"Still here," he replied once he'd finished checking all his body parts were still where they were meant to be.

"That's all I ask."

He considered what had happened. "I guess we don't have a competitor anymore."

"I guess not."

"And I guess, should we get tired of fetching ice, we can mine jewels whenever we like. So long as we're gentle."

"I guess so," she concurred.

"You know, Renee, other than the near-death part of the day, it hasn't been entirely terrible."

He thought he heard her say, "You make me smile," but he wasn't certain. Her voice was very faint over comms.

"You say something, Renee?"

She replied louder, "You remember, couple of days back, you asked why I stay with you?"

He said, "Uh-huh." He did recall the conversation.

"And I said how if'n you didn't know I couldn't tell you."

He repeated the "Uh-huh."

"Well, I'll give you a clue, Jay. I figure you deserve that much." She dared letting go of the rocky surface and hauled herself into a crouch, still anchored by her boots and the rope attached to the hook.

Then, she jerked her thumb in the direction of the beast's snapped-shut maw. "Because you ain't like Plover, Jay. Because you ain't like him."

He let his brain wrap itself around her words. Then he said, "How about we call it a day and crawl into our cot, Renee?"

"Yeah," she said, "and that's the other reason. Because you have some really great ideas. That one there, Jay, it's a doozy."

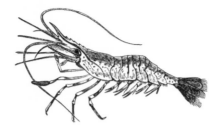

Mike Morgan was born in London, but not in any of the interesting parts. He moved to Japan at the age of 30 and lived there for many years. Nowadays, he's based in Iowa, and enjoys family life with his wife and two young children. If you like his writing, be sure to follow him on Twitter where he goes by @CultTVMike or check out his website, PerpetualStateofMildPanic.wordpress.com.

Narcissa, Her Dog, and the Diary

by

Jennifer Jeanne McArdle

FEBRUARY 14
   My sister gave me a diary before I left for Hapira. I haven't used it until now, though we've been here a few months already. Writing is good for managing stress, but I've never been very good at it. I like the smell of that thick glue that binds this book together; it's extra strong in the lab because the environment is kept super clean and at optimum humidity. But it's not totally sterile because humans need some microbes in our air.

(Also, there's a lot of dog hair, even with little robots that chase after it, clean it up.)

Samira gave Lev a rose earlier today. I forgot it's Valentine's Day. Lev said he forgot, too, because he doesn't like Samira back. Samira's gift *was* pretty oblivious. This is Lev's second time on Hapira. He used to work for a different company. Half of his team got exposed to an air leak in the lab, and now they're gone. One of Lev's former crewmates is now a vine resembling pink roses, of all things. They grow along the window near the south exit of our lab.

I wonder about Samira, how she made it this far in her career if she's such an airhead—you meet people like that sometimes. I live in a 3,000 sq. meter complex with her that I can't leave without a special protective suit, and I still don't know.

"Are we going to go outside today?" Patches, my dog, is always asking me and the answer is usually, "No!" because it takes too long to get the protective suits on her and me. All of the dogs have adapter collars that translate their thoughts into understandable speech. Sometimes I wanna turn them off, but I guess that's kind of rude isn't it?

Back to that rose. Why would you ever think anyone here would want a flower of any kind? Outside, all you can find is flowers: puffy ones, spikey ones, long ones, blooms shaped like hearts, and petals shaped vaguely like bats, etc. Once I leave here, I don't think I'll even want to see a flower for a year.

February 15

Esther is our project manager—she's been at Tanith for ages and has a not-quite-mean-but-brusque attitude of someone who's seen everything already. She plans to retire once this assignment is finished.

"We've got to get at least thirty more data sheets in this week or we won't meet our weekly goal," Esther reminds us over coffee. A many-petaled orange flower bloomed overnight and shaded half the window behind her. It distracted me from really listening to what she was talking about, but the resident sycophant, Raphael, was diligently typing her every word. Raphael is actually her son but kind of a shit scientist, so I guess he has to prove he's here for some reason other than nepotism. His dog, Medusa, a fluffy brown Chow Chow, whines, showing off her teeth. She doesn't talk often, but when she does, it's usually to tell everyone else to stay away from Raph.

Some background on our project: Hapira is a planet densely covered in red, yellow, orange, and pink flowers and fungus. Tanith Co, a pharmaceutical company, set up a laboratory here to gather data about life on the planet. The goal is to eventually develop medicines that make human cells more resilient and long-lived. Patches and I are part of a seven-person (and three-dog) research team from Tanith conducting research. I am the youngest member of the team.

"I don't understand. The totals don't make sense," Lev spoke up. "Pia's been working late every night. We have to have logged enough data this week."

Trials and trials and trials. We wake up early, we check on the ongoing experiments: the machines testing the chemicals, the things growing in the greenhouse and the outdoor garden. We fix issues. We run new tests. We record data, and we send that data off to corporate. Lev is right. Pia often works late. It's true that we're not developing any formulas yet. But we aren't expected to develop anything yet; we were told to just collect as much data as we can about human cells on Hapira over a six-month period. Month four started yesterday.

"Perhaps we shouldn't be relying on one woman to do most of our work for us. Some of us need to work faster." She, her son, and even their snobby dog glanced at me for a brief second. It's silly because Pia is a genius. No one works as fast as she does, and none of the other people on this project were selected with the expectation that we would be doing as much science, or as innovative science, as Pia is capable of.

Esther is here to manage, her son for admin (I guess), Lev because he has experience dealing with the hardships of working on Hapira, Troy to keep morale up, me to learn, and Samira…? I'm not sure. I guess we needed a seventh person. Esther, who, deep down is kind of a softy, probably felt bad no other managers wanted Samira, so she agreed to take the dingbat.

After the meeting, I went back to work. Pia had to go wash her hands and walk the length of the hallway a few times—even with all the breaks she takes, she gets more work done than the rest of us. Pia takes a lot of medication to manage her anxiety—I don't know much about what she's diagnosed with. It's not my business. Patches, though she's my dog, likes to follow Pia when she's pacing.

"Good steps. I like walk on two legs," is what Patches tells her every time, and I think Pia really likes to hear it. Patches, too, enjoys the routine. Pia wears her anxiety on her sleeve. But we all feel it.

It's hard to live on a planet that's so hostile—or maybe it's overly welcoming. Everything living and carbon based on Hapira, the plants, fungi, bacteria, protists, and viruses, works in harmony. When a life form that isn't balanced with the system is exposed to Hapira's ecosystem, like humans and dogs, everything works to integrate it. Hapira's life alters the alien cells, ripping apart and re-writing the DNA until the alien animal is transformed into a local flora.

February 16

Days on Hapira are about three hours longer than those on Earth. It makes me think of my grandmother, who always looked frazzled by housework, even with the helper robots trailing behind her.

"Never enough time in the day," she used to tell me with her hands on her hips, her hair frizzing out in all directions.

But longer days don't mean we have any more time in our lives, just that our rhythms are always a little off. The out-of-whack time gets to you after a while, along with the cramped space and threat of Hapira's flowers—I'm looking forward to the end this assignment. I was excited when I first got placed here. Hapira brings up so many questions, but no one cares about science for the sake of discovery anymore; everyone just wants to make money.

Outside my window, there are little clear stalks of fungi with black tips. They glow a light blue at night. I was drawing one and coloring it in with a robin's-egg-blue crayon (I didn't tell the others I brought crayons; they already make fun of me because I'm only 24 and still working towards my doctorate).

Suddenly I heard the sound of an explosion.

"DANGER DANGER," Medusa the dog's collar shouted as her feet thudded down the hallway. I got to my doorway in time to see her zoom past me. Patches leaned against my knee.

"Scared," her collar said. She whimpered, for emphasis. I looked down at her, and she tilted her head, her one floppy ear shaking, the straight ear bent towards the sound. When we got to the machine room, we saw that one of the machines running our tests had exploded and was covered with black soot. Luckily, nothing else was damaged.

"Narcissa," Raphael shouted at me. "Wasn't this the machine you were working on? Why didn't you do final diagnostics before leaving for the night?"

"I forgot once, weeks ago." I crossed my arms. Patches sat on one of my feet. "But check the logs. I never forget anymore."

"This is gonna put us even more behind." Esther's gray hair was loose for once, a ball of frizz surrounding her head, like my grandmother's. A blue light behind her made her look like a banshee. Raphael went to the main computer and verified what I said.

"Sometimes things break just because," Lev interjected. "Especially on Hapira. It happened with my last team."

"I guess we should just clean this up the best we can." Samira forced a smile. "Arguing about what happened on no sleep isn't going to help anything."

Troy was already gathering the cleaning supplies.

February 17

Today was not a good day. As much as I think the guy is a weirdo, I feel bad for Raphael. Esther was usually the first one to wake up every morning. We often found her sipping her coffee and looking out the large bay window in the dining area, the three dogs, who normally don't get along, calmly staring outside.

It must be so boring for them, really, with no insects or little critters to watch, just the bursts of pollen from fast growing fungus stalks. Why does a planet without pollinators need brightly colored flowers? Is it an evolutionary hold-over or perhaps the whole planet is a big flower and aliens are meant to be the pollinators... or prey?

Patches woke me up.

"Esther, dead." Her collar repeated the phrase over and over again. I couldn't understand it for a few moments. My brain was putting blocks together that wouldn't stay stuck.

Then I went to the dining room. Esther, her hair tied neatly and wearing her lab coat, was slumped over the table. Raphael had his arms around Medusa, holding his dog tightly. I could see the whites of her very open eyes as we each entered the room and came upon the scene.

"Raph, what happened?" Lev finally asked. Raph took a few seconds to respond before he leaned back from the dog, his eyes red and hair looking extra greasy.

"Someone poisoned her coffee. She's dead. I tested the coffee already. Kanapsis." Kanapsis is a poisonous flower first discovered on Roggets, a small colony some light-years from here. I had to look it up before I wrote today's entry. The poison is odorless, tasteless. Almost instantly deadly. It's pretty rare and most people have never heard of it. But we live in a lab with astro-botanists and chemists.

Raphael rubbed his eyes and stood up, stepping on Medusa in the process. She yelped, but Raphael didn't apologize. "Which one of you assholes did this?" he asked, his normally high-pitched voice coming out very low. "Which one of you dared? What do you get out of killing her?"

He started walking back and forth. "You idiots are mad she wanted you to work harder, huh? Was it you, you paranoid, little freak?" He pointed towards Pia. "You are smart enough to know about Kanapsis, unlike the rest of these idiots—"

Lev stepped forward and grabbed Raph's arm. "Man, don't bother her. You need to calm down."

Medusa started growling, her haunches up. Raph yanked his arm away from Lev. "Don't touch me, you bastard."

The dog jumped at Lev, pushing him against the wall. It was snapping at his face, Lev pushing her back with one hand and protecting his face with the other. Before the rest of us could act, he punched the animal's big head. She whined and fell back, but now Raph was lunging at Lev, a shock-baton in his hand, he smashed it into Lev's face. His thin body shook, wildly. Samira screamed. Troy rushed forward and grabbed Raph's shoulders, squeezing him tightly.

"Stop," he commanded, his normally soft voice reverberating through the walls. Raph struggled but couldn't break free. Lev was still tremoring. Samira rushed to his side. He was gasping, his face turning blue.

"Help me get him to the infirmary!" Samira shouted. I pushed Medusa out of the way. Patches followed us to the infirmary. We got him onto an operating table. Samira attached heart monitor sensors to his wrist; the machine emitted a low singular beep.

I scanned the room for the portable defibrillator.

"What need?" Patches's collar voiced with its robotic trill. I couldn't get distracted trying to explain a piece of tech in terms a dog would understand. I opened a cabinet, frantically pulling supplies out. "What need?" she repeated as she pressed her wet nose into my back. I finally found one, a blue and red disk, still in the clear packaging—we obviously didn't pay attention to all of our safety protocols when we first set up the base. All of these medical supplies should have been set up already.

Troy was in the room now, I could hear his hard breathing as he performed CPR on Lev's chest. After I frantically ripped the packaging off the device, Samira grabbed it from my hand and turned it on. It whirred awake and lit up. She pushed Troy to the side, pulled Lev's shirt collar down and pressed the device into his chest. His body convulsed a couple of times, and then the heart monitor began to beep.

We all took a deep breath. I reached down and sunk my fingers into Patches's soft fur.

"Lev, ok?" she asked.

The machine stopped its regular beeping. Samira slammed the device onto Lev's chest.

Again.

Again.

Again.

Finally, Troy put his hand on Samira's back. Sweat had soaked through her shirt. Her long hair was plastered to the side of her small face. Pia hiccupped and started crying.

"Lev, dead?" Patches asked me. I kneeled and hugged her. I looked up to see Raph in the doorway, his own dog leaned against his legs.

"I didn't mean to kill him," he whispered. "I—"

"Tensions are very high right now," I spoke up. Normally I don't like to make waves as I'm the lowest ranking team member, but they all know each other better and are more emotional. "I think before we start accusing each other of one thing or another, we need to take a beat before—"

"We should put the bodies away. So they don't start smelling. Narcissa, can you help me?" Troy interrupted. The atmosphere in the lab was sealed to the outside but the air still had Earth microbes. Decomposition would start to happen to some degree. And the dogs...

We stood awkwardly for a few moments, until finally everyone left the room, except for Troy, and me, and our dogs. We found bag big enough for a body and put Lev's body inside and then carried it into our walk-in freezer. For now. Then Troy and I went to the cafeteria and did the same with Esther's body while Raphael watched us. I know it's gross, but we didn't expect anyone to die. That wasn't the kind of mission we were on. I guess we expected our dead to just turn into plants or mushrooms, like the rest of Lev's old team.

Hapira was supposed to be the enemy.

But now two of us have been murdered. Patches's collar keeps just saying, "sad," "confused." I played with her with a ball in my room to distract her.

February 18

Last night, I couldn't sleep. The dog was antsy, too. She kept kicking me and moving around the bed. So I got up. I didn't put Patches's collar on because I didn't want her making too much noise. First, we paced around the lab a bit, just getting rid of excess energy, then, after I built up my courage, I held my breath and opened the door to the cafeteria. On the floor was the shock-baton that Raph had used on Lev. I crouched low to look at it. I can't believe he just left it there, but I noticed that the dial was turned up to a lethal setting.

So maybe he *did* mean to kill Lev. It's hard to say. It's also possible he didn't realize. But then I remembered a conversation I had with Raph, ages ago. He had been grilling me about my education. I said I'd studied and worked in an astro-botanical lab back on Earth's moon last year. He told me everyone else on the team had done their field work on colonies on other planets. He mentioned that he'd spent time on Roggets, the colony where Kanapsis grows. Would Raph have poisoned his own mother?

I went to Troy's room first, quietly knocked on the door and told him we needed to talk. Luckily, Bouvergard isn't a loud dog and didn't start barking. We then went to Samira, and finally Pia, who looked like she hadn't slept at all.

"We have to confront him," Samira told us.

"Has anyone contacted corporate yet?" I asked. "We need to get off this planet."

"I've already called." We heard a voice from the doorway to Pia's room. It was Raphael.

"We all know you meant to kill Lev," Samira shouted.

"Samira, no. Don't start fights." Pia put her hands over her ears.

"I didn't mean to kill him." Raph squeaked.

"Narcissa saw that the shock-baton was turned up to lethal—"

"What if Narcissa is lying? What do we even know about her, huh?"

"You're the only one who studied on Roggets. Do you know how hard it is to get Kanapsis in other places?" Troy's voice was hushed, almost a whisper.

"How do you know it's hard to buy Kanapsis?" Raph was hugging himself. Medusa let out a low growl. "Do you have a habit of trying to buy poisons?"

"Raph—you can't pretend like this all isn't suspicious. You were the first one to find your mother's body."

"Dammit. I'll make things easy, all right? Medusa and I will leave. I know from Lev that there's an old lab that's empty but still running a five kilometer walk from here. The protective suits should last the dog and me long enough to walk there. Corporate has already been called. Check the log. They're sending someone to get us, but it will take five days. I'll wait for them at the other lab. I won't get murdered, and if you all murder each other, it's not my problem."

Nobody argued with him because—well, I can't speak for everyone —but, I thought him leaving was for the best, to keep the tension down. I was relieved when I heard the buzzing and whirring, and scanners beep as one sealed door after another opened and let Raph and his dog out onto the planet.

February 19

I realized that no one even checked to see if Raph was lying about contacting corporate. So I checked the logs and confirmed. Someone killed Esther. That's all I can think about. Why would Raph kill his own mother? It didn't make sense.

"We have to get everything ready for corporate as best we can," Samira told us before we could even talk about what had happened. "Or they'll fire us."

Jobs are hard to come by nowadays. Scientists are a dime a dozen, though most of them aren't particularly talented. And a lot of the menial jobs are automated. Some colonies and countries just pay people to live, you don't have to work, but you have to get into those places. For someone like me and the others working for Tanith, losing a job meant losing even our right to live on any decent planet or country, too.

As part of our experiments in the outdoor gardens, we put various types of human cells treated with different chemicals in the outdoor growing spaces. Most had completely transformed, but some had managed to retain human features; leaves tipped with hard fingernails, stalks with patches of human flesh color, and human veins transported alien liquids inside the clear fungal bodies.

There was a problem, though. The remote-control robots we use to do most of the work in the outdoor gardens weren't responding.

"Do you think Raphael sabotaged these?" Troy asked the rest of us.

"I can't tell how to fix them. I can't concentrate on making repairs now." Pia was scratching her arms a lot. I could see all the harsh marks on her skin.

"Then let's just suit up and collect what we can. Better to collect some samples than lose all of them."

It took an hour for me and Patches to get into the protective suits. Each section of the suit had to be tested, then put on, then sealed. I kept missing steps and having to start from the beginning. But carelessness would lead to infection. I kept hearing Lev's voice in my head. And Esther's.

"Corporate won't be happy."

They were dead. Raph was gone. Even that bitch, Medusa, and her little whines. Gone.

When I finally was ready, Pia was leaned against the doorway, tapping her hand on the wall.

"Pia, are you ok? Do you wanna stay back?"

"No. We've got to collect as much as possible. I can't be fired. I'll lose access to my meds."

We worked for hours, in the oppressive humidity under bits of harsh sunlight that leaked through the floral canopy, collecting samples in sealed containers, getting disinfected, refilling our air, getting water, opening and closing all those damn doors, and then going back out again. Pia fainted at some point in the afternoon. I helped get her back on her feet. I made her go inside. We took off our suits.

"Can you go to my room and get me some of my pills? I left one out on the nightstand." she asked me.

I got her medicine and water, which she greedily swallowed. Her lips were so chapped and the circles around her eyes were so dark.

"You need to lie down," I advised and took her to her room.

"Keep an eye on her, Patches." As much as I wanted the dog with me for comfort, just getting my own suit back on was going to take a while. This time, I got the suit on faster and went back out to work for another couple of hours with Samira and Troy. The work was mind numbing. Testing the sample a final time. Putting the sample in a container. Sealing the container. Putting it next to the door. Carrying a few containers inside at a time. This planet is too damn quiet. No bugs. No birds, just the sound of a slight breeze, the slight whistle and rattle of wind through leaves and the soft explosions of pollen bursting into the air. I heard each of our footsteps, the fabric of our suits swishing, and the canisters opening and closing so sharply.

We stopped, finally, when the sun started going down.

"That's enough for today. Let's shower and eat," Troy told me and Samira.

We got back into the lab and showered. Patches wasn't there to greet me, which was odd. Bouvergard was pacing around, but he didn't have his collar on.

"Should we tell Pia we're eating?" I asked. We decided to go together, but as we got closer, we could hear weeping from the room. "Pia?" I called to her and knocked on her door. "Patches?"

"Pia sick," I heard from Patches's collar. "Patches scared. Very scared. Not move scared."

"Shit." Samira said behind me. "Pia, open the door." The electronic locks had been disabled but it felt like she had physically blocked the door.

She screamed. We heard a loud noise.

The dog collar yelled: "Stop!"

"I won't let you kill me," came a guttural noise vaguely resembling Pia's voice.

"Her meds must not be working," I suggest, but honestly maybe she was behaving rationally, given the fact that a few of us had *actually* been killed.

"Maybe not. We shouldn't leave her alone. Stand back, Pia. We're coming in." Troy tilted his head, suggesting we move out of his way. If my dog weren't locked in there with Pia, I'd have advised we leave her in her room. She could also be the killer, yeah?

So, I moved out of the way of Troy. He took a few steps back and then he charged his big body forward, right shoulder first, grunting as he smashed the door once.

He charged a second time, and this time, the door flew back, sending a chair flying. Patches yelped. But Pia was waiting for Troy. We heard her wail again. I couldn't exactly see what happened, but Troy screamed, too, and then he backed up a few steps. A brown liquid covered his face, dripping down his neck. I couldn't think for a few moments, the fluorescent light in the room shining through the smoke rising from his skin, the sounds of crying, screaming, yelping, *chaos* echoing far away in my ears. I felt I was drifting away. Disassociating. Losing myself.

"Narcissa!" Samira's voice rang loud. "Go make sure Pia doesn't have more acid. I'm taking Troy to the infirmary."

What?

She said my name again. I felt a wet nose on my hand. I tried to concentrate on what was in front of me. Pia was crouched in a tiny ball on the floor.

"I'm sorry," she was muttering to herself. "I thought he had come to kill me." I crouched next to her, careful to avoid the traces of the acid spilled on the floor.

"Pia..." I whispered.

"I can't. Nars... I don't know what's going on anymore."

My head was swimming. Finally, Pia stopped crying, and we sat in silence for a few moments.

"Most of my pills are gone. Someone took them. I skipped my morning dose and just took the one you gave me. Do you think Troy will be okay?"

Troy wasn't okay. Samira did the best she could to clean off the acid, but a lot of him had been burned. She got him on an IV, and he was in a coma.

"Can you leave the dogs with me tonight?" Pia asked. I didn't want to. Bouvergard should be with Troy.

But Samira answered for me. She said yes. Why should we trust Pia with the dogs?

February 20

Today wasn't a good day. Troy died. We couldn't save him. Pia insisted she needed the dogs to stay with her today, too. Samira said we should try to collect some of the samples in the indoor greenhouse. I only lasted a couple of hours. I kept worrying about Patches. What if Pia hurt Patches?

"We're going to get fired if we don't get everything set up for when corporate comes," Samira warned me.

"What is wrong with you? Three people are dead. Raph probably turned into a plant out there. Who cares about Tanith? We've already majorly screwed everything up. Our equipment keeps getting destroyed. At this point, boxing up more samples and experiments for them isn't going to mean shit. I'm getting the dogs."

"You can't take the dogs from Pia!"

Samira and I argued. I eventually took Patches but left Bouvergard. His collar kept repeating: "Sad."

I took the collar off. I figured it might set Pia off. I pet him, shaking his floppy ears back and forth.

"I'm sorry," I told the big oaf.

I stayed in my room for the rest of the day. I don't trust Pia and Samira enough right now to walk around while they're awake.

As I'm writing, Patches keeps looking at our bedroom door.

"Bouvergard smell strange," Patches's collar said just now and then she tilted her head back to look at me.

"Strange? How strange?"

"Strange. Not good."

Even with the collar, dogs can't explain everything in ways we can understand. Sometimes I think, maybe we should have a scent collar that lets us experience the world as they do, let us swim in thousands of tiny aromas.

It's funny. When I was first studying botany, we learned about symbiotic relationships, how lichens are really multiple species of life across kingdoms that work together in order to survive in the harshest of environments. Various species vastly different from one another working mutually together underpins Earth's entire ecosystem.

But what about dogs, the fungus to humanity's algae, in the lichen of our civilization? Together for thousands and thousands of years. To build what? Everything can and does colonize, growing and growing. We, too, are grotesque and weird life, by someone's metric.

I keep writing, but I don't feel any better.

February 21

An alarm ringing through the whole laboratory woke me up after just a few hours of sleep. I felt a pit in my stomach. It was the alarm for a breach, meaning, one of the walls or doors or windows had been broken, and Hapira was leaking into the lab. I went to my wall computer in my room and requested a status report. The breach was in Pia's room, but the system quickly activated fans to keep Hapira's spores and pollen away and robots had already sealed up the door to her room to stop any leaks.

At least our main protective systems were still working. Whoever had started all this hadn't been able or hadn't thought to mess with those. I slipped quickly into my temporary protective suit—not as advanced as the real one, but good for temporary exposure to outdoor Hapira. I commanded Patches to stay back, but she wouldn't listen. I prayed no spores had leaked inside.

Samira was already at Pia's door.

"I've overridden the security code." The walls into the bedrooms were made of a smart glass that could be lightened enough to make them see-through. We could see into Pia's bedroom now. I thought then that maybe I'd underestimated Samira. I didn't know she could figure out how to get around internal security that controlled access to view inside Pia's room. But maybe the breach made it easier to override things. I should have read all of our safety procedures booklet.

Anyway, we saw a pile of tools and that Pia had made a hole in the wall big enough for her to fit through. She was gone. Bouvergard was splayed out on the floor, his floppy ears up and exposed. He might have been sleeping. I've seen him sleep just like that. But he was dead. I'm crying, you know? He's not even human, but that damn dead dog made me sadder than the death of my colleagues. I don't know what that says about me.

"It's not worth going to look for her." Samira said without looking at me. "If she went out without a suit, it won't matter. Once the spores get to you, you'll start to turn."

Patches let out a low whine.

"You want a treat?" she offered a biscuit to the dog. Patches took it from her gently.

"I need some time to think. And pack the rest of my stuff. I guess it was Pia this whole time? You think her meds just stopped working?"

"It makes sense. We should have listened to Raph. Hopefully, he survived the walk to the other lab."

I felt a chill run through my body as I walked back over the hard, carpeted floors to my room. Once we were in the room, Patches spit the treat out of her mouth.

"Smells strange. Like Bouvergard."

"Patches?" I asked. She rested her chin at the edge of the bed and looked at me with raised eyebrows. "Yesterday, Bouvergard eat treats from Samira?"

She clicked her tongue. "Treat Samira, yes. He eat."

I couldn't sleep. I did what I should have done a while ago. Patches and I snuck into Esther's old office. It was actually unlocked. Her computer was also on. About a month ago, Esther had given me her password to get something off of her computer. Esther was old school in that she used a password and not biometrics, which she found creepy and annoying.

"We're all on the same team here. Not like some outsider can easily walk onto the lab and steal our secrets. I don't need to use an eye scanner."

Raphael didn't like that she gave me her password. She was always a little extra nice to me. I don't think he liked it one bit.

I tried her password, and it still worked. I looked at her emails. There was another company that wanted the data we'd been gathering on Hapira--not really a company, actually. A barely legal entity called Calato known for selling on the black market. Esther was nervous because someone from corporate had told her they'd spotted Calato ships coming and going from Hapira. She wanted corporate to end the assignment early for our safety. Corporate said we couldn't end until we met some milestones. If we got enough data fast enough, we'd be able to ship out sooner.

So we had actually been meeting our weekly goals. She just wanted us to exceed them so we could leave early. But she probably didn't want to worry us by telling us Calato was on Hapira. I thought back to what Esther had said about no one just being able to walk into the lab and steal our stuff. But what if the person who wanted to steal our information and corporate secrets was with us the whole time?

"Samira coming," Patches's collar spoke, and she growled. I ran my hand through her multicolored fur.

"Samira not good. Samira not friend." I tell her.

"I know," came the answer from the collar. If I weren't distracted by the situation, I'd be floored by the strangeness of the first time (I think) I've ever heard Patches use that phrase.

Near the desk was a cast iron pan. Esther was peculiar. She liked cooking for herself, sometimes in the middle of the day, as break from work. She was also kind of a slob. Traces of eggs and grease remained. I picked the pan up with two hands, as it was heavier than I expected. Then I turned to the door.

Samira was there, holding a shock-baton.

"You're a mole. From Calato." I gripped tighter.

"Calato is coming here. They'll be here in a few hours. It took you long enough to figure out it was me."

"You seemed like such an idiot," I told her.

"You don't have to die horribly. Calato will scan your brain—your consciousness will survive, digitally. They want all the data on the project they can get. I'll keep your dog, too, and make sure she's well taken care of. If you cooperate, they'll pay out the rest of your five-year contract and a bonus to your family. One of their scouts found Raphael already. I got Esther's brain scan. They found Pia, too, before she turned. Your brain would be a bonus. And can't have you reporting back to Tanith."

"Go away," Patches's collar yelled as she let out a loud bark.

"This damn dog," Samira lunged toward her, baton forward. Adrenaline pumping through my veins, I raised the pan and slammed it into her face before she could make contact with the dog, knocking out a couple of teeth and causing her to collapse before she could reach Patches.

Should have brought a gun, not a baton, to the pan fight.

I went back to my room. I'm writing this all down because I don't know what to do. Calato is coming. Now, the sensors in the lab are picking up that there are multiple vehicles some kilometers from the lab. They're moving slowly because of the difficulty of navigating through Hapira's plants. I should leave Patches, right?

February 22

Patches wouldn't let me leave her at the lab. I tried to explain to her many times that she will likely die if she leaves the lab with me. Her protective suit will fail before someone finds her. She will get infected and turn into a part of Hapira's ecosystem. If she stays, the Calato people might adopt her.

But no. She wanted to go with me. I don't know if she really understands.

Earth times and dates don't match Hapira's sun, which is out now. We've walked through the spikey and curly neon-green thickets, burning the path ahead with an acid spray and a laser-edged machete (also, probably a more effective weapon than Samira's stupid baton). Orange and black blooms with mum-like, almost dog-like faces hang over me, watching with disgust.

Samira did everything she was supposed to, but all good spies have the potential to turn again. Her family will get paid, which is probably why she agreed to the terms. Samira's consciousness, if she survived my blow to the head, will be likely absorbed by Calato's computers, just like what she planned for me. Wouldn't that be better than death? But I'd become boundless data, eventually. Everything and nothing. No, no. Best to end things on my terms.

There is a bog a two-kilometer walk northeast of the lab. The dead material in bogs builds up and keeps oxygen out, delaying decomposition. My diary is already starting to deteriorate as I write it in now, in Hapira's atmosphere. But I have a container, like the ones we used to store the samples from the garden. If I stick my diary inside the container and then drop it into the blog, it will preserve my diary for perhaps hundreds or even thousands of years. Some future explorer might even be able to read it.

Please excuse how poor my handwriting has become. It's hard to hold a pen with gloves on.

There is a tear in the left foot of my suit. The suit contained the tear by sealing off the part around my left foot, but Hapira's spores have touched the skin of my foot. Like a charismatic cult leader, Hapira's cells are slowly converting my cells to their side.

"Join us," Hapira compels my alien, mammal cells. "Wouldn't you like to take these chloroplasts from us? Wouldn't you like to make sunlight into food?" Its viruses have started editing my DNA. "Your cells no longer need to be flexible. You need walls."

Patches is panting and leaning against my back. I'm sorry, girl. But you always wanted to go outside more. Once I've filled up this page, I'll put this diary in the container and throw it into the bog, watch it sink. Before long, Patches and I will be plants or fungus. We'll grow together as part of the collective Hapira.

I'd like my cells to become a sunny, yellow flower, like Earth's daffodils. My flower face will stare at the bog as I grow, although the sludge is too murky and dark to reflect back my own image. But the diary will survive. The diary will be me—at least, the parts of me I want others to see. Isn't that what a self is? Choosing what you will show—the act of deception is the act of making the individual?

I'm not a philosopher. I imagine real ones would find plenty of holes in that statement.

Whatever.

You might suspect I've lied about quite a bit in my account of the events leading to my death. Everyone's death. Maybe you'll want to posthumously accuse me of awful, terrible things. Most likely, though, no evidence of what really happened will have survived by the time this diary is found.

So, you'll never really know for sure.

Jennifer lives in New York State with her partner and an agent of chaos (her dog) and works in animal conservation. In the past, she taught English in Korea and taught in Indonesia while serving in the Peace Corps. She has also worked with small nonprofits in Asia and the US. More info can be found on her website: jenniferjeannemcardle.blogspot.com/.

Under the Monument

by

John M. Floyd

AVE Keeton stood on the grassy slope just west of the Washington Monument, watching the sunset. He was in no hurry; his family had taken the late tour across the bridge to Arlington Cemetery, and wouldn't be back until seven. He was glad he'd stayed behind. This was their fourth day here—four days of sightseeing and museum visits and sightseeing and shopping and more sightseeing. If he had to hear one more fascinating fact about the nation's capital, he'd decided he would strangle the tour guide and flee the country and become a monk. Enough was enough.

Keeton had spent the past two hours strolling the sidewalks of the Mall, stopping now and then to buy an ice-cream cone or a lemonade or watch a frisbee competition. It had been a good afternoon. Hot and humid, sure, but Mississippi natives were used to that. The truth was, he felt good. Marge and the kids would appreciate the improvement in his mood.

That thought made him glance at his watch. His family would soon be returning to the Lincoln Memorial—the dropoff point for the tour —and he didn't want to be late. He took a last look at the Capitol and the Monument, then headed down the slope toward the setting sun.

That was when he saw the old man.

He looked to be about seventy, lined face, long white hair. He was sitting on an upright suitcase, reading a paperback. Another suitcase lay on its side in the grass beside him. The only remarkable thing about him was a wool suit far too heavy for the August heat. It did not, however, appear to bother him in the least. He wasn't even sweating.

Dave Keeton's path took him right past the old man, and his Southern upbringing prompted him to offer a greeting. As he drew abreast he smiled and said, "Great sunset, huh?"

The whitehaired man raised his head and studied him over a pair of thick glasses. "Exceptional," he said.

Keeton was friendly by nature, but not pushy. It was something in the older man's tone of voice that made him linger. "Looks like you're ready for traveling," Keeton said.

The old fellow looked down at his suitcases and nodded. "I am waiting for my transport." His voice was quiet and precise.

"Transportation, you mean?"

"Ah. Yes. Transportation."

Keeton glanced at the traffic on Constitution Avenue, a hundred yards to the north. This was a long way from a bus stop. Or a Metro station. "You're taking a taxi, then?"

"Not exactly." The old gentleman smiled. "I am not using—how do you say? 'Ground transportation.'"

They stared at each other a moment. Keeton started to reply, then something caught his eye. The paperback novel the man was reading was upside down.

The poor guy's missing some dots off his dice, Keeton realized. It made him feel sad, and a little embarrassed.

Somehow reluctant to leave, he said, "What brings you to Washington?"

The whitehaired man seemed to think that over. "Education," he said.

"I beg your pardon?"

"Education," he repeated. "Knowledge. Enlightenment."

"I see." Keeton hesitated, then asked, "Why here?"

"Why not here?" The old-fashioned eyeglasses turned slowly toward the white spire of the Monument, then to the bustling traffic, the grand old buildings. "Why not here, at the seat of government of the most civilized nation on earth? If one is to gather knowledge of a people, and has time for only one stop, would it not be here?"

Neither of them spoke for a while. Somewhere to the north, a siren wailed. Probably just some civilized American killing another, Keeton thought.

"And have you found it?" he asked.

"Found what?"

"Knowledge. Enlightenment."

"Oh yes." The older man's smile brightened. "My superiors will be pleased."

Keeton narrowed his eyes. Superiors? "Where exactly do you work?"

Another pause. "I am from Europa," the man said. That seemed to trigger a memory, and his eyes took on a vacant, faraway look. He turned again to his book, and its upside-down pages.

Keeton watched him, thinking.

Europa? Strange, the guy didn't sound—or look—European. In fact, he didn't seem to have any accent at all.

Odd.

Then again, the things he'd just said were pretty odd, too. Gather knowledge of a people? And this business about not using "ground transportation." What did he plan to do, plug a propeller onto his suitcase and zoom over to the airport—

But wait a minute. Wait just a minute here...

Wasn't Europa one of the moons of Jupiter?

Good grief, Keeton thought. The poor old fool thinks—

He thinks he's waiting for his spaceship.

Keeton sighed. Maybe this kind of thing wasn't that unusual here. After all, this was D.C. It stood to reason there'd be more loonies per square mile than in Vicksburg. Even Southerners don't go around reading books upside down.

Shaking his head, Dave Keeton finally turned his eyes—and his thoughts—away from the old man. He was about to check his watch again when he noticed something unusual. Two limousines had screeched to a stop at the foot of the slope—17th Street?—and a crowd was gathering just beyond, near the east end of the Reflecting Pool. Even as he saw this, he heard a deep, thudding roar over his head. Bright lights filled the darkening sky.

Keeton looked up, and his jaw dropped.

My GOD—

But as the lights swooped downward, he realized they were heading not for him but for the patch of flat ground beside the roadway. Half a dozen policemen appeared, herding spectators clear of the landing site.

Moments later the helicopter settled to earth, its downwash whipping the grass and the clothing of the onlookers. When the noise died down, an entourage of diplomats was transferred from the chopper to the limos, which whisked them away. The crowd began to disperse.

Still shaken, Keeton looked over at his companion.

The old man smiled. "That wasn't mine," he said. And went back to his book.

Dave Keeton couldn't think of a single response to that. Instead he sighed again, and looked across at the Lincoln Memorial. The sun was down now; streetlights were kicking in. He had a family to meet. Before leaving, however, he turned once more toward the old man. At that moment a breeze gusted in from the west, tugging at the wool suit and lifting the snow-white mane of hair back from the lined forehead.

"What are you called?" the old man asked, staring into the wind.

Keeton blinked. "My name is David Keeton."

The whitehaired man seemed to consider that. Finally he nodded. "Have a good life, David Keeton."

And then he smiled, a gentle, friendly smile that warmed Keeton's heart. The old guy might be crazy, Keeton thought, but I won't soon forget him.

On an impulse, Keeton took his digital camera from his shoulder-bag and raised it to his eye. The built-in flash lit up their little piece of twilight on the grassy slope. The old man showed no surprise. He just stared at the camera with mild interest.

"This way I can remember you," Keeton said.

The old man smiled again, the wind in his hair, and returned to his paperback.

As Keeton left, he looked back twice at the figure sitting quietly on his suitcase in the gathering dusk. Then, when he'd crossed 17th Street and the trees bordering the long sidewalk south of the Pool blocked the view, Keeton's thoughts turned again to his wife and children. Ten minutes later he was sitting on the tall steps at Lincoln's feet, waiting for the return of the Arlington tour bus.

Pleasantly tired, he let his gaze wander over the historic setting, pausing on the dome of the Jefferson Memorial and the distant Capitol and the shadowy statues of the Vietnam soldiers fifty yards away. Farther to the left, beyond the trees and lights of Constitution Avenue, he saw no really tall buildings, and spotted only one landmark: the Old Post Office tower. He had once read that Washington was the only major city in America with no skyline.

His eyes moved right again, to the bright needle of the Monument and its sloping meadow, washed now in the glow of streetlamps and floodlights. The old man was still there, dim but visible, a white-topped dot on a green background.

Keeton chuckled. A weird guy, that one. Marge would enjoy hearing about him. Then Keeton remembered the picture, raised his camera to look at it—

And something happened. Dave Keeton sat up, frowning and alert, the camera forgotten in his hand. He looked around, but saw nothing. It was more of a feeling, actually—a thickening of the air. He felt his ears pop, and heard a deep, pulsing buzz somewhere in the distance. It reminded him of the sixty-cycle hum he used to get when he switched on his CD player without connecting the ground wire.

And then it was gone. In the dead silence that followed (the handful of tourists around him didn't seem to have noticed anything), Keeton was struck with a thought. He saw a man nearby holding a pair of binoculars, and asked to borrow them. Snatching the glasses to his eyes, Keeton scanned the slope just west of the Monument.

The patch of grass was empty.

The old man—and his suitcases—were gone.

Keeton felt his knees go weak.

And then something else jumped into his mind. Something he'd glimpsed earlier, for a fraction of a second, as he stood looking at the old man for the last time. Something he had seen but hadn't quite... absorbed. Or had blocked out.

He realized the camera was still in his hand. Holding his breath, he pushed the button to display the photo he'd taken, and looked at the color image of the man sitting on the suitcase and smiling into the camera.

The picture was a good one, sharp and clear: wool suit, old-timey glasses, long hair swept back by the wind.

Swept back to reveal a pink, wrinkled forehead.

And pointed ears.

John M. Floyd's work has appeared in more than 350 different publications, including *Alfred Hitchcock Mystery Magazine, Ellery Queen Mystery Magazine, The Saturday Evening Post, Best American Mystery Stories* (2015, 2018, and 2020), *Best Mystery Stories of the Year 2021*, and *Best Crime Stories of the Year 2021*. A former Air Force captain and IBM systems engineer, John is an Edgar finalist, a 2021 Shamus Award winner, a five-time Derringer Award winner, a three-time Pushcart Prize nominee, and the author of nine books. He is also the 2018 recipient of the Short Mystery Fiction Society Lifetime Achievement Award.

Harvest of the Dandelion - A Taxonomy of Regional Variants (Annotated by Dr. Vasquez-Fox, of the Esteemed Venusian Collegiate Assembly)

by

Sarah Cline

S*PECIMEN* #1, Species: taraxacum mollusca. Subspecies: Coastal mollusca variant, "Queen Electric's Bloom," "The Queen Electric." Location: Most densely populated in the Azure Berms.

Description: Shimmering in electric blue hues, the shells of the most common subspecies of the taraxacum mollusca stud the fine-grained, steely shores of our new-christened colony, Heyoka. The Blue Mollusk subspecies, also referred to as Queen Electric's Bloom, somewhat resembles an Earthen seashell, hiding an iridescent, slug-like mollusk in its coiling folds. The Queen Electric is found all across the coastlines of the Heyoka colony's main continent, Nampendin[1]. These electric-blue shells rest in abundance on the iron sand, as if sunning themselves beneath the watery, white light of the planet's distant sun. The Queen Electric was among the first new species discovered upon human establishment on the surface of Heyoka. Thus far, they have provided an excellent and abundant source of sustenance.

Specimen #2, Species: taraxacum mollusca. Subspecies: Canyon mollusca variant, "The Green-capped Mollusk." Location: Sinner's Gorge.

---

[1] The name "Nampendin" has flummoxed historians since the discovery of the notebook circa 3178. Recently, my colleague, Dr. Enne S'Yoko-Flynn, of the Esteemed Venusian Collegiate Assembly (EVCA), has proposed that Wicasta may have been referencing a colloquial joke, as the primary continent where the colony established itself on Heyoka was in fact never given a formal name. Rather, an obscure reference to the single, remaining map of the continental region in archaic digital imaging bears only the title, "Name Pending A17."

Description: The spectacular diversity of the taraxacum mollusca species continues to enthrall me[2]. In the sinister chasms of Sinner's Gorge—seeming lifeless at first glimpse—one's patience is rewarded if, walking along the jagged edge of the canyon, with the shaded splay of red cliffs and chasms splitting the land beneath the lazy, dappling clouds, the barren landscape is suddenly transformed by a mighty gust of wind during what passes for spring on beautiful Heyoka, and flung through the canyons, weightless and spinning like petals in the breeze, come the ghostly Green-capped Mollusks.

Puffy and light, their shells thin and hollowed like balloons, one cannot help but laugh with joy at the sight of them, white-bodied and with a splash of green crowning the hollow, fluted twist of shell atop their heads, they resemble nothing if not onions, drifting on the breeze. A few white puffs, glimpsed as they rise between the rocks and float upward, aslant, traveling like dandelion spores. A few, then a dozen, then a hundred, and a hundred more, spinning up all at once from the deeper chasm, their bodies burning white as they catch the sunlight, spinning and drifting, drifting and spinning, in a most spectacular display. Beautiful and ludicrous and thrilling[3].

Unlike their coastal cousins, the Green-caps, while sharing the basic model of a soft iridescent body beneath a harder shell, have apparently evolved to live within the canyon ecosystem. They spend the majority of their time dwelling in the pools at the shadowy base of the canyons, where their bodies are heavy with water, and absorb nutrients from the fallen debris of dead plant, and sometimes animal, matter that live on

---

[2] The following note appears in the margins of the original document, apparently added by Wicasta out of a familiar, scholarly drive to validate her pursuits: "Deviating from my study of the coastal subspecies and following expeditions inland, I have already observed a variety of other subspecies of the mollusca, each perfectly adapted to its own environment. I now endeavor to provide a survey, however cursory, in order to establish the impressive evolutionary diversity and potential of Heyoka in hopes of securing materials, manpower, and funding for further study."

[3] This abrupt ode to biodiversity is uncharacteristic of Wicasta's passionate, yet typically more reserved, prose. One is forced to imagine the brilliance of the scene that must have erupted across the young scientist's consciousness when, exploring the canyons, her team happened upon the discovery of a new subspecies in such a dramatic fashion, as if the creatures had drifted up en masse to greet their visitors at the gates. Of course, no living specimens exist of this variant; we are forced to rely upon imagination, and the five low-resolution photos that have survived. These, unfortunately, do not appear to do justice to the spore-like triumph of the Green-caps rising in unison. More inspirational, in this humble academic's opinion, is the skeleton of specimen 1-2539-09HW, located in the EVCA Organic Repository, whose thin, almost translucent, bones, and delicately asymmetrical twist of dome-like skull, in its strangeness and grace, make the heart pump harder in the chest to gaze upon than any old images recovered from an ancient hard-drive.

the cliff-sides above, before, at the end of their life cycle, tumbling into the Green-caps' embrace. When the nutrients are depleted from the inhabited region of the canyons, the Green-caps move on; shrugging free of the pools, drying themselves on the dusty base of the canyon-floors, they lift their shells, puffing up their mostly hollow bodies, and take to the breeze in their preferred method of migration to a new and fecund part of the canyons. These floating displays are thus rare and unpredictable, occurring only when the Green-caps have thoroughly enjoyed their pools, and are ready to move on. Their skulls, with their subtle and elaborate network of fluted hollows, proved a passing fashion on Heyoka for some time, but the true value of the species was in the awareness they brought to these nutrient-rich, canyon pools, and the ample food supply subsequently harvested from the plant-matter growing across the cliffsides. Notably, the drifting-displays became more common in Sinner's Gorge when human competition forced the Green-caps to travel farther and more often for their supper, until, abruptly, they became much less common, and now are seen scarcely at all.

Specimen #3, Species: taraxacum mollusca. Subspecies: Volcanic mollusca variant. "The Cinderous Red." Location: The Lowering Crest.

Description: Along the southern ridge of the volcanic, mountain region beneath the Lowering Crest exists a unique variant of the taraxacum mollusca known for its high tolerance for heat and other extreme conditions which make the Crest naturally devoid of life above the surface. Its froglike body bulges beneath a thin, tortoise-like shell, tucked over its spine, and dappled red and black. Astonishingly, the Cinderous Red variant has been observed to exist largely within subterranean air pockets, submerged beneath semi-solid, molten earth that flows from the active peaks of the Crest mountain range. Even during periods in which streams of lava do not actively flow, subterranean chasms, filled with heat from volcanic activity, create a high temperature across the semipermeable crust of the region. The Red Mollusk exists, all but motionless, for a full 8-10 months of the year beneath the soil, subsisting on stored nutrient deposits accumulated during the rainy season—when the Red Mollusk, now thin and depleted of fatty deposits, slips its slim, tubular form from the earth with a succulent *pop* to gorge itself on clouds of rain-gnats that swarm the area as temperatures grow turbulent and storms rake the coastline.

Not long after the discovery of this wondrous subspecies, our scientists managed to extract a heat-resistant oil from the moist flesh of the Red Mollusk which, when used to coat our machinery and body-suits, has allowed us to explore the explosive heat of Heyoka's volcanic areas, and create a new version of our starships equipped to travel further into space, plumbing deeper depths of the galaxy, closer to the stars. As a result, the Red Mollusk variant has become more difficult to find, for so many of them have been extracted from the Lowering Crest habitat to harvest their oil[4].

Specimen #4, Species: taraxacum mollusca. Subspecies: Waterfall mollusca variant. "The Diamond Urchin," "The Silver Mollusk." Location: East Ridge Cascades.

Description: In the East Ridge Cascades exists a variant we've named the Silver Mollusk, for the hue of the froth and ice of the waters in which they dwell. This subspecies resembles the snail-like variant of the Mollusk first discovered on the shores of the new colony, the Queen's Electric, their slug-like forms tucked into spiraling, iridescent shells. But unlike their saltwater cousins, these freshwater variants may be encountered in the waterfalls that descend from the northern slice of fjords and river lands beyond the mountains.

Again, the diversity of the species is remarkable; the Silver variant, like an inverse of the subterranean, volcanic Red, lives submerged in an element too extreme for its cousins. The Silver Mollusk slumbers for the long autumn and winter seasons of the north, the Cold Season, locked in the ice of the many frozen waterfalls that can be found there, when the rapids distill, almost overnight, into crystalline, frozen beams cascading down the mountainsides. The Mollusks slink from their crystal-frosted caves as the seasons change, slow as starfish in their treacherous journey up the rocks, up and up to the highest mountain peaks, and submerge themselves in the waters near the top, just as the snows begin to fall. Sensing the imminent change in temperature, with their incalculable instinct for the shifting of seasons, they slide down into the waters at the river-founts just before the cold snap, only to drift along sluggish currents, and throw themselves into the massive cascades just as the Cold Season takes them.

---

[4]The modern formula for heat-resistant oil that allows for human machinery to traverse regions of intense heat is still in use, synthesized from the rudimentary oil Wicasta's team derived from the Cinderous Red variant. While no samples of the organic oil remain, reverse engineering from the original formula allows for the continued production of Cinder Oil to this day. With some discomfort, I acknowledge that not all long-term effects of the plundering of Heyoka were negative. Many discoveries have been made due to the use of the heat-resistant oil, and the freedom it has given us to exceed our previous limitations.

The Silver Mollusk, frozen in the ice of the waterfalls, can be glimpsed from afar when one knows what to look for; their iridescent shells, thrust downward in the silent plunge, appear to be dark diamonds, captured in the powder-blue ice. They slumber there, safe and sound, dreaming one-can-only-guess what dreams. Then, with the waning of the Cold Season, as the distant, white pinprick of Heyoka's sun returns, the waterfalls begin to melt, until, with a final, tremendous crash in the night, the waters are released. One can return in the morning, cold foam lashing pinkened cheeks, to watch them tumble through the meltwater like opals in the current, scattered amid the chunks of ice. Downstream, in the warm waters of the coast, the Silver Mollusk reach the rocky pools where males and females are thrust together amid those deeper waters, and the mating frenzy begins. Fascinatingly, when the bubbles have cleared, one can finally discern the males from the females, for half the shells will be empty, and the shimmering slugs within the other half fatten with growing young. These spawn gestate for a mere three or four weeks beneath the weak and gentle sunlight of the coast before the females birth their eggs along the bottom of the pools and wait, in their uneasy silence, for what comes next. After a few days, the eggs begin to hatch, and a second frenzy begins, red-tinged bubbles rising to the surface. A clutter of empty shells gild the bottoms of these pools as they slowly fill[5].

One wonders what will become of the Silver Mollusk when their spawning pools complete their evolution and, filled to the brim with the shells of mothers and fathers, at last become graves. In the meantime, the young begin to inch from the edges of the pools, and begin their slow, inevitable progress north, inch by moist, agonizing inch. A rarity among the taraxacum mollusca, a use has not yet been found for this variety.

Specimen #5, Species: taraxacum mollusca. Subspecies: Lunar mollusca variant. "The White Mollusk." Location: Heyoka's Third Moon, Idle Pines.

---

[5]Incidentally, Wicasta's interest in the ultimate fate of the Silver Mollusk was echoed by the team of EVCA researchers who made the singular return expedition to Heyoka in 3178—the same expedition which retrieved Wicasta's notebook. No evidence of the Silver Mollusk was discovered, nor of flowing water in the region identified as the Cascades, nor any shells in the rocky pools of the coast located downstream from what would have been the rivers described by Wicasta. However, ancient shells of a similar description were found accumulated on an island hundreds of miles from the shoreline of Nampendin, in the Unk-Maka Ocean, as if the waterfall variant was at some point forced to abandon its ancestral cycle, and seek solace in the sea.

Description: The third moon of Heyoka is the only one brindled in greenery. The other two, their pallid faces agleam in frosty sunlight, shimmer farther back in the atmosphere, pocked by craters. But the third moon, closest to the world and shrouded in tall evergreens best compared to Earth's redwoods and pines, tower across the landscape, hiding the moon's pockets of waters beneath their shadowy boughs. It is on this moon that the White Mollusk nest along the branches of the trees, like clumps of fresh snow dappling the pines after the first snowfall upon an evergreen forest. These little mollusks bubble from bough to bough by creeping up the tree trunks—an arduous but surefooted journey—to the tops of the trees, only to, with a rather unwonted burst of activity, flick themselves from the heights. The moon's lax gravity lends them the few extra moments required for the underside of this subspecies' bulbous, thin, and air-filled shell to bloom —expanding with the soft, filmy grace of a jellyfish puffing through the waters of the ocean—and float askance on lunar winds to strike the next tree trunk. In this manner, the variant is able to traverse the landscape of their little moon.

The White Mollusks—so named for their diaphanous, jelly-like underbellies—of the moon are, so far as we have yet noticed, the only living animal species to dwell upon the third moon. They feed upon the lichens that grow on their trees while their waste, trickling down between the ridges of the trees' bark in shimmering trails, pools amid the roots, and fertilizes the trees, and future bursts of lichen-growth. This ecosystem, perfect in its simplicity, appears to have been preserved from the ancient formation of the moon when its astral dust was seized from the early earth of Heyoka itself. Noting a rather large chasm in the colossal trench of the Unk-Maka Sea, our scientists theorize that the third moon is a byproduct of an ancient collision between Heyoka and a massive asteroid, the force of which striking the planet pried a large enough chunk from the world such that the two bodies of earth, swirling around one another in their gravity-drunk dance, formed a slightly smaller planet, and a new moon - one that still possessed enough living material on its surface to, miraculously, allow for the growth of the forest, as well as the ancestors of the White Mollusk now reigning there alone. One only wonders what these lofty and industrious specimens may have become if such a collision had never occurred, and thrown their evolution onto this brave new trajectory. While we have not yet secured funding for exploratory vessels to be commissioned for an expedition to the moon, we have thus far been able to study the White Mollusk quite well through our super-telescopes. As far as extending humanity's reach to these creatures in-person to further evaluate their use, such proposals are even now being drafted[6].

Specimen #6, Species: taraxacum mollusca. Subspecies: Plains mollusca variant. "The Dappled Bronze Mollusk," "Scavenger Mollusk." Also called, "The Fertile Bane." Location: The Hazy Scavenge.

Description: Of a matte bronze hue dappled by swirling bands of black and white specks, the shell of this subspecies is spiked like a warlord's helmet and houses lethal venom within its barbs. The Fertile Bane is so named for its widespread dominion of the plains lands ecosystem, and its surprising ferocity, for a mollusk. Unlike the majority of the other variants, which are roughly equal in size, the Bane is notably larger than most. Not only that, but unusually for Heyoka, the female is considerably larger than the male.

Lakes, not wide but deep, dot the plains and sahara of Heyoka, and it is at these lakes that the Fertile Bane dwells. They spend surprisingly little time in the water, though they like to plunge into the depths on occasion and leap back out, sunning their bulky underbellies as they sprawl in their fleshy piles along the rims of their lakes. Highly territorial, the Scavengers will—if hungry or bored—make their way across the land in the dead of night to seek out other lakes, where they set upon their own kind. A great ruckus can then be heard for miles around—harrowing screams in the night, for unique among the taraxacum, this variant has developed large jaws beneath the shells that cup their soft organs. Fanged in sharp teeth, their jaws hover over an octopus-like sprawl of thick tendrils, on which they easily traverse both land and lake. In the morning, stray tendrils can be seen, drifting sulkily on bloodied waters.

The term *scavenger* is accurate, but perhaps slightly misleading. The Bane will scavenge for food, a devourer of the dead—even corpses in advanced stages of decay are not safe from their apparently ceaseless hunger—but they are also hunters, brawlers, and cannibals. They will eat almost anything: living prey while its writhes and squeals beneath them, spindly legs thrashing over the wheat-gold tips of the plains grass; dead bodies, whose stale innards, half-spilt from their husk, are drying in the sun; or, in a fit of boredom, the females may turn upon the lower-status males, sometimes satisfied to bat them around, other

---

[6]In spite of Wicasta's efforts, EVCA has not been able to confirm that any human researchers ever landed on Idle Pines. Satellite surveillance indicates that life on the moon appears eerily unchanged in the centuries since Wicasta's observations were recorded, in spite of the overall desolation of the surface of the planet itself.

times their bites growing more violent as they taste blood, until there is no going back. Oftentimes, these males are quiet and submissive throughout the early stages of this battering, perhaps not believing, until the very end, that their mothers and sisters and daughters will devour them. Not believing, until they feel their bodies giving out on them. Then there is an explosion of thrashing and writhing, of whimpering and barking and biting, until the end.

If any loyalty exists from one to another within the society of this subspecies, it is of the daughter to the mother. Fiercely matriarchal, the society of the Fertile Bane is clustered around the dominant female, and, in a steep hierarchy, her daughters and sisters, and eventually, her sons and brothers. This loyalty does not, however, endure forever. As is typical of the Bane, power changes hands—or tentacles, as the case may be—through violence. When the matriarch's strongest, largest daughter reaches her peak maturity, she turns, quite suddenly, on the mother. Often, she lunges for the throat out of the blue, and a long, harrowing struggle follows. As mother and daughter wrestle in their death-grip, blood spurting down their fronts, violence erupts between the remainder of the females; the daughter's sisters and cousins turn with her, the matriarch's sisters lunge to kill the daughters and nieces with whom they fed side-by-side contentedly only moments before. The males scamper into the water, or into the rocks, and wait for it to be over.

When the struggle ends, many of the females are dead. A bloody culling, with only three possible endings; most often, the younger and stronger daughter will prevail and devour her mother's writhing tentacles in an orgy of newfound power, while her aunts surrender around her, and those too wounded to live creep off into the water, where their bodies will cool, and the remains slime down the throats of their sons. Less often, the mother will prevail, and reestablish her reign, attending her coronation gowned in the blood of her daughter. In the rarest outcome, both mother and daughter will fall, locked together in their death-grip. When this occurs, the strongest of the remaining females will assume the role of matriarch. There has never been a case observed in which one does not claim dominance over the others.

They are said to be mad, this variant of the species. Cooing to themselves as the hyenas of Earth were said to cackle their hysterical laughter, circling their prey in the night. That is the Fertile Bane[7].

---

[7]Here, Wicasta's notes appear to decrease in legibility, as if written in haste, or possibly in a state of distress.

Of note is that, among the variant subspecies of the taraxacum mollusca, this particular subspecies is, evidently, the only variant of the species not currently endangered by habitat loss, human competition, or resource harvesting. Initially, it was suspected that the Bane may decline in number as the expansion of the Heyoka colony pushed back the inhabitants of the plains region, and the loss of tree and grasslands decreased the population of the Bane's prey. Other predator species have declined in number due the narrowing of hunting lands. The Bane has proved more adaptable, reacting to increased competition and decreased hunting lands, by accepting a wider variety of food sources, and resorting to carrion activity, including digging partially eaten remains from the earth to devour, and growing more adept at stealing prey from other predators and humans alike. Indeed, unique among the inhabitants of Heyoka, the Bane have grown comfortable infringing closer and closer to human settlements as the colony expands, and have proven as willing to pilfer human garbage as they are to snatch children who wander too close to the edges of town. It is with increasing scorn that our settlers mutter the name of the Bane.

Unfortunately, it seems that this unusually violent aspect of the species is the only variant that is not only resisting endangerment, but thriving. We have not yet been able to get close enough to the Bane to ascertain its potential usefulness. Most of my colleagues agree it is probably of little feasible use for the purposes of Heyoka[8].

---

[8] It is the opinion of this scholar that the reluctance of Wicasta and her colleagues to pursue in-depth study of the Scavenger Mollusk is less a reflection of its uselessness, and more a reflection of the discomfort of the scientists in researching the subspecies. The fact that, singular among the variants surveyed by Wicasta and her team, the fiercest and most violent among them proved to be the best equipped to thrive in the hostile environment created by human interaction with the ecosystems of Heyoka, disquieted the researchers. For it forced them - as it forces us - to consider the kind of world we are creating when our work ensures that only the cruelest among us can survive.

Sarah Cline lives in San Diego, California, where she works as a writer and freelance editor. She has Masters degrees in English Literature, as well as Library and Information Science. Her writing has appeared in *Grim & Gilded,* and in *The Maine Review* and *Whetstone: Amateur Magazine of Sword and Sorcery* under pseudonyms. Read more of her work and learn about upcoming projects at: authorsarah-cline.wixsite.com/sarahcline.

A Dazzling World

by

M. Stern

SCIENCE took a historical wrong turn, as far as Dr. Kai Kingsley was concerned, when it forsook beauty as a central consideration. Anthony Hilder agreed. For Anthony, the elder microbiologist's outre theses and preoccupations resonated with the primordial truth of a signal excreted from a gland. Which is how he now found himself sitting at the desk in the man's home office, tapping the Erasmus Darwin bust on the desk, thinking back to the project's genesis.

"You're the first graduate student I've had who knows Erasmus Darwin's *Loves of the Plants*," Kingsley said. "Science and taxonomy relayed in the form of a poem! Could you imagine it today? These stolid STEM types don't even have passion for the field, let alone for the poetry pouring from the Earth. They could hardly appreciate an account of the world so—what's the word—"

"Variegated?" Anthony replied.

"I was reaching for *dazzling*," said Kingsley. "but variegated, I think, works also."

"They're both words you've used to describe our beloved *Coccinellidae*, aren't they?"

"I'm sure at some point," said Kingsley, laughing. "I've used a lot of words to describe a lot of things in my day."

"Specifically, in the paper you gave at the 2003 World Molecular Biology and Genomics Forum in Zurich."

"Found a transcript, did you?" Kingsley said.

"*We live on the cusp of a techno-biological revolution. In my work with the family* Coccinellidae *I see that horizon most clearly,*" Anthony quoted. "*It is a variegated world, a dazzling world, which contains within it colors, concepts, and truths more profound than anything seen through the astronomer's telescope. To understand the natural, microbiological processes within these beetles, colloquially ladybirds or ladybugs, is to carefully unpick and analyze the thread with which the Creator has woven beauty into our world."*

"A bit purple, wasn't it," Kingsley said. "Quoting me verbatim, Anthony? If I didn't trust your research skills I'd accuse you of flattery. Then again, how flattered can I be? That paper nearly got me laughed out of the profession. They said I sounded like a mad butterfly collector who had settled on an even more obscure entomological fixation. I told them the aesthetic refinement it takes to appreciate the distinctions in beetles is of a far finer order than what lepidoptery demands. I was told *QED,* and consigned as far to the margins as they could stick me given that I had tenure."

"Consigned to the margins by ideological conformists who can't see past horticultural utility and nursery rhymes," Anthony said. "Insect microbiology has more to say about the natural world than any anthropocentric scientific pursuit. As for ladybugs—well, the beauty of their taxonomic variance is worth appreciating on its own. Beauty is its own end. It's a good in itself."

"Tell that to the people funding grants," Kingsley said.

Anthony took a pen from the desk, held up one finger to indicate a pause, wrote a number on a slip of paper and slid it to Kingsley.

"What's that, the increase in tuition for undergrads this year?" Kingsley laughed. "More zeroes than I've ever seen."

"That's what we've got coming from The Castle Mountain Foundation," Anthony said.

Kingsley stood up, awed.

"I've been trying to get this research funded for decades and couldn't hope to ask for even a tenth of that! Not back when they were giving research grants away, and certainly not now. How in the world did you manage it?"

"Charm?" Anthony said. "And plenty of the humanistic gobbledygook that gets do-gooders and bureaucrats excited about research."

Kingsley's home laboratory was a floor below his office and in it, for years, the two scientists dug deep into their ladybug subjects' genes. They used CRISPR in ways no other researcher would have thought possible—or considered advisable. They broke new ground in understanding mutagenesis, protein synthesis, melanin formation, and heritability, and hypothesized ways to tinker with them well beyond nature's imposed parameters. Theory, though, outperformed practice.

Until, one day, Kingsley arrived home from vacationing in Boca to find Anthony sitting at his desk.

"Been working this whole time?" Kingsley said.

"Take a look at the table," Anthony said.

Kingsley walked over and looked. He scratched his head.

"What am I missing?"

"Look right *there*." Anthony said. He pointed in front of the bust of Erasmus Darwin.

Two ladybugs doddered on the desk. Their shells were precisely the same dark lacquered wood grain color and pattern as the desk itself.

Kingsley howled "*Eureka!*" He flailed his arms and danced around and Anthony joined him. They hugged.

"Think of what it means," Kingsley said, pulling champagne from the mini-fridge and popping the cork. "If we can understand these mechanisms in humans, the possibilities are endless. We could cure disfigurements, malformations, scarring... It's unprecedented, Anthony!"

Pouring the champagne, Kingsley did not recognize Anthony's shift in mood at his enthusiasm for innovations all-too-human.

"Unprecedented," said Anthony, taking the champagne. "Indeed."

Dr. Kai Kingsley sat slumped in the corner. Anthony had blasted the bust of Erasmus Darwin at his face with an amateur martial artist's strength and a beastly ferocity. The old man's head smacked the wall and left a dent. The crimson that streaked the wall was now drying. A welt disfigured the better part of his forehead inhumanly. Kingsley, turning blue, had one eye frozen in a half-open flutter as undignified as the pooled, terminal evacuation in which he sat.

As with Kingsley's final sentiment, Anthony found a grating humanness—a revolting lack of beauty—in his mentor's posthumous condition.

He threw a blanket over the man and replaced the red-splotched bust of Erasmus Darwin on the desk.

The ladybugs were ready. He brought them up from the lab.

They had been biologically altered to have a drastically sped-up reproductive cycle, an ability to generate pigments that varied millions of times beyond what was normally seen and, in order to do so, they were made capable of metabolizing any semblance of amino acid into color. They could, and would, eat anything.

He placed them under the blanket and sat at the desk, tapping on the bust of Erasmus Darwin.

In a few hours the blanket over Kingsley began moving. First with slight disturbances, then at a simmer. Soon it seemed they were feasting.

Hours after that, the floor was growing thick with the beautiful things. Generations of larvae hatched from eggs, ate, molted, pupated, emerged from their pupae as adult beetles, moved out from under the blanket and continued eating in microscopic bites.

Initially, they emerged mostly as familiar red beetles with black spots, or the yellow and black Asian variety; the brown and white ladybugs of Siberia and Mongolia, or thousands of other known types.

But as the rate of reproduction picked up and the thickness of the insect carpet grew, more unique colors and patterns began to emerge. First, Anthony noticed a few grape purple ones with green spots flitting lightly through the air. Then he saw a couple with shells the consistency of corrugated cardboard.

The hours stretched into days, Anthony sat there eating hors d'oeuvres, drinking champagne, and marveling at the new colors and new shapes of new nature.

Eventually, he could no longer eat or drink, because he could no longer lift his hands. The beetles had filled up the room entirely. It was a sea of constant, vivid movement. He lost count of the new colors of ladybug shells he saw; there were crystal-clear ones, lava lamp swirls, bugs that were bioluminescent blue, steely verdigris, polished chrome, speckled banana, black-and-white marble, translucent green glass, all varieties of plaid, paisley, stripes, and heaping handfuls of ice-cream colors pulled from a pastel rainbow just to start. There were countless new shell textures, too; he noticed ruffled crepe paper, mammoth fur, aluminum, denim, corduroy, different types of plastic, melted wax, sponge, linoleum, ones that were bristly, whiskery, wiry, and wrinkly. The conjugations of texture and color seemed to grow more endless by the second.

There remained, though, plenty of the familiar varieties mixed into the whirling spectrum, and the scent left no mistake that it was beetles filling the room. It was the thick, musty smell of the underside of dead, wet wood. The pungent stale odor of chitin shed at scale. And the earthy scent of a vivacious, frenetic pheromonal conversation going on around him.

Soon all he could do was smell and see. If that. The room had grown so full that the top layer of ladybugs was level with the bridge of his nose.

He breathed raggedly, drawing what air he could between insects. He felt tiny legs tickling his nose hairs as they explored his nose. He felt them brushing against and gingerly biting his lips like hundreds of tiny playful kisses. He heard the soft clicking and crackling in his ears, of the living blanket walking, working, busying itself.

Tears poured from his eyes and puddled in the moving, clambering landscape level with his eyes, as the beetle bodies blocked his nostrils entirely. Ladybugs bathed in the salty pool and sucked it up in their mandibles. He felt one glassy one meander up to his lower eyelid. He blinked at a scraping slash against his cornea that blurred his vision irreparably.

The light was dimming, and Anthony calculated the rate of reproductive increase and was thrilled at the potential variances on the beauty of the ladybug that would be born into the world. As they burst forth from this house's windows and walls, as they made their slow, deliberate, inexorable path forward. A rolling march toward more beauty. Filling the world with it. With nothing to stop them. Filling the world.

He imagined them collapsing through the ceilings of the seats of government like the roses of Heliogabalus.

He imagined landscapes rural and urban alike, blanketed, submerged, overwhelmed, reshaped.

Even the seas would fill up and become living, crawling mountains of unprecedentedly vibrant color and variety.

It was going to be a dazzling world.

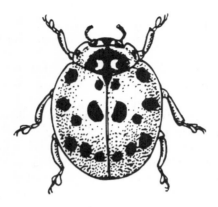

M. Stern is an author of speculative fiction and weird horror whose stories have appeared in publications such as *Weirdbook Magazine*, *Cosmic Horror Monthly*, *Startling Stories*, and a number of themed anthologies. For news on the latest creeping, crawling creations from M. Stern's imagination, visit www.msternauthor.com. Follow on Facebook at www.facebook.com/msternauthor.

The Tragedy of Amanitanalia

by

Michael Anthony Dioguardi

CAPTAIN Terrence Lefleur single-handedly consumed one-third of Amanitanalia's native population. He was a freaking fiend. This was a tragedy of both human and fungal proportions. Lefleur's astounding discovery and his ensuing madness resulted in the extermination of the long-lost humanoids, known in common parlance as the *mushroom people* of Amanitanalia.

It wasn't just him though—he had some help too. I mentioned that one-third of the Amanitanalians were eaten by our captain, the remainder were devoured by Lieutenant Melinda Wright, and me, Corporal Stanley Hager. The following details are a synthesis of ship recordings and personal computer data. All conversations are verbatim. Let this tale be a warning to curious forayers: *Know your mushrooms, and don't be a dick.*

The portobello stench seeped its way in through the walls of our cruiser. I wondered how that could be? Could smells escape the vacuum of space? Or was that just Lefleur's stinky suit? He hardly ever changed. There was no oversight in deep space and if your captain didn't mind, it spread like wildfire. Wright was our only saving grace; she had the motherly instinct to take care of us but even she was getting tired.

Captain Lefleur searched for years for the rumored mushroom planet. It existed only in legend until a few moments ago. I swear he never slept, spending night and day researching nearby star systems for evidence of large-scale mold. His insatiable hunger for chanterelles and morels engendered a sycophantic obsession within him—an insomniac with fungal yearnings.

I stared out the circular viewing chamber at the planet's murky atmosphere. I glanced at my forearm interface. *Temperature: 21-32 degrees Celsius. Atmospheric makeup: 50% Oxygen (damn, more than Earth) 30% Nitrogen 10% Carbon Dioxide 10% Argon.*

"Captain, this is most definitely it. It's doing that spinny thing that planets do."

Lefleur was easy to mess with. He would just tune out my asinine comments toward the end of each report. Lieutenant Wright was more of a straight arrow, keeping it business as usual on the bridge.

"Good, Corporal. Lieutenant, landing report," Lefleur said.

"Five minutes until we break through the stratosphere," Wright replied. "Containment and heat index operating at standard efficiency."

Our cruiser rumbled as a fiery halo enveloped its exterior. I nearly shat myself in excitement. I wondered how much of Amanitanalia's atmosphere was composed of pure spores? Is that why it was a yellow-brown color? And if there were spores everywhere, would that mean the population was constantly ~~ejaculating~~ reproducing into the atmosphere?

My spore theory held water. The tip of our cruiser barreled through the planet's stratosphere, plowing aside congregations of innumerable spores—a trillion grains of sand sprinkling against the ship's metal. The rattling subsided as we descended, unclouding our view of Amanitanalia's surface.

From our position, we could take in the entirety of the planet's intricate geography and urban arrangement. The urban center, *The Bolete Dominion*, was flanked by the surrounding *Amanita Forest*, the namesake of the planet itself. The *Basidio Ocean* swelled against the cold shores of *Protista Commons* in all its lime-green and testicle-shriveling glory.

Amanitanalia was a small celestial object; under our Milky Way classification system, it would be a relative of Pluto, clocking in at 2,228.6 kilometres. It had no moons and was tidally locked to its star *Angelica Blagojevich 9*. I wish that wasn't its name. At some point, the Earthen population started naming stars whatever they wanted. You could buy one and name it. The Amanitanalians didn't know, and they probably wouldn't care either. But *Blagojevich*? And there were nine of them!

Due to its tidal lock, one side of the planet was a scorching hellscape, while the other side was remarkably well-suited for fungal life. Their species' trajectory resembled ours, having evolved from single-cell organisms to multicellular intelligent beings. We shared a common ancestor: fungus. But they stayed the same while we mutated—or maybe it was the other way around.

"Communications are fuzzy, Captain. I can't get a reading. Descending at 933 KPH," Wright said.

She was panicking, but Lefleur was surprisingly relaxed. He scratched his leg and mouthed *ahh Cortizone* under his breath.

"Uh, just land the thing on that big white mushroom," he said.

There were thousands of white caps on the horizon. Lefleur's lack of clarity should have been a sure-fire indicator of his imminent insanity, but choices had to be made; we didn't want to crash and burn in front of the Amanitanalians.

Wright and I made eye contact. Her hand hovered above the landing gauge.

"Hold on to something!" she shouted.

She pushed the button, forcing the cruiser's front-side thrusters to kick in. I couldn't stay on my feet. I fell back a few inches from where Lefleur stood. He seemed unaffected by the gravitational forces, continuing to squint into the monitor while scratching his crack.

"Steady, Lieutenant. Try not to bruise the damn thing."

"Metal doesn't bruise, sir!" I replied.

"I'm talking about the mushroom, numb-nuts."

If it weren't for Wright's tactful maneuvering, the ship would've decimated a few caps and stems. We touched down on the mushroom's surface and could feel the cruiser sink into the spongy makeshift landing pad. The viewing chamber was blocked by a whirlwind of russet-colored spores.

"Yes, yes, I can taste it." The captain sniffed the air and shivered, tonguing his upper lip like an amphetamine-deprived space lizard. "Oxygen levels, Corporal Hager?"

"Same as before, I believe, Captain." I tapped my suit's forearm interface. "Teetering between fifty-one and fifty-three percent, sir."

"Good, good." Lefleur exhaled and shimmied his legs together. "Landing procedures then, I need a minute." He coughed and turned toward his quarters, walking like a duck while muttering to himself.

My stomach growled. I didn't want any more of that nasty bean dip casserole that came in a vacuum-sealed bag. I thought for a moment that maybe the Amanitanalians would provide us with some food, and then I remembered that mushrooms ate dirt, like worms.

"What do these folks eat, Melly?" I asked.

Corporal Wright gave me the side-eye and shrugged her shoulders. "Stanny, we don't even know if these guys are friendly." She cocked back her pistol and holstered it on her hip. "What makes you think they're going to be all nice and fuzzy toward us?"

"Yeah, you're right." The verdict weighed on me. But I ultimately decided to starve, for the time being, thinking perhaps due to our common lineage, we'd have similar diets.

I tightened my belt and peeked out the viewing chamber. The spore clouds whirled with the planet's wind, revealing a canopy of white-capped giant mushrooms. The spore ejections were so numerous that I could see torrents of spotted-white flow from the four-meter-long gills.

"We can breathe here, but we ought to be wearing masks," I said. "Unless you want a mouthful of mushroom seeds."

"Was planning on it," Wright replied.

Captain Lefleur stumbled out of his quarters with his pants just above his thighs. He rushed to pull them up, grunting as he secured his belt over his gut. "We ready, people?"

Wright stood stiff. "Captain, shouldn't we complete a biological survey before exiting the craft?"

Lefleur finished tucking his shirt and turned to Wright. "What? We got oxygen, we got a ship to go back to, and we got guns."

Couldn't argue with that logic. Wright rubbed the side of her head and reached toward the commissary to grab extra food bags. She knew she'd end up taking care of the two of us if things went south.

Lefleur was stoked. He had already overlooked just about every regulation on the books, and under normal circumstances would be an ideal candidate for a court-martial. But he didn't care. If I didn't know any better, I would've assumed he was inebriated, but that was just his normal behavior.

He strolled carefree to the hatch before bumping his fist against the release valve. Neither Wright nor I could react; a stream of spores blasted through the opening. Lefleur walked onto the cap like he was about to check his mailbox.

"Sir, you need a mask!" I shouted.

"Wh...need...goddamn..."

I couldn't make out the rest of his reply. He disappeared behind a sheet of floating spores. Wright begrudgingly strapped on a mask and marched out the door. Everything happened so fast, I didn't even have time to check the vicinity's air quality. I strapped on my mask and hit the hatch's button on my way out.

The commotion created by our landing kicked up a substantial amount of otherwise stagnant spore-litter, fomenting an exaggerated view of the planet's flora. Such was the case that after breaching the surrounding wall of spores, the view ahead was surprisingly unobstructed.

Captain Lefleur stood shivering—his legs visibly shaking as he reached out with his arms and reared his head back. Wright and I observed the strange behavior. I didn't understand at the time, but our captain was experiencing the same feeling that so many explorers had felt, a sort of triumphant euphoria begotten by being the first of his kind to do something never done before.

He crossed his arms and surveyed the horizon. We had landed at a niche location, at the edge of the Amanita forest and the south end of The Bolete Dominion. The urban conglomerate consisted of several massive king bolete mushrooms, hollowed out at various locations. The specimen nearest to us brandished an archway that resembled a primitive opening, with dozens of holes of different sizes serving as balconies and window fixtures. Interconnected mycelium knotted together, forming a series of highways and side streets, the largest of which ran between the most prominent boletes, ending at a bracket polypore monstrosity, a most fitting location for the Amanitanalian elite to meet and govern.

It didn't take long for the locals to investigate the mysterious object that had landed on one of their finest rural homes. At first, I swore I was hallucinating, but as I rubbed my eyes and stepped toward Lefleur, I realized we had indeed made contact with the mushroom people of Amanitanalia.

They came in all shapes and sizes. On average, they were about two and a half meters tall. The cap and stem species were the most prominent and most abundant, followed by the trumpets and phallic stinkhorns. A puffball eclipsed the edge of the crowd, about the size of a Routemaster bus. Corals twirled at its feet, each of them shimmying their way toward our ship in their unique dance. The mold crept to the forefront, providing a barrier between their brethren and us.

Like a Spaghetti Western, the three of us stood facing down the now-still crowd of animate fungi. A lumbering cloud of spores floated between us, clearing just enough for the details of their faces to emerge. I shouldn't have been surprised, but their faces were strikingly similar to ours: complete with eyes, noses, and gaping, mold-encrusted mouths. I caught a glimpse of the foremost russula blink while staring right at me; my body shuddered in response.

"Good mushrooms of Amanitanalia!" Lefleur shouted. "We are the people of Earth. We come in peace. I am Captain Terrence Lefleur. I must speak with your leader."

Could he have sounded any more like an alien film villain? I watched Wright out of the corner of my eye. She discreetly unlatched the pistol from her belt and tiptoed to Lefleur's side. Taking the cue, I did the same. Without an immediate response from the Amanitanalians, I didn't know what to expect.

"Have you no tongues good fungi!"

"Yeah, we hear you." A voice rang out from the crowd.

The three of us glanced at each other. I tightened my grip on my pistol.

"English? You speak English?" Lefleur replied.

"También español, güey."

Lefleur grit his teeth and turned toward me. "Why do the Spanish always get there first?"

"Sir, there appears to be no evidence of prior human contact," Wright said while tapping on her forearm interface.

"Impossible!" Lefleur said. "How would they know both languages?"

"We start pretty early."

"Damn, these guys are good." Lefleur regained his composure before addressing the crowd. "Okay, then. Fine, is there no one among you who can show us your great land?"

The crowd parted as if Lefleur himself was a prophet. In the middle of the rift stood a solitary Amanita Muscaria. Its cap transitioned from bloody-orange to sickly-yellow, flaking off in white drapes in front of its gills. Although it was presumptuous of me to assume their species was sexually-dimorphous, I had little doubt that this specimen was male, as the base of his stem was swollen and girdled; he was probably popular among his female counterparts.

Lefleur examined the mushroom from stem to cap and smiled. The amanita returned the gesture by bowing toward us, revealing his intricate network of scales. I admired the mushroom's poise and beauty. Once the amanita returned to his previous posture, his mycelium flared out in front of him, motioning for us to descend from the mushroom. I should have sensed it then and there—that Lefleur's motivations were questionable—but I decided against my hunch, even as the captain licked his lips for no discernible reason and glanced back at me with bloodshot eyes.

The pathway consisted of several descending caps, separated by a meter of height and length. Before attempting each descent, I'd scoot myself to the end of the mushroom and dangle my feet above the next cap. I experienced a child-like enthusiasm, hopping from mushroom top to mushroom top—stinky trampolines, little fungal bouncy balls. It was all very exciting. Not only had we successfully discovered a new species, but they were friendly too, and they spoke English!

Lefleur's landing on the mycelium-infested ground created an upsurge of spores. Wright and I trailed shortly behind, the two of us swatting through the thickets of spores that resembled swarming mosquitoes. Now that the distance had closed between us and the Amanitanalians, I could clearly see the apprehension on their faces. Unless I had interpreted their body language incorrectly, they looked terrified or appalled. In contrast to our immediate infatuation with their appearance, ours repulsed them.

The amanita that welcomed us stood behind a slimy line of green and yellow mold. He slivered forward—his mycelium like tentacles—and his stem swaying side-to-side like a tree branch in the wind.

"My name is Z z z s s s z z z s s." The mushroom paused and nodded. "But you can call me Eric."

Wright and I pulled up to Lefleur's side, still gripping our pistols. I glanced at Wright and read it on her face too; she was just as flabbergasted as I was. Lefleur's eyes widened and his pupils twitched as he analyzed the crowd and licked his lips again.

"Eric!" Lefleur shouted. The mushroom crowd in front of him collectively winced. Realizing how loud he was, Lefleur shrunk his head into his shoulders and whispered, "Eric, my friend. Please, show us everything. This place—this planet—it is a marvel. And I wish to know more."

Eric appeared to smile. I wish he hadn't done it though. His mouth was unnaturally wide, and the interior was as black as night. For a moment, all I could see was an unbridled predator. But as Eric's smile lengthened to fill out his stem, he demonstrated his initial relaxed posture.

"These are my assistants, Corporal Stanley Hager and Lieutenant Melinda Wright," Lefleur said, gesturing to us.

Not knowing how to properly greet the Amanitanalians (let alone any alien race), I couldn't help but form a half-smile and assume the *woogity* posture with my free hand: pinkie out, thumb out, shake it all about. Wright looked as if she was about to take on an army of Xenomorphs. She stood with her knees bent, shivering with both hands clutching her pistol.

Eric observed Wright first, then his eyes shifted to me. I gazed deep into his pupils. I felt him staring into my mind. How could something so peaceful be so off-putting at the same time? Wright played it safe, I thought that maybe I should do the same, seeing as our captain had nearly incapacitated himself in excitement.

The ever-patient Eric the Amanita Muscaria, squirmed over the bumpy road of mycelium leading toward the wider path ahead. The crowd dispersed, either too afraid or wisely prudent of the invaders. Their faces crowded the balconies among the upper decks of their king bolete mega-structures, watching our every move. I felt uncomfortable—like an intruder—but the astonishment at meeting this new and strange species was just starting to kick in.

The diversity among the Amanitanalinas could not be understated. During the long ride over to Angelica Blagojevich 9, I had plenty of time to familiarize myself with the most sought-after mushrooms in the mycological world. Being able to identify them in real-time brought me a unique excitement. I glanced to my right and made out the silhouettes of Black Trumpets gathered at the foot of their balconies. I imagined skewering them and roasting them over a charcoal grill, but I came to my senses, acknowledging that these beings were sentient and deserved to be treated with dignity.

Even Wright let down her guard, staring at the various groups of fungi now congregating around the openings in their bolete houses. I watched her scowl and refocus her attention forward as a trio of penis-shaped stinkhorns bobbed at the foot of the mycelium street. Lefleur walked with his hands in a fist below his chin, like a child in a toy store. I began to wonder how many spores he had inhaled at this point? Would they affect his judgment?

Eric slithered at a slow-pace up an incline leading to the polypore conglomerate. As we entered the shadows reaching out from under the bracket fungi, I noticed the sides of the bark leading to the entrance were guarded by the black knot fungus, *apiosporina morbosa*. Their eyes unpeeled in unison as we passed. Among the toughest of fungi, their placement was strategic. I was starting to catch on to the sophistication of their social hierarchies. It made sense. The tougher, more robust fungi handled security, from the mold that guarded the onlookers when we landed, to the knots that stoically watched our every move.

But their complex systems still befuddled me. I wanted to ask Eric how sentience was distributed among his population. For instance, how does one know if their offspring are to be sentient or not? It's kind of like the Goofy and Pluto problem, but with mushrooms. Imagine the dismay some of these fungi must go through, to see their children born as just regular ol' mushrooms. *Yes, honey, they'll make a fine house for us to live in someday.* It's actually quite morbid.

We entered the interior of the polypore structure; it had been hollowed out and fashioned into living quarters. Just enough light trickled in through well-placed holes in the ceiling. Their level of engineering was impressive. I had no doubt that in a few generations they would've achieved space travel, at least on the local level. The sides of the mycelium hill were dotted with openings to corridors. Four golden chanterelles waddled out from the exits and walked alongside Eric. As they approached, I heard them whisper in a language I couldn't understand.

Lefleur stopped in his tracks at the sight of the chanterelles. He let out a croaking noise and itched the back of his neck. Wright rushed over to Lefleur's side and supported him underneath his arms.

"Should've worn a damn mask, you buffoon," Wright said as she unlatched the medical tote on her belt and extracted a syringe. "Stanny, give me a hand here."

I forgot about the mission and our mushroom attendees as I knelt behind our captain. Wright stabbed Lefleur in the arm, then pulled the needle out before inserting its contents into a receptacle at the base of her forearm interface.

As the screen lit up, I noticed the mushrooms close-in around us. While Wright was distracted taking in the data, I caught a whiff of the rancid stench of a white-capped mushroom breathing next to me. A few sniffs revealed my worst fear: we were surrounded by death caps.

"Significant levels of alpha-amanitin in his bloodstream, Corpo—"

Lefleur fired off a shot at Eric. He turned around and fired three more. Shocked at the sudden violence, I stood frozen, watching the bodies fall at my feet. Captain was an excellent marksman. The death cap that fell next to me had a smoldering hole in the center of his cap. Eric writhed before us—his flesh transitioning from milky white to brown as he let out a sustained squeaking noise.

Lefleur gathered himself to his feet and turned to Wright and I. Sweat glistened on his cheeks as he put on a big grin. He reached into both of his pockets and pulled out a stick of Breakstone's Salted Butter, and in the other hand, an Opinel Folding Mushroom Knife.

"Where'd he...the butter? Wha..." Wright whispered.

Whatever our captain had inhaled during his brief visit to Amanitanalia, it had awakened a long-dormant hunger within him. A hunger that had no regard for intelligent life. Or maybe he was always that way because evidently, he stashed butter and specialized knives in his pockets.

With a surge of energy, Lefleur lunged after a fleeing chanterelle. He sliced through its stem before whipping his head onto its flesh. Like a ravaging shark, Lefleur shredded a yellow chunk from the mushroom's cap. He shoved the butter stick into the other corner of his mouth and bit down. After an initial swallow, he moaned and fell to his knees.

"More! More! I need more!" he shouted with bits of chanterelle sputtering out between breaths.

Having clearly established his intentions, Wright and I looked at each other, silently agreeing that we had three options:

1. Subdue Captain Lefleur, bring him back to the ship, apologize profusely, and get the hell out.

2. Ditch Captain Lefleur, fight our way back and get the hell out.

3. Or, join in the massacre and make the best of our time here.

You wouldn't believe it, but we actually went with option three. We gave one and two an honest attempt though.

Lefleur continued on his rampage, cutting caps and stems with gusto and gnawing on their detritus between mouthfuls of butter. Having recovered from the initial shock, I started after Lefleur as he hacked the chanterelles to pieces. More mushrooms crowded our position making it difficult for me to navigate toward the captain. I counted six morels (or at least I thought they were morels), both yellow and brown, surrounding Lefleur. They towered over him, but Lefleur was fearless. He circled his knife over his head, swinging the blade within inches of their porous exterior. A smaller morel grabbed a hold of his foot but swiftly met its demise when the captain gouged its stem. Lefleur ripped the knife up and cut the morel in two.

"You're not hollow!" Lefleur let out an exasperated grunt. "Gyromitra esculenta! Brain mushroom bastards! Morel wannabes!"

An adroit mycologist—Lefleur called their bluff. The gyromitras backed off once they witnessed the captain's savagery, but the crazed mushroom-hunter beckoned them for more.

"Have at me, you venomous leeches!" he shouted before leaping out with the blade facing downward, pressed between both of his hands.

Before I could reach the outskirts of the attacking gyromitras, a bramble of mica caps stumbled over me running in the opposite direction. They left their orange slime residue along the right side of my body and they managed to take my mask with them. I tripped to the side and had to reorient myself.

Dozens of mushrooms rushed around us speaking in strange tongues (but occasionally in Spanish). There were too many to identify. The majority of the crowd had chased after Lefleur, but judging by the flakes of mushroom being tossed into the air, I knew he was winning spectacularly.

It was at that moment I noticed Wright had not joined in Lefleur's defense. Between a crew of passing blewits, I saw Wright lying on her back with her head propped up against the torso of one of the chanterelles Lefleur had murdered. I assumed the worst, but under further investigation, she was actually smiling, even giggling at the massacre.

I ran to her side and tried to get her attention. "Melly! Melly! The hell's wrong with you?"

She turned her head to the side but could only muster a cluttered word salad. It dawned on me that maybe she had experienced a slight poisoning, similar to what she had confirmed on our captain moments before he began his fungicide. She had taught me the basic blood drawing procedures while we were aboard the ship, and seeing as Lefleur was having no hard time defending himself, the rightful triage of the situation consisted of me checking on Wright, then making a decision of who to return to the ship first.

I located the medical tote still attached to her utility belt and scrambled its insides. Finally, I found a fresh syringe, uncapped it, and plugged it right into the underside of her bicep. As the blood was being drawn, I lifted my head to assess the mushroom panic/mass murder.

Larger mushrooms—nearly double the size of the late-Eric—lumbered down the cavity from which we had entered. More of them marched behind the preliminary frontline, consisting of russulas over a meter tall, then king boletes with stems over a meter wide. Their mycelium slivered out in front of them like snakes searching for prey. Lefleur was busy cleaving the remaining gyromitra garrison; his skills were yet to be properly tested, but that was about to change.

I deposited the blood sample in my forearm interface and read the data as it came in. Wright began to laugh audibly. She pointed her finger out and mumbled, "Oh my god—there's like so many mushrooms over there!"

It all came together as she finished her profound statement.

"38 mgs of psilocybin... Lord help us..."

Before long, my interface started to vibrate and the colors began to sing to me. Their melody was a sweet one. The neon blues and greens were excellent at harmonizing. The mycelium beneath us shared our heartbeats for a moment. It was nice to know that there were still some fungi that were not hostile toward us. I looked Wright in her eyes. Her pupils were the size of silver dollars. She laughed in slow-motion and mouthed, "Mushrooms, man... Goddamn mushrooms. So freakin' hungry..."

I was really hungry too. Maybe Wright and I could eat some of the mushrooms, just for a bit. We'd only be borrowing their flesh, right? Eventually, we'd die and then they'd eat us. I remembered they ate dirt. So, it was all good. Russulas were edible—and we'd help out Lefleur in his foray anyway.

We did just that. Wright and I managed to locate our feet; having forgotten they were attached to our legs. There were so many fractal patterns that the earth-tone colors all mixed together rendering our puny-human vision to be less effective. All the mushrooms scurrying about created quite a racket. I swore I could understand their language if I listened hard enough, but I just couldn't focus on any one thing for too long. I remembered what we were doing as Wright dragged her feet out in front of me—her head twitching back and forth as if ducking from dive-bombing bats.

We didn't have any other weapons on us apart from the pistols, and I didn't exactly feel comfortable opening fire while under the influence of a gratuitous amount of psilocybin I had unknowingly ingested. We had to make do. Hands it was.

I passed Lefleur as he thrashed about like a mad man and made my way to the front line of russulas. Although they were twice my size and resembled an Earthen predator with their sunken black eyes and gaping mouth, I didn't feel any apprehension standing before them. They even looked cute in a certain way. I reached out and ripped a chunk off one of its stems. The russula's mycelium elongated beside me and shook violently, followed by the mushroom itself shrieking in pain. I knew that cooking was recommended, but I was just too hungry. I took a bite and tasted the distinct peppery flavor associated with yellow russula mushroom. Not bad—but not my favorite.

The injured russula was attended to by the surrounding squad— its shrieking yet to cease. I looked over my shoulder and saw Wright climbing on top of an orangey bracket fungus that had descended to assist in the planet's defense. Wright dug her fingernails into the top side of the largest specimen and reached down to pluck the moistened strand with her teeth. Chicken-of-the-woods—a fine choice; her knowledge impressed me.

I felt another wave of the psilocybin coming on strong, but I was lucid enough to remember that I had set forth parameters for my mission. It was hard to recollect them, but I knew I needed to press on. I tried to run after Lefleur, but could only muster a few steps as I noticed my feet had bifurcated into several looping fractal patterns. Walking it was.

Lefleur had gained some distance on me; he had nearly exited from underneath the bracket fungi where we'd entered. There were so many mushrooms attempting to stop him, that they combined together into an amorphous entity of color and sound. They crashed down like waves upon the captain, but he held strong, fearlessly annihilating them upon contact. I glanced back to see if Wright was following, but to my dismay, she had bored a hole in the meter-wide chicken-of-the-woods—her face and hands dripping with yellowy-orange fungal guts.

I managed to find my way back onto the main mycelium boulevard but couldn't believe what I was witnessing. The king bolete megastructures burned from their roof-caps. Hundreds of mushrooms—small and large, round and scrutumesque—all leaped from their windows and balconies. Some splattered against the mycelium road, while others survived the jump, eventually regaining their composure and running through the streets. It was pure chaos.

I heard giggling next to me. Wright had finished her meal; I had only eaten a bit of russula and was still itching to get my hands on something better.

The ground shook. Then there were two hulking shadows growing from beyond the confines of the bracket fungi capital.

Calvatia gigantea. The biggest mofos out there. The two largest puffballs I had ever seen rolled down the tops of the bracket fungi steps—their final defense; they were going to take us out *Indiana Jones style.*

The mushroom Gods read my mind. There was only one thing to do: ~~run for our lives~~ stop their momentum and eat them asap.

With her mouth still full of mushroom fodder, Wright cracked a dripping smile and drew her pistol. She fired at least a dozen shots (maybe fewer—counting on shrooms is incredibly difficult) at the puffball rolling down on our right. Noting her enthusiasm, I unholstered my pistol and fired at the one on the left.

The bullets riddled the fungi with steaming holes. Their structural integrity was severely compromised, evinced by their exteriors splintering like glass from their wounds. They exploded one after another upon making contact with the next polypore, splitting into several uneven slices of fungal shrapnel.

Wright gave me a cheery smile, her cheeks still somewhat inundated with leftover mushroom bits she was yet to swallow. I watched her saunter past some frightened parasols and make her way toward a banana peel-shaped slice of puffball. She lay down in its interior fluff and plucked chunks of the spongy fungus, tossing them into her mouth like popcorn.

I followed her footsteps up a crooked polypore and lay down next to her on a similarly sized edible mushroom blanket. I felt complete serenity. The skies were illuminated with intricate swirls of yellows and browns, and the smog from the burning mushroom buildings had dissipated slightly.

Wright and I must have sat there for hours, engorging ourselves with the delicious Amanitanalian population. As my consciousness ebbed and flowed from the accidental psilocybin overdose, it dawned on me that due to our continued inhalation of the mind-altering chemicals, we might be indefinitely stuck in this precarious state. Against my inclination to enjoy my trip and feast until I vomited, I decided that it would be a good idea to locate our ship at least—maybe Lefleur too—if he was alive.

I left Wright to her blissful ignorance and began my stroll through the carnage below. Few mushrooms remained on the street level. I imagined most were huddled away somewhere, perhaps underground. Every now and then, I'd catch a glimpse of a thin strand scurrying behind the smoky ruins of the Bolete Dominion. Our ship glistened in the faint light that managed to push through the cloud cover. Climbing up the white-capped and gigantic mushrooms was more challenging than I thought. I looked at my feet and noticed a red ooze slithering its way toward our ship. It hissed at me as I summited the cap.

"*We'll poison your existence yet! We'll scramble your brains more than the cubensis did!*"

"Don't listen to 'em, Stanny."

It was Lefleur. He was sitting against the ship's door. I approached the side of our ship and knelt down in front of the captain. He reached out with a soot-covered hand and waved me off.

"Captain?"

"It's just Ergot." Lefleur coughed and grit his teeth. "Must've accessed our archives and read about their descendants. They think they can render their lysergic acid into diethylamide"

He squirmed against the ship's side, wheezing and clutching his stomach.

"Ah, boy. They got me this time."

"What are you talking about?"

"Caloric deficit, Stanny…"

His voice trailed off to a whisper as he said my name. "Take care of Melly, will ya?"

"Captain, I don't read you. Captain!"

Lefleur's head slid on the curvature of the ship and rested on his shoulder. His belly deflated—the fabric of his suit scrunched up between his fingers.

Lefleur had eaten so many mushrooms that his body pushed itself to the limit in a desperate effort to digest the fungus. He probably mentioned it during our journey to Angelica Blagojevich 9, but mushrooms are a negative calorie food. Now, ordinarily, this would not be problematic. But when paired with a rigorous form of murderous exercise, and the thermal effect of eating while completing said activity, the combination could be deadly. Nonetheless, our captain had found a unique way to die.

Once Wright had come to and found herself atop the mushroom landing pad, we looked at each other and understood the full magnitude of our actions. There was no *goodbye* or *come again soon* from the Amanitanalians; a quick biological survey confirmed this, as their numbers appeared to be so diminished that only trace amounts of biological activity were detected.

We buried Lefleur at the foot of the mushroom's stem underneath a pile of spore debris. Over the mound of broken mycelium, I scraped into the stem:

Captain Terrence Lefleur – Of USA of Earth. The first man to make contact with the Amanitanalians – *Beat the Spanish.

"Computer, play Fleetwood Mac," Wright said, wiping a tear from her cheek as we skulked up the mushrooms back to the ship.

Landslide hummed softly from within the cabin. That might've been in poor taste considering the condition in which we were leaving Amanitanalia. But it didn't matter. We had failed our mission, succumbing to the worst qualities of human nature. Apart from the standard shuttle dribble, Wright and I said very little to each other for the first two days of travel.

On the third day, I broke the silence. "It's not right. What we did back there. What Lefleur did. We have to do something about it."

"What do you have in mind? We just up and turn ourselves in? Hell if I end up in some brig sweating my tits off next to some dwarf star."

"I got an idea." I stood up and nudged Wright away from the controls. I tapped the interface to scan the Blagojevich system. With Amanitanalia's planetary conditions punched in, the adjoining planets began to pop up on the big screen.

"I reviewed the flight data and suit recordings from Amanitanalia. I really feel like garbage. What we did to them was, like, not cool. But that got me thinking." I pressed my finger against the computer screen at Angelica Blagojevich 3. "Okay, see this one? S-type planet next to that star—"

"No. Just no. I see it, but your idea—"

"Come on! Just listen. Same atmospheric content, no life forms, just enough in that golden crisp zone—"

"The golden crisp zone? You mean, the goldilocks zone?"

"Sure—that thing. If we go there and…"

It was hard to communicate the haphazard plan I'd just concocted in my cottage cheese brain. Wright was already starting to cover her face with her palms.

"So, uh…with our bellies filled with the mushroom people *and* their spores… Maybe if we do our *business* there—" I squatted so she'd catch my drift.

Wright rubbed her head against her palms. "So…you're suggesting we use this planet as a bathroom and leave?"

She didn't immediately reject the plan. This one was a keeper.

"Precisely! It would be an *immaculate inoculation*—if you will. We'd be like their gods!"

"I wouldn't exactly call it immaculate, but whatever…"

Wright hesitated with her hands hovering above the interface. She turned in her seat and twiddled with the controls, adjusting our flight path to my recommended location.

"I suppose it's the least we can do before we pen our prison memoirs," she muttered.

"Yeah, yeah." I felt relieved but still guilty. It was the least we could do, as unflattering as shitting on a planet sounded at the time. I harkened back to my initial thoughts on the Amanitanalians and how their sentience was determined by a genetic dice roll. I imagined a planet filled with frolicking morels and lazy puffballs, all existing in blissful harmony.

When the deed had been done, we reboarded our ship and took off toward the Milky Way. There was just one last thing to do.

"Melly?"

"Yeah?"

"I really hate the name."

"Nothing you can do about it."

"Well, there is, technically. We can submit a request for a name change through the DMV."

"They do planetary name changes too?"

"I know, I know. They started with TNOs. What'll be next?"

"All right, so what do you got?"

I typed in the proposed name change and looked at Wright. I could tell she didn't like it, but also that she didn't care much either.

She sighed. "Screw it."

I pressed enter and sent the request.

We'd be incarcerated by the time the bureaucratic schleps would get to it. But it put a smile on my face to see the name displayed on the interface: *Captain Terrence Lefleur and Eric the Amanita's Fecal Garden of Hope Memorial Planet.*

Mike teaches and writes in upstate New York. Links to more of his published work can be found here: *michaeldioguardisciencefiction.tumblr.com*.

Welcome to Vega IV!

by

Simon Kewin

NOW the war between Earth and Vega is over, more and more Terrans are choosing to visit Vega IV to savour its distinctive culture. Keep the following guidelines in mind as you explore this fascinating planet:

1. Don't eat the food

More than one human has made the mistake of assuming the Vegans are vegans. The truth is quite the opposite, as their impressive arrays of razor-sharp teeth, body-spikes and chitinous claws perhaps make obvious. Vegans are top predators. Their diet consists almost exclusively of the fast-moving, soft-bodied madrats so numerous on Vega IV.

In a desperate attempt to avoid being eaten, madrats have evolved a highly toxic body-chemistry. Unfortunately for the madrats, the Vegans have evolved a digestion that doesn't care. Humans have not. Eat any local dish and you will die.

2. Don't drink the water

Vegan biology isn't based on H_2O like ours: Vega IV's skies rain sulfuric acid and consequently that's what Vegans drink. Don't make the mistake of trying it. Their alcoholic drinks are especially unsafe. These are acid mixed with concentrations of alcohol likely to slay any human within moments.

3. Don't breathe the air

Vega IV's atmosphere does contain oxygen and nitrogen. But it also contains very high concentrations of sulfur dioxide. Vegans consider this combination healthy and bracing. You shouldn't.

4. Avoid social interaction

Vegan hive culture is complex, hierarchical, and bound by social norms that few humans can hope to understand. An individual contravening any of a long series of frequently bizarre social conventions will be immediately killed, for fear of upsetting the social order. Don't be that individual!

5. Don't attempt to communicate
Vegan language consists of a rapid series of clicks, thrums and pincer-gesticulations. Any human attempting to converse in this fashion will inevitably make mistakes. It has been calculated by xenolinguists that around 80% of the Vegan language is devoted to dire threats. You are very likely to end up in an unfortunate position if you do attempt to communicate.

6. Don't even look at anyone
Direct eye-to-eye contact is considered threatening to the Vegan mindset. Unfortunately, the sight of a human face is very likely to trigger the Vegans' strong predation instinct, and they may well attack mercilessly and without warning. Remember, this is perfectly normal in Vegan culture and shouldn't be taken as a personal slight.

The similarity of human facial features to those of the madrat is perhaps an unfortunate coincidence in this regard.

7. Do admire the meadows
Perhaps surprisingly, Vega IV is blessed with many stunning flower meadows. These are a must for off-world visitors. Don't touch any of the flowers, though. Seriously, just don't.

8. Keep moving
You may well be tempted to linger as you admire the flower meadows or the Vegan's soaring hive architecture. Don't. Stationary individuals are generally assumed to be dead and therefore food in Vegan culture.

Follow these simple rules and your visit should be enjoyable and may even last as long as intended. Enjoy your stay!

Simon Kewin is a fantasy and sci/fi writer, author of the *Cloven Land* fantasy trilogy, cyberpunk thriller *The Genehunter*, steampunk Gormenghast saga *Engn*, the *Triple Stars* sci/fi trilogy and the *Office of the Witchfinder General* books, published by Elsewhen Press. He's the author of several short story collections, with his shorter fiction appearing in Analog, Nature and over a hundred other magazines. His novel *Dead Star* was an SPSFC award semi-finalist and his short story *#buttonsinweirdplaces* was nominated for a Utopia award. He is currently doing an MA in creative writing while writing at least three novels simultaneously.

Delectable

by

Robert Luke Wilkins

"IT'S certainly a pretty one-sided deal," said Leonard as he leaned back into his chair. "But what else would you expect? They're bugs, not attorneys."

The reporter nodded and scribbled a note in his pad. The dining table in the harvest facility's executive lounge seated twelve, but only three seats were occupied, by the reporter and the company's two harvester-team leaders.

In the middle of the table was a large wooden bowl of toasted honey-bugs. Tiny ant-like creatures, their sweetness was mingled with unparalleled flavor, and their shell yielded the perfect, lightly crispy crunch. But they were also incredibly rare, found only on the hostile surface of Khepri. All efforts to raise them elsewhere had failed, and per ounce they had become one of the galaxy's most expensive delicacies, beyond even Earth-raised caviar.

"It's a dangerous job you guys have," said the reporter. "The death-rate here is incredibly high."

"It was worse before the cutbacks," said Leonard with a shrug. "We lost a team almost every month back then. But it's been better recently, so the figures you have down might be a little high. Still, there have always been risky jobs, haven't there? We get paid well for our work, and nobody comes here expecting an easy ride."

That much was true. Everybody knew the job was hard and not without risks, though the loss of Alex's team last month had still come as a shock. It had been a timely reminder to them all that even experienced harvesters could pay the price if they were careless. Rumor said a replacement team was inbound, but in the meantime, the remaining teams were reaping better harvests than ever.

"So why not use machines instead?"

"They tried," said Leonard. "But the bugs don't like the machines, and they don't last long in this atmosphere anyway. No, the only way is with human feet on the ground. That's why our product is so valuable." He took a pinch of the lightly toasted honey-bugs and popped them into his mouth. They crunched between his teeth. "I admit it wouldn't suit everyone. But for those with the stomach, it's a way of life. I wouldn't trade your boring job for mine in a month of Mondays."

An hour later, Leonard and his two team-members stood in the facility's northern exit chamber. The processing facility itself was a dull-looking structure with armor-plated outer walls. They had nicknamed it Candy Mountain.

"So what did he want?"

"The usual," said Leonard, stripping off his clothes. Beside him, Ellis and Joanna were already naked. All three were shaved entirely clean of body-hair down to the eyebrows, and all were ridged with heavy muscle. "He wanted to know all about the most dangerous job in the universe."

They laughed. They loved that reputation—it made them the rock-stars of the new frontier.

Each of them took an elliptical facemask and a pair of ear-plugs from a long shelf against one wall. They inserted the plugs and fitted their masks carefully before heading through a nearby door into the closing chamber, where they waited to be covered.

The symbiosis of the bugs and their harvesters was a boon. The planet's atmosphere was incredibly corrosive, and little could endure it for long. Even diamond and titanium degraded quickly, and the finest custom-made protective suits lasted only a day.

But the bugs endured it easily. The scientists said it was down to rapid cell regeneration, far faster than any animal on record elsewhere. And by happy chance, they were attracted to humans. The tiny things, barely a quarter of an inch long, would crawl onto any open skin they could find and form a living barrier between the harvesters and the hostile atmosphere.

And then they ate them at the end of it. It was a perfect reflection of humankind. The facility would roast and pack up the majority of the harvest, but kept enough living bugs on hand to fully cover all outgoing harvesters.

The facemasks were disposable, and equipped with microphones that would transmit to the team's ear-plugs. Each would last for a single harvest only, and each contained tiny hyper-compressed air canisters, sufficient for a day's breathing. They were lightweight but durable, and damaged visor layers could be peeled away as necessary to help maintain clarity. The last three layers would crackle when peeled free, a warning to any harvester running close to his equipment's limit.

But aside from the mask and ear-plugs, every other part of the body was left naked to attract the bugs. The more skin you exposed, the more bugs you could attract. And the more bugs you brought in, the more money you made.

Nobody knew exactly what the bugs got out of it. Scientists had proposed several theories about human secretions, but nobody had been able to safely study the relationship. Still, whatever it was, the harvesters got the best of the deal—and all you had to do to get your share of the pot was let a million tiny insects crawl all over your naked body.

It wasn't a job for everyone. But if you couldn't stomach it, then you didn't deserve the rewards.

"Hey, Jo," said Ellis, as the bugs began to form a thick layer on his legs. "Do they ever get up inside your... well, you know?"

"Yeah, every time," she said. "Hey, it's all money, right?"

Leonard laughed, and started to say something about her being weird. But as the bugs climbed up over his groin, he closed his eyes and took a deep breath. Part of him always expected things to go wrong at that point. The first time they'd crawled over him, they'd actually given him an erection. That had been embarrassing enough—and in his mind's eye there were always visions of much, much worse.

But the bugs continued crawling up without incident, and soon all three were clad in living suits. The crawling sensation was itchy, but reassuring. It meant you were protected.

The lights turned green, the secure doors opened, and they marched out onto the planet's surface.

The job was simple enough, at least on paper. Head out, find a cluster of bugs, and lead them home. There were box-traps all around the base that would capture them once they were nearby, but live, close human flesh was the only thing that would attract them.

And even once the body was completely covered, the bugs would keep coming. They'd crawl on top of the others, forming a heavy, shifting mass around the harvester that could become several feet thick. Movement was difficult then, like marching neck-deep in molasses, and you needed strength, and fitness. It was no job for the weak.

"We'll hit the sixteenth quad," said Leonard.

"You sure? It's dodgy out that way."

"I'm sure. Alex's team was scheduled there this week, and nobody's hit it yet. We cleared out the western side yesterday, and Stu took his team South. I know it's a hike, and rough ground, but I think we've got a great chance of finding a large mass."

Ellis and Joanna simply nodded. Leonard's instincts were rarely wrong, and over the last two years his leadership had made them rich.

The sixteenth quadrant lay to the north-east, four miles away on the other side of a stretch of thick vegetation. The surface was tough on Khepri at the best of times, with unstable, uneven ground and one hundred and twenty percent of Earth's gravity to contend with. But the green areas were worse. Aside from the thick, vine-like plants that sprouted all over, there were some strange, lumpy things that emitted foul fumes, and hollow fungus-like growths that contained enzymes that the honey-bugs hated. If you fell into one of those they would scatter and leave you naked—after that, it was a dice-roll whether the enzymes or the atmosphere killed you first.

Neither was a clean death.

The atmosphere had left no trace, but the fungi were Leonard's hot pick for what had claimed Alex's team. Others had vanished in more barren areas, and those he put down to poor leaders who didn't know the ground well enough, or who had panicked when things went south.

But Leonard had a cool head, and knew the ground better than anyone. There were no surprises nor any tumbles into evil fungi, and within three hours they'd cleared it—good time for the terrain, though the return trip would be slower and tougher if they found the kind of mass he was hoping for. The vegetation yielded to an open plain —easier going, but it was a mixed blessing. There were no more evil fungi to contend with, but the ground in the Sixteenth was renowned for its instability.

"I hate this place," muttered Ellis.

"Don't we all," said Leonard. "But the honey-bugs love it. Let's spread out and find them. I'll bet both of you dinner that there's a good mass around here somewhere."

The trio fanned out, with Leonard heading north, and after ten minutes he spotted what he was looking for. A quarter mile ahead the ground was lightly rippling, the unmistakable sign of a large mass of bugs beneath.

"Ellis, Jo, get to my position." The pair both acknowledged. He waited, watching the shifting ground as the two made their way to him.

"Told you," he said, pointing at it. "What's that, a size-four group?"
"Looks like it," said Ellis. "Or damned close anyway. Man, I love
your instincts! It's only a shame they're underground."

"It beats not finding them, right? Let's lead them back to the
Mountain."

They walked closer, every step slow and careful. With the bugs
gathered underground in a thick mass, it would be even more unstable,
and more than one harvester had lost their life when the ground
collapsed. But after several cautious minutes they drew close to the
edge of the colony, and the first bugs began to crawl out towards them.

"We've got them," said Leonard. "Hang back here for few minutes,
and then—"

There was a sudden stiffness to his arms. The bugs could be heavy
at times, but instead of shifting, flowing and crawling as they usually
did, they all began to freeze in place. More bugs continued to crawl up
onto him, all freezing still, until he couldn't move at all.

"Wait up, guys," he said. "My bugs are acting all weird."

"Mine too."

"Same here."

Leonard frowned. This was new. In six years of harvesting, he'd
never seen them act this way. So what had changed? He looked around
for anything different in their environment, some kind of unknown
predator, but saw nothing. It all seemed normal, almost dull.

Slowly and ungainly, Leonard's legs stretched out forwards, carrying him in an unsteady step towards the colony.

"Whoa, whoa," said Leonard. "What the hell?"

"Hey, what happened to hanging back?"

"It's not me, it's the damned bugs." Leonard fought to hold his legs
in place, but the bugs were shifting, the living suit settling into its own
rhythm as it marched him forward. "I can't stop them!"

"Nor can I," said Ellis's voice over the intercom. "What the hell is
going on?"

Leonard was silent. He didn't know.

The bugs marched them out over the shifting mass, and though Leonard
expected them to sink into the unstable earth ground, the bugs beneath
formed a firm platform that kept them up. Leonard had some sense
of his direction, and though he didn't know exactly which quadrant
they were heading towards, he knew they were heading towards those
at the very edge of the facility's harvest boundary.

On the side of his mask was an emergency beacon button, but he couldn't lift his locked arm to push it. As far as anyone in the base knew, they were simply out hunting for a good mass. They'd rarely been out for less than twelve hours at a time, and had often come close to the full twenty-four—nobody would start worrying about them for hours. Beads of sweat were forming on his face, and his mask had begun to mist up.

"We've got to do something," said Ellis. "Anything!"

But there was nothing to be done. None of them could move, or resist the relentless marching of the bugs.

As they crossed an unfamiliar ridge, the broad entrance to a tunnel came into view, and they were marched straight down into it. Leonard expected utter darkness after that, but narrow blue veins in the rock glowed lightly, their dim fluorescence enough to see by.

The tunnels twisted and turned, and the bugs marched them along relentlessly. Leonard's body moved more quickly under their power than it ever had under his own. It was efficient but clumsy, and as they rounded one corner he felt his ankle twist painfully. The bugs didn't slow. They kept on marching, jarring his ankle over and over.

At last, the tunnels opened up into a single broad chamber, and within it sat six bugs—but vast ones, unlike any Leonard had ever seen, all facing a broad, four-foot tall stone pedestal in the middle. They were similar in form to the honey-bugs, but far larger—each was easily ten feet in length from head to tail, and six feet high as they stood. Their front legs were extended forwards, but instead of ending in simple points they splintered into long, delicate-looking fingers, three on each hand.

The pedestal itself was intricately carved with unfamiliar symbols and shapes, and on top of the pedestal were six silvery platters. Each was a little over half the size of a man.

The bugs coating him suddenly moved, crawling up over his face mask. For a brief moment he was blind, but then he felt it being pulled from his face and they all scattered, leaving him naked but for a simple pair of now worthless earplugs. The atmosphere stung his skin and eyes, but it was softer here, far less corrosive than the atmosphere at the surface.

He stumbled on his twisted ankle, and as he fell to the ground, he looked around quickly for his mask, hoping that he could grab it and push the transmit button to send a distress call. But all three of their masks were being carried around the edge of the chamber by a group of scuttling bugs. When they finally stopped, they dropped them against the far wall in a pile with dozens of other identical, corroded facemasks.

Leonard stared at the pile, and then back at the six giant bugs. They were all looking at him and his companions, but had not moved. He turned to the exit, looking for any way out, but the entrance was blocked by a seething mass of honey-bugs. They couldn't hope to run. Their only hope of escape was to get to the pile of masks, and—

Something hard grasped his arm, and then his ankle, and he was lifted into the air as though he weighed nothing at all. He heard Ellis and Joanna screaming and yelling, and then heard their voices suddenly muffled, but he couldn't look to see what was happening to them. He was lowered down, and felt cold stone beneath his naked flesh.

He looked down at his body. One of the giant bugs gripped his ankles, and then he felt something starting to pull on his arms. His limbs were drawn out against each other, and he screamed as he felt the bones of his shoulders and hips dislocating. He heard Ellis and Joanna screaming as well, and all too late as his flesh began to tear apart, he knew the truth about the honey-bugs of Khepri.

The deal wasn't so one-sided after all.

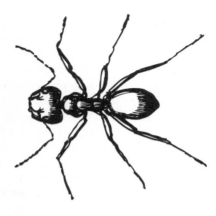

Robert works as a software engineer by day, and writes by night, with his stories having appeared in *PodCastle*, *Stupefying Stories*, *On Spec*, and others. An ex-pat Englishman, he now lives with his wife in Nevada, where their cats Mochi Luna and Teddy Logan do all they can to disrupt the tranquility of their lives. You can chat with him on Twitter at @RobertLWilkins.

Sky Tears

by

Mike Adamson

THE scientist in charge was more than a little attractive, but I had to stay focused. Professionalism demanded it, so I kept my eyes on my work and my tongue between my teeth. After all, being called in to find and destroy a drone, criminally harvesting the sweat of the skybeasts, was not an everyday occurrence.

To be asked for by name was an accolade—recognized as the best damn drone controller this side of the military—which I was. My experience was in asteroid exploration, guiding fleets of extractor bots through the mineral smorgasbord of the star-reefs, sniffing out the rich lodes and bringing back the bounty in gold, molybdenum, rothnium, and a score of other metals upon which the human colonial endeavor depended. So, being tasked to a biological sortie was something new.

The shuttle brought me direct from orbit to the science platform, a grubby, wind-blasted assembly of tanks, modules and girders floating in the lavender sky 200 meters over the lush meadowlands and lakes of Delphi, one of the colonies settled in the mid-24th century as part of the Magellan Group. I crossed to the platform as a robo-porter delivered my packaged gear—the kill-drone I would use for the shot. The command interface I carried in my com, which never left my person.

"Dr Laura Dryden," the boss began, extending a fine hand for a cool, dry shake. "Welcome aboard, Mister Relph." She was as tall as me, a dark ponytail down her back, clad in a leaf-green bodysheath, with the look of a fitness earned and kept over many decades. I had looked her up in the company database and knew she was well post-reju, five times my own meagre forty years. I'd not been home in ten of them, but family was as close as the subspace datalink, and an irritating kid-sister had monopolized my transmission time *en route* to Delphi. I considered myself about as normal as a human being could be, which made this woman, with her hundred-fifty years as a planetary scientist dealing with all manner of strangeness, deeply interesting.

I inclined my head so the wind, fragrant with the scents of the blossoming forests below, lifted long, sandy hair from my eyes, my long dark coat tugging like a sail. "Thanks for calling me in, I appreciate a different challenge."

"You've never been to Delphi, have you?"

"No, ma'am."

She hesitated, something in her manner speaking silently to me that all was not as it seemed. "You were briefed on what to expect, but for some the first time can be traumatic." She gestured to a hatch at the edge of the embarkation platform and we headed inside as the shuttle stood away, and the platform's service robot took charge of my gear.

The craft drifted over a wide, bucolic valley where the afternoon sun glimmered on a languid river, and we heard the chorus of the rainbow-hued flying creatures of this world. The air was warm, humid and seemed, to human senses, to threaten a storm. But we were not alone in this alien Eden, humans had adapted well and called it home.

Calmundra City lay low on the dusky horizon, a domed expanse a dozen kilometers across, floating serenely where it perched on the mooring tower of Mount Komarov. The cities—Ranthambor, Praxiteles, Memphis and others—were the glory of Delphi, eclipsing New Cambridge, the original planetary capital, in their extravagance. They were helium-filled carbon-foam structures, cities of no fixed locality, which wandered the globe, providing eternally fresh vistas for their inhabitants, and to the high-intensity tourist trade which brought so much to the local economy from all over the Middle Stars.

"It's our skybeasts," Dryden said softly as the door hissed to and I found myself in the relief of air conditioning. She showed me to a comfortable couch overlooking the vista below through a wide, oblate transparency. She sank in at my side and I made myself concentrate on the job; her charms were certainly distracting.

"The skybeasts," I repeated. "They gave me the full package before I left the Susa asteroids. Whale-sized critters that drift around the world, people come from all over to watch them, it's a whole industry. But it has a downside."

"Just so. *Aeronektonicus subliminus*, the Linnaean name tells all. They are naturally lighter than air, generating hydrogen gas in their tissues, they're living blimps. This means they can afford to be huge. They're colorful, benign, inoffensive, and humans totally adore them." She sighed softly through flared nostrils. "But there is a dark side to every rainbow, Mr Relph—"

"Anders, please."

"Anders." She smiled, just for a moment, a warm expression. "This particular one casts two shadows. The first is why you're here."

"*Sky tears.*" My whisper hung in the air for a long moment.

"The excretions of the pregnant skybeast," she began, with an air of explaining the facts of life. "In the later stages of pregnancy, the species generates complex molecular chemistry and emits some from their pores. Now, water vapor is normally condensed in their tissues as ballast and they have an evapotranspiratory cycle which keeps them both hydrated and neutrally buoyant, but if they need to gain lift in an emergency they simply pass water, they are, literally, living clouds that begin to rain. But when pregnant... Ah." She stirred uncomfortably. "Their chemistry leaches from them and they begin to sweat a rich brew. It's toxic to humans, but there are many alien species which can metabolize the complex molecules and to them it constitutes a rare and potent tonic. This makes it valuable."

"'Delphian Gold,'" I whispered, giving it the common name. "Thus, the black-market trade." My observation seemed to cover all the bases and she could only sigh. A moment later she touched her ear com and whispered a reply, then rose and beckoned.

We went up a companionway to the next level, passed through a security door, and I found myself on the command bridge of the platform. Several ergonomic workstations were ranked in tiers before a panoramic window and she escorted me to the rail within that crystal arch—and the sight took away my breath.

The platform was advancing down the great valley, and spread in a languid herd ahead were a dozen of the creatures. They were almost indescribable, being oblate, vast, with primary-colored streaks and splotches, randomly distributed lobular processes, a propulsive siphon running the length of the body on its central axis, which pulsed like a living jet, fins almost fishlike with their sail-sized membranes stretched between radial stiffeners of cartilage. I felt strange as we approached, quite unable to take my eyes from them.

"It's their infrasound," Dryden whispered, touching my shoulder fleetingly to draw me back. "Everyone feels it, their voices pass through us as if we're not here. But some part of us can hear them, just a tickle in the lungs, the gut."

"Which of them is pregnant?" I asked, a wry smile betraying my sudden attempt to imagine these beasts coupling.

"None. They become solitary when the time approaches. Our girl is out ahead."

We cruised gently by the magnificent leviathans, and I saw a tourist craft standing off a few kilometers away. The small platform was maneuvering to place the giants against the gathering colors of evening for sheer spectacle.

"If it's valuable," I asked obliquely, "why isn't it gathered legitimately?"

"It's dangerous. The stuff is rank poison to us. Oh, it oxidizes in a few hours, naturally breaking down into harmless gunk, but when fresh—and potent—it's nasty stuff. And the various peoples with whom we share this quadrant of space take rather a dim view of such exploitation. If every pregnant *Aeronektonicus* was attended by industrial drones catching every drop of xeno-sweat, it would come very close to harassment by their definition."

"Yet they buy the stuff."

Dryden smiled as if my youth made me adorably inexperienced. "Humans are not the only race to have a criminal class, or scruples which can become elastic."

I coughed softly to cover my flash of embarrassment, as much as my sudden impression that she was telling only half-truths. "So, the cartels use drones. They have a mothership somewhere here, running dark, ready to recover the harvest and beat a quick retreat. I was told there would be a small drone somewhere on the critter's hide, gathering the sweat. My job is to find it and dispose of it."

"Just so. We've tried before but our shoot-down rate has not been good." Dryden gestured to an area to one side of the windows. "Enough space?"

"Fine. As soon as the kill-bird is launched I'll operate through its senses. Don't worry, I'll find the thing."

I took my input gloves from a belt pouch and drew them on in anticipation, brought up the imaging display in my com, screen extended and flipped around before my right eye, and found the signal from the kill drone, already unpacked out on the deck and ready to fly on my command. Yet, as I did so, I sensed in the scientist's words, as much as in the expressions of the other command crew on the bridge, that something dire was left unsaid. A thrill of unease made its way up my spine as I watched the herd recede off the starboard side, and we moved on in quest of our lone mother; and I then recalled from the data package that this species was asexual and parthenogenetic—every daughter was a clone of the parent. And I frowned silently as I also recalled the warning in the data that the event could be disturbing to the uninitiated.

Still, I was not here for that. Just let me bag the harvester drone and my job would be done.

One's intentions may be pure, but reality has a way of altering the course of events, even of life. After many years working among the rough and ready mining communities of the asteroids and barren worldlets which were the mineral bonanza feeding the human race's insatiable hunger for resources, I thought nothing could surprise me.

I was wrong.

The moment the drone came online I became immersed in its sensory input, far more than visual information coming in through my right optic nerve. I felt the moist air, the warmth, the latent stormy character as sunset approached, Delphi's calm, main-sequence star slanting west through clouds, stained colors seemingly unknown on many another colony world. The immersion was so visceral, so powerful, against the cold emptiness of space in which I usually worked, it was momentarily overpowering, as if I had become a flying creature myself. But, more than this, the leviathan herself was... I could not put it into words in my own head, but she commanded my attention in every sense.

The platform had found her a few kilometers further on, well away from the tour craft—I wondered abstractly at that, a thrill of foreboding going through me, but tried to concentrate. I sent the drone off the deck in a whir of drive fans that gave the machine the agility of a dragonfly against the neutralized weight provided by its AG sled. My physical body stood to one side of the bridge viewport, my eyes half-closed, hands gesturing before me to manipulate systems only I could perceive, and the sky beast framed in the forward view came to me through the drone lenses, growing swiftly as I closed in.

She was vast and rotund, sluggish—she carried weight low down, her clone offspring a dead weight as the baby had not yet produced much hydrogen. Junior could not afford to bloat too far or the parent would die, and that moment must be reached in its own time.

It was close.

Toxic sweat rained from the struggling titan in an endless patter of droplets, and I felt a deep swell of pity in my gut as I sensed her distress, her clear knowledge of what would soon come to pass. Were they sentient? Perhaps not in the sense of mechanistic converse and brain processes such as manipulative species share, but I knew instinctively, they felt, they feared, and were bound helplessly by the realities of their own biology. Humans had long since transcended the same limitations, but non-technological species would never develop alternatives to mortality, and their philosophy of being would never encompass them.

I felt Dryden's feather-light touch at my shoulder. "Focus," she whispered, and I silently thanked her for the perspective she brought, as if she knew automatically where my mind was going. The drone feed was probably on screens, maybe in her own com, and the targeting of my attention would be obvious.

The giant hung against the late afternoon clouds, moribund and calling mournfully, tugging one way or another, wandering listlessly in an exhausted, pointless way. I sent the drone in slowly, I had no wish to stress her any more than necessary, and began a cautious probing. I was scanning for a low-level EM field such as an AG drive would produce, the chemical signatures of refined metal and plastics. These would be subtle traces, the drone would be both small and stealthed to the best ability of the field so as to go unnoticed to the likes of me. No wonder the scientists' shoot-down rate had been poor.

Dryden whispered at my side, her words coming to me as if from a dream. "The closer the giant comes to birth, the more potent the chemistry. The drones have a semi-active A.I. that reads the physical state of the beast. They harvest slowly at first, then go for maximum loading only in the minutes before... Before culmination."

Her euphemism made me blink and I thought back on the briefing. I had not been very concerned with the biological issues, I was a dedicated drone man and not interested in much else. Perhaps I should have paid more attention. Whatever. I pushed it mentally aside and scanned, sending the kill-bird in long, sweeping passes beneath the bloated creature. Her hide was stretched tight over a great doming in the underside. Compared to the healthy creatures, this one was distorted, and I felt a tinge of sympathetic pain. Against any divorced judgement, I found an unexpected tide of pity for the creature's suffering, as suffering she undoubtedly was.

My preoccupation almost caused me to miss the target. The metal detector blipped, and I sent the bird back, looping hard for a crevice between engorged gut and a sail-like control fin, and there it was. The harvester was small, smaller than the drone I had brought, four jointed limbs seemed to be snagged into the hide, so it walked slowly on the underside like a fly on a ceiling, a collecting nozzle sweeping back and forth over the perspiring tissues to soak up the rich perspiration, transferring it to a storage tank on the machine's back. It reminded me loathsomely of a tick, sucking blood from some unlucky animal, and I dodged my drone into the cover of the fin to avoid the harvester registering it. The weight of the harvester sagged the tissues to which it was attached, suggesting the tank was almost full, perhaps ten liters —a fortune when translated to gold through the medium of illicit interstellar trade.

"It'll disengage soon," I murmured, assuming Dryden was still beside me. I brought up the engagement interface, selecting the visual outline of the drone recovered from cam memory. Now the system would recognize it instantly and use it to key a motion-based tracking solution. I stayed zoomed in hard on the small area of the leviathan's flank, ignored the mournful groans and trills which were increasing in frequency and power, and my hands hovered over the COMMIT legend in my field of view.

"Wait," I heard Dryden whisper, an odd note in her voice, as if she was fully as stressed as myself. "Wait... We're just in time, she's about to..."

The harvester drone dropped free and drive fans extended as the legs folded away. It turned on a dime, streaked away toward the blind side and I dabbed a hand through the legend in my glowing interface. A hi-ex projectile disengaged from the kill-bird and went after it faster than the eye could follow. I dropped the drone hard to reacquire line-of-sight, and was in time to see a sharp detonation, a ball of flame and a cracking report through the muggy air as the "Delphian Gold" was vaporized.

"Got it!" I exclaimed with a balled fist, then the cries of the leviathan caused me to turn, look up—and the remainder of my life would forever be lived in the shadow and memory of that instant.

Being linked to the drone's perspective placed me up close and very, very personal with something I had never imagined and certainly never wished to see, and my body went cold, then hot in turns, as I watched, stunned...

The great beast spasmed, a shudder rippled through the flesh from end to end, and the belly split open in a hideous travesty of birth. Blood and other fluids rained, and the creature gained lift for a few seconds before the newborn oozed free under the force of gravity, a small, pale, puckered infant whose lifting vacuities were insufficient to support its mass, merely to slow its plummet as it fell hundreds of meters to an ungentle impact with the rich meadow by the river. But the real horror was enacted above, as the parent, bereft of the weight, careened skyward, out of control, its cries diminishing as its ruptured body hemorrhaged in a cataract. I backed off, watched her go, horror rising in me as I saw what remained of the giant swelling again, realized the hydrogen lifting bladder was no longer regulated, but was expanding as air pressure reduced.

The moments were agony to watch as surely as they were for the doomed creature, and the end was both grotesque and mercifully quick. When the hydrogen vessel ruptured, the body was blown to shreds and came falling back to earth like the torn remnants of a sail in a storm gale, turning over and over, bloody tatters where once there had been the serene beauty of their kind.

The body collapsed horribly into the valley a few hundred meters from the infant, and I felt myself shaking from head to foot, trying desperately to set aside a spectacle I could never un-remember. I set the drone to return automatically, then looked down from its lenses on the pathetic sight, knew tears were wet upon my cheeks, and the last thing I saw was the infant flopping and rolling single-mindedly toward its dead parent. And I remembered from the briefing, it was not from any sense of familial concern or need—merely that the deceased giant constituted a fabulously rich source of nutrition, which the infant was equipped to harvest until driven into the air for the first time, to become a filter-feeder, to avoid the scavenger organisms which had evolved to specialize in clearing away the remains of sky beasts.

I felt myself steered into a seat to one side of the bridge, and my com lifted off by Dryden's gentle hands. The scientist sank down beside me and put a hand on my shoulder, engaged my gaze, and in that moment, I was like a child in want, for all the horror I had just witnessed needed to come out. I was profoundly glad of the experience and strength of her two centuries, for she helped me through the moment, my hand over hers.

When I could stand, she took me back to the observation lounge a deck below and we looked out on the herd which drifted unconcernedly, way off toward the distant outline of the city on the mountains, the setting sun coloring all deep golds now.

"That's why the tourists are kept away," Dryden murmured, passing me a drink brought by the service robot. She smiled in a sad, helpless way, and shook her head. "Humans and aliens. Sometimes we understand each other easily, other times not at all. Nature takes no stock of human constructs, and it's as cruel here as anywhere else, by our standards. Other races have different outlooks... What can I say? Their biology is as you see it—one for one generational replacement. Only in times of exceptional abundance are twins born, and thus the species increases by an extra individual. The parent is forfeit, the

offspring requires no guidance or care. The new replaces the old..."
She was whispering, holding my eyes with her own, which I saw were
also moist.

"People come from all over the colonies to see them," I said softly,
taking off my VR gloves slowly, methodically. "But nobody knows
this?"

The lovely woman sighed, choosing her words with care. "They
can't afford to know. *Aeronektonicus* lives centuries but can, of course,
only ever reproduce once. In them, humans have found a metaphor
for peace and stability, for inoffensive beauty, for a living majesty
that suggests to us the need to follow our own higher callings. Few
who come to visit the herds leave without being emotionally, even
spiritually, touched—and that effect runs on into the course of one's
life. Untold thousands have said they have been made better people
merely by encountering the sky giants of Delphi.

"Now, imagine how they would feel if they knew, much less were
exposed directly to, the facts of life as they are for this species."

"Wonder would turn to grief. Love perhaps to loathing." I spoke
in a flat, quiet way, still more than a little in shock. Dryden pressed
the glass to my lips again.

"More than that." She took her time. "This planet is one of the
most hospitable of all the colonized worlds. It's one of a handful that
may be called *Edenic*. The giants are an integral part of the biosphere.
In the early days there was much soul-searching—on one hand, did we
want to cohabit a planet with a spectacle so gruesome it challenged
our philosophic underpinning? On the other, how could we pass up
the chance of settling a terrestrial world with an existing carbon-based
biome?" She shrugged. "It was a choice without a choice, and in the
end, we settled for a gently-preserved lie. We appreciate the giants and
let them take on all shades of meaning for the human experience—this
is our own species-wide, willing spin on things. We simply look away
when the difficult times come."

"So wide a prohibition? How can it be enforced?"

"With the full participation of all those who actually know. It's
one reason most of the cities on this planet are mobile—they can avoid
the spectacle. And the ranger ships, like this one, monitor the herds
and know when an individual is about to undergo *generational renewal*.
That's the euphemism we use. A nice, clean obfuscation for suffering,
blood and—to us—horror, on a scale we, as a species, are long unused
to.

"You see, the experts, a century ago and more, were very afraid of something. People are very plastic when it comes to outlooks. Point of view changes easily, opinions can invert if given a substantial shock... If people in general were aware of the horror inherent to their beloved sky giants, it was feared this planet may breed a kind of existential mania, a sense that beauty and peace are meaningless." She spread her fine hands and smiled again, the desperate, helpless need to keep even a modicum of control over a situation which threatened to become unstable. "Imagine. Beyond ennui, a kind of devolutionary path may occur, in which the higher qualities become worthless. I confess I do not follow the philosophic wrangles, I'm a biologist, not a social scientist, but I accept the need to avoid such an outcome if we can."

I sighed, finished the drink and wiped my eyes. "I never bargained for this when I took a drone job. And now I'll never view the universe quite the same way again."

"There is good in this, for you live in a wider world than yesterday."

"I could have got by without these revelations."

"I understand. But the job had to be done. The giants *are* inoffensive, beautiful, and do not deserve to be harassed and *parasitized* in their direst moments. Much less taken into some ghastly captivity to be exploited for their fluids—force bred in a rapid turn-over to maximize yield." I shuddered as she spoke. "The Colonial Administration has placed them under close and constant protection, we cite the whales of Old Earth as precedent, but really... we're downplaying some rare but awful truths."

I rose and stood at the curved viewport as the setting sun filled the valley with shadow and the city on the mountains caught the low rays in a bright gold. Truly this was the juxtaposition of beauty with horror, and the human psyche struggled to reconcile one with the other. Perhaps willing self-delusion was also a deeply human trait, one of the coping mechanisms our species had always needed to deal with a world—a universe—so far beyond our understanding, let alone control, that it made us aware of our own infinitesimal nature. I had signed a confidentiality agreement before embarking for Delphi, and now I understood what it really covered.

Dryden rose and came to my side, sensing I still needed support, and I smiled my thanks to her as we watched the day reach its end. I knew I would be processing for some time, but now I belonged to a circle of humans privileged—cursed—to be the shepherds of a secret, and I accepted the responsibility with more fatalism than I had known I possessed.

Perhaps a shock has always been necessary to help some people, finally and at last, to grow up.

Mike Adamson holds a Doctoral degree from Flinders University of South Australia. After early aspirations in art and writing, Mike returned to study and secured qualifications in marine biology and archaeology. Mike has been a university educator since 2006, is a passionate photographer, master-level hobbyist and journalist for international magazines.

FROM THE AUTHORS

All of these authors and I would like to thank you for coming along with us on this journey among the strange flora and fauna. We hope you enjoyed the book, and if it was worth your hours of reading, then please spend a moment more and let it be known. All reviews are greatly appreciated, as they not only bring in more readers, but help in allowing all of us to justify the immense amount of time we spend on these endeavors.

Jessica Augustsson, www.JayHenge.com

Made in United States
Troutdale, OR
10/29/2023

14124503R00213